BROKEN SOULS

MIRANDA GRANT

BY MIRANDA GRANT

BOOK OF SHADOWS
(dark mafia PNR with all the triggers)
Madness Behind the Mask
Cursed to be Mine
Tethered Souls
Broken Souls

DEATHLY BELOVED
(fantasy romcom that's utterly bonkers)
To Have and to Lose
Death Do Us Part
For Better or For Worse
To Love and To Perish

WAR OF THE MYTH
(epic fantasy with smut)
Elemental Claim
Think of Me Demon
Tricked Into It
Rage for Her

FAIRYTALES OF THE MYTH
(dark Grimm-esque, open-ended fairytales with no HEA)
Burn Baby Burn
The Little Morgen
Bjerner and the Beast

BROKEN SOULS

This is a work of fiction. All characters are products of my imagination and should not be seen as having any more credibility than fake news does. Any resemblance to organizations, locales, or persons living, dead, or stuck in purgatory is entirely coincidental.

TRIGGER AND CONTENT WARNINGS

Stop at chapter 52.

When writing *Madness Behind the Mask,* I thought it was dark but not, like, painful. Terrible shit happened, but because Sau was so traumatised and it was so constant, to mimic that overwhelming despair where you feel like life will never get better, there was this distance between what happened and what you felt. She was deliberately unrelatable. But Micha... Fuck. This just sucks. It just flat out fucking sucks.

So why did I write it? Because sometimes we just need to know that despite the shit we go through, someone has it worse. Is that wrong of us? Maybe. But it's fiction, and it's healing us when nothing else can.

So yeah...take care of yourself and put the book down as often as you need to. Hel, **don't read past chapter 52** if you want to end with a HEA. Or at least, don't read past that until you have the next and last book in the trilogy.

Find the full list on my website:

https://mirandagrant.com/broken-souls-triggers
(these are also spoilers)

To You, Dear Reader:

I am not responsible for your therapy.
But I am so very sorry.

YOU'LL WANT A 0% SERIOUSNESS PALETTE CLEANSER ON STAND-BY

Suggestion: *My Queen, My King*

I wasn't really having sex with my executioner; I was seducing my executioner to kill him, and that sounded infinitely better. Classier. Way less slutty.

OR FOR A SLIGHTLY MORE SERIOUS ROMCOM WITH HATE SEX

Read: *To Love and to Perish.*

"I have learned necromancy just to kill you over and over again."

"Awww. That's so sweet. No one's ever obsessed over me that much."

"I'm not – No, die!"

WORLD KNOWLEDGE

THE THREE GANGS OF ST. AUGUSTINE

1. **Shadow Domain** – this is the gang the series follows. They are witches, and the main family who rules it can turn into shadows, travel the Plane of Monsters, and use their shadows as a storage unit. Every witch also has an innate magical ability and is tattooed with personal runes to help them cast their favorite spells. Their Boss is Varius Shadow.

2. **Blood Fangs** – these are the vampires. There are two types: born and sired. Only the head of a vampire coven can create sired vampires. Sired vampires are infertile and they cannot phase like born vampires can. All vampires can daywalk, but strong sunlight irritates them to various degrees (a high noon sun will turn sired vampires into ash) due to the world they're originally from not having a strong sun. Their Boss is Aleric Zadar.

3. **Death Hunt** – these are the werewolves. The pack is mostly made up of females and a few beta males. They can shift at will, are bipedal, and are seven-and-a-half feet tall on average. They have broken the peace treaty of the last forty years by killing the Blood Fangs in vast number after a two-thousand-year power stalemate between the three gangs. Their Boss/alpha is Antonio Garcia.

MAGIC SYSTEM

1. Every witch has an innate ability, one they are born with. The Shadow Family is special, however, due to an ancient pact they made with a djinni to give them the ability to shift into false shadows (these shadows cannot move vertically up surfaces), travel the world of the Plane of Monsters, and open a portal to said plane. It is extremely rare, but a strong Shadow can call forth monsters from their shadows.

2. All magic causes a backwash of energy on the user. If the user is too weak or exhausted, that energy can seriously hurt them or even kill them.

3. Magic kills the weak regardless of one's age. If you cannot control it, it will turn on you, more so if it's dark magic. For this reason, many witches struggle to carry to term, so they have a saying: *vorum van del mona*, which translates to: the little shit's being fussy. Meaning: the soul of the baby doesn't like the body you're making and would like you to try again. Many believe this to be a good sign that the child will be successful once they finally arrive, due to their demand of high standards.

4. There is 'magic' and then there is 'dark magic.' Dark magic is extremely easy to use (though not control), but requires a larger blood sacrifice than the spell's benefit. Many cases of people vanishing into thin air, such as the Roanoke settlers, can be traced to them being used as sacrifices for dark magic. Sacrifices can be taken from anywhere in the world. They do not have to be beside the witch when the spell is cast.

5. Witches are born with magic in their blood, but they can't cast any spells until they hit their ascension (magical puberty).

6. Custom wands are normally only used by witches in training. More experienced witches prefer to tattoo runic designs on their body to help them control their magic.
7. Premade wands can be used by those who can't use magic, as long as they have reached their ascension. Before this, they don't have enough magic in their blood to activate the wands. AKA: young kids can't use them unless they are witches. All premades are legally required to be triggered by the word, "Iactus." Black market wands don't use this word.

BLOOD BOND

1. This is a spell only witches can cast. They can bind with either another witch or a non-witch, but all the witches involved have to make a payment.
2. It is very rare for someone to enter a blood bond as the price required for it to work has to be something that will tear the couple apart. So for someone who is over the top jealous, possessive, they might have to allow all their brothers to fuck their girl. Or watch her come on her crush's cock while she screams their name. The payment is unique to each person and is up to the witch to decide on what it is. However, if the payment is not harsh enough, then the blood bond will be rejected, and the person who started the blood bond will die unless they kill the other person first.
3. At the end of the blood bond, each person involved will be able to feel the emotions of the other person. They can erect a temporary wall to stop this.
4. They will be tied together forever, in this life and the next, reincarnating with each other.
5. Most couples who blood bond turn into archnemeses

within a year due to the payment required.

MENTIONABLE TERMS

1. **Archangel** – seven men who govern the gods. They do not normally get involved in mortal affairs, but if they do step in, they are viciously efficient.
2. **Human** – all creatures that were created in the gods' images. This includes all supernatural creatures too, as long as they have the ability to take a humanoid form. This term was later taken by Earth humans to mean just them when the portals to the rest of the Seven Planes were cut off and they forgot about the rest of the worlds out there.
3. **Hybrids** – sups that are a mix of two creatures. These are extremely rare and are victims of extreme hate crimes. They are often cut out of the womb and then they and their mother are burned or killed in some other fashion. Most do not make it to puberty due to being hunted. Though the archangels haven't officially ruled them to be illegal, they will not stand for an army of them being made.
4. **Portals** – gateways that allow travel to the other Seven Planes. Most were destroyed during the Great Extinction in order to protect Earth humans from being killed. The only one in the U.S. is controlled by the Shadow Domain. It connects Earth to Blódyrió.
5. **Premades** – premade wands that are manufactured and loaded with pre-programmed spells in a limited number for non-witches to use.
6. **Ricks** – short for 'erections'. This is the street name for the incubus drugs that change a person's dick (or gives them one or more), giving them various bells and whistles for their appendage(s), such as ridges, cum sacks, the ability to knot or vibrate, etc.

7. **SCU** – Special Crimes Unit. An Earth human group that governs the supernatural world here on Earth. The are a branch of the Elv've'Nor, the interplanal equivalent of the CIA or MI6. There is a rumor that they have a direct line to the archangels, and so they are feared by all.
8. **Sup** – supernatural creature.
9. **Vs** – street name for succubus drugs that changes a person's vagina and vulva. They can vibrate, make your belly expand when you're jizzed in, help with pregnancy by storing cum inside for weeks or longer and more.
10. **Wolf** – short for werewolf.

CHARACTERS

SHADOW BROTHERS (FROM OLDEST TO YOUNGEST)
1. **Varius** – the Boss of the Shadow Domain. He is paranoid as fuck and trusts no one as he has been the target of numerous assassination attempts taken out by his own gang ever since he failed to develop any magic. His senses are enhanced though, and he is faster and stronger than other witches to make up for his lack of magic.
2. **Leno** – he controls plants in every way, able to draw out enough poison from a single belladonna berry to kill an entire city. A werewolf blinded him when he was a kid, and now he sees through his dog Krypto. He can also feel and taste what Krypto does.
3. **Khalid** – the reaper of the Family. He's tasked with killing those who turn traitor, including friends and family. He is not really close to anyone due to this. Everyone fears him.
4. **Talon** – a capo who has his talons in every part of

the business. Due to his childhood lover being killed and marked as a 'witch's whore' by the vampires, he hates them with a passion. He controls electricity.

5. **Enoch** – a telekinetic and Ezriel's twin.
6. **Ezriel** – a telekinetic and Enoch's twin.
7. **Rudy** – Varius sees him as a son as he practically raised him when their father walked out. He hates violence but is the strongest Shadow brother due to his innate ability to make one's greatest fears real. However, he does not like violence, so he has been given the role of cleaner. He was born mute due to magic hitting Sau while he was in her womb.
8. **Maddox** – the interrogator. He's a shapeshifter, able to change into any person as long as he has enough time to study their DNA. Everyone but his brothers try to avoid him due to fearing him 'taking their face' and the fact that he's a little shit. Often smells of onions.

OTHER MAIN CHARACTERS

1. **Aleric Zadar** – Boss of the Blood Fangs (vampires)
2. **Antonio Garcia** – Boss of the Death Hunt (wolves)
3. **Micha Black** – Varius' fiance. She's a witch assassin – or was before Varius purchased her for her womb. Now she's a breedmare – a Shadow term for women who are bred. They're not broodmares because, in Sau's words: "They will respect us more than they do a fucking horse."
4. **Sau Shadow** – the mother of the Shadow Brothers. She was cursed by their father before he died. If she uses any magic, it'll drain her life away. She is the strongest healer on this side of the Atlantic.

MENTIONABLE SIDE CHARACTERS

1. **Dayne Killeen-McCarthy** – Micha's best friend and ex-assassin partner.
2. **Vlad Laska** – Aleric's second; he isn't interested in ruling the Blood Fangs despite everyone wishing he did. A born vampire.

STORYLINE
(TETHERED SOULS SPOILERS)

WHAT JUST HAPPENED:

1. Varius learns the reason he doesn't have magic is because his mother stripped it from him using dark magic in order to save his life when he was a baby.
2. The Shadow Domain found out Antonio (the Boss of the werewolves) is trying to make hybrids, which is extremely taboo, so they attacked him last night. They failed to kill him, and Talon almost died.
3. Micha and Varius (MCs) just started a blood bond. She also just tattooed her name on his dick.

ONE

HIM

My dick is still burning from the tattoo she just gave me, but fuck, I need that pussy. My fiancee's lying in my arms, stroking her fingers between her lips, touching what I want. What I *own*. **Property of Varius Shadow** is inked beneath her black curls. *Mine*.

She turns her head into her pillow and sucks in a little breath, trying not to wake me. She knows I need my sleep after the shit that happened last night – our attempt to kill the Boss of the Death Hunt gang led to one of my brothers nearly dying under his claws.

But the scent of her cum-stuffed pussy's getting stronger. It's tickling my nose, filling my lungs until I'm consumed by the idea of rolling her onto her back and sinking into her balls deep.

"*Micha*," I growl, trailing my hand from her breast to her stomach. She stills rather than jumps, her assassin training locking her muscles down despite her surprise. "Did I give you permission to touch yourself?"

"I don't need –"

My fingers wrap around her wrist and pull.

She tries to resist, but I am much bigger than her, much stronger than her, and I force her fingers up to my mouth. Flicking my tongue out, I taste what's mine.

A groan rumbles from my chest.

A soft whimper escapes hers.

"Whose name is on your pussy?" I growl, stroking her fingertips across my lower lip.

"Some neanderthal who thinks he can just say, 'Grr. I man. Grr. You woman.'"

My smile twitches into existence, then falls as my cock hardens. "Say my name, Micha."

Her spine stiffens against my chest. My little monster – so damn defiant over any order, no matter how small... My blood heats in anticipation of getting her to submit.

Sucking her fingers inside my mouth, I twirl my tongue around them. She shudders. Then wiggles her pert little ass against my cock, making me hard.

Relaxing my grip on her wrist, I skim my fingers down her arm, trailing goosebumps across her ribcage. Her hip. I dip towards her pussy, and she spreads her legs on a little moan.

But instead of touching her there, I go up to tease her breasts, feathering my fingers across her A cups but not touching her nipples like she wants me to. She's so damn sensitive there, often enjoying the pinch of clamps.

"Tell me who owns your pussy," I growl, having finally released her hand from my mouth.

My blood pounds in the thick veins of my cock. I rock my hips forward. She sucks in a breath, and I know she is close to breaking.

I graze my fingers over her nipples, checking that they're hard before dipping my hand south. I tease the top of her pussy lips, circling around but not going in. She rocks her hips in invitation, but if she doesn't say her pussy is mine, I am not going to give her what she wants.

Grabbing my cock, I slide it between her thighs, building her up but denying her that final finish. Her pussy slides across the length of me, feeling so damn good despite the burn of my new tattoo. She lowers a hand to the front of her thighs and rubs the head of my cock as it pushes out.

I groan at the feel of her. I fondle her breasts, letting my palm graze her nipples just barely. Her breathing grows ragged and harsh as I slide my dick back and forth between her thighs.

She tries to sneakily touch her clit, but I'm on her before she can apply any pressure. Locking both her arms above her head with one large hand around her wrists, I bite her shoulder. "That's two strikes against you, Mrs. Shadow."

She whimpers as her name rolls off my tongue. We are not married yet. She has not officially taken my name, but she will. There's no changing that even if she can't give me the heirs I wanted when I purchased her four months ago. Micha Shadow is *mine*. If anyone tries to take her from me, I'll kill them. If she tries to run, I'll just drag her back.

My free hand roaming around her nipples again, I keep pumping my cock between her wet thighs. She squeezes me as she whimpers and moans. Desperate and needy but still so damn stubborn.

"Tell me who owns your pussy, little monster, and I'll let you come."

She sucks in a ragged breath. She tries to tug her arms free as I stroke my fingers across her clit too gently for her to find true pleasure. My grip tightens. My cock quickens, but my finger stays feather-light.

"You better hurry up," I moan as my pace increases even more, "or I'm going to come between your thighs."

A strangled noise breaks past her lips. With a defeated

groan, she rasps, "*Varius.*"

My fingers push down on her clit, rewarding her as a smile –

"*Men.*"

I still, despite my consciousness not having worked it out yet. But then I do. I put it together. I pull my finger out *fast.*

She giggles.

Actually fucking giggles.

"You think your pussy is owned by *various men*?" I growl as I flip her over onto her stomach.

She turns her head, a cute little smirk on her lips that quickly spreads into a wide O as I shove my cock into her pussy in one hard thrust. She cries out, a flash of pain in her eyes. She's wet, absolutely soaked in both her cum and mine from earlier, but she's still so damn tight. It's only been relatively recently that she's managed to take all eight inches of my thick, girthy cock. She wiggles, trying to get comfortable, but I hold her ass down in both hands as I pull out and ram back into her. I can hit her deeper in this position, and with each thrust, I hit her cervix *hard.* I lift her hips up just off the mattress and pound into her like I want to rather than in the way she needs.

She digs her hands into the sheets as her cries get louder and louder, and I can feel her body shaking as she hangs on the pinnacle of her release. A roller coaster about to drop.

But she can't drop.

Can't come.

She needs outside stimulation.

Which is why her pussy is off the sheets, denying her the chance to grind against them as I rail her hard and fast. My cock is burning, but I don't give a shit. All my focus is on filling her with my cum until she's begging for forgiveness.

She reaches a hand down towards her clit, but I release her ass and grab both her arms. Wrestling them behind her back as she whimpers, I lock them together with one hand, then continue to fuck her like I hate her.

"You think your pussy belongs to *various men*?" I growl as I lift my free hand and slap her ass. A red mark blossoms across her cheek; my jealousy bleeds out in another hard slap. "You think another man gets to enjoy *this*?" I fuck her so hard, the bed slams into the wall, the headboard cracking the plaster, and white dust rains down on the pillows.

She cries out, shuddering, and I grab her chin and turn her so I can see her face. Her eyes are closed. Tears seep down her cheeks. Her mouth is open in arousal now, not pain, but her brows are pinched in frustration. As turned on as she is, as wet as she's making my cock, my little monster needs outside pressure on her pussy to come.

"I..." She starts, but whatever she was about to say dies on a moan as I release her chin to spank her ass again.

"Hands on the headboard," I demand, and she instantly obeys, her submission easing a bit of my jealousy.

Good girl, I growl inside my head, but I don't say it out loud, don't want to reward her yet. If she wants to be a brat, she can damn well take the consequences.

So I don't stop, don't slow down at all as I ram in deep and fast.

Leaning forward, I place two fingers in her mouth. She sucks on them, her tongue and cheeks working hard, and my cock jerks inside of her. When my fingers are fully wet, I pull them out and use them to trace the rim of her ass. "You want multiple men inside you at once?" I growl, and she tenses, already too full with my cock. There's no space for my finger in her ass, and we both know it. We tried it with a toy much narrower than my dick once, but my little monster is just too small.

"Wait –" She cries out as I shove in. Her ass clenches the tip of my forefinger, trying to stop me, and that gets her another slap across her cheek. I push in deeper, timing my invasion with the withdrawing of my cock, then pulling out as my cock goes in. I work her holes fast and rough until they start to loosen, until I can get in both at once.

She's screaming and bucking against me, but her hands never leave the headboard.

"*Varius, please,*" Micha begs, her legs shaking. She's so damn desperate to come.

My cock jerks inside her, the fresh tattoo she gave me burning with every thrust. But the pain is fucking worth it when my little monster becomes a sobbing mess. Adding a second finger to her ass, I stretch her even further. She cries out, her knuckles going white.

I groan as I orgasm inside her pussy, the tightness just too damn much with that extra finger. I close my eyes, my balls releasing so much cum that it starts to push out the old. It gushes down my balls, and as my cock goes down, I manage to get in that second finger.

I'm breathing hard as I stare at her ass, at the way she's clenching around my fingers. I'm going to buy her a dildo, a cast of my own cock, and I'm going to fuck her with it while I'm inside her. Then I'll get a third for her mouth. *Various men. Various fucking men.*

"How many men own your pussy?" I hiss as I piston my fingers inside her.

She cries out, unable to form words.

"Three?" I push another finger in, causing her to thrash about as she whimpers.

But still her hands don't come off the headboard; she doesn't tell me it's too much.

"*Four?*"

She slams her right palm against the wood of the bed. Over and over as I work that fourth digit in.

My cock starts to harden, and now I'm really stretching her. I can feel my four fingers on the other side of the wall. There's no room for more. No room to *move.*

And now her hands are trying to drag herself forward

and off me.

"Don't you dare," I hiss as I grab her hip with my other hand. "You wanted various men inside you, then you can damn well take it all."

She cries out as I start to thrust my fingers up her ass. I can't push deep, can't get them in that far, not if I want my cock to stay buried against her cervix.

"I'm sorry," she whimpers as she presses her ass into me, getting into the rhythm I'm forcing on her. She squeezes me with both holes, pushing out more cum from her pussy. "I... Just you, Varius." She squeezes the headboard with both hands as she rocks faster against me. "Only ever you."

"Damn fucking right." I slap her ass. "Because you know what will happen if you even *flirt* with another guy?"

She nods as she pants. Her knuckles turn white. "You'll kill him," she breathes.

"*And fuck you on his godsdamn corpse.*" My cock fully hard again, I pull out and thrust back in. She screams as her entire body shakes. As I fuck her at a speed that puts more holes in the wall.

Growling, I pump my digits inside her. They slide against my cock, felt through the wall between her pussy and ass. I'm owning every part of her body. Filling her up so no one else ever can.

Various fucking men.

Reaching forward with my free hand, I shove my fingers into her mouth. She sucks on them. Licks them.

Without any hands to balance me now, I'm forced to slow my pacing. So I fuck her *hard* instead of fast. Just the way she likes. Where I pull out slowly, then hesitate before slamming in deep in one smooth move.

She cries out around my fingers, her saliva dripping all down my hand as our mixed cum drips all down my cock. I fuck all her holes until I feel my second orgasm building. She screams my name as I bury my cock all the way inside her pussy and my fingers all the way inside her ass and mouth.

Collapsing against her, I squeeze my eyes shut on a series of growls and groans as my cum shoots free. *Fuuuuck.* As my entire body shudders with the last of its release, I bite her shoulder, marking her with my teeth. She arches her neck, asking me to do it there. So everyone can see she's mine.

A low growl vibrates out of my chest as I sink my teeth into the base of her throat. She jerks against me. My tongue swipes against her skin, easing the sharp pain, and she stills on a moan.

My fingers fall from her ass and mouth, but I keep my cock inside her as I press her body down onto the mattress. My eyes close as I start to drift asleep.

She wiggles beneath me, and worried she's being crushed given how much smaller she is, I roll us onto our sides. My cock stays in her, where it fucking belongs.

"Please," she begs, the word raw and raspy as she pushes her ass into me. "I need to come."

Using the hand that was in her mouth, I reach around to cup her pussy. "Who owns this?" I ask.

"*Varius fucking Shadow.*"

"Good girl," I breathe against her skin, my lips curling into a cocky smile. I stroke her pussy lips, feeling how wet she is, how much she is actually mine.

"But you're not to come until morning," I growl.

As I fall asleep, the last thing I hear is her whimper.

But the last thing I feel is the burn of my cock, the words tatted there:

Property of Micha Shadow

TWO

HER

Fucking.

Hel.

My pussy's pulsing around his cock and against his hand, trembling with the need to come. The blood bonding ritual we just started, which will bind us as mates for all eternity and allow us to feel each other's emotions as our own at all times unless blocked once it is completed, let me feel how good his cock felt when he came – just for a moment, a spark of connection between us that's now gone. But it was enough for me to know that I want that. Need that. Am so desperate for that same release.

But I don't reach down between my thighs. Don't play with my nipples as I imagine his mouth on them, sucking and licking and nibbling. Even when I sense him fall asleep through our budding bond, I don't disobey his command.

No coming until the morning.

Fucking.

Hel.

But Varius clearly wakes up easily – unsurprising given how paranoid he is – and he will not hesitate to punish me again. My ass burns from the stretching he forced upon it, but my pussy kegels at the memory of him doing so. His ability to brush up against my line between pleasure and pain, between forcing and coaxing me to take more has left me fucking *wrecked.*

Rocking my pussy against his hand, I bite back a small whimper before stilling my hips. As much as I want to fuck him into oblivion, I'm a bit worried about the punishment he will give me. The memory of the two anal plugs he came into my room with a few months ago pops into my mind.

One had a fox tail attached to it, and had I disobeyed about wearing underwear to our engagement party, *while wearing a dress that was damn near mesh,* he would have made me wear it.

In front of my *entire* family. His entire family. All twelve of his capos and their seconds. All the assassins I trained with. And some of the most powerful Families in America.

So I don't move as I lie in his arms. Don't take what I want as he sleeps.

I close my eyes and pull on my training. I nearly died three months ago after having my side ripped open from my breast to my hip. My organs fell out, and I died for a few minutes. I survived that, so I can handle this.

I can...

My thighs clench, and I whimper.

It takes me hours, but I finally manage to fall asleep.

I dream of him kneeling behind me, with my pussy in his face. His tongue is inside me, scooping up his cum and mine before he spits it all over his cock. Using it as lube, he fucks me in the ass. Hard and feral. A second cock grows out of him and fills my pussy. One of his new tails slides between my breasts, then feathers down my stomach to enter my pussy too. The other tail presses against my lips. Something sucks on my clit.

My thighs shake. My toes curl.

And unknowingly, outside of the dream, I come *hard*.

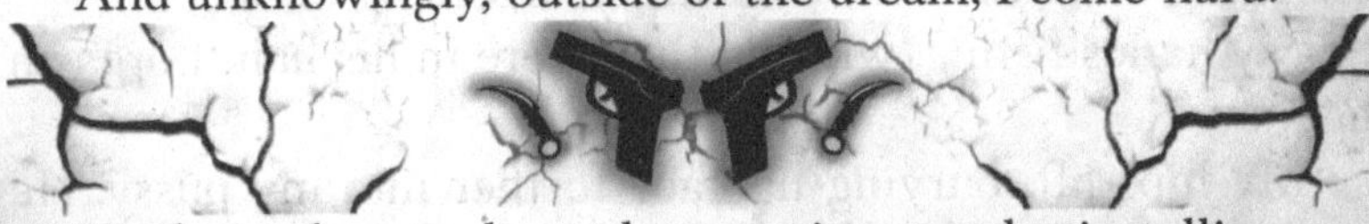

I jerk awake, my heart hammering, my brain telling me there is danger. I try to sit up, but I find my hands are bound above my head, spread out to each corner of the bed. And there is a towel folded under my hips.

"I told you this pussy is mine," Varius growls.

"What are you –" I cry out as pleasure erupts from my pussy. I arch off the bed as my thighs clench around his head. He buries his tongue between my lips, licking me in one long stroke before latching onto my clit and humming. I jerk off the bed, my hips the only thing rising for my legs are tied down too, silk wraps around my ankles. The buzz of his humming has me crying out, then screaming.

I twist against my binds as an orgasm builds fast. I try to hold it back, worried I'm not supposed to come, but I can't stop it.

His mouth doesn't let me.

Crying out, I jump off the edge of cloud nine and swan dive into paradise.

"Given you're so desperate to come," Varius says as he lifts his head and kisses my thigh, "I'm going to let you."

My eyes open wide as I stare at the ceiling. I'm breathing hard. My pulse is racing. And my brain is still telling me there is danger despite my body feeling utterly amazing.

He licks my clit, and I try to jerk away, too sensitive to be touched. But my binds don't let me move far, and he is back on me before I can stop him. My toes curling, I thrash under him. "*Varius*," I pant as my body trembles.

Locking his mouth around my clit, he starts to hum, then

suck. I try to squeeze my legs together, to deny him access so I can breathe, but he doesn't let up, doesn't relent. There is no mercy, no world outside his lips. I can't concentrate on anything other than the pleasure he's forcing on me.

My hands fisting, wishing they were in his hair, I orgasm again.

My hips lift, burying his face further into my pussy. He pushes a finger inside of me, and the tremors of my orgasm has me squeezing around him.

Another finger joins the first, and I cry out. It's too soon, too much. I need him to wait, to let me come down before he fucks me with his fingers, before he rubs my clit with his palm, but he doesn't. My toes lock tight. My legs grow rigid. And after a few minutes of merciless attention, he forces me to come again. My body arches off the bed. My eyes close as I moan.

"That's it, little monster," Varius growls before licking me between my soaked lips. "You're going to come for me until you pass out."

My clit is aching, pulsing, seeming to draw all my blood to it, and I can't quite make out the words he said. I'm too consumed by the feeling of his tongue in my pussy, by the close proximity of his mouth to my over-stimulated clit.

But then they click, and I whimper.

Licking his way up my stomach, he removes the fingers he has inside of me and rubs my cum all over my asshole. They dive back into my pussy just as his tongue reaches my breasts. He licks between them, and I tug on my binds as I try to find words to tell him to wait.

"I can't..."

"*Please...*"

"Varius..."

"You can," he growls. "You can take it."

"*No... I...ca...ahhh!*"

I moan as he sucks on my breasts. My nipples are hard

and aching and too damn sensitive. My entire body starts to shake as he builds me back up to a climax. It's a longer trek this time, nearly a godsdamn hour of constant licking and sucking and nibbling and biting focused on my breasts. His fingers are in my ass, thrusting in and out slowly, and the towel under my hips gets completely soaked.

"Fuck…"

"Shit…"

"Varius…"

"I…"

"…need…"

"Ah!"

"*Please…*"

Tears flood down my cheeks as even my brain becomes overwhelmed, no longer able to string words together in any way that makes sense.

His free hand kneads my right breast as he sucks my left one entirely in his mouth. His tongue strokes me, flicking across my nipple back and forth until I scream. I arch off the bed as he pinches my other nipple, then relaxes his grip, then pinches again. He works me until my head goes dizzy and my breaths come in ragged pants. I'm so fucking close to another orgasm, but I can't handle it. I *can't.*

"*Varius,*" I beg, half-crying, half-screaming as he sucks on my breasts without mercy. My arms and legs tug hard on my black silk binds, but he's wrapped them well, and I can't move. Can't escape. I can only lie here and take what he is determined to give me.

Which is fucking everything.

Screaming out his name, I come with his teeth around my nipple.

He groans around my hard bud, then moves his mouth to my other breast, trailing the hand that was there down to his cock. He jerks himself off as he holds himself up with his other hand after pulling it away from my ass.

I whimper.

I sob.

I beg for him to stop.

But he doesn't.

And an hour later, my body flushed and shaking, I come once again from him playing with my nipples. I'm so utterly exhausted, so desperate to sleep. My eyes roll back into my head, which is fuzzy and dizzy and unable to make out any of the words he's been saying to me. All I can think about is the next orgasm. The buzzing of my clit. The achiness of my nipples.

Grabbing the pillows out from under my head, he slides them beneath my hips, under the towel. Then he pushes his cock into me, bends his back to bury his teeth in my neck, and fucks me slowly as he growls. I'm so soaked, he goes in easily, no burn, but within a few thrusts, the world starts to spin.

He keeps his pace consistent and slow. His cock fills me. He bites me in numerous places. His hand goes between us, and he rubs my clit. I cry out, too sensitive, too hot, and in another few seconds, I am coming so hard I see stars.

My pussy clenches around him.

My toes curl as I lift off the bed.

He groans against my skin as he continues to fuck me. Slowly. Lovingly. And my heart skips a beat as an emotional orgasm rips through me.

"Var..." I sob as I shake beneath him.

He doesn't stop, though, doesn't change his pace. He just fucks me, murmuring words against my throat, my ear. His teeth mark me. His body claims me. And another orgasm is forced from me.

And another.

And another.

Back to back now, unrelenting.

So much pleasure, it hurts.

My body a shuddering, sobbing mess, I black out.

THREE

HIM

Seeing her faint makes me fucking feral, and I pick up the pace until I'm fucking her hard and fast. She oscillates beneath me, her tits jiggling as I pound into her. Her body is completely relaxed and at my mercy.

She could've fought me. She could've used her magic to throw me off as I only bound her wrists and not her fingers. The fact that she didn't makes my blood hot. She trusts me in her vulnerability. Trusts that I won't go too far. That I won't hurt her while she can't protect herself.

And that gifting of her safety, that blatant show of her belief in me unravels something inside my chest. Groaning, I slide in all the way. My balls grow tight. My cock jerks, feeling too damn good. But right as my orgasm is about to release, I pull out and shuffle up her body. I slide my cock across her tits. At the feel of her hard nipples, I sag forward with a growl and my cum sprays all over her chest and face, painting her as mine. Gripping my cock, I jerk out more cum for her, every last drop, before collapsing against the wall, one arm resting on it as I kneel over her.

Breathing hard, I stare down at the woman I love. The one I purchased four months ago merely for her womb.

"I don't need a wife, Micha," I told her that day in her father's office. *"All I need is an heir."* I shake my head at the memory. What an utter fool I was. *A neanderthal...*

My lips curling, I reach over to the nightstand and grab my phone. There's a text notification from Aleric Zadar, the Boss of the Blood Fangs, that I've been waiting on, but it's a one word response, so I ignore it. Grabbing my dick with my other hand, I drag my cock all over my fiancee's body and snap a few pictures of it next to her cum-stained cheeks and breasts. My breathing increasing, I trail my cock down her stomach, ignoring the pain born from its sensitivity.

I jerk my hand back and forth, getting myself hard again, then I bury the head of my cock inside her pussy. I groan at the sight of her taking me, and I snap a few more pictures. I'll paint this one day – capture just how her soaked lips hug me. Then I turn it onto video mode as I fuck her slowly, focusing on how beautiful her pussy accepts me into her body.

A soft sigh escapes her lips, and I point the camera at her face. A few seconds later, she opens her eyes. I push deeper into her, going in further than my head, and her lips part in a pretty little O. She doesn't wake though, so I angle the camera back to her wet pussy before changing my mind and focusing on her face once more. I'd rather capture the color of her cheeks, the heated desire so clearly painted there. The little moans and whimpers she makes as I fuck her while she's out.

Shuddering, I come inside her, but my balls have already been drained so damn much, the orgasm is practically dry. Following my hand with the camera, I scoop up the cum on her face with a finger, then push it between her thighs after

I pull out. She lifts her hips on a little sigh, and I push more into her until she's clean. Kneeling between her thighs, I place the phone there to watch the cum seep back out of her pussy and down her legs. Groaning, I push it back in, then end the video.

Tossing my phone on the bed, I shuffle down to lick her pussy. She tastes like mine, and my cock twitches even as it begs me to leave her alone. It is aching from the pain of the new tattoo. A small bit of blood and ink is even now leaking from it, so with a last kiss to her thigh, I shuffle off the bed and head into the ensuite.

My pulse quickens as I wipe away the mess on my cock, worried her name's no longer readable, but it's there in solid bold. **Micha Shadow**

I run a finger across it. She'll have to redo the **Property of** though, and my cock twitches at the thought of her marking me again. Claiming me like I have her.

My chest tight, I head back into the bedroom to untie her so she can get comfortable. She sighs as I place one of the pillows under her head. I leave the towel under her hips.

Standing over her, I hesitate for a second, then lean down and kiss her forehead. "I love you," I murmur. The words feel alien on my tongue, a bit too heavy, a bit too risky to admit to an assassin. She could be manipulating me, making me fall in love with her just so I put my guard down. There has been a bounty on my head since I was a kid, and she is more than skilled enough to pull it off. But fuck, do those words feel right.

Pivoting, I grab my phone off the mattress, throw on a pair of sweatpants, and head for the door. As much as I want to crawl back into bed with her, that text from the Boss of the Blood Fangs demands my attention.

Four months ago, we found out that Antonio's gang, the Death Hunt – the third and final gang with a claim to St. Augustine, Florida, was kidnapping members of the Blood

Fangs and killing them in some gruesome experiment that led to all their skin falling off their bodies and their organs turning into mush. My seven brothers and I thought they were developing a poison or a new disease that they would eventually use on us.

Aleric, the Boss of the Blood Fangs, tried to keep it all a secret, not trusting we wouldn't attack them too while they were weak. But we grabbed one of his tortured men after the Death Hunt dumped his body like yesterday's trash, still barely alive. Unfortunately, Jerry was so far gone, he wasn't able to speak due to choking on the bits of flesh falling off his tongue and the walls of his cheeks and throat. So we then grabbed Cid, Antonio's youngest son, for information about what his father had planned, and it is worse than we ever imagined.

The fucker is trying to make *hybrids*.

If any of the archangels get wind of this, we're all dead. They will not limit their killing to just his gang. They are responsible for keeping the balance of the Seven Planes, of which Earth is one – albeit it is ignorant of that fact, and an army of hybrids will threaten that balance as they are more powerful than either of their parents, almost putting them on par with a demigod. One existing isn't an issue to the archangels. But an entire army? Every sup in this city would be worth sacrificing then – simply kill everyone to make sure you get them all.

So I need to take measures just as drastic. I need to strike an alliance with the Blood Fangs. Our two gangs might be at peace now under a fragile treaty, but the war before was long and bloody.

Mother was born as a breedmare only a hundred years ago, gifted away to our father before she was even named. On their wedding day, the Death Hunt attacked the venue and killed her dad. She, in turn, killed their Boss' mate and their unborn pups.

She had fourteen children during that time of war. None of them survived long enough to see their twenty-second birthdays, most having been brutally killed by the other two gangs. Aleric even sent their butchered bodies back to her, cut up and packaged to be delivered through the mail as he couldn't pass the ward around our house. Rightfully angry, Mother then retaliated by killing a hundred of his vampires in a single night, gaining her the name Reaper of the Sired.

Any alliance between us and the Blood Fangs is going to be hard won, but hopefully it'll give us the edge we need to catch Antonio off guard and kill him.

Whatever it takes, we must stop him before he makes his army and damns us all.

Stepping into my office, I open the messenger app and see the text I sent Aleric a few hours ago:

Varius: *I know Antonio is planning on making hybrids.*

As well as his answer, which was delivered when I was sucking on Micha's tits:

Aleric: *k*

I didn't expect him to break down and immediately ask us to help him now that we're in the know, but I expected more than a 'k.' His gang is being slaughtered, and although Aleric cares for no one but himself, he is smart enough to understand that he won't survive this coming war. Either Antonio will kill him or the archangels will.

Varius: *We should talk.*

Aleric: *k*

Varius: *Today?*

Aleric: *k*

My eyes narrow. I was about to suggest meeting him behind the library – a traditional place of parlay that is still honored, even by Antonio, but his Ks are really starting to piss me off.

Varius: *When and where?*

Aleric: *k*

Varius: *That isn't an answer.*
Aleric: *k*
Varius: *We ran into Antonio last night. He's jacked up on something hard. You can't win alone.*
Aleric: *k*

My fingers tighten on my phone as I resist the urge to toss it on my desk and give up on this damn conversation. But as annoying as the Boss of the Blood Fangs is, we need his gang as much as he needs ours. Antonio is now faster than a fucking bullet – something that shouldn't be possible. Whatever he's doing to himself, whatever dark magic he's messing with or whatever drug he's pumping into himself, it's made him too strong for us to kill on our own, especially since his kind is naturally resistant to magic to begin with. So we need the Blood Fangs as canon fodder.

But I don't want him to think we're just as desperate as he is. When it comes time for us to negotiate the terms of our alliance, I will do it from a position of power.

Varius: *Enjoy your final moments then.*

He doesn't immediately reply like he has been.

Just as I start to think he won't at all, he texts: *Finished jacking off to a picture of your mom. You should try it to get that stick out of your ass.*

My blood boils.

Aleric: *My house at three. And bring me a picture of Sau. I wrapped this one around my dick and now it's all torn. Got a bit too rough. Also got too much jizz on it.*

Varius: *Insult my mother again, and I'll kill you myself.*
Aleric: *k*

Inhaling sharply, I hold it for a few seconds, then type: *I'll be there at two. I have other shit to do.*

I don't, but fuck him and his schedule.

The three blinking dots pop up on my screen, telling me he's writing a long message this time.

...

Aleric: *k*

Glowering at my phone, I half wish Antonio will find a way to kill him before our meeting. Dealing with Vlad, the vampire's second, would be so much easier. He, at least, acts like a fucking adult.

FOUR

HER

When I wake, I am alone. There's a glass of water on the bedside table though, alongside a chocolate bar and a note. My engagement ring sits on it. A slow smile curls my lips as I roll onto my back and stretch out my entire body. I feel like a cat lazing in the sun.

When Varius Shadow purchased me four months ago, I never thought I'd fall in love with the neanderthal. All the stories around his name painted him as a ruthless monster, and although I do not doubt that claim, having seen him not hesitate to torture his own family, I've also seen a different side to him. The one who is fiercely loyal to those who give him their loyalty. The one who will protect what's his with the merciless cut of his knife.

Stroking my fingers through my lower curls, I trace the tattoo hidden there.

Property of Varius Shadow

My chest squeezes, and though I would be the first one to

reject the idea that women are property, with him, the ink feels stronger than any wedding vow. More permanent. He gave me an engagement ring because he *had* to in order to legitimize his heirs. He inked me because he *wanted* to.

My pussy kegels in memory of last night, of how he had to own me to sate his jealousy. But as fun and as hot as that was, I won't ever tease him like that again.

There was a flash of uncertainty in his eyes. Too many people have pretended to love him only to try to kill him. To a paranoid man like Varius, giving him any reason to doubt me could be a death sentence. Perhaps even more so now that we have started the blood bond.

"It's a dangerous thing to fall in love with a dangerous man."

"If you break his heart, Micha, he'll kill you for it."

My best friend's warnings come back to me, and I heed them. All of Varius' past experiences, all his harshly taught paranoia won't just disappear because I've told him I love him.

But he is worth the time and effort it'll take me to break through his thick-ass, barb-wired, booby-trapped walls.

I'll probably need multiple lifetimes to accomplish that anyways.

Turning over onto my side, I face the wooden bedside table and reach for the chocolate bar. I peel it, eat it, then sit up to drink the water. Feeling loved, I slip on my ring, then pick up the note.

My smile falters when I read it though.

BE DISCREET WHEN YOU GO BACK TO YOUR ROOM. DON'T

MENTION THE BOND TO ANYONE.

My chest hurts as I stare at the black scrawl. He isn't rejecting me in the morning light, isn't trying to hide me from his family like I'm some great sin. He simply doesn't trust them to know that I'm a weakness. Doesn't trust that they won't hurt me to get to him if they knew they could.

Last night, I told him someone is trying to blackmail me into stealing the Family ledger – the book of records that can put every single Shadow Domain member away for life. Although I haven't yet told him about my suspicions that the culprit is either one of his seven brothers or his mother, Varius has recently been burned by someone close to him. Now he trusts no one.

Hating that he doesn't have sanctuary even in his own home, I burn the note with my magic, then stand to collect my clothes. I need to figure out who this blackmailer is so he doesn't have to. So I can stop them before they hurt him to the point of no return.

After getting dressed, I slip out his bedroom window. He is on the second floor, but I know how to roll the landing so it doesn't hurt. Sneaking around to my room, I ease up the window and climb inside. I shower and change into a fresh dress, then head out of my room to make breakfast before the sun has properly risen.

I stop in the archway of the kitchen, my eyes snapping to the wooden counter splitting the room. Magic hums from it, and I recall coming home last night to a commotion in here. I didn't stop to see what it was, having been away for a few days and only wanting to go upstairs to see Varius.

He surprised me with his desire to claim me as a mate, and I knew then something bad had happened, something serious enough to have triggered a drastic reaction in him. Death has a way of causing such things... I wonder which brother made him fear dying with regrets.

Please don't be Rudy, I think instinctively, liking him the best. No one who takes the time to help ducklings cross the road deserves to die.

Feeling a presence behind me, I turn to see Maddox, the

youngest Shadow at twenty-two, enter the vast living room, which is connected to the kitchen through the archway I'm standing in. He doesn't look like he's lost a brother, and the tension in my shoulders eases a little. Whatever happened last night might have been serious, but it wasn't lethal.

Maddox looks me up and down, then flashes a cocky grin. "Well, you look like you've been properly fucked," he says.

My neck heats, the marks Varius left on it burning hot. The ones on my thighs and breasts tingle to awareness too, but I tell myself he can't see those.

"I'm surprised you would know what that looks like on a woman," I say. My eyes widen as my brain suddenly catches up with my mouth.

He laughs. Then winks. "Only because I have them rail me in front of mirrors."

My mouth drops open as my blush shoots all the way up my cheeks and to my ears. Maddox is a shapeshifter, able to take the form of another – male *or* female.

"Are you saying you..." The rest of my words turn into a strained noise. Deciding I don't want confirmation, I blurt, "What happened last night?"

His smile evaporates as his eyes shift to the long wooden counter humming with magic. "Talon nearly died."

"How?"

"We tried to kill Antonio."

"We being you and Talon?"

He snorts. "All eight of us."

My mouth hits the godsdamn floor. "And you *lost*? With Khalid there?"

He's the Family reaper, a badass motherfucker who hunts down those who turn traitor. Meaning he's the best of the best. His soul magic is utterly terrifying. With it, he's able to kill from anywhere in the world as long as he has their DNA.

With all of the Shadow brothers attacking Antonio, that should've given Maddox enough time to study his molecular makeup so he could shapeshift into the werewolf alpha and then give Khalid a part of 'him' to use in his soul magic. The fact that the Boss of the Death Hunt isn't dead? Means he had an ace up his sleeve that no one knew about. Which begs the question, what other surprises does he have?

"Khalid got distracted."

"*Khalid?*" I stress, shaking my head. "Mister Won't Even Glance at a Supermodel's Boobs got *distracted?*" I have legit seen that happen. One of the capos brought his mistress to dinner a couple months ago. She was absolutely gorgeous, so much so that even *I* looked when her dress accidentally slipped when she reached down to grab a dropped napkin.

Unfortunately, that ended up killing her as Varius caught me looking. Which was a shame; she had great boobs before he cut them off and then slit her throat.

But Khalid didn't even glance over with a quick side eye, not when she bent down nor when Varius killed her. He just kept eating his steak. His focus is insane.

"By what?" I ask incredulously.

Maddox sighs. "You want to cook while I talk?" he says as he glances behind me. "I'm fucking starving. Been out all night babysitting the fucker."

I blink.

Blink again.

Then I turn and head into the kitchen while he follows me.

"Is Sau okay?" I ask as I start pulling out what's needed to make egg and bacon sandwiches for the entire household. Normally, their mom is up before me – the role of a female Shadow being one of servitude. But Sau is the only true healer in this family. If Talon was that fucked up, she would have ignored her curse, which requires her to sacrifice time off her life in order to use her magic, and healed him.

"Yeah. Ma's fine. She's just exhausted after saving T's ass." He settles on the counter, seemingly indifferent to the black magic electrifying the air around it. Me? I keep my distance from it, using the other side of the kitchen to do my prep work.

"Counter's fine," he says with a grin. "It ate enough blood last night to keep it sated for months."

I look at it warily. I want to ask him what the fuck that means. Sau hasn't explained why it hums with so much dark magic – a family secret I'm not trusted with yet, but I don't want to get distracted from what happened last night. Varius might have instigated the blood bond, but that does not mean he's going to treat me like a partner in the Family business. A woman in the Shadow Domain is nothing more than a breedmare; she doesn't need to know anything other than when her husband wants her on her back. Perhaps one day I can change that, but it will be two thousand years of tradition I'll be fighting – as well as Varius' paranoia about a coup.

He's survived too many to not instantly see my innocent attempts at becoming his equal as a veiled threat.

Hurting for all the shit he has been through, for all the paranoia that has been forced on him since he was a kid, when that first knife went into his back, I pull out the stuff needed to make waffles. They're his comfort food. And they are quickly becoming mine too.

"So why were you babysitting Khalid?" I ask as I crack open the eggs and separate the whites from the yolks. "He get hurt too?"

I look up to see Maddox shake his head. In another bowl, I start mixing the egg yolks, milk, butter, and vanilla extract into a batter.

"Nah. Turns out the dumbass bonded to a fucking WALL member, and he's been chasing her all night. Varius wanted me to stick with him so he didn't do anything stupid."

I stare at him dumbly, my mind incapable of computing any part of that. The WALL are humans who hate sups so much that they vivisect us and call it God's work. I know Khalid has been obsessing over some girl for the past three months, but a *WALL* member?

"Let me guess, she knows how to kill a werewolf with a toothpick?" I finally manage.

He laughs.

"Wait a sec," I cut in just as he starts to say something. "Varius asked *you* to keep Khalid in line. *You*?"

"Hey!"

"You have a six-inch-tall sex fiend as a pet in your room. You keep her in a fish tank, and she humps her tower. You cannot possibly argue you were the best pick for the job."

He starts to try, then he grins. "Yeah, I just happened to be in the wrong place at the wrong time."

"And did you?"

He cocks his head. "Did I what?"

"Stop him from doing anything stupid?"

"Depends on your definition of stupid."

"Will Varius be happy about it?"

"The guy's never happy."

I open my mouth to tell him that's not true, but then I shake my head. If someone knows what makes you happy, they'll know what will break you. And Maddox specializes in torture for the Family. Varius wouldn't be happy with me sharing anything about him at all.

"Have you never seen him happy?" I ask softly, my heart hurting over just how distant he has to be with everyone.

"I haven't, no. By the time I was born, he was how he is now. But the others say he used to laugh a lot. He used to read them bedtime stories and show them bugs he found."

"Did he have a favorite bug?" Maybe I can get him a pet for his birthday. *When is his birthday?*

"You'll have to ask Leno. Or Talon. They know him best."

"Not Khalid?"

"Obviously Khalid, but he ain't gonna share shit."

I laugh as I go back to making the waffles. Of course he wouldn't. But I like that about him, that he has Varius' back all the way.

"But I wouldn't ask either of them," Maddox says softly after a few minutes of silence. The batter has been mixed and is cooking in the waffle maker. I have a pan of omelets going and another sizzling with bacon.

"No?" I ask, not turning around as I focus on keeping everything from burning.

He shakes his head. "Varius doesn't like snooping, and I would hate to see him become suspicious of you."

My heart aching, I realize getting him a pet would be a bad idea anyway. Insect or dog or cat – it doesn't matter. Pets are clear weaknesses. Hurt them, hurt Varius.

He would never let himself love it.

And with that realization comes another one.

Feeling cold, I flip over the bacon.

Varius has no real understanding of what love is. So how can he ever truly love me?

FIVE

HER

After breakfast, I start to clean up, and Sau joins me in the kitchen.

"Are you sure you should be up?" I ask her. She looks just as flawless as always – her long black hair beautifully shiny and lush, her green eyes highlighted by dark eyeliner, but there's a heaviness on her shoulders that seems to bow her inwards despite the strict posture of her back.

"I'm a single mother of eight boys. It's going to take more than a curse to keep me down." She gives me a look that reinforces that statement, and I smile at her.

"I don't know how you did it," I say, shaking my head as I stack the dishes in the dishwasher. "I know there's over a decade between them all, but how did you ever survive their teenage years? Especially Maddox's?" I shudder.

She laughs as she grabs a dishcloth to start wiping down the table. "With a lot of weed."

I glance at her in shock.

"I used to 'hide' a stash in my room. The boys would find it, do it, and then I'd get a blissful few hours of peace as they zonked out. Though once, Rudy and Talon watched a snail for three hours as it tried to climb a wall. They were torn between rooting for it every time it went higher and being sad that it was going further away from any food source. The next morning, I find out they spent the night attaching shelves to the outside of the house, then stacking them with all our fruit and vegetables. I was livid as Varius was hosting his first meeting here, and all the shops were closed so I couldn't restock. Thank gods, none of the capos were vegetarian then."

I laugh. She comes over to the sink and shakes out the crumbs she collected on her cloth.

"You weren't worried about weed leading to the harder stuff?" I ask as I turn on the dishwasher.

She gives me a look. "We run a drug empire, Micha. If they wanted to try something, all they had to do was throw their last name around. Everyone wanted their favor."

I incline my head.

Hanging the dishcloth over the sink to dry, she turns to me. "We're making healing potions today. The boys used a good amount of them last night, and they will need more by the time this war ends."

"Can Varius use them?" I ask as I follow her out of the kitchen.

"Of course."

"So it's just premades he can't use?" I press. I know she traded all his magic to save his life when he was a baby, but there's just something about that story that is bothering me. I don't know what, so I'm just fishing for information.

Premades are wands created for non-magic users to use. They work by pulling on the dormant talent of the person wielding it though, so not everyone can use them. Most humans from Earth (rather than the collective 'humans' that cover anyone who's been created in the image of a god) can't use them. Nor can any sup who hasn't passed their ascension – a sort of magical evolution that hits during puberty, as they don't have any magic in them before then to activate the wand. Unless that sup is a witch; we are born with magic. It is a part of us, entwined with our blood, our souls.

So if Varius was a vampire who'd never hit his ascension or a werewolf or a dragon or one of the thousands of other humans out there (those who have a humanoid form gifted to them by the gods), then it'd make sense why he couldn't use a premade.

But he is a witch.

Sau might have traded his magic to save his life, offering it up as payment in some dark spell, but she couldn't have ripped it from him without killing him. And in evidence of that, Varius' brothers are able to use him as a sort of battery from time to time, topping up their supply with his.

So I know he still has enough magic inside him to be able to use a wand, and the puzzle is driving me insane.

"It seems to be so," she says.

"Why is that?"

"I don't know."

"But you cast the spell." I try not to make the words come out accusatory, like I think she's hiding something. But a part of me wonders if she is.

She glances at me as she takes that first step down the stairs, heading for the basement. "Have you ever used dark magic, Micha?" she asks.

I shake my head. I've heard stories though; every witch has. The amount of power you can gain with it is legendary. Witches use it to extend their lives, to sink entire cities into the ground. To create plagues that can wipe out a third of the population, to change into great beasts much bigger than themselves.

With regular magic, you need physical access to the extra mass or the ingredients needed for the spell, but with dark magic, you can take it from anywhere. There are cases of large groups of people going missing – the crew of the Mary Celeste, the settlers of the Roanoke Colony, the fifty-thousand soldiers of the Army of Cambyses. These mass disappearances can normally all be linked back to a witch playing around with something they shouldn't.

Such cases draw the attention of the archangels though, and no amount of magic will save you from their wrath.

"When we cast a spell," Sau says as we descend into the basement, "we control it. We shape it how we want it to act. We limit it in its entirety so it can't run free. But with dark magic, it controls *you*. You can give it an idea of what you want, but the outcome is never guaranteed. There's also a good chance it kills you instead of doing whatever it is you want."

"You must have acted quickly then, to stop it from going wild."

She smiles tightly as we reach the door to the spellroom. "I guess so."

"You guess?"

Opening the door, she steps inside. "Honestly, I do not remember much. One moment I was focused on Caden as he screamed in his nightmare. The next..." She trails off. Her lips draw tight, a haunted memory beating inside her skull. "Caden was a strong telekinetic," she says softly. "He ripped Varius into so many pieces, I'm not sure how I found them all to even cast the spell."

I shudder, my stomach knotting at the idea of him being in so much pain. Or perhaps there was no pain then, death having taken him quickly.

"Did you have to bring him back from Purgatory?" I ask as I follow her to the cabinets where we keep the potions and their ingredients. Necromancy is a hard-learned skill, taking two to three decades to master. As far as I know, Sau doesn't know the first thing about it – just like most people don't. It's one of the rarest skills out there.

"I guess so."

I frown. I know Sau loves her children, and I can't think of a single reason for her to lie about what happened to Varius' magic, but you don't just get lucky at necromancy. You bring back a twisted mess – *if* you manage not to die in the process in the first place.

"Or maybe I kept him alive long enough with my healing magic," she says. "His head and torso was still together – at least, it was above the heart."

My stomach churns at the thought of a baby looking like that, but it's the only thing that could be possible. Sau is a damn strong healer. If she reacted within seconds, she could have made sure he didn't bleed out or die of shock while she reattached his other parts with dark magic.

"It's a good thing you didn't panic then," I say. "Seeing that, I don't know many who wouldn't have."

She looks at me sadly. "I panicked the previous times."

The words are a sucker punch to my chest. Varius might be her firstborn, but that is a moving title in the Shadow Domain, passing down to the oldest survivor. There were fourteen other kids before him. I do not know the details of their deaths, but I can see the pain in her eyes. They did not go gently into the night.

Feeling like shit for bringing all this up for no reason other than my own curiosity, I turn to the shelf of unused vials. "So how many healing potions do you think we should make?" I ask.

"As much as we can," she says as she picks up a box of them. "Before the treaty, Antonio targeted our healers first, the rest of the women second. You kill a man, you kill one soldier. You kill a healer –"

"You kill everyone they can fix."

She nods. "And if you kill a breedmare –"

"You kill the next generation."

"Exactly. So we shall make enough not just for my boys but for as many women as are in our Family." She picks up an entire box of empty vials, then pauses. "I killed Antonio's pups and his mate all in one day. Even when he signed the treaty, I knew his desire for revenge had not been sated. He will not stop until all my sons are dead." She swallows, then looks into my eyes. "I half hope you don't get pregnant until this war is over."

My blood chills as my fingers itch to press over my belly. My period is normally irregular, but I just had it a couple weeks ago, although it was lighter and shorter than usual, so I know I'm not carrying, but I feel an instinctive need to protect my womb.

"Though with the way Varius is going..." Sau says with a sudden smirk, "we better kill the Death Hunt quickly."

My cheeks on fire, all I can do is nod.

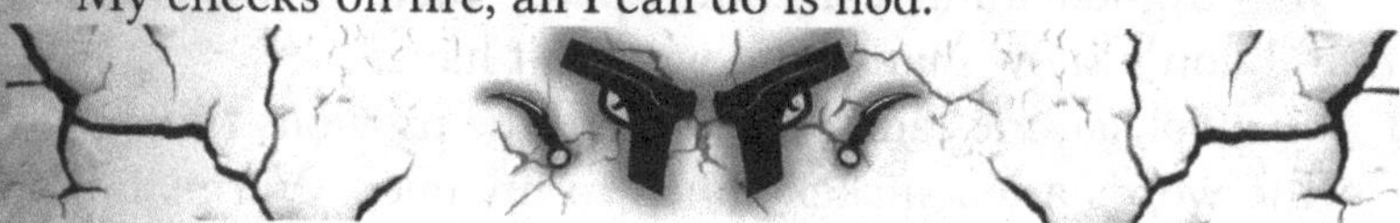

In the last three hours, I have made more potions than I have in my entire life. Before I was purchased by Varius, I was an assassin who went out on missions with my best friend. He was my spotter, the plan maker, and healer, so I only carried healing potions for the jobs where we had to split up. Mine aren't great for fixing major damage, but they held me over until I could get back to him. Dayne isn't as advanced in his healing magic as Sau (no one is), but he knows his shit way better than I know how to make healing potions. He's done well over the years, patching me up whenever I got stabbed, shot, or hit with a particularly nasty spell.

"Don't be stingy with the sideritis," Sau says as I very, very carefully add pinches of the ground perennial to the pot of glacier blue liquid. Fog rises off it, smelling strongly of mint and ice.

"You literally just said it could blow up in my face if I get it wrong." Which really makes me think this healing potion recipe is a farce. Dying while making one should *not* be a possibility in my book unless you really fucked it up. But then, this recipe is Sau's own. Not only is she the best healer in all of North America, but she also survived a bloody war and has crafted her technique over decades.

"I can heal you," she says simply.

"Khalid will kill me if you use your magic." He told me so. Very, very clearly on the first day I got here. I might be engaged to his brother, and Khalid might be his bodyguard whenever Varius is out, but Khalid is also the reaper. And I am absolutely terrified of him.

"Khalid will do no such thing. He –"

"No." I shake my head. "Not risking it. I'm just going to add this in very, very slowly... It'll just take an extra two, three seconds and –"

"*Stop*," Sau demands, and I jerk my hand away from the pot, careful not to drop any more of the sideritis into it. My heart hammering, I wait for the thing to explode.

It does not.

Thank the fucking gods.

"Good. Now add your magic to it."

"While thinking about happy, funny things," I murmur. Magic feeds on emotions. Stress-free treatment is better for one's recovery, and laughter is the best medicine. The brain releases an increase of endorphins, natural painkillers, and neuropeptides when you laugh, and all those things help with the healing process.

Ducking my head, trying to pretend Sau isn't standing right beside me, I place a hand into the pot. As my magic pulses out of my fingers, I think about what Varius did the first time I got my period.

"*Why didn't you come to me?*" *Varius growls as I exit my ensuite, wrapped in a towel and fresh from my shower.*

My brain glitches out at the sight of him naked on my bed, his cock hard and in his hand. He's stroking it, and I can't breathe. He's fucked me for hours every night for the past few weeks. I should be able to see it without losing the ability to think by now. But dear fucking gods, it just does something to me, seeing it in his hand. Seeing him take the pleasure he wants.

I try to think of something sexy to say, but of course my mouth decides to go in the complete opposite direction.

"Because the monthly hillbilly has come to town," I blurt, *"and it's murdering all the – actually, no, that doesn't work, does it?"* I laugh awkwardly and high-pitched. *"Because it's normally the bimbos going into his hometown in horror movies. So the monthly girls are getting slaughtered…"* I cringe. Oh my gods, why isn't he telling me to shut up? *"My period,"* I croak. *"I'm on my period."*

He stares at me without blinking. His hand doesn't stop stroking his thick cock. "And what do hillbillies slaughtering bimbos," Varius deadpans, *"have to do with why you're not riding my cock right now?"*

I blow out a breath on a nervous giggle even as heat flares through me. "Okay, one, that sentence should never exist. You can't start off with a horrible analogy for one's period and then transition into something that hot. And two…um…it's messy?"

He stands up, then walks towards me, herding me back into the ensuite. The intensity of his eyes never waver. "Get in the shower, Micha. I'm going to fuck that hillbilly right out of his own damn town."

I giggle, both in my memory and now in the kitchen. The neon blue liquid starts to froth, churning back and forth as if it's laughing too. But I didn't laugh for long once he got me in the shower. I didn't do much other than scream and –

"That's good," Sau says, and I blush hard. Yanking my head out of those 'happy thoughts,' I pull my hand out of the pot. My magic fades from my fingertips, and I grab the hand towel on the counter to dry my hand. Feeling slightly dizzy, the continuous use of magic starting to drain me, I make my way to the refrigerator and pour myself a cup of juice as she fills up the next set of vials with a pipette, then seals them with a cork. Making a single batch of potions doesn't use much magic, barely any at all, but we've been at this for hours, and I have been fueling the bulk of our creations.

"This batch will go to the soldiers of the Family," she says as I rejoin her. That's a polite way of telling me I didn't do that great of a job. The ones she made will stay here with her sons, those potions being stronger. Although I have been following her instructions to the letter, magic is often fickle.

"Think of funnier things," she says as she finishes up. "Thoughts of sex might send out dopamine, endorphins, and oxytocin, but laughter really is the best medicine."

A strained noise escapes me as my face full on explodes in a blush. "Noted," I squeak. I don't think I'll ever get used to how open this family is when it comes to discussing sex.

"But other than that, you did a great job."

"Thanks. These are much stronger than anything I have ever made."

"They're still not as good as a mediocre healer for most things." Using a healing potion is like shopping for clothes at a department store when you're a foot above average or between sizes. Yeah, you can find things that cover you, but the chances of an off-the-shelf dress hugging your specific curves just right or a long-sleeve shirt actually stopping at your wrists rather than half-way up your arms is pretty low. The magic is too generic. It doesn't have the proper focus needed to fix bones and reseal wounds to the point that no other recovery is needed.

"Better than most human treatment though," I say.

She inclines her head as she corks the last vial.

My phone buzzes in my pocket, and I dig it out to see a text from Varius. "He's calling everyone back for a meeting at lunch," I say. I glance at the clock in the kitchen. Twelve fifteen. He likes to eat at one. My eyes narrowing, I text back.

Micha: *You couldn't have given a better head's up?*

Cooking for eleven (the eight Shadow brothers, me, Sau, and Leno's dog, who absolutely does not get dog food given Leno can taste everything he eats) takes fucking ages. At least at breakfast, only half of them ever show up. Maddox is rarely awake at that time. Rudy and Enoch like cereal. Ezriel only drinks coffee, and Talon usually isn't here at all.

He doesn't reply, and I roll my eyes as I shove my phone back into my pocket. "Lunch meeting," I tell Sau.

She doesn't react with the same annoyance I did. She just nods gracefully, ever the polite fucking lady – the one I am supposed to be learning how to be.

Biting back a muttered curse for a certain neanderthal, I start to pull out the ingredients needed for a stir fry.

SIX
HIM

As my seven brothers and I all sit around the kitchen table, waiting to be served by Micha and Mother, we discuss the shitstorm we ran into last night. Antonio is faster than a fucking bullet – something that shouldn't be possible and which caught us completely off guard.

His Family has always eaten the dead members of their pack as a way to keep their "souls" with them. Somewhere along the line, though, that ritual turned into actual magic, and with every soul consumed, they gain a small boost of power. But the keyword is *small.* Antonio would have had to eat a whole pack, if not more, to gain the strength and speed he has now.

"You think he's captured a rival pack?" Rudy, my second youngest brother, signs. He was born unable to speak due to Mother having been hit with a blast of magic while she was pregnant with him.

It's a good question. Although the magic only works if

the werewolves eaten are part of the pack, he could have forced them in as omegas – those whose entire purpose is to be bullied to strengthen the rest of the pack, before he killed them.

Talon shakes his head, then signs, as we all do in respect to Rudy. "We would've heard something if he had."

"He could be eating his own?" Maddox throws out as he glances at me.

"He would have been challenged," Leno says. He is the second eldest and sees (and can also feel and taste) through his dog Krypto, having lost his eyes to a werewolf when he was a kid. Despite his injury though, he doesn't hate them like Talon hates the vampires. If anything, he's fascinated by their culture and knows more about them than most of us do.

However, even I know a werewolf isn't born as an alpha. That is a position that is fought for, and most of the pack is made up of women he gets to fuck. If Antonio started killing his own pack just to eat them as a power source, they would have turned on him.

"So if it can't be outsiders because we haven't heard of any attacks," Maddox, my youngest brother, says, kicking back in his chair until it rocks on two legs, "and it can't be his own pack because they would have killed him, then who the fuck does that leave?"

My attention flickers away for a moment as Micha walks towards me with a plate of stir fry. I breathe in deep until I can smell her raspberry and cream body wash beneath the spicy aroma of the Schezwan beef. The tattoo on my cock burns as it starts to harden, and I am so godsdamn close to calling this meeting over so I can fuck her on the table.

All morning, I have resisted the urge to text her to come upstairs to my office so I could bury my tongue in her pussy while I thought of how to divide Antonio's territory. After we started the blood bond last night, all I seem to want to do is laze the day away between her thighs. But I have a family to protect and a Family to run. So I force my gaze to roam around my brothers rather than go to her. "Regardless of who he's eating," I say, "Antonio must be killed before he manages to make a hybrid. That gives us only a few months max." My gaze stops on Khalid, my brother and bodyguard and the reaper of this Family. "Which is why you and I are going to visit Aleric today to make a deal."

"What?" Maddox shouts as he drops his chair down on all fours. The *thump* of it hitting the wooden floorboards is accentuated by the shattering plate beside Leno. He flinches. Krypto's eyes were on me, so he didn't see what happened. Mother is standing there in a mess of stir fry.

"Varius," she starts, but I cut her off.

"We cannot allow hybrids to be made whatever the cost. I understand your disliking of him with everything you two have been through." Her lips tighten into a thin line. "But this is not a discussion. We will eliminate the Death Hunt together, then divide their territory and business." I've spent all fucking morning working out how we'll split everything between our two gangs. We'll capitalize on taking over the majority of their drug trade, and Aleric will get a monopoly on human trafficking.

"Why not kill them too?" Talon sneers as Mother bends down to clean up the mess she caused. His hands fist on the table in front of him. There isn't a plate there, not yet, Micha having only served Leno and me so far. She'll move to Khalid next, then Talon, working her way down the table from oldest to youngest. "What they have done to this Family demands retribution," my brother growls.

Despite his word choice though, I know he means what they have done to *him*. Talon's hatred of them is surpassed only by Mother's. Jackie, his childhood sweetheart, was a bloodbank – one of the humans the group feeds on. Unlike cattle – the humans that are bled dry in one go, bloodbanks hold rank in their gang. It is the lowest rank, but it is one nonetheless and they didn't care for one of their own falling in love with the enemy. So they stalked the two of them on their first date, and when my brother left her alone for two seconds, they killed her and painted 'witch whore' on her forehead in her own blood. Talon got back just in time to watch her die in his arms.

He hasn't forgiven them in the decades since and has constantly toed the line of our treaty, pushing against it as hard as he can but not quite enough to break it.

Holding his gaze, I say, "The Blood Fangs haven't broken any terms of the treaty, and they make up almost half of the police department." He starts to say something, but I sharply add, "*And* a good chunk of the local court system. Weeding them all out will open positions for WALL to fill. A drawn out war will have more chances of bringing in the SCU."

"They haven't visited this city in decades."

"Thanks to the treaty Mother got Antonio and Aleric to sign. That is now gone, and they will return if we drag out another war." The Special Crimes Unit polices our kind here on Earth, but their numbers are stretched thin. So they leave us alone as long as we only kill other sups and don't reveal our existence, but we can't involve the humans in our death tolls. A war will not discriminate nor will it give us time to hide the bodies we kill with our magic under the blade of a knife. Such deaths will puzzle the local community, and they will call in the Special Crimes Unit. The humans don't know that the private international company, famous for solving weird cases, is actually part of a world they know nothing about. But if we draw them back here and they get wind of Antonio trying to make fucking hybrids? They are a branch of the Elv've'Nor – the interplanal equivalent of the CIA or MI6, and they have a direct line to the fucking archangels.

"Our business does not clash with the bloodbanks and sex trafficking the vampires do," I say to my brothers. "They will avoid hunting and dealing in our territory after this meeting." I sweep my eyes across the table. "So until they become a threat, we will leave them be. There will be no more attacking them" –my gaze settles back on Talon as he seethes in silence– "nothing to break the deal I make with Aleric today. Do I make myself clear?"

Jerking his head, my brother gives me his obedience. He isn't happy about it, but he knows ignoring a blatant order will see him dead. Traitors are not given second chances in this Family. Blood or not.

Feeling the weight of a recent loss, the torture and death of a man I trusted, I find Micha in my peripheral vision. She turns to me with a small smile, and I look away, not trusting my family to know she's become more than just the womb I purchased her for.

The rest of my brothers all nod, though the tension of my decision does not dissipate as we eat. As the rich spices of the Szechwan stir fry fill my mouth, I can't help but wonder if this decision has just damned my family.

If Talon or Mother or any of them breach the terms of this agreement, Khalid will be forced to kill them. But we cannot survive without the Blood Fangs' alliance.

I can only hope they come to understand that.

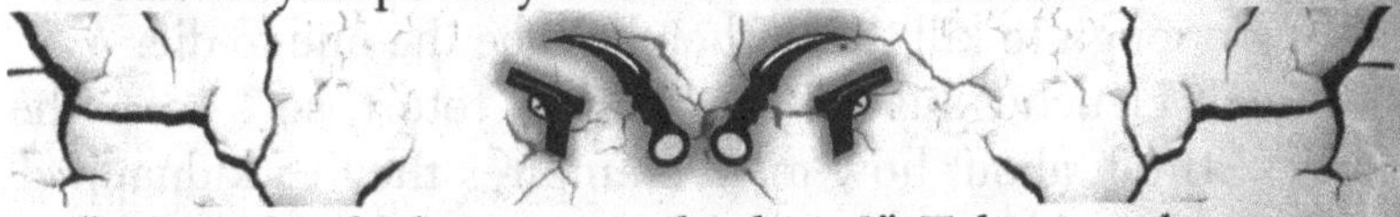

"What the fuck are you thinking?" Talon seethes as we discuss this in his room after lunch, just the two of us. I knew he would be the worst one to get on board, especially given how much he loves to fuck with the Blood Fangs' operations. He sabotages their wares, steals their clients, and has even killed a few vamps – those of lower rank only though, whose deaths won't break the terms of the treaty.

"We should just let Antonio kill all the Blood Fangs," he spits.

"And live harmoniously with the Death Hunt after?" I ask flatly.

"We can kill them after they deal with the vamps."

My eyes drift over the pink slashes across his shoulders. "You think we can handle them after what he did to you?" It took Antonio less than thirty seconds to rip Talon apart. His arms and legs were nearly hanging off him, cut so deep only slivers of skin remained. I could see his heart beating under the crushed cavity of his ribcage.

"He only managed this because he caught me alone," he says. "If we hit him all together –"

"He's too fast for even Enoch and Ezriel to grab." Given they are both strong telekinetics, having inherited Father's innate magic, they don't have to be close to something to grab it. But by the time they spotted Antonio, he was gone.

"If we trap him with magic –" Talon starts.

"Which barely works on him." Werewolves are naturally resistant to magic, and Antonio is more immune than most. At his current power, I'm not even sure if Khalid's soul magic would work on him. My brother can usually kill a person from anywhere in the world as long as he has their DNA, but what no one else knows is it's always a battle of power between the strength of their souls. If Khalid isn't strong enough to kill them, then he'll be the one to die.

Talon clenches his jaw but has no retort, so I press the issue. "Think about how many vampires they've kidnapped, T. Antonio can't have overseen every grab himself, so there has to be other members of his pack who are just as fast as he is." Born vampires have the ability to phase. In less than a second, they can vanish. With their keen sense of smell, they'll spot a werewolf a mile away; no wolf is sneaking up on them without magic.

"They could be setting traps," he counters, and the hairs on my neck rise. He is being too defensive of the Death Hunt, having excuses ready for why we should leave them be.

My voice deadly calm, I say, "Is that what they're doing, T?"

"They could be. I don't –" His eyes widen as he gets what I'm actually asking. *Did you buy into their bullshit when you were undercover at their brothels?*

"I'd *never* betray this family," he growls, his spine rigid.

He holds my gaze strongly, and I am reminded of the 'brother' he recently lost. He was his best friend, as close as solid blood, but when he turned traitor, Talon walked away from him, leaving him to be tortured. His loyalty to this family has never been in question – only his loyalty to me. Though even that was unfounded.

Still, someone is blackmailing my fiancee into finding and stealing our Family ledger. And though I do not think it is any of my brothers due to them all knowing where the ledger is, Talon has the ability to fuck with technology. He could have easily hacked her phone to send her the threats.

"Fucking hel, Varius," he spits. "You know my stance on hybrids. I ain't backing Antonio if he's messing with that shit."

If there's one thing Talon hates more than vampires, it's hybrids. They are the scum of the earth according to him. Abominations that need to be put down. It is a view shared by most people; those pregnant with halfbreeds are hunted down and their fetuses ripped from their bellies and burned.

"So we are in agreement then. Siding with the vampires is better than dealing with hybrids."

My brother's lips flatten as he runs a hand through his dark hair. "Fuck. Fine," he snaps. "I'll honor the treaty."

"Good," I say, "because you're coming with us to the meeting."

"The fuck I am!"

I don't repeat myself, and he curses.

"Why?" he demands.

"To show your support of this alliance. I know it's you who's been killing the lower vamps."

I can hear his teeth grinding, but he doesn't protest.

"You have fifteen minutes," I say as I turn. "Then wake Khalid."

Our brother has been up all night, first killing wolves, then killing the people who hurt his girl. He needs his rest before we walk into the belly of the beast. Opening the door, I leave Talon seething in anger. Pulling out my phone, I text Micha to come to my office.

Micha: *Yes, sir.*

I can practically hear her sarcasm, and my lips twitch as I slide my phone back into my pocket. She arrives less than a minute after I enter, closing the door behind her as I prick my finger with a needle.

"You want a quickie?" she asks hopefully.

My cock jerks up, saying yes despite the pain (although I have now wrapped it), but I shake my head. "Come here."

Her smile falling a bit, she crosses the room as I squeeze out a large drop of blood onto my fingertip.

"Who do you think is blackmailing you?" I ask, knowing she has been trying to figure it out.

She stops on the other side of the desk. There is a flash in her eyes, a look of guilt that causes my paranoia to rise. "I don't –"

"Don't lie to me," I say, catching her gaze for a heartbeat before turning away to smear my blood onto the keypad of the safe behind me. The painting that normally hangs over it leans up against the wall below it. My blood is eaten by the magic protecting the metal safe as I key in the access code, then the ward grants me access. I open the door and pull out the leather notebook inside. Turning to Micha, I drop it on my desk.

She stares at me, a wariness in her eyes.

"Tell the blackmailer you have the ledger," I say.

"And how would I have gotten it?"

"You think he'll want to know how?"

"You think it's a guy?" she asks, just as sharp.

I smile. My cock jumps, turned on by her brain. "Do you not?"

She hesitates, studying me. A flash of pain darts across her eyes before she buries it. I keep my face completely free of my thoughts even as my blood freezes in my veins. What is she worried about? What is she hiding?

"The blackmailer texted me when the house was empty," she says slowly. "Your brothers –"

"All know where the safe is," I say, my eyes narrowing slightly. "As well as how to get into it."

"I didn't know that," Micha says, but she doesn't sound convinced it isn't one of them.

My fingers itch with the need to clench into fists and go a couple rounds with the bag – or an opponent I can make bleed.

"Who do you think it is?" I ask. I don't want to believe her, but nor do I want to believe that she's trying to get me to turn on them. To divide us so her Family or someone else who might have hired her can come in and fuck us over as we fight among ourselves.

"I don't know." She shakes her head. "But whoever it was knew the house was empty when they texted me."

"So you think it's one of my brothers?" I ask flatly. And then it clicks. Her question about the blackmailer being a male. "Or my mother?"

"Who else could've known?" she says.

You.

The blackmailer had 'conveniently' deleted all evidence of their existence from her phone. She claimed they were using Dayne, her best friend, to manipulate her, but I had a guy watching him for months, knowing that the easiest way to get to Micha (and, in turn, to me) was through her best friend. No one had threatened him at all.

Is she lying about the whole thing?

I hate that I am having these thoughts. That even though we've bonded, I still can't trust her.

I search inside myself, looking for the first tether of that bond, for any sort of emotional connection at all.

But there is nothing.

Did she even really start it? Or was that just a lie to get me to lower my guard?

My blood runs cold, but now that I've had that thought, I can't shake it. I should be able to feel *something* even with the mere few drops of blood we supposedly exchanged, and yet there is nothing.

Not one iota of her emotions runs through me.

Does she have any for me at all?

"How are you supposed to get in touch with him?" I ask.

"He gave me two weeks."

"That deadline passed."

"Yeah…" she says slowly. "Yeah, it did."

Yet there has been no repercussion… Almost as if he does not care about the ledger. Or if he does not exist at all…

Silence descends, taut and heavy and fucked crushing in its presence. I want her to give me a reason to trust her, to say something that answers all the questions now in my mind. To prove to me that she isn't a mole. Hasn't just made things up to get close to me, to get the ledger I've just tossed onto the table between us.

"If he's watching your phone, taking a picture of it might suffice," I say, no longer comfortable with her taking it out of this office, even if it is a fake.

"Yeah…" she says with a small nod as she digs her phone out of her purse. "We'll see if they get in touch." She snaps a picture. "They'll probably want to see a few pages of the inside."

"Have a spread in mind?"

She glances up at me with her head still pointed at the book. "Have any allies in there you don't like?"

The tension in my chest eases a little at the sly smile she gives me. "Everyone. I'm not the biggest fan of people."

She laughs, and my muscles relax just a bit more. I open the book to a random page that doesn't incriminate any of my brothers or my mother. The chances of the person being able to decrypt my code is low. The chances of them using this information in any way whatsoever is even lower given the entire book is filled with false information. The crimes in it might be real, but everything is just slightly tweaked so nothing in it can be matched to any evidence.

The book might say I killed John and buried his body in the garden of Client A (as we run a legitimate landscaping business just for that), but in reality, I was down in Miami when Talon killed him and chucked his body in the sea.

I flip through to another page, this one dealing with the names of the people we're blackmailing – politicians, CEOs, celebrities, anyone with cash or weight. We have lured them to the hotels we run so we can document their affairs, their drug taking, their purchasing of whores. We also take their DNA to use at crime scenes or in my brother's soul magic, making them our bitch forever.

She slips the phone into her purse, and I pick up the book to put it back in the safe. As I turn though, she stops me. "If it *is* someone who lives here, they might ask me to take more photos when they know you're not home. Just as solid proof I actually have it."

"Then stall."

"Do you not trust me with it?" she asks outright, and I turn, the book in my hands.

"I won't risk my brothers' lives for anyone."

"You're not risking anything with a fake though, are you?"

I still. Not even my family knows the ledger is a lie.

"I know how paranoid you are, Varius," she says softly. "You wouldn't have let me take incriminating photos even of your enemies."

"I would to save you."

Her mouth drops open slightly.

Turning, I toss the ledger into the safe, then shut its door and hang the abstract painting back over it. I step around the desk to head for the hall. She moves into my path.

"You know I love you, right?" Micha asks as she tilts her head up to hold my gaze; she's much shorter than me, the top of her head only reaching to my chest.

I want to say yes, but the word stays stuck in my throat. I try to feel something, anything through our bond. But still there is nothing.

I nod. But I don't know if that's a lie.

Stepping around her, my chest tight, I leave her alone in my office.

SEVEN

HIM

I head downstairs to talk to Mother, needing to ask her a question before I meet with Aleric. I find her in the kitchen, sitting at the counter, her hands pressed to the wood as she hums. She's talking to it – or rather, to *her*. To the monster who died and whose ashes have been magically mixed into the twisted knots of the zebrano – an old companion of hers called Olivia.

She looks up as I enter the kitchen. She slides her hands across the counter in a farewell, then stands as I reach her.

"You can't trust him," she says.

"You trusted him to save Khalid," I counter, referencing a call she made to him three months ago. For how much she claims to hate the vampire, he was the first one she thought of to help her.

"I have something he wants," she says tightly. "You do not."

"I have the resources to save his Family."

"The only person that fucker cares about is himself," she scoffs, for once not being the perfect pleasant lady she was raised to be.

"Then why would he agree to the meeting?" I ask.

"To lure you in and kill you."

I shake my head. "He can't afford a war on both sides."

"He'll sacrifice his whole Family for –" She stops as she presses her lips into a thin line.

"What does he want with you?" I ask softly.

She shakes her head. "That's between me and him."

"Will it interfere with the alliance?"

"No."

"The meeting?"

"No."

I want to trust her, but she's lied to me for too long about other things. "What did he ask you for in exchange when he saved Khalid?" I ask again, this time not as a son but as her Boss.

She lifts her chin. "Please don't press this."

I don't say a word, letting my silence speak for me.

"He wants me to put on lotion every night."

My eyes narrow. "Lotion?"

"Yes." The word is ground out, and I know there is more meaning to the simple action. Something she despises.

"That's what he asked for when he risked his life to save Khalid?"

My brother was on a job as the reaper, hunting down an ally turned traitor. He was cut to pieces, nearly lost both his hands, and only managed to take down his opponent by using the reckless power of a spoken spell before he passed out from blood loss.

But I saw the two marks on the traitor's neck when I collected his body. There were teethmarks beneath the cut of a knife, and Aleric had blood on his mouth that night. Khalid didn't kill the traitor – or at least, he didn't kill him fast enough. The man would have ended him in his final moments if Aleric hadn't arrived and ripped out his jugular.

Which he supposedly did simply in exchange for Mother applying lotion every night?

It doesn't make fucking sense.

Unless it's just a power play.

Gaining pleasure from forcing her to obey.

Feeling pissed he thinks he can fuck with my family, I turn for the door to kill him. Fuck the meeting. Fuck using his gang to protect my own. I'll find another way for us to –

"Varius, wait."

I stop instinctively, the tone she used ingrained within my soul, demanding obedience.

"He's forcing you –" I growl with my back to her.

"My entire life, *I* have been *forced* to do things."

My fists clench. "I can stop –"

"But I am not forced in this," she cuts in. "I *chose* it to save Khalid. It is mere lotion," she says strongly. "He cannot force me to think what he wants me to."

To think about him while she applies it, she means.

My stomach churns at the thought of him obsessing over her. Jacking off to her. Then plummets at the sudden arrival of a memory.

Not too long ago, I entered her room, thinking someone was in there while she was out. But the noises I heard were from a porno playing on her TV. With a woman that looked like her. There was a bottle of lotion on her nightstand...

That was the day Micha was blackmailed.

The day someone knew we were all out.

The day Aleric called me away to a parlay held in the center of town and then failed to show.

"Can Aleric pass our wards?" I ask.

She jerks back. "Of course not. Why –"

"How did he drop off Khalid when he saved him?"

"He came and got me. You saw him grab me –"

"He's broken past our wards before."

"Decades ago. We've strengthened them since. Where is this coming from?"

I pause, then force out the words, trying not to imagine them as I say them. "The day we were all out of the house, you left the TV on in your room." Another pause. "It was playing a porno."

Spinning on her feet, she picks up the dishcloth hanging over the sink's faucet. She soaks it, then starts to wipe down the pristine counter, her back facing me.

"Mother."

"I left it on," she says. "I...asked him for another favor, and he –"

"I'll kill him." I turn.

"Don't."

That damn tone again stops me.

"We need this alliance, Varius," she says.

"You were originally against it."

"I wasn't thinking logically then; you aren't right now."

My jaw clenches, but I know she's right. I just want one fucking excuse to kill the guy. He irritates me like no one else can.

"I'll make him end your deal," I say. "As part of ours –"

"Don't."

I spin back around, and she is facing me now, the wet cloth pinched between her fingers.

"Why not?"

"Because Aleric has a twisted mind. The lotion doesn't bother me, but take that away from him, and he'll think of something worse."

Like a fucking child throwing a tantrum.

"We could back Vlad –"

"He does not wish to lead."

"Then why is he with him?"

"Aleric had a son once."

"Did he kill himself?"

"No. Caden killed him in revenge for Aleric killing ours. But his name was Colton, and he was married to Vlad's sister," she says. "He stays around because Aleric is all he has left."

"It would be better to be alone."

"Agreed." A small smile flicks the corner of her lips up as I sense the arrival of my brothers.

I clench my jaw. All the other questions I have are going to have to wait. It's time to make a deal with our enemy.

EIGHT

HIM

Twenty minutes later, we park in front of Aleric's multi-million dollar house on Vilano Beach. All the members of his gang who live in the city are on this street, and each house had a vampire on its doorstep, watching us as we drove past in the afternoon sun. It is a myth, started by vampires long ago, that they will turn into ash at the barest touch of a ray. Them being unable to enter a house without permission or not having a reflection are also lies despite the WALL believing them. It makes it easy for a vamp to 'prove' they are human.

None of them followed us though; they just watched, so it is only Aleric who greets us here.

He stands in the doorway, his dark-gray eyes lingering on me as Talon, Khalid, and I climb out of the car. Maddox stays in the driver's seat. We've brought him with us just so Aleric knows we're not sneaking him in as a fly, that this meeting isn't a trap for him to study his body enough he can shift into him.

A glint of sunlight reflects off the horseshoe earring in his nose, and I instinctively glance away from the bright light. My gaze happens to go to Talon beside me, and I see all the shit I was smelling in the car – his rush of hormones, of anger and violence and adrenaline, clear in the clench of his fists and the tightness of his jaw. In the daggers he's glaring at Aleric, no doubt envisioning his death in a thousand different ways.

I know Aleric can sense it too. He looks too damn happy as he leads us into his [slaughter] house. It's the definition of modern living with dark grays and whites, full of wide open spaces with high ceilings and vast rooms.

Yet, it still manages to feel claustrophobic.

Or perhaps that is just how it feels when entering enemy territory.

Turning to me, Aleric smirks. "It is a new era when the head of the Shadow Domain visits my home," he says. "And without any guards either." He glances at my two brothers, making sure the dig hits home. Khalid ignores it, but Talon is damn near ready to kill him for it.

Aleric's smile widens, and I can see his desire to keep poking the already irritable bear.

"It became a new era," I reply flatly, "when the Death Hunt started massacring your people."

"Yes, quite." He doesn't seem concerned with it though, but at least it gets his attention off my brother.

Moving through the living room, he enters the kitchen, then continues on through to a study on the upper floor. The two walls perpendicular to the door are covered in books. The one opposite us contains a wide double window view of the ocean, with an alcove to sit in. A desk fills nearly a third of the room, and a black leather swivel chair sits behind it. Only one other chair, positioned in front of it, is available. I take a seat as my two brothers stay standing behind me.

Kicking back in his chair, Aleric places his feet on his desk. "I want Anastasia Island, his territory in Miami, and his stretch from Georgia to North Carolina. That basically gives you all of Florida."

"But leaves us surrounded by your territory."

He smiles.

"I'll give you," I say, taking great pleasure in watching his smile fall at the idea he is not in any position to barter, that all he can do is take what I gracefully feel like giving him, "Anastasia Island and his streets in Miami, as well as his stretch from Tallahassee to Atlanta, which will strengthen your hold in Alabama. You can have the coast of South Carolina and the range of mountains all around Asheville, but the rest of Antonio's territory is ours."

Aleric's gray eyes flash with a hint of mahogany – the first sign I am irritating him. If he gets properly pissed, his irises will turn a bloody red. "You drive a hard bargain," he says.

"We can always help the wolves wipe you out."

His smile is back, and I don't fucking like it. "You think Antonio will stop with our extinction now that he's made hybrids?" he asks.

I still, my muscles growing taut, my skin growing tighter. I want to move, but I refuse to acknowledge that we didn't know this. That we only thought he was trying to make them. That we had months before we would have to really act. My tone flat, I ask, "How many has he made?"

"Four."

"We'll kill them tonight," Talon growls from behind me.

"No need," Aleric says calmly as he leans further back and puts his hands behind his head, clasping his fingers. "He consumes them soon after birth." A lazy smile mocks me as he purrs, "I'm surprised Sau hasn't felt the imbalance. She was always so *sensitive* to such things..."

Talon's fury is so prominent, it's making my hairs rise.

The crackle of his electrically charged magic fills the air, but *I* am the one nearly an inch away from killing the bastard in front of me. If Talon knew what I did, what games he was playing with our mother, the vampire would be a splatter of red across the fucking walls and ceiling.

But we need this alliance. At least until we finish using them as bait and cannon fodder to discover what weapons Antonio has at his disposal.

"Is she sick?" Aleric asks innocently.

"No."

"Is she grieving for that turdstain she called a mate?"

Talon shifts behind me, and I turn to look at him. "Do you need to step out?" Father has always been a sore spot for him.

He shakes his head, his jaw locked hard. But he exhales, and his magic quiets, the charge in the air reducing.

"I'm not here to talk about her," I say, facing him again.

"So she is." His lips tighten, and there is a flash of red in his eyes that makes me cold. "Maybe she should have run away with him when he begged her to," he says.

"Father was not a coward," Talon growls.

He lifts his eyes to T's, mocking him, teasing him. "Being a coward was your father's defining trait. Why do you think Sau had to take her own revenge for her dead children? If she had been allowed to lead, we would be living in a very different world."

I watch him closely, picking up every minuscule change on his face. And there is pride there. In *her*.

A knot grows in my stomach, the pieces of the puzzle falling together in ways I do not want them to.

"I will accept the dividing of territory you proposed," he says, his tone now strictly business. "However, there is one thing I need to discuss with you first – in private."

"Out," I order.

As soon as the door clicks shut behind them, Aleric drops

his feet from the desk as he leans forward.

"How many males do you have left?" I ask before he can say anything. If the count is too low, then fuck him and this alliance. And he'll die today for playing with Mother.

"Ninety-six sired," he says with a shrug, "half of which are under twenty. You saw everyone else, minus those at work. There are three hundred and seven female vamps, many of which are born. Unlike your women, mine can fight." He grins; I don't. He inclines his head. "Though more men will arrive tomorrow." He says it casually, but I hear the acknowledgement beneath it. He knows he will lose this war without our help.

As will we.

The Blood Fangs used to number over a thousand in this city alone. If the Death Hunt is capable of killing hundreds in only a few months, then it isn't just Antonio we have to worry about. He's shared his new powers with others. There is no doubt about that now. The only question is how many super werewolves are fucking out there? How many with his new speed? His strength?

"But all this talk is meaningless," he says with a grin. "You have a traitor in your Family, and until you deal with her, I'm not signing shit."

"I don't know what –"

He waves his hand. "Someone wants Khalid gone. A call came in an hour ago saying your brother doesn't have an alibi for last night's murder and that there is a witness the police can interview."

My brother spent last night torturing and killing those who'd hurt his girl. He assured me this morning that he had dealt with all the evidence, having gotten Talon to wipe his image from the hotel's security cameras before the tapes were dropped off at the police station. There was one man who'd passed him in the hall – the witness Aleric speaks of. Killing him then would have caused more issues given he hadn't seen anything. But he knows when Khalid entered the premises. Knows the time of his alibi is a lie. Now he won't live to see the sunset.

I keep my voice flat, my face expressionless. "Who called it in?" *Is it the same person blackmailing Micha? Are they after the ledger to find leverage on the reaper?*

"You bring me a picture of your mom," Aleric says, "and I'll tell you."

"You mention my mom again, and I'll kill you."

He stills. "So protective..." A flash of red fills his eyes. "Are you fucking her?"

I'm on my feet, but he's there first, his hand around my throat. My knife touches his side, but he doesn't fucking care. I can see it in his eyes. Faster and stronger, he'll kill me before I can kill him, and he won't give a damn if he loses his entire Family for doing so when mine retaliates.

"Touch her like that," he says, "and I'll force you to blood bond with a pig." It isn't a growl. It isn't a wild threat. It's a simple promise. A godsdamn fact.

One way or another, he'll make it happen.

Now I know Aleric isn't just playing with her.

He's obsessed with her.

In love with her?

And then I see it.

The answer to all my questions.

Feeling sick, I shove him away. He lets me go, and I put my knife in its hidden sheath. "I'll deal with the traitor," I say. "Be ready to wipe out the Death Hunt in two weeks."

Yanking open the door as soon as he nods, I step out into the hall. Talon is a tight wad of energy ready to explode, but Khalid is deadly calm. His eyes flick over my shoulder to look at Aleric. I wouldn't be surprised if the fucker waves.

My brother looks back at me with a silent question, but I don't answer him as I walk away. We get in the car without any trouble, no vampires coming to ambush us, but the knot in my stomach doesn't relax. The hairs on my neck don't settle.

There's another godsdamn traitor in my Family, someone who wants my brother dead, but that isn't the issue that has hold of my tongue, that's making it hard to form words.

It's that Aleric is in love with Mother.

And I have powers no witch should have, but which are all too common in vampires.

No. I'm being too fucking paranoid. We don't even look anything alike.

But now that the thought is there, I can't get it to leave.

Especially since the one constant with Mother is that she will do anything to save her children – even if one was the son of Aleric Zadar. A hated enemy. Even if that boy was a rape baby. An abomination. A fucking *hybrid* that should never see the light.

She is a strong witch.

She could've cursed me...

Bound both sides of my true nature so only slivers of them remained.

You're being paranoid...

But all the puzzle pieces are sliding together.

Why Father – *Caden* couldn't look at me when I didn't hit my ascension. How he changed from a loving, smiling man to a drunkard who lashed out at Mother and I.

Why she never took me to see a specialist about my lack of magic.

Why Father ended up cursing her even though he loved her.

How the most recent traitor had failed to kill me. Mother claimed the blade had missed my heart, but that man never missed.

You simply can't kill a born vampire that way. You have to cut out their heart entirely. Or cut off their head.

My mouth runs dry as too many pieces fall into place, as

a memory of a blood-drained woman floods my mind. I saw her in the alleyway I was attacked in. Aleric thinks a rogue vampire killed her, but he's never found them.

I glance down at my hands. Feel the pulse in my teeth.

Feel the truth in my fucking heart.

Aleric Zadar is my godsdamn father.

And I'm a fucking hybrid.

NINE

HIM

When we get home, my entire body is taut with energy. I step out of the car, and my fingertips burn with the need to clench, then go eight rounds with a bag. But I keep my face expressionless, my discoveries secret as I signal Khalid to follow me. Stopping down by the lake on our property, away from all ears, I fill him in on how many vampires are left in the city. I don't tell him about the traitor. Don't tell him about Aleric's demand for a picture of Mother. And I sure as hel don't tell him about potentially being a hybrid or about being Aleric's son. I trust Khalid with my life as Boss of the Shadow Domain. But as a hybrid? As an abomination that is hunted before they're even born? I don't trust anyone.

When Khalid leaves me, I don't head back to the house. I know Mother will find her way here, too fucking worried about what Aleric might have said to me. So I stay by the lake, soaking in the peace and quiet of the lapping shore. I do not have to wait long before I catch her scent in the breeze.

My lips tight, I turn to face her as she reaches me. Her eyes tell me everything I need to know, but I ask anyway, wanting to hear what fucking lies she comes up with this time.

"Is he my father?" I ask softly. "And do not fucking ask me who."

Her lips purse together, and she turns her head towards the house. Looking back at me, she then gestures further down the lake. She doesn't wait for me to follow, her legs as restless as mine, perhaps, despite the grace she still moves with.

We walk for fifteen minutes, heading along the water in heavy silence. Just as my patience starts to evaporate in the heat of my anger, she whispers, "Did he tell you he was?"

"Answer my question." I'm not in any mood to play any of her games, to give her anything in exchange for what she gives me. She can suffer over her lies.

"Varius –"

"Answer," I say softly. "The. Fucking –"

"Yes."

I stop, then move again, too restless to stay still. I knew it. I figured it out in the car, but even still, hearing her say it. Hearing her admit that she's lied to me all this time. Lied to me again when I asked her for the truth a few months ago.

"He doesn't know," she says as she walks alongside me. Her voice is light, hard to hear even with my hearing, even with us being this close. "I've been so afraid since he found all your blood in the alley, that he might recognize it even with my magic." She trails off. Takes a deep breath. "I'm sorry I lied to you, but I did it to protect you."

"Because I'm a hybrid."

"Yes."

My throat suddenly feels swollen. "Can I have kids?" I ask, swallowing down the rest of the question, the real one.

Will I ever be able to marry Micha?

"Yes."

I scoff. Hybrids are infertile. "Another fucking lie –"

"It's not. I realized you were a hybrid in my womb, and I…" She trails off. Stops. Turns to stare out at the lake as she wraps her arms around herself. Her eyes are distant. I want to keep moving. *Need* to give this burning energy inside me a way out, but I stop too.

"You what?" I demand.

"I changed everything about you." She swallows. "Your face so you wouldn't grow up looking like him. The smell of your blood so he wouldn't be able to identify you as his. I even changed your DNA slightly. Not a lot, just enough so you could conceive. You know it's the absence of one little gene for hybrids…"

"I don't fucking believe you." My entire body is vibrating, and I clench my fists with a need to destroy something, but I bite back that anger, control it. I need to think, to make sure she isn't just telling me more lies. To hide something even worse. "Shit like that requires dark magic," I say.

She folds in on herself. Her right arm slips down so her palm presses flat against her stomach. She says something, her lips moving, but I can't hear it.

"Mother," I growl, the first show of anger in my voice.

She flinches. "You were a twin," she says loud enough for me to hear.

"*What?*" I rasp. I swallow hard, work my tongue around my mouth to try to get the sudden ash-taste out of it.

"I had to make a choice – lose you both or save one of you."

"So you killed him."

"Her," she whispers. "Her name was Uri, and I gave birth to her before you. Your father was so broken when he saw her come out dead. I think he might've suspected since then that you two weren't his. She looked so much like *him* even then, but Caden loved you. He loved you so much, he didn't care."

"Then why did he leave?"

She flinches.

"*Why?*"

"Not because of you," she says.

"But he couldn't look at me when he came back."

"It *wasn't* because of you. He just saw you after we had a fight. He left –" She swallows, takes a moment. "He left because we completed a blood bond, and it broke us. After everything we went through, he couldn't handle..." A bitter note hits her voice.

My blood stills, but I don't push her. My thoughts fly to Micha. Every blood bond requires a sacrifice; what if we do not survive it either?

The silence stretches between us. Not quite as heavy as it was before we started, but it's still thick and muggy and crushing on our shoulders. The truth can only lift it so much when the lies have piled on year after year after year.

"What are the limits of my curse?" I finally ask.

"You can't use magic in any form. You can't phase. You will never grow fangs. You will age and scar. The only time you can feed on blood is if you're dying." She glances at the two rings I have on my hands. The ones that give me the strength of a vampire. "And those are just placebos; you don't need them to do what you do."

I glance down at them, feeling the weight of their lies.

"And you can never fall in love."

My head jerks up. "What?"

"If you do, the curse lifts."

I stare at her, more shocked about this than anything she's said so far. "You chose a fucking *fairy tale* as the curse breaker. Why? So I would be happy even when my world is falling to shit?"

"Because you're firstborn," she says simply. "We don't

get the luxury of knowing what real love is. We are too paranoid, too targeted, too fucked up by our position. It is something that will never happen."

I stare at her in disbelief. "But you love us." *And I love Micha.*

Her heart breaks in her eyes. "I love you as much as I know how. But I've lost so many children that I fear giving you all I have." A dry laugh leaves her lips. "I don't even know if I have it in me to give. Caden didn't think so at the end..."

She hesitates for a moment, her eyes wet, her lips tight. Then, "The type of love that will break your curse is the type that will utterly destroy you if they get hurt. I have to divide my love across multiple children. Have had to choose between who to save first... To *try* to save... And you'll have to make those same choices as Boss. You can't ever know what love is. Our responsibility does not allow it; you can't break over one death when you have others to watch out for. I'm sorry."

"But you loved Caden enough to start a blood bond."

Her shoulders sag, and she is the oldest I have ever seen her. "I loved him as much as I knew how. But I was given to him when I was a child. He named me. Owned me before I even knew the meaning of that word. Of any word. And then he was all I knew. After what Antonio did to me... I latched onto him because he was all that remained of my old life. All my brothers and sisters were dead. And my mother had raised me to love him before that. She'd built him up as this great prince... this great honor...

"I did love him. I still do. I gave him everything I had; it just wasn't enough. I never learned to love him like he loved me."

"But he was Boss and a firstborn," I counter.

"And he loved me as an obsession, only giving his love as long as I was his. The love I cursed you with is one without restriction, without conditions. You love regardless of how they love you, how they treat you. If Caden loved me like that, he never would have cursed me when he learned –"

She stops.

Hugs herself again.

There is a difference to her silence this time, though, less guilt directed at me. Whatever she's hiding, it is her secret, not mine.

But I am not ready to give her the trust of my ignorance again. Not ready to let her keep her secrets.

"When he learned what?"

"Varius, please, don't push this."

"You lied to me for decades. You lied to me about what I *am*."

She turns to me and drops her arms. Then she lifts her chin. "I did it to protect you. I am not sorry for that, and I will not suffer for doing what I thought was best to save my child. I am simply sorry you have to deal with the sins of your father. That you have to keep a secret so big from the people you care about."

My body stills.

If T found out...

He'd hate me so much, he'd side with the wolves.

Antonio might be breeding hybrids, but he's doing it to use them, to torture them. He's not treating them as if they are humans.

Volatile energy burns up inside me as more pieces of the puzzle slot together.

"One of them already knows," I say. "Someone's been blackmailing Micha for the ledger. Now why would any of my brothers do that when their crimes are in there too?" My gaze turns venomous, my blood to ice. "Unless they want to use it as an in into another Family. Give us up in exchange for their favor and a high position in their ranks."

"No one would trust them if they betrayed their own."

"Antonio doesn't need to trust them to use them."

Her jaw clenches as she glares at me, and for a moment, I see the Reaper of the Sired, the one who took on Aleric's gang all on her own, right in the heart of their territory, and nearly succeeded in killing them all. I see the future Aleric said we could have had she been allowed to lead.

She forced peace on this broken city.

What more could she have done if she had been trained from birth? If she had been seen as something more than a breedmare?

"Antonio," she spits, "will not deal with him. He wants nothing for this family but for us to suffer for what I did to him."

"And yet, he lets Talon into his brothels when no other witch can enter."

"Your brother is not trying to steal the ledger," she hisses. "It won't give him any leverage over what he already has in his head."

I bite my tongue, unable to deny the accuracy of that statement even in my anger. Talon has his fingers in nearly every section of the Family. He might not know everything that's in the ledger, but he has more than enough to take to Antonio.

All my brothers do.

"But think about it, Varius," she pushes. "There's only one person in the house who will benefit from selling it to the highest bidder."

I still even though every nerve inside me explodes with motion, an itch beneath the skin that wants *out*.

Micha.

No, she wouldn't...

But the fucking seed is already there, its roots shooting deep. The plant budding. Growing. Blossoming into a thorn-lined rose.

Why would she start a blood bond if she's planning on

stealing from me? I argue with myself. With us bonded, I'll always be able to find her. There will be nowhere for her to run.

No, *Mother* is wrong. She's fucking meddling, trying to split us apart so I never fall in love.

"I can't fucking trust you," I growl.

"Then don't," she says without hesitation. "Look into her yourself."

Bordering on the edge of desperation, I do. I search for the bond Micha claims to have started. To prove that she is mine. That she would never –

My heart trips.

Tumbles all the way down to my fucking feet.

There is nothing there.

No bond.

No connection.

Nothing at fucking all.

It's because we're too far apart, I decide. We didn't share much blood. We didn't share enough to cross the distance from the house to here.

I look towards the two-story mansion lying behind the field of flowers. Then I start walking towards it, every step a mix of hope and fear. Hope that with the next step, I'll feel the bond. Fear that I haven't yet. That I never will.

Because it isn't there.

Because she lied to me.

Is planning on stealing the ledger.

When I get to the house and still feel no bond between us, I storm up to my office. I spend the rest of the day and all of the next looking for the traitor, for someone to blame other than my little monster.

Everything I find, though, points to Micha Black.

To my chosen mate.

To the woman I thought I could trust.

Because there's only one person who isn't in the ledger,

so they won't be burned if it's handed in to the police.

Only one person who doesn't have the intel already in it, so they need the physical copy to sell.

Only one person whose account ID on a black market site matches the one that accepted the job to steal our ledger two weeks ago.

And only one fucking person who doesn't love Khalid, who'd be okay with framing him to get what she wants.

My vision growing red, I yank open my office door. As much as I want to punish Micha myself, to deal with her as is my fucking right as her mate, I am duty bound to inform the reaper of her sins.

So I cross the hall and knock on his door, not caring that it's well after midnight. That he's probably asleep or in the middle of fucking his girl – who he brought in this morning, unconscious in his arms while he bled from multiple holes in his body. He made another fucking mess for me to clean up, having blown up a human's house, but at least his girl is here now, under his protection so there is hopefully no one else for him to kill.

When Khalid opens his door, naked and without shame, I ease into telling him about Micha being the traitor.

"I'm sorry," he says, but I force my agony down, keep my pain hidden. If he knows I have claimed her as mine, he will not do the duty he is required to do. That I *need* him to do because I'm pretty sure I fucking can't.

"Her life does not matter," I lie. "But if her dad planted her, then this will mean war with the Blacks."

I say that to remind myself just how much she needs to be punished. Although we do not need the Blacks' support in our war against Antonio, if we have to fight both of them at once, we might not survive. Throw in whatever gang or police force she sells the ledger to – whether for money or a clean slate, and we're fucked.

Khalid's jaw tightens as he looks over at his girl. She's

asleep in his bed, and I know he wants to go to her. But he wants to protect her more, and there is a traitor in the place she sleeps.

Terrified he might go after Micha now, I order, "Get some rest. I will look further into Micha and let you know when I need you."

I shut the door behind me, closing him off, blocking his path to my girl. But in the loneliness of the hall, where there is no one she needs to be protected from, I clench my fists.

I need to punish her for her sins.

Hurt her like she's fucking hurting me.

Stalking down the hall, I head to her room, where my little traitor is fast asleep.

TEN

HER

I'm yanked out of bed by a heavy hand. Reacting on pure instinct, I throw a fist into my attacker's body. He grunts as I connect with whatever part of him I hit, but my focus is on the grip he still has on me. Grabbing his thumb, I wrench it back as I twist my arm to free myself.

His other hand wraps around my neck and shoves me back down onto the mattress. His body quickly crushes me, and for a second, primal panic consumes me. But then his lips are on mine, and familiarity washes through me. I know this mouth, the roughness of these hands as he gropes at my breasts.

"Varius?" I rasp in the darkness of my room, my pulse spiking as he presses a hard thigh between my legs.

He has been avoiding everyone since he got back from Aleric's, but I've felt his rage and pain through our bond. I tried to go to him, to knock on his office door while he was locked in there these past two days, but he never gave me permission to enter. So I've been forced to wait until he came to me.

"Do you want to talk –"

He sucks my tongue into his mouth, forcing me to shut up. His fingers tighten around my throat, making it fucking clear what he wants from me.

My body, not my words.

Pressing his thigh harder into me, he snarls, "Fight me."

A shiver rushes down my spine. I don't hesitate. Don't dare disobey by asking questions. Couldn't even if I wanted to, my flight-or-fight response kicking in as if I'm really in danger.

I wrench my mouth away from his; he moans as he licks the side of my face. I swing my fist into his side, aiming for his smallest rib. He grunts and releases my neck to grab both of my hands. So I send fire down to my fingers, but he snuffs them out with the large palms of his when he crushes my hands into fists.

I cry out, the thrill of submission exciting me even as I worry that I've burned him with my flames. But he doesn't seem to be in pain. Or, at least, he doesn't seem to notice it, his attention back on my mouth as he forces his tongue inside mine.

I bite him, and he hisses. He pulls his tongue back, but it's just to speak. "Harder," he rasps before plunging back between my lips.

My teeth close fast, but before I can do more than brush his tongue, he's released one of my hands to grab my jaw. He forces my mouth to stay open, my teeth just scraping his flesh as he takes what he wants.

With my free hand, I swing for his rib cage again. He stops kissing me as he grabs that hand and pins it back over my head. Wrapping one large palm over both of mine, he holds me firmly so I can't move.

I stare up at him, my chest heaving, my body shaking at

the thrill of his conquest.

Staring at me, darkness swirling in his eyes, he trails one hand down my naked body. Goosebumps flare everywhere he touches, and I arch up into him when he gets to my breasts, my nipples so sensitive they hurt.

"You like that, don't you?" Varius growls as he cups me. "Such a naughty little thing. I bet I can make you come just from playing with these." He pinches my nipple, and I cry out.

Leaning his face to my neck, he licks the full length of it as he continues to play with my breasts. His fingers stroke and cup and knead and pinch. His mouth licks and sucks and bites and kisses. I writhe beneath him, growing hot as my orgasm starts to build. My chest tingling with way too much sensitivity, I squeeze my thighs together. But my legs are still wrapped around his, and so I rub myself on the hard muscles of his thigh.

"That's it," he growls as he nibbles on my neck, his hand still feathering back and forth across my breasts, teasing one, then the other, never leaving them alone. "Show me how you're mine."

Whimpering, I rub my pussy lips against his thigh. The area soon becomes wet, and I close my eyes as I chase the high he's giving me. His mouth trails down my neck in little kisses, and with every touch of his lips, I suck in a harsh breath. The anticipation of him reaching my breasts grows, and by the time he gets to them, I'm a complete mess, my orgasm so damn close already.

I glance down at him, watching as his lips trail across the top of my breasts. My nipple hardens, begging him to take it in his mouth. His breath feathers across it as he blows on it, teasing it, teasing me, teasing my godsdamn orgasm as it's ready to explode.

"Varius, *please*," I beg as I tremble beneath his body.

"Please, what?" he asks, a bite to his words that vaguely

registers in the fog of my brain. There's a dangerous edge to him tonight, a monster beneath the lust, and for a second, I pause, but then his thigh presses harder against me, turning on the button that switches off my brain, and I moan.

"Please put my nipple in your mouth."

Parting his lips, he does exactly as I say, but he's opened his mouth too wide, and his lips aren't anywhere close to my aching nipple. I try to twist my body to feel the touch of them, but he just lifts his head back up. I whimper.

"Not like that," I rasp, shaking my head. "Suck on it. Let me come. I'm so close, Varius. *Please.*"

His lips latch onto my other breast, and I arch off the bed. He pinches my other nipple in between his fingers, then releases my hands to touch my pussy. His thigh moves out of his way while he strokes me. I shudder beneath him. My eyes squeeze shut tight. My breaths come out shorter and shorter, harder and harder. Until I'm –

He pulls away.

Jumps out of bed as I'm left crying in frustration. "No," I whine. "Please come back. I was so close. I need –"

I start to cup my breast, but he grabs my arm and yanks me out of bed.

"Run."

Cursing, I jerk my arm away from him and bolt out of my bedroom. If I can just get far enough before he catches me, I can finish myself off…

Running through the house, I yank open the door to the outside, then head for the woods, hoping to lose him in the dark. I can hear the heaviness of his footsteps as he chases me though. Can sense just how close he is.

My pulse spiking, I run faster, pulling on everything I have. The trees start to fill in the space around me. I dart left and right, switching directions like a terrified rabbit being hunted by a wolf. And still he stays on my tail.

Frantic, I jump for the branch of a tree, thinking to lose

him if I climb, but just as my hands wrap around the bark, he barrels into me. The skin is torn from my palms. The air is slammed out of my lungs on impact. The primal fear that was tickling my senses now full on attacks it, and I throw my elbow at his face as he spins me to face him. We hit the ground.

He fends me off as I fight him. My pulse spiking, my body flush with too much adrenaline, I curl my legs up to shove him off. He grunts as he stops them from wrapping around his neck, then again as he shoves them down and forces them apart.

I cry out as a tendon in my thigh blares with sharp pain but not enough to worry me that he's snapped it.

Ignoring my hands, he kneels between my thighs, his boxers now gone –taken off before he chased me, perhaps– and grabs his cock. In one quick, hard thrust, he fills every inch of my pussy.

I moan as I place my fingers flat on his chest, knowing he still isn't comfortable with leaving me 'armed' when he is vulnerable. A witch cannot use their magic without their fingers to safely conduct it, shape it into what they want. And with the darkness swirling around him right now, I know he needs that safety net more. Lifting my hips, I take him deep with every rocking of his.

He wraps his fingers around my throat as he fucks me. He thrusts into me so hard, my body makes an indent in the ground. Leaves crunch, and twigs snap around us. My pants turn into screams. I stop trying to match his rhythm as my entire body arches up, that orgasm he denied me right on the edge once more.

Choking me, he growls, "Don't you fucking come."

He thrusts in slow and hard in just the way I like, and I whimper, then cry, then bite my lip, my head jerking side to side as my entire body shakes, trying to obey. To be the good girl he wants me to be.

His fingers tighten around my throat. My air is cut off as he pounds into me. Pleasure and terror mix together, but my orgasm doesn't come. I fight it back. I lock it away in my lungs that can't breathe.

Our hips slap against each other.

The crickets chirp around us.

The full moon glitters through the trees, but slowly, it starts to fade away as the darkness rushes around me.

My eyelids flutter.

And then I'm suddenly allowed to breathe.

I gasp in air as he slams into me balls deep, hitting the back of my cervix, bruising it, claiming it, marking it as his. He grabs both my arms and pins them back over my head. He leans and bites all the flesh he can reach, from my wrists to my elbows. He wraps his fingers back around my throat.

I jerk beneath him, each bite making me hotter. I love it when he marks me, when he tells the entire fucking world that I'm taken. His.

Varius fucking Shadow's.

As his teeth dig into my arm hard enough to make it bleed, I cry out. He sits up and hauls me onto his lap. He guides one of my hands down to my pussy.

"Burn the hair off," he growls as his hips pump into me.

I freeze, the demand shocking me. He's always loved my curls, has even punished me for shaving before. The worry from earlier comes back, that there's real danger in the air tonight.

A desperation.

A darkness.

A madness.

Whatever happened at Aleric's meeting, I don't think it's caused this.

He almost seems mad at me? Like he's punishing *me*.

My heart plummeting, my spine shivering, I look into his eyes.

A monster glares back at me.

It's dangerous to fall in love with a dangerous man.

The hand he has on my throat suddenly feels too hot.

He squeezes me.

I panic.

He loosens his grip, allowing me to breathe.

But that panic doesn't get washed away by the flooding of air into my lungs. It's gripping its claws in me tight.

"I love you," I say as I burn the hair off my pussy, hoping I can appease him with my submission. With my love. That whatever has caused this darkness inside him can be fixed with a simple reminder that I'm *his.* His to take care of, to protect, just like I will him.

The sulfuric smell of burning hair reaches my nostrils. My magic warms my pelvis. His cock jerks, and so I rock my hips, taking him in deep with every thrust. I keep my fingers flat on his shoulders, unthreatening as I ride him in slow, deep penetrations.

My eyes dip to his lips, wanting him to kiss me, to show me that everything between us is fine. But his eyes are on my pussy. On the words emblazoned there.

Property of Varius Shadow

"I'm yours," I whisper, my hands seeking his. I entwine our fingers, giving him control of my magic, making myself vulnerable despite knowing he is on the crumbling edge of a dark crevice.

But he needs this. I can see it in his eyes, in his harsh breathing. He has always been so alone, betrayed so many times, he's learned not to create connections. Not to give them a way to hurt him. He's learned to be wary even of the people he loves. Never able to trust them fully because no one has ever stayed in his corner through thick and thin.

But I will.

"I'm here," I murmur as I lean forward to kiss his lips. Gentle. Tenderly. Lovingly. "I'm not going anywhere."

He tenses beneath me for half a second, his muscles rigid beneath my body.

Then he's fucking me like I'm a sex doll, as if he just needs to *move*. Burying his teeth into my neck, he bites me hard. His cock slams into me. He releases my fingers to grab my hips and move me. Up and down. Up and down. Up and fucking down.

I ride him on ragged pants despite the pain in my cervix, trying to give him whatever he wants. Whatever he *needs* in this moment, so he can step back from the edge urging him to jump. To run away from the relationship cornering him on the ledge.

I know he's just running scared, so uncertain with what it means to love someone so much, it's terrifying. He needs reassurance that this is *right*, that this relationship isn't scary despite the big leap we've just taken – bonding before we're even married. Before we've even known each other for a year.

So I hold on as he uses me. Punishes me. Hates me for making him feel this vulnerable, for breaking through his walls and seeing him in all his rawness.

His hands squeeze my hips tight. He lifts me up. Slams me back down.

And then he's coming inside me on a roar of emotion that squeezes at my heart and lungs and throat.

I thread my fingers through his hair, holding him to me.

He brings his head down and kisses me. It's rough. Wild. Desperate.

I kiss him back, my tongue dancing with his, letting him feel every inch of me to know that I'm not going anywhere. That I'm here. For him. For us.

"I love you," I murmur.

His lips rub against mine. Our breaths mingle.

Then he pushes me off him and says, "Run home, little monster."

I hesitate for the barest of seconds, watching his face, but then I'm gone. Running through the woods on shaky legs that drip with his cum. I reach a hand between my thighs, then bring it to my lips. Sucking his taste off my fingers, I moan.

The snap of a twig behind me makes my pulse jump. The sound of him chasing me makes me hot, and I wonder if I can even make it to the house. Or if I'll collapse in a heap of arousal and exhaustion, my lungs no longer willing to suck in air.

But soon, the house comes into view, and with the last drop of energy I can wring from my tired legs, I run up the side of the building below his room, latch onto the ledge of his window, and pull myself up onto it. My core clenches as I balance on an inch-wide ledge, the anticipation of a fall making my adrenaline spike. But then I'm pushing up the window, having unlocked it with my magic, and rolling inside Varius' room.

I barely make it back to my feet when I feel him behind me. His arms wrap around my waist and lift me. Pivoting, he throws me onto his bed.

I bounce, my jaw slack as I pant, my eyes hot on his toned, naked body standing in all its glory in front of me. My mouth waters. My chest heaves.

And then he's on me, shoving my thighs apart as he buries his face between my legs.

Arching on a cry, I grind against him as he eats me out. Wrapping his hands around my legs, he rolls onto his back so I'm above him. I sit down all the way, riding his face until I'm quivering in pleasure. Then he lifts me off him and spins me around. One thick forearm on my back pins me to his stomach, my face right in front of his throbbing cock.

I reach forward and grab it. My fingers can't reach each other, he's so big. But I squeeze him tight and lean forward as much as I can without coming off Varius' mouth. My tongue flicks out along his head, tasting him for the first time.

He groans into my pussy, and the vibration of it causes me to gasp. Moving his arm up from my waist to the back of my head, he guides me onto his cock. I take as much of him as I can, but just his tip is stretching my lips too much. I gag around his head, and he jerks into me, sliding past my lips to go even deeper.

I struggle to breathe as my saliva runs down my chin to wet his balls. But I don't stop, bobbing and jerking my head, trying to please him as he pleases me.

His tongue flicks between my lips, building me up until I'm close to coming again. Wanting him to be inside me when I do, to connect us in that most primal of ways, I wiggle my hips in a request for him to release me. To let me move.

His hand on the back of my neck applies more pressure for another few seconds, and I take him as deep as I can. Then he's releasing me, and I'm crawling down his body until my pussy hovers over his cock. Grabbing the thick-veined beast, I rub it between my lips, which are wet with my arousal and his cum and saliva. He slides against me. His hands squeeze my hips, urging me on.

Holding him tight with one hand, I slowly lower myself down on his cock until I'm fully penetrated, fully his.

Moaning, I start to ride him. He's inside me so damn deep. My hands on his knees, I lift myself up and down his gorgeous cock. His fingers dig into my hips as his breaths come out faster behind me. My pants growing shallower, I squeeze my eyes shut as pure ecstasy courses through my body.

"Fuck, baby, you feel so good inside me," I pant as my thighs tremble from the pleasure. My fingers squeeze his knees as the entire area where we're connected becomes soaked with my arousal. "I love your cock so much."

Shuddering, I squeeze my pelvis muscles, gripping him tight. I'm so fucking wet, I'm sliding up and down him in a sloppy mess. I groan every time he hits me just right.

"Fuck, baby, fuck me harder," he groans as his fingers knead my flesh. But he doesn't force me. Doesn't move me himself. He waits for me to do it. To listen. To obey. To give him my submission.

Whimpering, I fuck him harder.

And harder.

Until I'm riding him so fast I see stars. Until my limbs no longer seem to know how to work, they're so exhausted, so poised on that edge of ecstasy.

He sits up behind me, his cock hitting me at a new angle, and I cry out in utter pleasure. One of his hands reaches around me to rub my pussy, applying pressure just the way I like it. The other tightens around my throat.

His breath tickles my ear. His teeth latch onto my lobe. "Don't you fucking come," he growls as he tightens his hand around my neck.

He removes his hand from my pussy to force my head to turn to the side so he can kiss me, then puts it back, his fingers stroking me slowly as his other hand grips me too tight. His tongue dives inside my mouth, stealing the last of my air. Taking my breath and making it his. I try to kiss him back, to keep riding him as he needs me to, but all the oxygen has left my lungs, and my limbs are becoming too heavy. My brain too sluggish, then too loud as it screams at me that I'm dying.

That he's killing me.

That the person I love is too dangerous a man.

No.

No, he loves me.

He's just scared of the vulnerability I make him feel, but he loves me.

He won't hurt me.

As the last of my consciousness starts to fade, I rub my lips against his, mouthing, "I love you. I am here..."

I will always be here.

ELEVEN

HIM

She's a fucking liar.

She doesn't love me.

Doesn't want me.

She's just trying to manipulate me.

She never even started the blood bond. I've tried these past two days to connect with her, to find it, to use it as a reason to ignore all the evidence painting her as guilty. Every fucking hour I tried searching for it, as if the past forty-odd other attempts were somehow done wrong even though that's impossible. A blood bond involves soul magic; a person just has to want it hard enough to make it real. No curse can stop that.

So *this* is what the bitch deserves for fucking betraying me. For tricking me into loving her until I showed her the ledger. Until I let my guard down. She pierced my heart with her fucking barbed arrows, and I need to pull them out despite the pain.

So I squeeze her neck harder. Keep her air supply cut off even as she passes out. I just need to do this for a couple minutes longer, and all this *pain* inside me will be gone.

"I fucking loved you," I growl.

My fingers clench a little bit more as my lips move across hers. She doesn't kiss me back. Doesn't move at all.

She's dying.

I'm killing her.

And my heart can't fucking take it.

With a guttural cry of pain, I release her neck. She sucks in a breath immediately.

I'm sorry, Micha. Fuck, I'm so sorry. I hold her up as she sags against me, locking my arms tight around her. Her eyes flutter open to find mine, and there is trust there, like she knew I would stop even when I didn't.

My throat thick with words I don't know how to say, I grab her thighs and hold her above me. Then I start fucking her hard and fast and feral. But now it's desperation driving me rather than rage.

Fuck.

I should be willing to give up everything to protect my brothers. I promised them that when father – when *Caden* walked out on us.

And yet...I can't do it.

I can't give up on her.

Can't give up on *us.*

She groans as she places both her hands over mine, her fingers flat against me so I can feel their every movement. Even now she is giving me what I need. Her submission. Her vulnerability. Her godsdamn trust despite almost dying at my hands.

I hate that. Hate her. Hate how it makes me hesitate in what I need to do.

Wrapping my fingers back around her throat, I inhale deep, expecting to smell fear but only smelling love. How the fuck can this not be real?

Growling, I jerk her down. My cock rams into her cervix. Bruising it. Hurting her. She jerks in my arms as she cries out, but whether from pleasure or pain, I don't know. And I don't know which one I truly want her to feel.

Lifting her off me, I spin her around so I can see her face. Her knees on either side of me, she fucks me just as hard as I'm fucking her. Her hands thread through my hair as she leans back and brings my mouth down to her breasts. I suck them into my mouth, able to take one in entirely. It's so godsdamn small.

She's so small. I could snap her like a twig.

Instead, I move to her other nipple, suck on it until she screams. Then my lips are back on hers. My tongue is in her mouth. My cock is inside her. She might be planning on betraying me, she might be lying to me all the fucking time, but in *this*, in this fucking moment right here, she is *mine*.

"Fuck, little monster," I growl against her lips as my cock throbs inside her pussy.

She pulls back and opens her eyes, searching the dark depths of mine. Then understanding blossoms there.

"I love you," she assures me, clearly thinking that I need this. That I'm running scared after we took a huge step in our relationship. After I opened myself up to be vulnerable.

But I'm not.

I'm not.

I would have given her everything.

Now I will take it all from her instead.

For daring to harm my brothers.

For lying about the blood bond.

My grip tightens around her throat.

Then loosens, allowing her to breathe.

I can't.

I fucking can't.

I'll punish her in ways other than death. I'll lock her in a luxury cell. Make it so her entire world revolves around me. Around when I come in to feed her, clean her, fuck her until she screams. So she never gets the chance to betray me. To hurt my brothers in her greed.

She whimpers as she rides me. Squeezes me. Marks me as hers with her pussy, then her teeth as she leans forward and bites my shoulder. I groan as I grab the back of her head and hold her to me, wanting her to break the skin.

Wanting her to prove she wants me. Wants *this*. That the ink on my cock, though half-fucked and needing redoing, is the truth.

Property of Micha Shadow

She is my wife.

Even though we're not yet married.

She is *mine*.

Her teeth dig into me.

Mark me as her husband.

My fingers kneed her ass, rocking her faster.

Increasing the friction of her pussy on me until my balls become tight.

Groaning, I watch her tits jiggle as she slams down on my cock.

Over and over until I come inside her on a roar.

She jerks her hips a few more times, then slams down all the way as she screams into the crook of my shoulder. Her pussy clenches around me, shaking and shuddering as she gives herself to me completely.

Yanking her head up, I sink my teeth into her neck. She groans, threading her fingers in my hair. I kiss and suck and nip. Lifting my lips, I look her in the eye. Her gaze's slightly unfocused from the intensity of her orgasm. But even still, there is love inside those depths.

A fucking lie.

"You came," I growl, wanting to punish her for making me believe she cares.

"Yeah, I did." She grins as she raises a hand to her neck. "That was fucking *intense*." Her eyes widening, she shakes her head. "Uh, I mean – I'm sorry," she says as she lowers her gaze, acting apologetic but looking way too pleased with herself. "I'm such a bad girl. Maybe you should spank me."

The blatant manipulation makes me want to deny her, and for a moment, I almost do, but I want her at my mercy more. Want her to become reliant on me so she can never run. So she can never leave.

Pushing her off me, I order, "Stand on the side of the bed and bend over."

She moves quickly, and I stride over to the dresser full of toys I purchased over the past couple months. I seemingly bought at least one of everything, wanting to try them all to discover what we like, to share those firsts with *her*. Now it all almost feels like a mockery.

I open the top drawer and rifle through the items to find what I'm looking for. Paddles and whips call to me, but I ignore them. I don't trust myself not to really hurt her in this moment. I don't know if I'd stop once I started. If the session would end with her dead and bleeding out on my bed.

The hairs on my neck rise the longer I have my back to her, so I work quickly, shoving aside dildos, vibrators, nipple clamps, and everything else the shop sold until the toy I want is in my hand.

I turn to find her facing away from me, her ass in the air, her forearms flat on the bed. My cum dribbles out of her wet pussy and down her left thigh. My cock twitches with the need to slide back inside her. Just to rest. To connect with her while she sleeps. While she's vulnerable.

Instead, I stop a foot from her. I stand there, letting her feel my presence. She starts to squirm, her thighs bunching as she curls her toes in anticipation. Her breaths come out a bit harsher. But there's no fear seeping from her pores. No terror that I'm at her back, a monster in the dark, an enemy who's found out she is an imposter. *Why isn't she afraid?*

Finally, she breaks, turning her head. I slap her ass before she can look over her shoulder. She jumps on a small gasp. I spank her again, my hand a bit heavier. The sting bites my palm as the *whack* resonates in my chest. Her body jolts over the mattress. She moans and wiggles her ass again.

Grabbing her hips, I pull her away from the bed so I can reach around her pussy. I know she can feel the piece of metal and silicone against her leg because she starts to turn, her head angled down to see what's in my left hand. As she stares at it in shock, I secure the chastity belt around her pussy, then lock it.

"Is that a witch's snare around the hip?" she asks.

The locks chastity belts come with might be good enough for humans, but a witch can easily break them. What one can't escape is a witch's snare – a golden chain imbued with magic that makes it impossible to remove without the "key."

So she'll die with the fucking thing on if she betrays me.

My body tight, I slap her exposed ass. Her cheek jiggles, and my cock twitches at the sight of her bound so only I can give her pleasure.

Fuck, little monster. I would have given you everything.

"Yes," I say.

"How long will it stay on?" she asks as she twists around to face me.

"Until you're sorry enough to beg."

TWELVE

HER

I freeze at the growl of Varius' words. There's a darkness clinging to them beneath the heat. A danger lurking under the pleasure. Something has been heavily weighing on him these last two days. I thought it was caused by Aleric or him being scared of how fast this relationship was moving, but now?

The bruises on my neck suddenly feel different. They're no longer a symbol of trust. They're a warning of what's to come.

Raising a hand to my throat, I swallow and feel the pain.

"Varius?" I ask softly, my nerves frying under adrenaline. I glance at the open window in my peripheral but keep my eyes on him. On the lion staring at the buck. "Please talk to me. What do you think I've done?"

He doesn't say anything. He just stares, sending chills down my spine.

I try to think of what he could be suspecting me of. His

paranoia has kept him alive all these years. It's well honed and well trusted, and now it's pointed directly at me. If I can't soothe it, I know he will fucking kill me. He'll see our love as nothing more than an attempt at manipulation, his experiences harsh and unforgiving. His first and only crush before me tried to kill him. He was just betrayed by a man he thought loved him like a son. By family he thought he could trust. I am but a stranger in comparison.

So when he still does not speak, as unnerving as that is, I take comfort in it. Because I'm not dead. He could've killed me at any point tonight, but he didn't.

Which means he wants to talk. He *wants* me to fix this thing that's broken. He just doesn't trust me enough to tell me what the problem is.

But I have years of experience dealing with kids just like this. Those whose parents had hired me to kill them. But instead, I faked their deaths and gave them a new name. Sometimes, a new face. And I set up a bank account with half the fee I got for their 'assassination' deposited into it, accessible for when they hit eighteen.

"Is this about the blackmailer?" I ask. The whole business hasn't settled right with me. Who half-asses a thing like that? "Because I was thinking that it's a red herring. They don't want the ledger at all."

He doesn't speak, but he also doesn't tell me to shut up. So I continue, laying out my reasoning so he can pick it apart as he needs to. "One, they didn't grab Dayne to use as collateral. They just sent a picture stolen from the guy you had tailing him for his protection. Two, they haven't tried to threaten me into getting it since. The deadline passed, and nada, no further threats, no nothing even though I've acted like I don't know Dayne's alive and well and nowhere near them. Three, they haven't responded to the pictures I took of the ledger. I have the product they want. Even if they know it's a fake, they should have replied back to tell me to keep looking. And four, I can't think of a single reason why anyone in your family would want it other than using the information inside it against you so they can leave this life and be left alone. But even still, they don't need the ledger for that; they can just use what's in their head."

Taking a deep breath, I let it out. My skin tingles under the force of his silence. But I get it now. Why he's pissed at me. Laying out all my ideas like that has led me to only one conclusion. "Their goal isn't to take the ledger," I say slowly. "It's to set me up as their patsy."

"Or you used the cover of a blackmailer to get my trust," he counters. "Make me believe you are a victim, so I'd work with you rather than against you."

"If I was doing that, I would've had Dayne go into hiding and applied more pressure on myself to really play it up. But I didn't."

The smallest show of doubt pulls at the corner of his lips.

"But what motive do you think I have for stealing it?"

"To sell it. Your accounts are low."

I scoff. "Wow. Elitist, much." I have millions of dollars spread across my accounts. Then I shake my head. "But that is another point in my favor. My closet here contains more money than what I made in a year as an assassin. If I was greedy, it'd make more sense to do everything I could to stay here. Like having sex all the time to baby trap you."

His eyes narrow.

But that means his mask is starting to break. I'm on the right track of getting him to trust me again.

"I don't have a reason to leave, Varius. They could offer me billions of dollars for the ledger, and I wouldn't take it. I want to be here. With you. The *only* way anyone could get me to do anything to change that is by threatening Dayne or my sister Lou, but they are both safe."

"Then why did you accept the job to steal the ledger?"

I blink. "I didn't."

"I had someone hack the site you use – Black Marks. Your username is the one who accepted the job."

I shake my head. "Why the fuck would I agree to steal it for a price if I'm being blackmailed to give it up without payment?"

"Because as you said, they don't have Dayne. They just planted a seed in your head, making you realize you might be able to steal the real thing."

"Fuck, Varius. Do you think I would seriously be dumb enough to give you a head's up, saying I would steal from you, even if I trusted the anonymity of that site, *before* I actually did it? Also, whoever put up the request for the ledger thinks they are dangerous or big enough or just plain fucking *stupid* enough to take on the Shadow Domain. I am not telling them I'll *get* something. I'd get in touch after I already had it so they don't have a reason to blackmail me."

"Hindsight is a –"

"No, *you're* being a bitch." I snap my mouth shut as I realize what I just said. Fuck's sake. I shouldn't have let my anger get to me; all that's going to do is get me killed. I take a breath, then try my best to keep my voice level. "I like your brothers and your mom, Varius. I don't want to think any of them would use me as their patsy, but if I *am* right, just think about what that means."

My eyes softening, my heart hurting for what he's going through, I ask, "Can you think of anyone who might need a patsy for any reason?"

I hold my breath, half expecting him to say me.

But he doesn't.

His eyes flashing with rage, he snarls, "Mother."

THIRTEEN

HIM

How many fucking lies has Mother told me? How many fucking truths has she kept from me?

Despite how Micha might have taken my answer last night, I don't think Mother needs a patsy or wants the ledger. I just think she's a meddling bitch who wanted to cause a rift between me and my mate. So I don't fall in love. So I don't break the curse she wants to keep hidden. Even though she sounded so fucking sure I could never know real love.

My rage burns too hot as I think of all the lies she's fed me, which is why I haven't gone to her yet. If I confront her while I'm this angry, I'll kill her, and we need her healing magic in this war. So I focus on writing up a new alliance with the Blood Fangs and then setting up a meeting with Aleric for tomorrow afternoon.

A couple days ago, I checked the police records and traced the anonymous call I was told of to the soldier we had on reception at the hotel Khalid visited that night. He ran. Now he's dead. I thought Micha might have killed him before I could talk to him for no other reason than the fact that I suspected her of trying to play me. But it seems that isn't the case, and the traitor Aleric was hinting at was just some low-level soldier, most likely looking to give Khalid up to the police in exchange for witness protection.

It isn't until midnight that I'm able to finalize the pact I've drawn up for Aleric to sign between all the other jobs and responsibilities I have. I save the file on my laptop, then print out two copies for tomorrow and give him a call to set a time for the meeting.

"Calling to ask for my email address?"

"What?" I ask.

"For where to send your mother's –"

"Finish that sentence, and I will take my chances against Antonio alone."

He laughs. "She rarely lets me *finish* either."

My fingers tighten around the cell phone as I see red.

"She's always interrupting me." A pause. "Thinks I don't have anything worth hearing."

"Just fucking shut up and listen."

He sighs. "Like mother like son."

But not like father...

I force my hand to relax. As much as I hate the fucker, we do need the alliance. I want to trust Micha's reasoning last night, but if she's lied to me, if the Blacks are planning on stealing the ledger or killing me to take over, we need allies. "Meeting. Tomorrow. Four o'clock," I say.

"Six."

"Four."

"Five."

"Four."

He gives a drawn-out sigh. "Fiiiine. But I want all your brothers there to sign. You might have caught this traitor, but you seem to attract them like flies to honey. That way if you die, the agreement is still valid."

"Leno will be enough." He's the one who will rule if I die.

"You clearly don't know Antonio. He isn't going to stop until you're all dead. I want to make sure when he takes you out one by one, to hurt your dear ma as much as he can, that I still have the best chance of survival. Really, I don't even know why he's targeting me. I sent him a birthday cake this year and everything." He laughs with utter delight. "Probably shouldn't have iced it with a placenta and placed three fetuses on top of it though, huh?"

My stomach knots, knowing damn well he isn't talking about cake toppers. He's speaking literally. Giving that to a father who lost his three pups and mate in one blow... Aleric is a fucking monster.

Like father, like son...

My jaw clenching, I say, "Fine. We'll all be there to sign."

I hang up before he can say anything else, not wanting to talk to him anymore than I have to. My fucking father...

Fuck.

If I'm lucky, he'll never find out I'm his son. I can barely stand him now. If he starts cracking dad jokes, I really will kill him.

Rubbing my neck, I give myself a moment to breathe, but instead of relaxing, with every minute that passes, I just get more and more pissed, thinking about all the lies Mother has told me. Thinking about all the damage she could have done between Micha and I.

Cold with rage, I stand and start stripping off my knives, removing every single temptation I have. Stepping out into the hall, I head down the stairs and to my mother's room. She opens the door before I can knock; her sixth sense has always been sharp. She seemed damn clairvoyant when I was a kid, always knowing whenever my brothers and I did stuff we weren't supposed to do.

I wonder if she knows why I'm here.

Her face paling, she steps back and lets me in.

"If you were anyone else," I say as I turn to face her, my voice soft, cold, lethal, "you would be dead right now."

"I don't know what you're accusing me of."

"Do not play games with me," I say, deliberately staying vague in case there's anything else she has done that I don't know about. "I'm already on the verge of kicking you out of this damn house."

"Your brothers won't –"

"They're not the Boss."

She glares at me as she bites her tongue. But I'm not the young boy she was able to break with her silence. "When I saw you laughing with Micha," she says, each word pulled from her, "I panicked. You haven't looked that happy since your father left."

I don't correct her about who my father is. I'd rather be Caden's son than Aleric's.

"So two days later, I messaged her anonymously, using a spell Talon taught me. I just wanted her to act weird enough to trigger your paranoia."

My blood runs cold at her words. "And what would have happened, Mother," I asked softly, my words flat, lethal, "if she had tried to steal it? Would you have let me kill her?"

Her face softens. "It would have been regrettable, but I will trade any life for yours. Including a breedmare's –"

Grabbing her arm, I shove her back into the wall and pin her there, my fingers biting. "She's my *fucking mate*," I hiss, the words coming out before I can stop them.

She stares at me wide-eyed, and I can smell the fear on her. It makes me sick, but I don't let her go.

"You've bonded?" she breathes.

My grip tightens on her arm as that question rams into me. I don't know if we actually have; Micha didn't bring it up as a reason I should trust her. And I didn't ask, afraid what the honest answer is.

"Yes," I say with all the conviction I want to believe in. "If you *ever* try to come between us again, I'll kick you out of this fucking house. I'll send you to some gods forgotten town in South America, and you will never come back. You will never see any of your sons again. Maybe, I'll send a fucking card when a grandchild is born."

Her eyes track across mine, and I don't blink, letting her see the truth. That if she forces me to choose between her or Micha, I will take the side of the one who hasn't stabbed me in the fucking back. Who hasn't lied to me over and over and over again.

"Varius, you can't fall in love with her –" she starts.

"As you said, it's impossible for me to," I cut in with a sneer. "So you have nothing to fucking worry about."

Leaving her room, I only *just* manage not to slam her door off its fucking hinges.

FOURTEEN

HER

I'm on that verge of wake and sleep, that dreamlike state where reality hasn't yet quite dug its harsh fingers into me. Something feathers across my skin, igniting pleasure along my nerves, waking them up but only just – aware but not *awake*. That something dances along my body, touching me here, touching me there. I sigh in pleasure, but that pleasure isn't chased. Isn't sought. I'm not waiting for the next touch on my body. I'm not anticipating. I'm just *existing*.

Just existing in this beautiful, delicious state of pleasure.

And then that something moves me onto my back, and I go with it without resistance; I'm just being exactly what it wants. Because fuck, it feels so damn good.

I'm rocking back and forth now, like a paper boat in a creek, the gentle movements of the current controlling my entire world. And it is pulling...pulling...pulling me away from the streams of the dreamworld and into the rivers of the living.

My eyes slowly opening, I find my chastity belt has been removed and Varius' dick is already inside me.

I groan as that pleasure I was feeling before intensifies as I focus on it, chase it. Capture it between my thighs as he rocks into me slowly. I'm not as wet as I normally am, so I can feel him rubbing against every inch of my pussy. A slow pull out. A deep ram in.

"Varius?" I ask as my hands come up to press against his chest.

"Sorry, little monster," he says, going as deep as he can. He holds it there for a second, then pulls back. "I couldn't wait."

"It's okay. I –"

He groans, and one thrust later, he comes inside of me. Wrapping my arms around him, I hold him as he shudders through the strength of his orgasm. He pants above me, and I crane my neck up to look at him. His eyes are closed, but there is so much pain in his face, and I know he's been to see his mother.

"Are you okay?" I murmur, reaching up to run my hand through his hair.

His eyes open.

He looks at me.

And for a moment, there aren't any walls between us.

Until there are.

Rolling off me, he pushes me onto my side so my back's facing him. Then he rubs his dick between my lips, pushes it in, and wraps an arm around me, pinning me to his chest.

"She knows to leave you alone," he murmurs.

I frown. "I'm sorry for causing a fight between you two. Did she say why she did it?"

"Yes."

I wait for him to elaborate.

But he never does.

My heart heavy, I wrap both my hands around the one

he has across my chest. He doesn't trust me again yet. Maybe he never trusted me to begin with. He is, after all, Varius fucking Shadow.

A paranoid man.

A dangerous man.

A broken man pretending he isn't.

Snuggling against his chest, I close my eyes and hope like hel that the broken pieces of me can slot into the broken chasms of him, and together we can be whole.

Knowing he won't be able to fall asleep until I do, I focus on my breathing. In. Then out. In...then out...

FIFTEEN

HER

I am used to being behind enemy lines. Dayne and I have accepted numerous contracts to kill government officials all around the world. So when I head down to make breakfast the next day, and Sau is already there (as she always is), I smile at her as if I know nothing of her animosity towards me.

She smiles back.

And there is no crack in her mask.

Nothing to tell me she hates me.

My skin prickling with just how deep behind enemy lines I am, I grab five packets of bacon out of the fridge.

"Oh, thanks, but I don't need any bacon out. I'm making waffles," she says, nodding at the bowl of mix in her hands. Waffles are Varius' comfort food. An apology for whatever she was planning to do after she blackmailed me – as she absolutely does not need what's in the ledger to fuck her sons over. She ruled this Family for over a decade, between when Caden left and before Varius was of age, and there are rumors that she ruled before then too – behind closed doors, behind her husband's face.

The fact that she isn't dead, though, tells me she wasn't planning on hurting any of her sons, so I'm not a straight-up bitch to her. I'm just mostly one.

"He wants bacon and egg sandwiches," I say.

"Did he say that?"

"He likes burgers." That's what he told me the first time he tried to flirt with me, and on our first date, we went out for burgers. That ended with him emasculating the waiter and tattooing my pussy. *Aw. Romantic, loving times.*

I shrug. "These are kind of burgers."

"He likes waffles."

I shrug. "Guess you could make some waffles to go with my burgers, but that'll probably make him feel like you're trying to make him choose between me or you."

Her eyes narrow ever so slightly.

"And he sure as hel chose me last night."

Her lips purse. "You know."

"Yep." Not quite true. Well, a blatant lie, really. He hasn't told me shit other than having said her name in answer to my question, but she doesn't need to know that. I grab a knife and stab it straight into the first packet of bacon, then rip it down the full length of the plastic.

A smile twitches at her lips. "If that is an attempt at a threat, girl, you –"

"I don't know what you're talking about. I'm making breakfast. What I'm *not* doing is causing a rift between you and him. So –" I smile brightly as I gesture at her with the knife. "Make your damn waffles."

Her smile falls. She puts the bowl down. Varius must've properly ripped into her last night.

"I'll get the eggs then," she says.

As much as I want to tell her to fuck off and watch me

serve him and be everything he wants, I don't. One, Varius does not show his affection publicly. And two, I have to live with the bitch. She could have just decided I wasn't good enough for her boy. Varius is the first of her children to get married as far as I'm aware. There was one other kid of hers who got close, but he got murdered at the venue. Antonio killed him while she was gone – where, I don't know. Her past is pretty private, and I've only picked up bits and pieces about Varius' siblings in the four months that I have been here. I get the feeling, though, that even her sons do not know most of her tale.

So as much as I want to hate her for blackmailing me, I don't let myself. It's not like Dayne and I started off great, and I trust Varius to have actually handled it. His mother or not, she has to be scared of him just a little. He has the ability to shut off even on those he loves.

Like Khalid.

And that fucker terrifies me.

"Thank you," I say.

"Mmm."

I turn on the frying pan. Get it hot. And as the bacon starts to sizzle, I decide to break the awkward silence. "You know, when I first met Dayne, he bit me, then stabbed me, the fucker, and now he's my best friend."

"By the sounds of it, he's your only friend."

"Wooow. Someone really is a bitch."

"I'm a mother, which you will understand one day."

I glance down at my flat stomach as she turns on the other stove to cook the eggs. When cooking for a house as large as this, four rings just doesn't cut it.

"It's been four months," I say, and still no baby.

"It's not uncommon for a witch to struggle to conceive. Magic kills the weak. Have you tested yourself?"

"No need. I just had my period two weeks-ish ago."

"Period or spo–"

"Micha," Varius says as he passes the entrance of the kitchen. He didn't bother coming in, but his tone told me to get out there, so I glance at the bacon sizzling in front of me and then at Sau beside me.

"Will you please not burn these?"

She stares at me for a second, then nods. "Go."

"Thanks." Wiping my hands on my unicorn and rainbow-shit apron, I head out to find Varius.

He's in the living room. Seeing me, he walks out onto the front porch, and I follow.

"You're leaving today. Going up north to talk to your father."

"Was there something wrong with his meeting with the Mattos twins?" I was up there a couple weeks ago, setting that up. They hold a monopoly on Ricks distribution in the entire eastern half of the USA. Ricks are magical drugs that change the user's penis into something *fancy.* You can get ridges, vibrating parts, cum sacks, G-spot hooks – you name it. They can even change the taste of both the appendage itself and the cum that shoots from it, and if a guy is really feeling lucky, he can double stack them to grow a second dick.

I haven't tried one, bit too scared of them, and Varius doesn't do drugs. Drugs lead to addiction, and addiction is a synonym for weakness. But I can admit to being curious. And potentially up for trying Vs – the vagina equivalent. They vibrate, taste delicious, and rearrange your organs so you can take monster dicks without being split in half, so you can get fucked in your cervix or have your belly balloon with cum. Some of them even help with pregnancy, storing sperm for weeks and releasing them at the optimal time of a woman's cycle.

"No. But we need men for this war. I don't want to rely on Aleric for everything."

"Your meeting with him is today?"

"Yes."

"So shouldn't I wait until tomorrow? Otherwise, it's just your mom here." I lower my voice even though there's no one else outside. "Do we trust –"

"Yes."

I really want to ask him why she blackmailed me then, but I know he won't answer. Being the wife of a Boss means accepting not knowing most things. So I bite my tongue and nod. "I'll pack a bag after breakfast." It's an eight-and-a-half hour drive one way. "Will you be removing the belt?"

He grins. His eyes dart to my pussy beneath my dress. "No."

"But –"

He steps in close. Ducks his head to my ear. "When you come back, little monster, you can beg me for its release."

"Ahhh." I swallow hard.

His nostrils flare and then he pulls me into his arms and kisses me.

I'm so shocked at his show of affection outside of our rooms, I don't kiss him back.

Not until he growls.

Then spanks my ass, telling me I fucking better.

Smiling against his lips, I do.

Unfortunately, The kiss is over before it really starts, but it's still the hottest one I've ever had.

As he leaves me standing on the front porch, I lift a hand to my lips.

And realize I'm still wearing my stupid fucking grin.

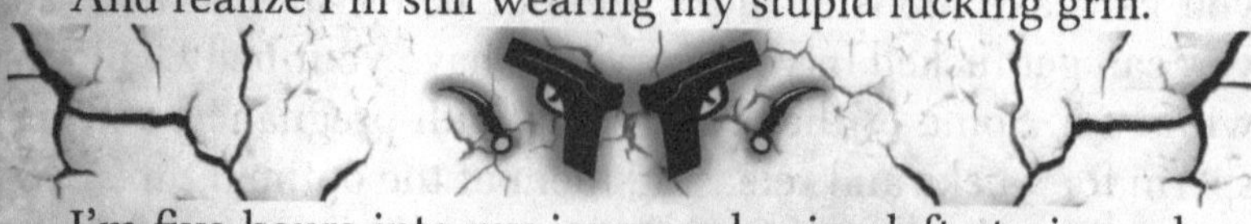

I'm five hours into my journey, having left at nine, when I get a text on my phone. It interrupts the song playing on the radio as it's connected to the car's stereo, and a robotic voice reads out my message.

Varius: Head back to the house now. Don't trust Mother. Watch her while we're gone.

My eyes dart away from the road to check the screen on my phone, needing a second confirmation that what I just heard was correct. It's two o'clock. The meeting is in two hours. Given he hasn't called it off or is thinking of leaving one of his brothers behind, he can't be that worried. He's probably just being paranoid.

He has to be.

There's no way Khalid would be willing to leave his girl there if there was any real chance of it being dangerous.

Speaking aloud, using the microphone-to-text option on my messaging app, I tell him I'm on my way. At the next opportunity, I turn the car around, and my original eight-and-a-half hour drive becomes nine due to a bit of speeding.

I'm exhausted by the time I make it back, having not even stopped for a coffee break just in case I arrived too late. I'm also hungry, so I park the car in the empty drive – the meeting with Aleric will most likely run late– and head inside, making my way towards the kitchen.

Which for some reason is smelling like a fucking sewage. Gagging right before I step through the archway, I look towards the stove, expecting some gross-ass but extremely deadly potion boiling away on it. I wrinkle my nose.

"Gods, that's an awful smell," I say.

A chair squeaks at the table, and I turn to see Khalid's girl sitting there. She jumps to her feet, looking nervous, and I can't help but wonder if Sau's tried to turn her against me already.

A pang pierces my heart at that thought. What the hel did I do so wrong to make her hate me? I really thought she liked me. The only time we ever had any tension was when I asked her about Varius' lack of magic.

A thought tickles the edge of my consciousness, but the godsawful smell coming from the stove makes it run away before I can probably think it. Lifting both hands, I weave a spell around the pot, curving the air in a bubble around it to trap the sewage smell inside. *Gods, that's so much better.*

Turning to Khalid's girl, I smile and try to make small talk, but I don't know what to say to a woman I don't know. She's been here for three days, but Khalid has kept her in his room all this time. Honestly, I'm surprised she's able to walk given I've seen the bulge in his pants and know he was celibate for the last two years. Plus, I bet the boy's into some freaky shit.

Knowing I can't say *that* though, I pick the first thing that comes to mind: blood bonds. It's the only thing I know we have in common – even if no one knows it.

On second thought, though, which, of course, only occurs well into the conversation, I realize that talking about witch stuff is freaking the hel out of her. She is clearly human and has very limited knowledge of our world.

Great.

I probably just got myself put on Khalid's short list.

A list I'm sure gets culled all the fucking time because he's just so damn efficient at killing people.

Fuck.

"Hey, Khalid really cares about you. I know that," I say, trying to pretend that I didn't just infer that he didn't care with my whole 'then why hasn't he told you the truth about blood bonds' speech I just made. "And I don't doubt for a second that he will do anything for you. But the men in this family can be really callous and selfish sometimes, so just keep that in mind. I know it can be overwhelming when they focus on you."

She looks at me for a moment longer than is comfortable before softly asking, "Which one's yours?"

I laugh, my heart skipping a beat. "No one is *mine*. But I'm engaged to Varius fucking Shadow." At her blank look, I ask, "You haven't met him yet, have you?" I nod. *Duh.* "Of course you haven't. Otherwise, you'd understand."

"You like him though, don't you?" she asks.

I still, wondering if these are her questions or Sau's. I do not know why she tried to blackmail me, but I don't like her knowing my personal shit. Before I can straight up ask her, the bitch in question comes in with a black leather grimoire in her hands.

"Here's a – *Micha*, you're back," she says as she walks towards us with a smile fit for a shark. "I thought you were out until tomorrow."

"Yeah, I got back early," I say with a cheerful grin right before telling her that I'm here for security because she's so damn useless with her curse. Gods, I am being such a bitch, but fuck it. This is karma.

"You're cursed?" Khalid's girl asks.

Sau turns to me, her teeth bared. Some would call it a smile, but I sure as hel wouldn't. Not with that look in her eyes. "Yes. I can't use magic without it draining my life, but that doesn't mean I *won't* use it."

Bitch, did you just threaten me?

My gaze locked on Sau, I start to stand. "I know you will die protecting her, but if I'm here, you don't have to." If the werewolves happen to come while the boys are gone, I can burn them all with my magic. "The wolves –"

"*Don't?*" Sau cuts in, the air electrifying like a coming storm.

"Did I say that?" I cock my head to the side, but my mind is already off the conversation. I've just felt something – a crawl of danger across my skin, raising my hairs. My eyes flick towards the window, trying to discern what's caused my sudden paranoia. Is it Varius through our bond? He's with Aleric. That'd be enough to make anyone –

No.

There's a break in the air. It's like the white noise I never noticed has now quieted. Like the wards –

My eyes widening, I throw up a shimmering blue shield of magic. Dark-red bolts crackle around the edges of it as I stumble back. The tendrils reach for me, searching for my flesh, and I send a pulse of fire into my shield. Purple flames race out from my palm in all directions. As soon as it hits Sau's magic, it intensifies in color and length, consuming every drop she threw at me. If I wasn't so fucking pissed, I might've found all those colors beautiful.

But I thought we were friends. I thought Sau liked me. I never thought she'd blackmail me. Never thought she'd try to attack me while the boys were out. To fucking blame me for tearing down the wards – that break in the air, that halt of white noise I felt earlier. I can hear exactly what she's planning on telling Varius when he gets back.

"I know I lied to you before, but you know *I would never take the wards down. I wouldn't risk it."*

Fucking *bitch*.

Lowering my hand, I watch as she runs from the kitchen. I let her go. Let her take those first few steps away from me because I am going to enjoy hunting her down. Then I am going to catch her and beat her into a godsdamn pulp.

My rage building, I take that first step. Purple fire flickers between my fingertips. I open my mouth to call her name, to let her know I'm coming, but just as the S hisses from my lips, it's killed by a chorus of howls.

I stop, my head snapping towards the window.

They sound close.

Too close.

And the timing of this can't be a coincidence. If it was just one wolf, then maybe. They could've been watching the house. Once the ward went down, they saw an opportunity to sneak in and kill the women who've been left on their own. A dumb strategy, but men wanting to climb the ranks and impress the Boss have done dumber things. But this isn't just one wolf. It's the entire fucking pack.

Meaning Sau must have gotten Antonio to be here either through trickery or by making a straight-up deal with him. Either way, I'm killing her for it. Because she clearly doesn't want to merely frame me for her sins. She wants me dead. Or worse, taken by the wolves.

What the fuck did I do to make her hate me so much?

Biting back the urge to set the house on fire, to kill the bitch that way, I run out into the living room. I veer towards the hall, and as I enter it, I catch sight of the two women up ahead.

I start to call my magic to my palms. The wall explodes right in front of me though, sending plaster and splinters of wood flying everywhere. A werewolf's arm has smashed a hole through the side of the house, blocking me from taking a shot at Sau.

Snarling, I grab hold of its wrist. "Get out of the fucking way," I snap as I shoot fire up its arm, burning it into ash.

The wolf howls as it yanks away from me, leaving behind the smell of burning hair and meat. A flurry of ashen flakes drift to the floor in front of me.

Stalking through them, I catch sight of Sau just as she reaches the stairs. Pissed as all hel, I throw a black ball of magic at her. It feeds on my anger, growing in size, taking up nearly half the corridor. She turns at the last second and catches it. Then dispels it like it was nothing. I don't know how much life she just burned through doing that because of her curse, but I hope it was fucking *years.*

"Keep going!" she snaps at Khalid's girl. "The stairs are just there."

Gods, that must be the panic talking; the girl's one foot away from the stairs. In fact, I'm pretty sure they ran down a few steps before running back up so she could fend me off on level ground. Good. I hope Sau is fucking terrified I will kill her. Because I'm going to.

"I'll hold Micha off," she says.

"But –"

"Go! And after you shut the door, call Khalid."

My heart trips over my feet. *Khalid is in on this?* As terrified as I am of him, of how he can kill me without even being here, it's pain and grief that fills me. I'm going to die, and Varius is going to believe whatever lie his mother tells him. Worse, the brother he trusts, the only one left he has to trust, has also betrayed him.

Now this is fucking personal.

They're going to hurt what's *mine*.

They're going to hurt my fucking mate.

I call on the fire I was born with, the one that eats magic, the one that can't be put out by anything other than me, and I stalk towards Varius' mother.

"I'm going to kill you," I snarl as purple flames dance between my fingers.

"No, girl," she says softly. "You're going to die trying."

SIXTEEN

HIM

Aleric leans back in his chair, his feet kicked up on his desk, his ankles crossed. Normally, the constant movement of his foot as he taps it in the air would annoy the hel out of me as I'm trying to read, but my thoughts are already too scattered to focus on the page in front of me. We've just spent the last two-and-a-half hours going over the contract, changing A to B, then B to C, then C back to fucking A. It's like he's been deliberately wasting our time, keeping us here and out of our house. I've been telling myself he needs our aid, that he won't sabotage his only chance at getting help in fighting Antonio, but Aleric has always done what he wants, to hel with the consequences.

And what he wants is Mother.

Who's home alone. With no magic to defend herself.

But he's also here, and although he could send a team to attack our place, I know he won't. Aleric is playing a game with her, and when it comes time for the next round, he'll be getting her himself.

Still, there's an itch across my skin, something telling me to leave and get back home. That something isn't right. So I flip to the last page of the contract and sign it quickly, then toss the file onto the desk and stand. Leno steps in to sign it next, and I hold my hand out to take Aleric's copy. He looks at me, and for a moment, I see how he is my father. There is a familiar need to dissect everything around him. He knows something has me on edge, and he's about to start pulling threads randomly to see which one unravels.

"Fucking sign it already," I say. "We have shit to do."

He stares at me for a second longer, then signs his copy with a flourish. He offers it to me. "May this alliance not fall apart too quickly." He smiles, and I know the fucker's telling me he thinks I'll be dead soon.

"Break any part of it, and I'll kill you myself." I sign it and toss it back to him as he laughs.

"You are your mother's son." He cocks his head to the side with a smile. "Will no doubt fail like her too."

He glances at Talon, who has just stepped forward to sign the ledger. My brother's knuckles are white around the pen, and I know he is thinking about stabbing it through the vampire's neck.

That won't kill him though. Probably won't even annoy him. Aleric's smile widens in a dare.

"T," Khalid warns. And just like that, Talon signs both copies, then steps back.

Aleric whistles as his eyes dance with delight. "Don't see dogs trained like that anymore. Do you beat him or suck him off to get him to obey that way?"

"He don't have a dick to suck," Maddox cuts in, drawing T's anger. He gets punched in the shoulder as I grab our copy of the alliance and turn for the door before my brother realizes Maddox just played him like a fiddle.

My brothers follow me out. Talon's anger seeps out of his

pores like a beaver's dam about to break. I glance at him as he yanks open the front passenger door of our car.

"I didn't do anything," he mutters. "And I won't as long as you keep me the fuck away from him."

Without a word, I climb into the back seat. Khalid settles in across from me, his jaw tight. Maddox takes the wheel, and my other brothers and Krypto fill up the second car.

I turn to Khalid, watching him as he checks his phone for the hundredth time. He seems to be on edge even more than I am, but I know it's because this is the first time he's left his girl alone. I wonder if that worry is amplified because he thinks Micha might have returned while we were out. I have not told him that she isn't the traitor I thought she was, not fully trusting that she isn't. Not trusting myself to be able to make that call.

The things she does to me...

I can't fucking think straight when I'm around her.

When Khalid frowns at his phone, that itch across my skin flares into a full-on rash. But he is bonded to his girl and can sense her emotions. If there's anything wrong at the house, we'll know about it immediately.

He doesn't text her for an update, doesn't need answers for anything he might be feeling through their link.

So it's just my paranoia playing up again.

Everything is fine...

And yet, as the streets of St. Augustine roll slowly past, a part of me is screaming that it isn't. That this ride is taking too long. That I need to be home *now.*

Feeling unsettled, I glance at Khalid.

But he isn't panicking. His knuckles aren't white on his phone, and I wonder if I'm simply on edge for the same reason he is. Micha is away on her own, driving up to her father's. The car has a tracker, and I have a duo following her for safety though – neither of which she knows about, but I still don't like her away from me.

Deciding that's the issue for the itch of my skin, I pull out my phone and check the notifications.

The men have claimed she's arrived at her father's. No trouble on the way.

The tracking app also says she's there.

But there's no text from –

My phone buzzes.

Micha: *Arrived. Spotted goons. Need better tail training.*

A small smile hides behind my flat lips.

My girl is safe.

Everything is fine.

SEVENTEEN

HER

Holy fucking shit, I'm going to die.

My back slams into the wall as I trip over my feet. The large claw I was dodging pierces the ground in front of me, cutting through the floor like it's butter rather than wood and concrete. The creature looks up at me, its beady neon green eyes actually fucking hypnotizing, and I tear my gaze away before it can make me freeze.

Rolling away from the wall just as its other claw swings for me, I hear the sound of a gun being fired. The claw digs into the plaster, no doubt piercing all the way through to the outside, and a bullet grazes my arm. I twist, my feet dancing a wild beat. My knees give out, and I drop like a stone, trying to make my movements unpredictable; I roll towards the monster. My heart is in my throat, getting this close, but it has both its claws stuck, and – *Fuck.*

It's claws are *not* stuck. It's ripped the one in the floor free, and now it's shooting down towards me, right in line to split my head open, to stab me like a shish kebab from one temple to the other.

Activating a rune on my side, I throw up a quick shield. I still grunt beneath the force of impact, it's so fucking hard, but I stop the claw from reaching me. With my other hand, I aim a blast of fire at the monster's bat-like face, its wide gaping mouth hissing in frustration – a clear shot.

But a sudden flash of black near my feet has me aiming my hand down and blasting at the floor instead. I shoot across it like a rocket, away from the shadows that were swirling at my feet, ready to suck me into the Plane of Monsters. An instant kill, and the place where this fucking gorgon-bat thing came from.

Its body is that of a gorgon – dark green scales across its serpentine body, with patches of light green. Two massive wing-like claws curve out of its upper body. Its head sort of resembles a bat on crack with a longish furry snout that has a mane like a lion, except within it are a hundred black tube-like *things* – like if Medusa slicked all her snakes back. So far, they haven't moved, so I'm pretty certain they can't, but I was also pretty certain I could kill Sau, so I'm not taking anything as fact anymore.

But fuck, I can see how she's a named sup – basically a title for a "badass mother fucker," one of only seven here on Earth. The Reaper of the Sired is about to add one more name to her list of kills, and as I'm dodging gun shots and stabbing claws, I wonder if this is how she killed all of Aleric's sired children and why the *fuck* no one mentioned it on all the blogs that talked about her.

Because this would've been brilliant information to know three minutes ago when I charged her like an idiot. I knew she would try to use her shadows to suck me into the Plane of Monsters. I knew to keep an eye on the floor while I wore her out with my own magic. But what I didn't fucking know was that she could use minimal magic, and thus, minimal life force, to open a portal to that place and call out one of the monsters living there.

So now she's still fresh as a daisy, shooting at me from her place in front of the stairs, while I'm expending all my energy and magic just trying to stay alive.

Fuck.

My.

Life.

Arching my back, I jump to my feet, change my mind, then flip backwards just as a claw swipes the air in front of me. It catches my leg, and I find out it can cut as well as stab as pain flares up my body. Shooting my magic down my leg, I stop the bleeding. It isn't healed, but it won't be the first thing to kill me.

Pivoting, I land on one hand, push off, then twist onto my feet. I dart to the side immediately. Throw up a shield to catch Sau's bullet. It pings off. The air behind me shifts, and I know a claw is coming up behind me to skewer me in half. I drop to the floor, belly down just as the *whoosh* of a blade-like object slices where I just was. I roll immediately in the opposite direction the claw is going, drop my shield, draw fire to my palms, and blast it into the creature's exposed side.

It hisses in outrage as it twists back around to face me. Not trying to stab me, just trying to backhand me with full force.

My shield comes up.

Just barely in time, and as the "elbow" of the claw hits it (fuck monster anatomy), I'm thrown across the hall. My head slams into the wall. Plaster rains down on me. My vision blurs. My skull pounds.

There is a roar.

A scream.

I don't know if it's mine.

Can't seem to think, to make things out anymore.

Gritting my teeth, refusing to die in a way that will mean Varius will believe I betrayed him, I raise a hand to my head and push healing magic into it. It's not enough to heal any damage I might've taken, but it's enough to reduce the pain. It's enough to get me back on my feet, my arms up, a pale-blue shield in front of me while I take my bearings.

My eyes widen. Fuck, I got lucky. A werewolf must have tried to join the fight while I was down because they're now pinned beneath one of the monster's claws, and the tube-like things on the back of said monster's head are all ripping into it, tearing fist-sized chunks out of its body. The wolf is screaming, howling in pain, throwing its arms up trying to defend itself. But it's hopeless. The wolf is already dead; it just doesn't know it yet.

I turn to Sau, wondering why I haven't been filled with bullets, and the reason is instantly understood.

The dead werewolf isn't the only one who has joined the fight. There are two others, and they're both attacking Sau. She doesn't have her gun anymore – either tossed aside or smacked away, I don't know. But she's burning through her life now, using her magic to defend herself against the fast claws and teeth of wolves. So far, it doesn't look like they've managed to touch her, the shadows swirling at her feet keeping them back as she launches balls of magic at them, but it's only a matter of time. She can't keep up with their speed, and she can't use her shadows forever.

And if one of them touches her, it will only add to her 'evidence' against me.

Fuck.

I have to intervene.

Glancing at the monster, making sure it's still occupied, I then drop my shield and line up a shot at one of the wolves attacking Sau. Just as I'm about to release my magic though, a blur to my right distracts me. I turn my head, but I'm not fast enough, and I'm shoved into the wall by a body thick with muscle and power. A human, not a wolf.

One of their arms is around my waist. The other hand is cupped around the back of my head. Before I even know what's happening, hard lips come down over mine.

My eyes widening, I try to push magic into my fingers to throw him off me, but then I realize they're behind my back, pinned under his arm. My heart jumps into my throat and pounds wildly. I could be dead right now. He moved so fast, moved *me* so fast. I never had a chance of surviving if he didn't want me alive.

He's off me in another second. I push back from the wall, trying to figure out what the fuck is going on. Sau can't be working with him if she's fighting his men. Which means she manipulated him into coming here, somehow letting him know the wards would be down today without actually telling him. So she could use her enemy to do her dirty work in killing me, use him to give credence to her lies. That makes sense. I get that.

What I don't understand is why the fuck did he kiss me?

Before the next thought can form, my brain melts from what I'm seeing. Antonio jumps, still in human form, over the moat of shadows Sau's erected up around her. He shifts in mid-air, too fucking fast and without the agonizing cries that normally accompany a werewolf's change, his bones breaking, his skin tearing, tendons and ligaments and every other part of him being ripped to shreds before reforming into a bipedal monster with vicious teeth, knife-like claws, and long red fur. His teeth latch onto Sau's shoulder, and white light flares around his face. They topple to the ground, sliding across the floor. Her shadows wrap around him, and he yelps as monsters from the other plane start to eat him alive, but he's killing her faster than she can kill him, his claws ripping into her chest, her stomach, every place he can reach, just tearing chunks out left and right, no finesse to his movements, no beauty. Just raw carnage.

My jaw drops open as I watch her heal just as fast, closing holes, restitching flesh. Black magic forms on her hands, and she shoves them through his chest. He cries out, releases her. Stumbles off and back. The other two wolves jump into the fight, not giving her any time to regain her feet. To rebuild her energy. She's burning through so much of her life, and even though I hate her for what she's done to me, I can't stomach watching her get torn to pieces.

She is Varius' mother.

So I raise a hand, forming a ball of red energy. The air crackles around me. I move my hands together, building up the magic, making it the strongest it can be. In this time, in the three seconds it takes me, she's already killed one of the wolves, and the other is screaming in agony. Antonio lunges back in just as I start to throw my spell. But it never hits him because I'm forced to twist and send it sideways as the fucking gorgon-bat thing slithers towards me, hissing in its desire to eat me.

The beast catches my attack in its mouth, and there is a moment of pain in its bright green eyes a second before its entire head is set on fire. It burns with such intensity, it turns into ash within seconds. I instinctively close my eyes so none of it flies into me, then wipe a hand across my face. By the time I can see again, though, it's too late.

There's nothing I can do to help Sau.

Antonio is kneeling on top of her, and he has both his hands inside her chest, stopping her magic from healing her. As I watch, helpless and exhausted, he rips open her rib cage, cracking bones and flinging blood in all directions. The shadows that were wrapped around his legs fall free, leaving behind gaping wounds.

Sau cries out for the first time, but it's weak, fragile. A final breath of life.

And then her head flops to the side, the light in her eyes fading. She looks straight at me, and I don't know if I feel happy that she's dead or not.

But I'm not dumb enough to just stand here thinking about it.

Running for the stairs as Antonio finishes her off, I head for the basement. A wolf darts in front of me, coming in through a hole in the wall, but it didn't look both ways. It hasn't seen me, its focus entirely on the basement stairs, no doubt able to smell the fear coming up from it as Khalid's girl, a woman without magic, cowers inside.

By the time I make it to the top of the stairs, it's already at the bottom, trying to tear its way inside. The magic in the wood is stopping it though. As long as the ward is activated, no one is getting through but Shadow blood. Which means I have to bring the ward down if I want to get inside. For a second, I hesitate – wondering if I should risk Khalid's girl for my own safety. As long as she's in there and the ward is up, she'll be safe. She won't survive with it down.

But I don't want to die, especially not if she tells Varius I'm the one who took the ward down. If he thinks I am the traitor due to whatever lies Sau told her.

I will trade the entire fucking world to keep what I have with my mate, and so I press my palm against the wall and push my fire into the runes.

It takes everything I have, all the energy holding my legs up, all the strength keeping my arm from wavering. Sweat pours down my face, and the pounding in my skull from my earlier fall intensifies. I am giving it every last drop I have, and yet, it is not enough. My fire eats magic, but the wards protecting the safe room are powerful.

Too fucking powerful.

Gritting my teeth, pulling on the fear of death, I open myself up to my flames. Pain shoots through my kidneys, my fire turning back on me. Eating me like it's eating the runes, and I falter, my legs giving out. I tumble down the stairs, smacking my head and every other part of me.

But there is a beautiful sound in my ears. The sound of splitting wood as the wolf tears through the door in its frenzy. I've broken the ward.

If I can just get to my feet and get inside, we still have a chance of surviving until the boys get here. Varius has to know something is wrong. He will have rushed back; he's probably coming up the drive now. I just need to buy us a few more minutes, and I can do that with the arsenal of potions in the basement.

Dragging myself to my feet, I watch as the wolf shoves its arm through the door, finally breaking through. It pulls back, then places its eye against the hole, only to jerk away again on a high-pitched howl, its fur smoldering as a smell so fucking nauseating and sweet fills the air. A potion has been tossed in her face, and it's burning through her like acid. She'll be dead in a few seconds when the potion eats its way to her brain.

Still, I don't think I have a few seconds to spare. I have already taken too long breaking through the ward. Antonio has to be finished with Sau already, even if she somehow managed to heal from when I last saw her. She's a strong witch, named when he is not. It is possible she survived, is still alive, but if by some miracle she is, she can't be for much longer. I can't rely on her buying me anymore time.

So I place my hand on the back of the wolf's chest, right behind her heart, and push my fire into her. Pain shoots across my kidneys, and I know my magic is eating me alive. Not for the first time, I wished our magic worked like it did on TV, where we could use it without risk, without worry. But Hollywood always lies. If we use it too much, it'll kill us like it's currently killing me.

I'll recover. Eventually. Unless I push it too far, too fast.

So I need the potions. I need to get into the basement.

As I start to drag the wolf out of the way, a white arm reaches through the hole in the door. Khalid's girl pours another vial of acidic magic onto the wolf, finally stopping its screams.

I don't have the energy to tell her I'm coming in. I can't figure out what words it'll take for her to believe I'm not going to hurt her, assuming Sau told her I would. Instead, I just shove the door open as soon as she pulls her arm back and stride in.

She tries to throw a whole handful of potions at my face. Expecting something of the sort, I throw up a shield. The vials hit it and fall to the floor as she stumbles back, her eyes wide in terror. She trips over her feet, then lands on her ass just as the glass potions shatter in front of her.

I am protected from the splashes of acid due to my full-length shield. She, however, is not, and as drops of the red liquid eat through her legs, she starts to scream. Then jerk, the pain all too crippling and sending her into shock.

Turning from her, I concentrate on the open entry in front of me. She might think I'm a bitch for not helping her, but I need to prioritize my jobs, or neither of us are going to be alive long enough to argue over my choices.

Pulling on my last reserves, I throw up a ward over the door. It isn't as strong as the one that was there before, and any sup other than a werewolf can now enter, but it'll buy us time, and that's all I need. Just more time. The boys are on their way. They'll be here soon.

Rushing over to the shelf of potions, I grab a healing potion and neck it. Grab another and do the same. The icy-blue liquid slides down my throat, then expands with the warmth of a hug. The pounding in my skull starts to fade, and the cut in my leg threads itself back together. A burst of energy fills me, giving me my second wind, and I grab a few more vials of various types, then kneel down beside Khalid's girl. I pop off the cork of a healing potion and hold it to her lips.

"Drink," I demand. "It'll stop the pain."

She groans as her body jerks in utter agony. She doesn't raise an arm to grab the vial, perhaps she can't, but she does open her mouth, so I pour it in.

She shudders once, then her shaking stops. She opens her eyes and looks at me. But I'm already leaving her, on my feet and heading for the door. I don't have time for niceties, don't have time to ask her how she is. I need to build up our defense before the next wolf comes down.

"Why did you save me?" she asks.

I don't turn to her, don't look at her, my eyes on the only door in and out of the basement. Thumps and snarls come from above, just out of sight. Sau must still be alive if the wolves are still fighting up there. Unless the boys are back...

Hope jumps into my throat, but I squash it down. I can't get lax until I see one of them for myself. So I place all the vials but two attack potions down on the ground beside me.

"Micha?" she asks hesitantly.

Hating that I have to even defend myself, I say, "Because we're on the same side."

"Then why did you take down the wards?"

"I didn't."

"But Sau said —"

"She was misinformed," I snap, not wanting to get into an argument now. I need to be on my A-game. Antonio can react faster than a fucking bullet, faster than I can throw. If I'm to have any hope of getting out of here, then I need to concentrate on survival and not correcting lies. That can come later. *If we're still alive.*

I will be.

Because I'm not leaving Varius before I even get to know him. I want to hear him laugh without restriction, without that fear of happiness choking the life out of him. I want to see him dance when no one's looking, feel the touch of his hand when it's covered in wrinkles. I want a lifetime with him. I want the bond to be completed.

So I can't die here today.

I have too many things I want to –

Thud!

The loud bang in the ceiling has me pivoting on my heels and looking up. I warded the door. I didn't ward the fucking ceiling. My eyes narrow as I try to figure out where they're going to come in from, but then they widen, and the two potions slip from my fingers. I don't know if they shatter. Don't know if the contents inside them get on me.

Because all my concentration is on the pain exploding in my stomach. A nest of fire ants. The impact of a bus. The tearing of a chainsaw as it digs into one's flesh. I don't think any of those things feel as bad as this.

My eyes roll back as my vision blurs. I'm vaguely aware of blood bubbling out of my mouth. I can taste the copper, can smell the iron.

Someone is screaming, but I don't think it's me. I don't think I have the ability to do anything other than breathe, and even that is a struggle.

Dropping my chin, my head unable to hold itself up, I peer down at my stomach. A clawed fist is poking through the right side of my body. A large presence is at my back. But before I can even question what the fuck went wrong with the ward, the darkness starts to take me.

No! No, I need to fight – Varius...

"Shhh," Antonio whispers in my ear, his words so soft I can barely hear them. "Just relax. Don't fight it." Spreading his claws out, he rips his hand back out of my body. Chunks of me splatter at my feet, and my knees buckle in an instant. He lowers me to the ground, his lips still by my ear. "I'm not going to kill you now," he murmurs. "First I'm going to take the bitch in front of you."

My eyes find her at the shelf of potions. She's grabbing handfuls of who knows what. I want to yell at her to turn around, to not give him her back, but I can't do anything other than gurgle up blood.

My cheek hits the floor. Antonio slides his hand down from my shoulder, where he was holding me up, to my back, below the hole he punched in me. His breath chilling my ear, he snarls, "Then I'm going to come back for the bastard in your womb."

My eyes widen.

His hand wraps around my throat.

Get up, Micha! Get up!

"I will make you suffer like I have."

He squeezes, and the darkness closes in on me. My brain screams at me to get up, to protect this child he's hinting at.

But my limbs won't work.

And my vision isn't clearing. Isn't coming back. It's just falling to the darkness like I'm falling to him.

No!

No, godsdamnit! Get up! Get...up...

"I will show you what it's like to be a parent without a child."

My blood spikes. I want to scream, but all I can do is lie beneath his hand and bleed out.

"And only then, Shadow whore, will I kill you."

Get...up...gods...damn...it

Get...u...

EIGHTEEN

HIM

Khalid's girl isn't picking up.

He has his phone to his ear. His shoulders are tense. His knuckles are white, and I can hear it ringing from my side of the car.

Riiiing.

The hairs on my arms rise as I stare out the window, a sudden thought occurring to me. *Fuck.*

Riiiing.

The beat of Khalid's heart picks up, and so does mine.

How the hel did I not realize this before?

Riiiing.

I can smell the panic being pushed out of his pores, the rush of adrenaline pumping through his body.

His phone drops.

And my heart stops.

The reaper is never afraid.

My head turns to him.

"What's wrong?" Talon asks, but I don't give Khalid time to answer, barking out a quick, "Go."

And he doesn't hesitate. Doesn't try to tell us what he's realized or sensed or felt. He just shifts into his shadow and leaves. Whatever he's afraid of, he needs to address it *now*, is terrified that if he stops to give us even a two-second brief, that he'll be too late. And that same fear is damn near squeezing at my lungs because I've just realized Aleric can get past our godsdamn ward.

It's species specific – created by Mother and Caden when they built the house we live in to keep out all non-witches.

Except I'm not a fucking witch.

I'm part vampire.

So if I can get in, then so can my father.

My jaw locked, I pull out my phone and dial Enoch. As it connects, I say, "Maddox, Talon, follow Khalid."

Talon shifts into his shadow instantly, but Maddox waits for his relief.

As soon as Enoch answers, I say, "You're driving."

"Got it."

I hang up as Talon's shadow slips out through the cracks in the floor. A few seconds later, another black mass appears in the footwell. I lean forward to grab the wheel as Maddox shifts, then chases after his brothers.

Enoch forms in the driver's seat, his shadows swirling up around his muscled body, all the way up to his ginger hair. His forearm flexes as he grabs the wheel "What's the sit?" he asks.

"Force it."

He glances at me, seeking answers, but he doesn't push before he makes the car speed up. He weaves in and out of the traffic, using his telekinesis to move people out of the way just enough for him to cut through gaps that are barely there.

"Khalid's worried about his girl," I start dialing Mother's

number.

He groans. "She probably can't reach the top shelf or something. He fucking dotes on her. You know Leno caught him picking some flowers last night? Dude was *not* happy. And I'm not happy Khalid's still breathing."

I raise my phone to my ear, listening to it ring as my brother keeps talking.

"You remember when I tried to pick a rose for Mother's Day when I was *seven*, and the damn thing strangled me, its thorns all digging into my neck? He left me there for hours until Mom came home! Then every time I stepped out of the house for the next week, the damn plants attacked me! But oh no, Khalid picks *half* a bush, and all he gets is a stern, 'Don't do that,' and the flowers taken away. He deserved losing a hand at least."

"You knew the flowers are for protecting the property," I say. Leno has cultivated each plant since it was a seed or bulb, adding his magic to its roots, letting it grow with his essence inside of it. He can connect to them from afar, but he needs to concentrate, needs to be able to touch the soil, which is why he always carries a bag of home dirt with him.

As the phone continues to ring, I send him a message to check in with our second line of security. I don't tell him the wards might be compromised, don't want to go down that rabbit hole of explanations if I don't need to.

"It was *one* flower," Enoch continues. "And Khalid -"

My lips tighten. "Mother's not answering."

"Maybe she can't? They were making potions -"

"Scry."

He huffs, but for all his thoughts that everything is fine, he doesn't hesitate to obey. Releasing the wheel with one hand, he traces a sigil in the air, leaving a line of dark-teal behind. An eye appears with a swirling pupil. He releases the wheel with his other hand, and with both, he creates a scry over the rearview mirror. The eye presses into the glass for half a second, then is gone. I lean forward as an image of our house appears.

"Shit," Enoch swears, then steps on the gas. His magic wraps around us in a bubble. He turns down a side street, then another, the other car with our brothers following close behind. As soon as there are no witnesses, he activates the bubble of magic, and the car becomes invisible.

A second later, we lift in the air, cutting straight above the city, the view in the mirror urging us faster.

Corpses of werewolves lie under crawling plants whose stalks and limbs sprout through flesh, rooting them to the ground. But there are more enemies on the roof and porch of the house, slashing their claws through the wood, trying to terrorize those inside rather than truly trying to get in. A foolish endeavor. Mother is afraid of nothing but the death of a child, and we are not there.

"Scry the –" I start to say, but then stop as Khalid arrives in our yard. He shifts into his human form and instantly throws a wave of heat at the werewolves on the roof, boiling them alive, their fur melting, their skin beneath bubbling and slipping free. He drops to his knees, spitting up blood, and I curse. He's at his breaking point already. How much fucking magic has he been using these past few days?

My lips tightening, wanting us to already be there, I twist in my seat and pull the back of the one beside me down, giving me access to the trunk. "Scry the kitchen," I say over my shoulder as I pull out an M4 and a loaded mag pouch. I strap the belt around my waist as the mirror in front of me shimmers.

Our kitchen comes into view. My jaw clenches when I see no one there, which means Mother didn't manage to dump Khalid's girl in the basement and get back to a strong defensible position. The grain of the counter shifts, drawing my eye as it moves restlessly. But the monster inside it is unable to rip free from its binds. A chill comes over me as I seem to catch its gaze. Although there's no face beneath the grain, I can almost hear it screaming for me to let it loose. I know it's panicking over Mother. *Our* mother – the bond it shares with Sau that of a child. A monster sister. A third defense that hasn't been used.

Holding its "gaze," I load the M4, pushing the magazine straight up until it clicks, then giving it a little tug to check it's locked. I pull the charging handle back and release it, my pulse calming at the familiar sound of the sliding metal. My world reduces to the gun in my hands and the wolves I'm going to kill with it.

"Shit," Enoch curses, his tone nervous, his body on edge. He doesn't wait for me to give him a new order. The mirror flickers between various rooms, the scry connecting to any reflective surface he can grab hold of with his magic. We're unable to see into the basement due to the ward keeping all magic from passing through, but we land on a view of the hall that leads to it.

He sucks in a breath.

A serpentine monster is lying dead on the floor, its head a charcoal so black, I just know that the smallest gust of wind will have it falling apart. Drifting ash. Lost evidence to the battle that took place.

"What the fuck does Antonio have that can do that?" my brother asks as a tightness coils in my stomach. There's only one person I know with flames that hot, but she's up north in Tennessee.

My grip tightens on my phone as it buzzes. Ignoring the new message, I open the tracking app on Micha's car. It says she's nearly five hundred miles away from here. I glance up at the text notification to see if it's from the men I have following her. But it's from Rudy, telling me Leno's one with the plants in our yard, but that our brothers are already inside the house. I start to type in Stefaan Black's number, but Enoch's sudden shout of, "Mom!" has my fingers stilling and my head snapping up.

"Fuck!" he rasps, and I lean forward to get a better look.

She's sitting up on her bed, her white sheets soaked red, her head hanging down as we look at her through the small mirror on her dresser. All of her clothes have been ripped away, leaving her naked and vulnerable. Her arms have been spread out to either side and nailed to the bed frame with dozens of nails in her wrists and hands.

"She's breathing," I say, my voice calm. Enoch glances at me, and I hear the words he doesn't say. *Do you care at all?*

But now we're above our property. There's no time for questions. No time for judgement as he starts to put the car down by our front porch. My eyes scan the house, looking for any werewolves or our brothers.

Spotting a wolf, I shove open the car door. We're still ten feet or so in the air, but I don't hesitate as I leap out. My gun comes up, the safety is switched off, and as I start to fall, I fire at the werewolf that has just barreled out of a hole in the wall of our house. He's running for the woods, but my hail of bullets hits him in the back. He stumbles. I hit the ground and roll, switching on the safety until I'm back on my feet. My thumb pushes the lever down. I'm ready to fire again, and I do so as the fucker starts crawling away.

The car thumps on the ground as it lands behind me.

"How the hel did you react like that?" Enoch asks as he hops out.

"I train. Now grab him," I say, gesturing at the wolf I just shot. "I want him alive for questioning. And tell Leno to go to Mother."

As the second car lands, I turn to the house. Keeping my gun up, I step inside and head towards the basement, drawn towards the monster I saw in the scry. To what its black-ash head might *mean.*

You're being paranoid.

And yet...I can almost make out a whiff of my mate. Of

the blood I have tasted.

Fucking hel, Varius. She's up in Tennessee.

Making my way through the house, I sweep my gun back and forth, ready to shoot any werewolf that's still here. My pulse stays steady. My thoughts do too, but just beneath the surface, they are screaming.

Because as I walk through the carnage in the hall, I can't deny the smell of her blood anymore. It fucking assaults my nose as I make my way up to the serpentine beast.

My girl has bled here.

Fought here.

What the fuck is she doing here?

And why did she kill one of Mother's monsters?

Maybe it wasn't a tame beast. Maybe Mother just opened up a portal and plucked out the first monster she could find. Or maybe Micha misfired. Was aiming for Antonio when the beast got in the way? That has to be it because she can't be a fucking traitor. I just cleared her. Just started to fucking trust her.

The hairs on my arm rising, I make my way down the basement stairs, following the trail of her blood. A female wolf lies at the bottom, half her face melted away. There's a burn mark on her back too that makes me breathe a little easier. Micha must have attacked her, which means she wasn't fighting *with* them. She isn't a traitor.

But then my chest squeezes again, my breath flees from my lungs. Because I've just noticed that the ward protecting our safe room has been broken. A werewolf couldn't have done that. It had to have been done by a damn strong witch.

Like Micha...

Stepping around the massive red bulk of fur, I enter the basement.

And now my blood is rushing out of my skull.

Filling up my lungs.

Until I can't breathe.

Can't think.
Can't even feel the fucking gun in my hands anymore.
Because my mate is lying on the ground.
And she isn't fucking moving.

NINETEEN

HIM

My entire world pinpoints in on her. For a moment, there is nothing but the heavy weight of silence crushing my shoulders. An absence of life, of meaning, of understanding.

And then there is noise, a sudden explosion of sound as my brain screams for me to run to her.

And when I take that first step, my gun starting to drop, my calf muscles flexing, I realize it isn't my brain that is screaming.

It's me.

My mouth is open.

My throat is raw, emitting a noise that is the sound of a heart breaking from pure terror.

She can't be dead.

Not when we haven't even started our life together. Not before she even knows that I love her.

I take that next step, a near fucking leap, even though a loud part of me is yelling at me to leave her. To clear the zone. To make sure there aren't any surprises hidden in any of the other rooms. That she isn't bait left alive to trick me into lowering my guard.

Because I can hear her breathing now, can see the rise of her chest even if it's faint.

And that part of me that's screaming, that intelligence that has kept me alive all this time, gains momentum. Yells louder. Tells me if I kneel down beside her, if I drop my gun to feed her a healing potion, then I'll be attacked by the wolf that's clearly hiding somewhere in this room.

But for once in my life, I ignore it. With that hole in her stomach, Micha doesn't have time for me to clear the zone.

So I shove my gun behind me, leaving it to swing on the shoulder strap, and pull out a vial from my pants pocket.

"Micha," I rasp as I drop to my knees beside her. Popping open the cork, I pour the healing potion between her lips. It doesn't seem to do anything, telling me there's too much damage inside for it to focus on stitching together her skin.

"*Micha.*" Her name is a hiss now, a fucking order as the pulse that has stayed calm all this time jumps up into my throat. Seeing my mate so pale, so lifeless even though she breathes is making me fucking *weak*.

Fucking *furious*.

I'm going to kill whoever did this to her.

"Varius!"

My head snaps up at the sound of Enoch's voice coming from the hall above. "In here!" I shout as I slide my arms under my mate and lift her into the air. By the time my brother makes it down here, I'm at the door.

"Move," I snap.

"Let me –"

"Don't you fucking touch her."

His eyes widen, but he steps back quick, pressing himself against the wall to give me space to leave. I stride up the stairs, doing my best not to jostle her despite the harsh pace.

My brother hurries behind me.

"The wolf you shot –" he starts, but I cut him off.

"Is Mother conscious?"

"No. She's –"

"Then get me Leno."

"But he's –"

"*Fucking get him*," I snap as I reach the landing.

Feeling his eyes on me, I force my anger down. My want to attack everything around me isn't going to fucking save her.

"*Enoch*," I growl as I step out into the hall, the burnt monster a terrible stench in my nostrils.

"Yeah, okay." He pulls out his phone and calls his twin. Leno won't answer if he's in the middle of treating Mother. He relays the message, informs them about the hole in her belly, and by the time I make it to Micha's room and lay her on her bed, Leno is striding in with a pint-size brew in one hand and Krypto beside him. Swirling his other fingers over the glass, Leno mutters a spell beneath his breath, and the dark-green liquid brightens.

"Hold her down," he says. "This is going to burn like hel."

Steeling myself to seeing her pain, I press my hands on her shoulders. Enoch raises his to use his telekinesis, but my low growl has him dropping them again. He steps back and shares a quick look with Leno.

Clenching my jaw, I snap, "Fucking hold her." As much as I don't want him anywhere near her, I'm not going to let my feelings get in the way of her comfort. She could hurt herself thrashing about, cause more damage than Leno can heal with his magic. He isn't as good of a healer as Mother. She could die if I don't let another man touch her. *Another man? He's my fucking brother.*

Stepping up to the bed, Enoch weaves his hands through the air, wrapping his magic around Micha's body, making her stiff, board-like. I know I can release her shoulders, that

I'm not doing anything to help her, but I don't.

Can't.

She's fucking mine.

Realizing I'm not moving out of the way, Leno shuffles beside me, then lines up the glass to the hole in Micha's belly. He glances at me side-eye, and I'm just about to snatch the potion and do it myself when he slowly starts to pour it in. For a second, she does nothing, lost too deeply in her unconsciousness, but then she screams.

Her eyes snap open.

Glassy and unsure but full of anger.

And pain.

So much fucking pain.

Releasing her shoulders, I grab her hands. I act like it's for her, so she can squeeze them as she needs to (Enoch's magic is only on her limbs), but the truth is, *I* fucking need this connection. To feel her warmth, her strength, her *life*. To know that she is alive. That we're not killing her despite how much she looks like we are. For the agony in her eyes is matched only by the breaking screech of her screams.

"Fucking finish it," I snap at my brother, my voice too raw to be familiar.

Leno glances at me as he pours more of the potion inside her. My new position has forced him to twist awkwardly around me, but I can't move. Can't give him the space he needs to work comfortably. Can't fucking let go of my mate.

He tips out more of the potion, but he doesn't dump it in all at once like I want him to. If my hands weren't wrapped around Micha's, if I weren't giving her my strength and taking hers in return, I would wrap them around his fucking throat. "*Leno.*"

Krypto growls, his teeth bared at me, his ears flat.

"I can't go any faster; I need to heal her layer by layer," my brother says as he reaches with his free hand to ruffle his dog's head between the ears. "It's fine, boy. He's just got his panties wedged up his ass. There."

The last drop falls.

My attention jerks off him and flies to Micha's stomach. The skin is red and raw, but there is skin where there wasn't before. Her eyes are still glassy though, still unfocused like she isn't really aware, and her breathing's harsh and ragged, but she doesn't look like she's one breath away from dying anymore. Doesn't look like I'm about to lose her.

My breath catches as her eyes find mine. I want to tell her I love her, but the words are trapped in the tightness of my throat. I work my tongue around my mouth, but by the time I start to open my lips, her eyes flutter shut and her breathing deepens.

Her fingers stop squeezing me.

But I don't stop squeezing them.

Can't.

Still fucking can't.

Closing my eyes, I lean down and press my lips to her forehead, feeling the warmth of her body, the taste of her sweat.

She's alive.

She's fucking alive.

"Right," Leno says as he drops the glass to his side. "I'm going to see to Mother."

My attention's back on him – or, rather, on the answers he can help me get. I straighten, lock my emotions down, force myself to be the logical Boss I need to be.

But I still don't release Micha's hands.

"Send her in when she's awake," I say.

He frowns. "She would've used a lot of ma–"

He cuts himself off at the look in my eyes. He knows I'm not asking. I need to know what happened with Mother's monster – the one Micha seems to have killed. I need to know when she arrived. Why the fuck she's back.

Leno lets out a breath as he nods. Then he turns on his

heels and leaves the room with Krypto right beside him.

A second after he disappears, Maddox comes sliding in, his breath harsh and ragged. "Antonio took Khalid!"

I'm on my feet in an instant, finally letting her go. Leno and Krypto come running back into the room, no doubt having heard the news.

"Alive?" I snap.

"I think so. I didn't see him." Maddox shakes his head as he pants with his hands on his knees. He cranes his neck up. "Talon shouted it as he ran out of the back before you all got here, saying he was going after Antonio."

"Fuck," Enoch says. "I haven't seen T since we arrived." Meaning he's not back yet. Might not ever be coming back.

The fucking fool.

"I tried to tell him to wait for me," Maddox says, "but by the time I got Zita chained up, the fucker was gone."

"You could've shifted into a wolf and tracked him," I say.

He looks at me like I'm an idiot. "What the fuck do you think I've been doing? But all the plants are so godsdamn excited, throwing out perfume left and right. I can't smell anything else. I saw the direction T ran off in, and I still ended up going in fucking circles."

"Talon doesn't stand a fucking chance," Enoch says, his face turning pale. "Antonio nearly killed him the last time."

"Maybe he won't care that he's following him?" Leno says, always so damn hopeful. "Talon can't keep up with him even in his shadow, and if Antonio's taken Khalid, then he'll want to get him back to his compound before he heals enough to fight back."

Maddox shakes his head. "Khalid's girl's gone too. I think they took her. Even if he's fully healed, he's not going to fight back if it puts her in danger."

"Fuck. What if she's in on it?" Enoch says, and all our heads snap to him. "Someone had to have let the wolves in," he pushes, "and Khalid kidnapped her. Maybe she killed the wards in exchange for her freedom."

Maddox snorts. "Been watching too much TV, Eno."

He bristles. "She's a fucking WALL member. They hunt *all* sups. Just because Khalid forced her to blood bond with him doesn't mean she likes him. She hasn't once been out of his room to meet us."

"Antonio nearly killed her," Leno cuts in. "Why would she side with him?"

Maddox rolls his eyes. "*Bruh*, if you're going to be on my team, don't come in with a piss poor argument any monkey can tear apart." He straightens. "She hates *all* sups. If we're too busy fighting each other, we're not going after her. Uh, fucking *duh*." He glances at me. "But I don't think she's the traitor. She never asked for steak."

My lips tighten as Enoch asks, "What the fuck does steak have to do with anything?" in exasperation.

But as much as I want to think Maddox is just being a little shit for the sake of it, I know he isn't. He might fuck about ninety-nine percent of the time, but during that one percent that matters, he's the most focused of us all.

Proving just that, he turns to me. "I knocked Zita out and chained her up in the garage. We can trade her for Khalid." She's Antonio's granddaughter, but that doesn't mean he gives a damn about her. Still, it's the best chance we have of getting one of them back.

Shoving a hand in my pocket, I pull out my phone. "Get as much info out of Zita as you can before she leaves," I say.

The grin Maddox gives me is full-on insane. He has been itching to get his hands on her for weeks now. As he turns to leave, I scroll through my contacts and press on Antonio Garcia.

"Enoch, get me the wolf I shot," I say, raising the phone to my ear to listen to it ring. My eyes shift to Leno. "Go heal Mother." There's a good chance we need her soon.

Leno leaves, but Enoch shakes his head. "I tried to tell

you earlier. That wolf killed himself. Took a poison or some shit before I could get to him."

My eyes narrow. "Where's Rudy?"

"Re-engaging the wards."

"Leave him, but get Ez. We're leaving in ten."

He spins and heads out. The phone keeps ringing, and I turn to look at Micha. As Enoch said, someone had to have let the wards down. Although Aleric once broke through them with the help of another witch, that was decades ago. We've heavily strengthened them since, and breaking them with brute force would've left massive damage behind. But none of the trees are on fire. The ground circling our border isn't dead. So there's another traitor inside this house.

Don't you fucking be it.

The phone clicks over to voicemail, and I hang up. My eyes stay on my mate for a second longer before I turn and head for the door. I have two brothers to find; I can't waste another second in getting answers.

But when I step out into the hall, I don't turn towards Mother's room. Maddox is coming back in from the other direction, and Talon is with him, leaning against him, one arm slung around his shoulders. His clothes are stained in blood in multiple places, and every time he puts weight on his left leg, he winces. His face looks pale as hel.

"Leno!" I shout as I head towards them. "T needs you."

"I'm fine," my brother says with a wince as he pulls away from Maddox. "Just got a claw to the thigh this time."

"And a cracked skull," our younger brother adds.

"No, I didn't –" He yelps as Maddox clips him around the back of the head. *Hard.*

"What the fuck?" T snaps as he stumbles away, one hand to his head. His knee buckles when he puts sudden weight on it, and he twists towards the wall to catch himself. He isn't graceful, and the crash makes his cut bleed more. He groans as he places one hand on the wall and pivots around to face us. But Maddox clearly doesn't give a shit about his pain.

"That's for being an idiot and running off on your own," he shouts. "I told you to fucking wait."

"He had Khalid!"

"Exactly! So why the fuck did you think *you* had a chance against him?"

"Enough," I cut in calmly just as Leno joins us. "Where is Khalid?"

T's annoyance dies under the emergence of pain and sorrow. He shakes his head as Leno rummages in his bag. "I don't know. I was following one of his capos. Antonio's – Holy fuck! What the fucking hel! *Fuck!*" He screams like a little bitch as Leno presses what looks like mushed up peas into his wound.

"Stop being such a pussy –"

"Ballsack," Maddox cuts in. "Pussies can take a pounding, you know?"

"Stop being such a *ballsack*," Leno corrects.

"Where were they heading?" I snap.

Talon grits his teeth as he presses both his hands on the wall to keep his balance. "South," he rasps, the word shaky.

I glance at Maddox. "Zita. Now."

"No." T groans, leaning his head back as he closes his eyes. "You want Micha."

I still. Then ever so slowly, I turn my gaze back to him. "Why?" I ask, my voice soft, lethal.

Leno glances at me, and I can smell his nerves, but T doesn't catch on, in too much pain perhaps. Too fucking *stupid* perhaps.

"She took down the ward," he says as he pants through the pain of his thigh. "She let the wolves in."

My blood runs cold as I step right up to him. "How do you know this?"

He looks at me, and I finally smell it, that first tinge of

fear. His eyes widen as he catches my gaze – the darkness there that's ready to tear him apart if he's merely guessing about what went down.

"Fuck, V, I'm sorry, but she's the reason Khalid's gone. She attacked his girl, and then he pierced her through the back, but Antonio took him out a second later. I tried to stop him, but he knocked me back."

"You're not dead," I say accusingly.

He glances away, his lips tight. "He said I wasn't worth the fucking hassle."

"It would've taken him less than a second."

His nostrils flare as he glares at me. "I think that was his fucking point."

I inhale, breathing in his pheromones, searching for any trace of a lie. He's on edge, but his sweat doesn't have that specific smell it gets when he's fibbing his ass off.

Fuck.

Stepping back, I say, "Get the twins and head south. I'll send you a destination soon."

"If Maddox comes with us –" T starts.

"He's needed here," I say softly, such a contradiction to the screaming inside my skull. I fucking *trusted* her. Love her. I would have given her everything if she'd just given it back to me.

Gesturing with my head for Leno and Maddox to follow me, I stride down the hall to Mother's room. She's no longer nailed to her headboard, but the circular wounds up and down her arms are still bleeding. Leno's focused his magic on somewhere else, an internal injury perhaps.

"Wake her," I order.

"That'll damage –"

"She'll heal. Now *wake her.*"

"Varius –"

I glance at Krypto, letting him see the full force of my gaze. The dog actually steps back and whines, ducking his head.

"Shit. Fine. But you're only getting a few minutes. She's suffered severe brain damage. If we need her to heal Khalid later, then she needs her rest."

Reaching out a hand, he calls his dog to him. Krypto looks at me warily before slowly slinking back over. Once he's in position, acting as Leno's eyes where he wants him, my brother cradles her head with his hands. He breathes in deep while my breath stills, stuck in my throat, unable to move in either direction.

White light flows from his palms, surrounding her head, encompassing it completely. He mutters incantations under his breath, speaking faster and faster, harsher and harsher until he sags forward. Kyrpto whines, then turns his head to nudge him. Ignoring him, Leno keeps pouring more magic through his hands, healing her as much as he can before he forces her awake.

As soon as her eyelids flutter, he collapses completely. Maddox moves in to catch him before he falls on her, but in my impatience, I shove them both away.

"Why did your monster attack Micha?" I demand.

She blinks up at the ceiling, her gaze unfocused.

"Were you not content with blackmailing her?" I hiss as I lean in and grab her jaw, forcing her to look at me. "Did you try to kill her?" *Was it fucking self-defense?*

She blinks again, but there is awareness there now. And pain. The sorrow of a mother who can't protect her child. "I wish I could tell you yes..." Shaking her head, she grabs my hand. "But I'm sorry, son; she's with Antonio. They...kissed."

I rear back. "You're fucking lying. You're just trying to keep us −" I stop, aware that my two brothers are still here. That I don't have the privacy to speak about certain truths. "You're *lying*," I say again.

Her eyes start to drift. "I wish I was. I never wanted..."

Her hand slips off mine, and I step back, my movements

jerky, my skin too damn tight for my muscles to move.

"That's it," Leno says as he shoves forward. "She needs her rest."

But I don't care. Because all I wanted to know was who the traitor is. Khalid's girl or *mine*.

And now I fucking know.

Turning on my heels, I make my way to Micha's room, but Maddox darts in front of me just as I reach the doorway.

"Don't," he says, his voice sharp, his eyes serious.

"Get out of my way," I growl, my words a low warning about what will happen if he doesn't.

He shakes his head, his eyes never leaving mine. "I'm not going to let you do this to yourself, V. You've started to have something with her, haven't you? Don't throw that away. We can rebuild her. We can turn her so she's on our side. Just don't ruin this."

"Why do you care?" My eyes narrow. "What. The. *Fuck*. Is she to you?"

He ducks back into the room, outside of range, and holds up his hands as I walk in. "She ain't shit to me, bruh. *You* are. You've been there for me all my life. Been there for all of us. Mostly in an annoying way, but still, and you've never let anyone look after you, not even Mom. But you're not alone, bruh. You know that, right? You're not fucking alone. I care about *you*, and this is the first time I have seen you passionate about anything. You need this, V. You need her."

"She lied to me," I say flatly. "She's the reason Khalid's gone, why Mother's stuck in bed. She betrayed us." She fucking kissed another man.

"Yeah. Yeah, she did. And you can punish her for that later but not like this."

"A traitor's punishment is death."

"You're the fucking Boss. You can change the rules." His voice softens. "But what you can't do, V, is come back from this. You know it."

I stop, the truth in his eyes rooting me still. Breaking her will break me. I will feel every cut upon her skin like it's my own. I will feel the cracks of our relationship, the ones that can never be repaired until they shatter into sharp pieces that cut me further. I will lose the last part of my humanity when I'm standing over her lifeless body. When I scream over the fact that I can't even take her into my shadows, to lay her to rest in a way where she'll always be with me.

But I will have saved my brother.

I will have learned where he is.

That has to be enough.

"Get out of my way, Maddox," I say softly.

He shakes his head,

"Let me talk to Zita," Maddox says, his voice soft and low. "I'll get the information we need out of her. We'll go rescue Khalid, and then when we get back, we'll break her. Together. So you can rebuild her into what you want. Into a faithful breedmare who will never betray you again. You know I can do it. Let me do this for you."

I look past him, my throat tight, and my gaze settles on my girl. I don't want her complacent, nothing but a doll or a true breedmare. I want *her.*

I want all her fire and passion and her inability to listen to any order. I want her loyalty, her love, the fucking blood bond she told me we started.

But everything I want is a fucking lie. An act.

So I dart forward before my brother can react and slam my fist into his jaw. He stumbles back. I feel the change in the air, the ripple of magic he's trying to use, and I push forward with my other foot, spin, and snap the back of my heel into the side of his skull.

Crack!

He crumbles to the ground, and I am there to catch him before he hits. He is a little shit, but his heart's always in the right fucking place.

But mine is too.

Because I have a duty to this Family, a duty that takes priority over my own desires. I have to save my brother. To bring him back home.

But perhaps in the next life...

Perhaps in the next life, I will find her again and we can start over.

Closing my eyes, fighting back the unfamiliar touch of tears, I lay my brother down on the ground.

And then I stand.

Walking over to Micha, I remove the witch's snare that's still snug around her waist. She won't need it anymore now that she's never leaving this room. Going back over to my brother, I tie his hands behind his back, binding his fingers so he can't use his magic when he comes around. Then I shut the door. Lock it.

And turn to the traitor lying still on the bed.

TWENTY

HER

I'm vaguely aware of the rustle of someone in my room. The conversations. The touch of someone's hands as they move me. But I saw Varius the last time I opened my eyes. I know I'm safe. The way he looked at me, the way he held me, squeezing my hands like he could never give me up... He won't let anyone touch me. I can sleep for a little longer, get some much needed rest now that the pain in my belly –

I freeze.

The pain in my belly.

My belly...

Sucking in a sharp breath, I press a hand to my stomach, checking it over, trying to see if my baby is alive. If it's even real.

Or, at least, that's what I tried to do.

But my hand won't move. Something is stopping it – a band cutting into my wrist. More smaller threads cutting into my fingers.

I open my eyes and find I'm sitting upright in my room, in my desk chair with my hands strapped to its arms – leather belts around my wrists, shoelaces around my fingers. Someone is in front of me, but my attention is on my belly, on the baby that's supposedly inside. I lean down – *try* to, but a strong hand wraps around my throat and shoves me back, pinning me to the chair.

My eyes widen as panic starts to set in.

Because I've finally clocked who's in front of me.

It's Varius, but it also isn't.

This isn't the man I know.

The one I've fallen in love with.

The one who held my hands as I screamed, whose eyes whispered words of encouragement, of heartfelt pleas for me to be okay.

This man's eyes are utterly blank. Empty. All emotion in them is gone.

And in his place is the monster that even monsters fear.

Varius.

Fucking.

Shadow.

TWENTY-ONE

HER

"I would have given you everything, Micha," he says as his fingers tighten around my throat. "I would have risked more than you will ever fucking know just to be yours. For you to be mine." He leans in, his breath fanning my ear and sending shivers down my spine. "But you lied to me. You betrayed me. So now I will give you what you deserve."

My fingers dig into the wood, shoving splinters under my nails. I can't breathe. Can't tell him that he has it wrong, that whatever his mother fucking told him are nothing but lies. My mouth just moves up and down, a useless hinge that just keeps trying to suck in air even though it knows it can't.

"I will kill you in this chair, Micha. You are not surviving this, but you can make it easy on yourself. You can stop the pain before it even starts." He pulls back a little, looks me in the eye.

His are still so flat, so cold. A monster that's stepped out of the dark, and I am of no illusion that I'm the prey.

Moving back, he releases my neck, and I instantly lean forward, hacking up my lungs even as I'm trying to suck in air. Two actions working so strongly against each other that for a moment, I can't do either. My nails dig deeper into the wood as I try to get control of myself. My shoulders shake. My eyes water.

But then I manage it.

One breath in.

Two.

The fuzziness that's poured into my brain starts to lift, making way for a killer headache that's begging me to fall asleep. To bypass the pain in my dreams, but Varius isn't making empty promises. If I can't convince him that I didn't let the wolves in, then I'm dead.

So I lift my head and try to focus my thoughts. Varius is standing by my bed, his back to me, his gaze on the items he's spread out there. My grab bag sits empty beside his feet, and my heart kicks up into my throat. There was cash in there and new identities I never told him about. Cards to offshore accounts. Keys to safe houses all across the USA. Magical cuffs, even a witch's snare, and various tools and weapons, alongside my favorite mementos.

My pulse hammering inside my skull, I jerk against my binds. I know how it looks – like I was always planning on betraying him, having my bag packed and ready to go. "I wasn't..." I cut off as the syllables burn across my throat.

He turns around to face me, having picked up two items off the bed – the first presents I ever received – a hammer and a screw. Dayne likes to joke that even when faced with a screw, I'm still stubborn enough to hit it with a hammer, and my heart breaks, knowing that Varius is about to taint one of my favorite memories.

"Please, Varius, don't do this," I beg as he walks towards me. "I wasn't leaving you. I swear, and I didn't take down the wards. Your mother –"

His fist with the screw backhands me across the face, and my head jerks to the side as a bloody line tears across my cheek. The cut burns, but it has nothing on the pain from being hit by someone I love.

"Varius, please," I push out, my voice cracking as I try not to cry. Pain, I can deal with. I suffered through worse when being trained by my father. But Varius is hitting me where father never could. He is tearing apart my soul with his refusal to even listen. Everything we were, everything we could have been, it is dying here along with me.

"The rules here are simple, Micha. You lie to me, you get punished. You tell me the truth, and I won't touch you until I kill you. Now." He pauses, letting me feel the weight of his words, the honesty within them. "Tell me what happened tonight."

"I came back because your mother tricked me." The text might have said it came from him, but I now know without a doubt that bitch lured me here. "Then she took down the wards and attacked me. I only fought back in self-defense."

"She would never do that."

"*I* would never do that." I look at him, trying to push my love down the bond we share. "Please, Varius. You know me," I murmur.

"I know a liar." His jaw tics. His voice drops. "And a whore."

"I'm not a whore." I realize my mistake as soon as the words are free, that I didn't protest to being a liar too, but I can still feel Antonio's lips on me, his tongue in my mouth, and that violation makes me sick – second only to the man I love accusing me of being a whore.

I start to open my mouth to correct my statement, but his hand flies across my face. My teeth slam together, radiating pain all up and down my jaw. The end of the screw tears a new jagged line across my cheek.

"You kissed him," he says. "Have you fucked him too yet? Or is that to be a celebratory act?"

"Fuck you."

His hand wraps around my throat this time, and he leans in, his face so close to mine. "Perhaps I should kiss you now," he murmurs, but there's no passion in those words, no desire. There's not even any anger of a lover wanting make-up sex, of an enemy wanting to punish. They are just flat, entirely and utterly empty. "So you can die alone, with not even your lover's lips to comfort you."

He keeps his face near mine as he chokes me, his eyes boring into me, letting me feel the force of his anger even as they shut me out. Panic floods my system, and if my hands weren't bound, I'd be clawing at his throat. My head goes fuzzy. My vision starts to blur.

But just as I start to pass out, he releases me and steps back. I lean forward, gasping for air even as the voice in my head tells me it's pointless. Why bother with trying to live when I'm not making it out of this room?

Because you're not fighting for just you anymore.

Those words come out of nowhere and steal away the breath I've just regained. Antonio said he was coming back for the child in my belly. He hit me above my womb, and there's no blood between my thighs.

My heart rate increasing, I lift my head and blurt, "I'm pregnant."

For a moment, the world freezes as he stares at me.

But then he twirls the hammer in his hand, his eyes so fucking empty. "I told you what would happen if you lied to me," he bites out, and my pulse jumps a wild beat inside my veins. I tug against my binds, willing my magic to free me. But he's tied my fingers down tight, leaving me completely helpless.

"I'm not lying. I'm –"

His knuckles slam into my chest, hitting me right in the

solar plexus. I lean forward, gasping for air as pain radiates across my chest. He switches the objects in his hands. The hammer is now in his dominant one, and seeing it there terrifies me. He isn't planning on hitting me with his fist anymore.

"Varius, don't do this," I beg, coughing up spittle as I try to wheeze. "Please. I didn't do this. Just listen to me. Varius, please."

He places the long screw on the back of my hand, and my heart jumps into my throat. He raises the hammer, his eyes cold.

"Don't. Varius. Varius, please, look at me. I love you. I –"

The hammer comes down, slamming the screw all the way through my flesh.

I scream, my voice cracking, pain radiating up my arm and across my vocal chords. The hammer resonates across the screw again, pure agony shooting through my body as the metal digs deeper into my flesh, the ridges causing even more damage, making the hole ragged and torn instead of clean.

I look up at him on a cry, and for the first time, he isn't wearing a mask. His face is twisted in equal parts agony and rage, and I know he cares for me. He cares for me, and his heart is breaking thinking I betrayed him. This is killing him, killing us.

But I know he will not stop.

It's because he cares that he's punishing me so severely. He's punishing himself for daring to believe in me. To trust me. To let himself be manipulated by me.

"I swear, Varius... I didn't let the werewolves in," I try again, my voice shaking as bad as my hand.

His eyes mist. His arm holding the hammer trembles. As his chest rises and falls rapidly, his Adam's apple bobs with a wail he'll never release. Then finally, he speaks, his words raw and cracked. "You attacked Mother," he says. "You were here when the werewolves came, knowing we were all out. And you can't..." He breaks off, his face twisting with so much agony before he controls it, flattens it. "You can't be *that*."

He places the claw of the hammer around the screw. His lips tremble. My gut twists in anticipation of the pain.

"Varius! *Please*! I'm telling the truth! I'm –" I scream as he rips the screw free, tearing out chunks of flesh, spraying blood high up between us.

I arch against my binds, screaming as my toes curl, the pain rocking through me in an overwhelming wave. "I did not let them in," I cry, my head hanging, tears flowing down my cheeks. "I did not let them in."

My hand's throbbing too hard for me to feel the touch of metal against my skin again, but I feel it when it goes through another part of my palm. I feel it embed into the arm of the chair. I feel him rip it back out. Slam it back in again somewhere else.

"Tell me where Khalid is," Varius says, his voice tight with his own pain.

Khalid? "He was with you. He wasn–" I break off on a whimper when he moves the screw to my other hand. I jerk against my binds, but it's a futile, pathetic attempt. I can't escape. I can't stop him. "I'm not the traitor," I say, focusing on the facts I know. "I'm not the traitor. I told you about the blackmail." Even though his mom didn't really want it, I told him instead of stealing it. That has to count for something – that honesty, that truth.

"To gain my trust," he spits. "Admit to something small to hide something big. It's a classic trick."

"No –" I shake my head. "No, that's not –"

The hammer comes down.

My back arches off the chair as I spasm in agony. My cries are shrill and cracked, ripping my throat raw. "Just feel the bond," I beg. "Just feel it. I love you. Varius, *please*."

His hands shake as he holds the screw against my skin. Its sharp end scratches me as his arm vibrates, but I am happy for that pain if it means he'll believe me.

His eyes close. He swallows hard on a shudder.

Hope flares in my chest, but when he looks at me again, it plummets into the acid of my stomach.

"I feel *nothing*," he says. "Now where is Khalid?"

"Varius –" My face twists under the strain of pain and panic. "How can you not feel anything? I love you. We're bonded. I –" I scream. I jerk. I thrash inside my binds as he slams the screw over and over into my hand.

"Where is Khalid?"

"Tell me where Khalid is."

"*Where is Khalid, Micha?*"

"I don't know. I swear I don't... But, Varius, stop, please. I'm p–"

My arms jerking against my binds, I scream.

And this time, I cannot stop.

TWENTY-TWO

HER

It is a terrible thing to be in love with the person who's hurting you. To feel like you can reach them even through their rage, that if you just remind them of how much you love them…that they'll stop. That they'll remember that they love you too, and you can go back to how you were. Just a blip, a misunderstanding. He's afraid for his brother. He thinks I deserve this. So he doesn't really mean it. He's just angry right now, but soon it'll stop.

Soon he'll remember that he loves me.

That I love him…

But Varius doesn't stop.

That hammer rams down dozens of times.

That screw imbeds into my hands, into the chair beneath, and is yanked out, taking muscle and flesh and bits of bone with it.

I can't move my fingers anymore.

Can't even feel them.

And still he does not stop.

"Where is he, Micha?"

Whack!

"Where is Khalid?"

Crack!

He throws the hammer across the room, then turns on his heels. I don't see where he goes, my head hanging too low, my vision too unfocused from the pain. It radiates up my arms and through every part of me, churning up my stomach.

"This much stress..." I say, my voice wavering, my words sluggish. "...is not good... for the baby."

He's in front of me before those words even finish being said. His hand's around my throat, squeezing it shut. "Don't fucking mention it again. You're not pregnant, Micha. Now just tell me where my brother is, and I can make all this stop."

He releases me, but the fear of pain won't stop me from trying to protect my baby. "Your mother..." I say, my voice cracking. "Just get her to check. Please...Varius. The stress..." I cry out as I suddenly feel a wetness pooling between my thighs. "Varius, please!" I shout, shaking in my binds. "Get your mother. Get your mother and have her check."

The words are flowing out in a panic as I try to squeeze my legs together. I look down, hoping like hel that I'm just imagining it. That the stress overloading my body is merely fucking with my mind.

"I told you to stop lying about the baby!" His words are harsh and ragged, his control finally snapping, and he slams a knife down on my fingers, cutting off the tips of three of them. I scream. I feel the blood seeping down my thighs, and my scream increases in both pitch and frequency.

"Varius, *please*! I'm losing him. I'm losing him."

"Shut up!" he roars as the knife comes down again. He hacks off my fingers bit by bit, but all my attention is on my lap. On my baby. *Our* baby... Sobbing hard, I try to squeeze my legs together, to get the blood to stop, to keep him in, but I'm too exhausted. I'm too weak from the blood loss. I can't keep him in. I can't save him on my own. I need help. I need a healer.

"Please!" I scream. "Just get your mother. He's your son, Va–"

His hand is around my throat. A flash of metal stained red rises high in the air. I struggle to free myself from his grip while I keep my legs together, but it's impossible. The panic just keeps on building.

The blood just keeps on flowing.

Holding his gaze, I beg him with my eyes. *Don't do this. Please don't do this.*

His face twists with rage and pain. The knife arcs down, but just as it grazes my chest, a large furry creature tackles him off me. The knife clatters across the floor. I turn my head, trying to figure out what the fuck is going on. Why a werewolf has just come in to save me. Is it Antonio? Does he want me to live so he can kill our child himself like he promised?

"Get the fuck off me!"

A loud *thump* sounds, and the vicious snarls the wolf was making turn into a whimper. It staggers to the side, shaking its head, blood spitting from its mouth. Its eyes are glossy and violet in color. They lock onto Varius as he rises, his hands coming up. He's covered in my blood, sprayed in it all across his body, and the rage he was just taking out on me in the violent swings of his knife – *my* knife, has been locked down. Only a cold monster remains. The werewolf will not survive.

And yet, it moves between me and him, blocking Varius from getting to me. It whines low, almost pleading, and it clicks then that this isn't a real wolf. It's Maddox in wolf form.

Has he tracked down Khalid? Has he come to tell Varius that I'm not the traitor? Hope erupts inside me at the idea that this is almost over.

My body shaking, I open my mouth to tell him about the baby, to plead with him to get Sau. But before I can get a single syllable out, Maddox turns and runs for the door.

I cry out as he leaves me alone with his brother.

Varius looks at me for a moment, his face expressionless, his emotions locked down.

"Please, Varius" I beg. "Just check my legs. I'm bleeding. I'm not lying. It's your son. It's your son."

His eyes dart to my lap. His nostrils flare as he breathes in, and for a moment, I pray that he has the ability to smell blood, to smell that I am with child just like Antonio can, even if that makes him a hybrid.

An abomination.

I will love him still as long as he saves our child.

"Please."

He walks towards me.

"*Please*."

He bends down and picks up the knife.

My heart jumps into my throat.

"Spread your legs," he says as he approaches, and I start to, only to instantly stop. I can't do that. Can't risk that being the final act needed to kill our child.

"I can't," I rasp. "Please just check."

He stops in front of me. My blood drips off the knife. My hands are so damn painful, and every nerve in my body is erupting with the urge to flee, to get away from the monster who's been hurting me.

But I lock my thighs together and lift my chin. He bends down in front of me, hikes up my dress rather than going down through the hole Antonio made in the middle of it. My legs tremble at the feel of his touch on them. His eyes give nothing away as he traces his fingers along my skin.

He pushes up to the V of my thighs before pulling back. He lifts his hand to his face. There's blood there, a lot of it, and I cry out, terrified that that is all I'll ever see of our child.

"Get Sau," I cry. "Please get Sau."

He stares at his fingers, his face going pale. "Micha..."

"Go!"

He jerks away from me.

"*Go*!" I scream, throwing every last part of me into that word. All my prayers. All my hopes. My fears. My trust that he will do this for me. That he won't just leave me here to bleed out with our child even if he thinks I'm the traitor.

My head sagging forward as he leaves, I close my eyes.

Please... I beg as I squeeze my thighs together.

Please don't let me lose him.

TWENTY-THREE

HIM

She's a fucking whore.
She kissed Antonio.
The child probably isn't mine.
It might not even exist at all.

I stop, only three steps from Mother's room, my thoughts whirling, my jaw tightening. Micha could simply be on her period and is using it to get me out of the room so she can make her escape. When was the last time she bled?

Sixteen days ago. Periods can occur that close together, but you can't bleed while pregnant.

My lips tight, I spin on my heels and stride back to the room before she can make her escape. Her sobs aren't as loud now, aren't as dramatic, and I curse myself for falling for her –

"Varius!" I turn at the sound of Mother's voice behind me.

Maddox is helping her out of her room, one arm around

her waist. His eyes find mine as they come down the hall. The challenge in them is unmistakable, as is the worry. *For me like he said or for Micha?* Is he fucking her too? They have always seemed so damn cozy together, laughing with each other, talking so easily.

"You can still fix this," he says softly. "Just let us in."

"She's faking –"

"You fucking paranoid –" Maddox starts, but he cuts off as Mother's shadows lunge for me. I scramble back into the room, the only way I can go, and she moves in, pulling free from Maddox as she does so.

"You can either leave us and call Aleric to find Khalid, Varius, or you can spend the time in the Shadow Domain, but you *will* get out of my fucking way so I can save my grandchild."

"It's not your gr–"

Her shadows swirl around my feet, but it's Micha's cry that shuts me up.

"Sau!" she sobs. "I can't stop the bleeding. *Please.* I can feel him leaving me... *Please.*"

My heart twists in my chest, but I fight the instinct to go to her, to soothe her in her pain. But nor do I stop Mother from reaching her even though a part of me whispers that I can find Khalid's location if I just deny Micha care until she tells me where he is.

He's my brother. I should be able to endure anything to save him. But this? Hurting the woman I love even though she is a traitor...

I feel fucking sick.

Moving slowly, Maddox comes up to me. "Let's go talk to Zita," he says softly. "We can call Aleric on the way over."

"We shouldn't leave Mother alone with her. She could be faking."

"You destroyed her hands, Varius. She's no threat to her. Now come on. Let's go find Khalid."

My tongue is heavy with more words until I realize they are just excuses for me not to leave her.

Micha is a traitor who let the Death Hunt into our home so they could kidnap my brother and his girl. As much as I want to forgive her for this, I can't. If I don't kill her, Khalid will.

And then I will kill Khalid for hurting her.

I look down at my hands, the blood on them mocking me for that statement.

Clenching my fists, needing to *move* due to the sudden tightness of my skin, I push past Maddox to get to the door. As I move down the hall, I rub the two fingers I ran between her thighs, those marked with the blood of her child, on the back of my left bicep – a clean patch of shirt in case the baby turns out to be mine and all I have left of him is that stain there.

My throat tightens as Micha's screams intensify behind me, and I close my eyes briefly, wondering if she lost the child.

Antonio's child?

She kissed him in my fucking house.

How many times has she spread her legs for him? Told him she loved him? Moaned his name as she came on his godsdamn cock? Was she even a virgin when I met her, or has everything out of her mouth been a fucking lie?

And is her father in on it? Her whole fucking Family? Has the Death Hunt made alliances like we have with the Blood Fang?

"Get Zita talking," I snap as Maddox comes up beside me. I don't want to hear any of his fucking thoughts about how I can't kill Micha until she gives birth. How in those five, six months, I can salvage what I've broken.

She's still a traitor who hurt Khalid's girl. Once that child is out of her womb, there'll be no stopping my brother from killing her.

As Maddox peels off to head to the garage, I pull out my phone and text Aleric.

Varius: *House has been hit by the Death Hunt.*

Aleric: *k*

My jaw locking, I call him. When he doesn't answer, I only just manage to stop myself from throwing my phone. Forcing my rage down so I don't do anything stupid, I text him again.

Varius: *Use your pigs to find Khalid. Antonio took him.*

Self loathing builds at the sight of that message. I could have fucking texted him earlier, could've tried to find Khalid without hurting my girl, but instead, I wanted to punish her. Wanted to hurt her for kissing Antonio, for letting him fuck her behind my back.

For making me fall in love with her when all I was was a mark.

For trusting her when I shouldn't have.

She might be with child, but she's still a fucking traitor.

Shoving my guilt down, I call Talon.

"Where are you?" I ask as soon as he answers.

"Ocala. Did you get a location from Micha?"

"Not yet."

"Shit. What are we going to do if she doesn't break?"

"She will."

"Before Antonio kills Khalid?"

My voice flattens. "Maddox is talking to Zita, and we'll raid every one of his fucking compounds if we have to." He wouldn't have taken Khalid just to kill him immediately. He probably wants him for his – "Shit."

"What?" he asks, sounding panicked.

I hang up and run towards the basement. Khalid's magic targets the soul, which allows him to hurt all creatures, even werewolves despite their natural resistance to magic. He can also kill someone anywhere in the world if he has their DNA and alexandrite – a material that is rare on Earth. Our supply of it is extremely limited, having all been brought over from the other Planes when our family first migrated over to Earth. Micha knows we have her DNA, that we can kill her even if she runs. There's no way she would have accepted this job if she didn't have a chance of living after.

So I leap down the stairs of the basement and run inside. As soon as I cross the threshold, an electric shock hits me. It isn't enough to make me stumble, but it causes me to pause nonetheless. Pivoting, I turn to face the door frame again, my eyes narrowing.

There is a slight tinge of blue in the air – an active ward.

Was it there the first time I came in?

It had to have been. I just must not have felt it in my grief, when I saw Micha lying in her own blood.

Because the ward doesn't have the same feel as any of those made by someone in my family. I've been hit by all of them over the years. I thought they didn't like me crossing through them because I didn't have any magic, so they couldn't tell I was a witch. But now I know that the reason was because I'm a hybrid. So I have felt each signature of my brothers' wards, as well as Mother's. This wasn't any of theirs.

But the only witch Antonio had here was Micha.

And I can't think of a single fucking reason for her to have warded the door against everyone but witches. Sau can pass through this. As can Khalid. It's almost as if –

My stomach drops and I race back up the stairs, ignoring the original reason I came down here, which was to check on our supply of alexandrite – the green stone Khalid needs to make his soul dolls.

Pulling out my phone, I text Aleric: *Check for Talon* just as Maddox comes in from outside, looking pissed. "Zita's gone," he says. "And she didn't escape on her own because I used fucking silver."

My pulse racing, I say, "Micha isn't the traitor."

He glances at me, but there isn't any surprise there. He figured that out already. His face grim, he says, "Talon."

The fucker who set her up, who made me believe it was her in the first place. When I get hold of him, I'm going to kill him.

But first I need to save my brother. If he dies because I've lost my head, I would've tortured Micha for nothing. *Fuck!*

"Fucking idiot letting Zita go," Maddox mutters as I force myself to breathe. "We might not have figured out it was him if –"

"He knew he was fucked when he told me it was Micha." When he saw how I was ready to kill him if he was lying to me about her. Now they all know that she's a weakness, that they can target her to get to me. Or perhaps a silver lining has come from this whole shit show. After what I did to her, what I proved I was capable of doing to someone I loved... Maybe they won't bother her at all.

My lips tight, I call Enoch.

Maddox grabs my arm as it rings. "If Khalid finds out you tortured her," he says, his voice low, "he'll kick the shit out of you. Might even kill you for it."

Khalid might be the reaper and my bodyguard, but he has one rule he never lets anyone cross. A man takes care of his girl. Once she's claimed, he better give up his fucking life to save her.

"So we'll tell everyone it was me," Maddox presses.

"No."

"Varius –"

"I didn't just hurt her, Maddox. I fucking tortured her." I damn well deserve anything the reaper wants to mete out.

"Yeah, you did, and you need to apologize to her for that, but you can't do that if you're dead."

The sly mother fucker. He always knows just where to hit to get the thing he wants.

"Hello?"

Jerking my arm free as Enoch comes on the line, I ask, "Where are you?"

"Down near Orlando."

"Head north."

"You got an address?"

My lips tighten. "Not yet."

Maddox starts to leave, heading down the hall to grab Leno and Krypto, and I turn my attention away from Enoch. "Have Mother heal Micha's hands," I say to my youngest brother. "Then tell Leno to grab a fuckton of home dirt. I want him connected to it the entire time we're gone."

Maddox nods as Enoch asks, "What's going on?"

"Micha isn't the traitor," I say tightly.

"What —"

"It's Talon."

"Shit. Fuck —"

"Call Ezriel and get north as fast as you can," I cut in as my phone buzzes with another call, and I pull it away from my ear to check the caller ID. Hanging up on my brother, I accept the new one.

"What have you found?" I ask Aleric.

"Well, hello to you too, gorgeous."

"Cut the shit —"

"Pretty hard to do when I'm shitting diarrhea. Ever tried cutting soup with a —"

"Do not fuck with me right now, Aleric."

"Sure thing, beautiful. I will make a date to do so later." He turns serious in the very next breath. "Didn't see a thing concerning Khalid, but Talon was spotted in Jacksonville."

I open the driver's door of my car. "Where in —"

"Morn Tower. Meet me at the museum before the river."

The line goes dead, and I climb into the car. The door to the house opens just as I'm about to shut mine. As I wait for my two brothers and Krypto to join me, I text Enoch and Ezriel our destination. My eyes narrow as I stare off into the distance, wondering what Antonio wants at a building that isn't his. *And why would he take Khalid there instead of to one of his secure compounds?*

"You get anything from him?" Maddox asks as he climbs into the backseat. Leno takes the front, passing my gun back so he can sit down. Then Krypto jumps in between his legs.

"Yeah," I say slowly, still rolling it through my head as I throw the car into reverse. "Morn Tower."

"What is that? A bank?" Leno asks.

"I don't know of a bank called that. But why would they be holding Khalid at a bank anyway?" Maddox asks.

"For the vault? Easy holding cell."

"But that would mean this was a last minute job. This doesn't feel like that."

No, every step of this has been planned. If not by Talon, then by Antonio. So what's the significance of having our brother there?

"Well, they sure aren't using him to hack into any of the servers there." Leno chuckles. "He doesn't even know what a server is."

"Server?" Maddox says, mimicking Khalid's voice. "Like the people with the menus at a restaurant?"

"Are you telling me they're all robots?" Leno jumps in, his voice impression worse than Maddox's but still pretty damn accurate. "So can I hack one to get free dessert?"

"One with more strawberries?"

"And cream?"

"No, not that cream…"

I easily tune them out as I head down the drive. Years of getting into 'the zone' makes it second nature – that place where nothing exists outside of my mission. But what is harder to block out is the fear that with every turn of the wheels, I'm getting further and further away from where I want to be. My chest tightens as my eyes flick up to the rearview mirror. I watch the house as it fades into the night, then disappears behind the trees peppering the drive. I want to turn around and go to her. Drop to my knees and beg her forgiveness. But I can't.

I can't risk breaking at the news the baby didn't make it or the look in her eyes when she says she'll never forgive me. So I keep driving, doing my best to ignore the wild beat of my pulse as it gets harder and harder to breathe.

A sudden touch on my shoulder causes me to tense.

Maddox leans forward in his seat behind me. "Oh, by the way, bruh," he says. "Congrats on being a future father."

"What the fuck?" Leno shouts as I suck in a harsh breath. The world starts to blur around me as my eyes burn. I blink and swallow down the tears, but one still manages to slip free. The feel of it on my cheek is so godsdamn foreign, but I don't reach up to wipe it away.

I want to feel it. Feel the emotions riding me hard.

The fucking joy and relief that he made it, the little bit of hope that I haven't entirely fucked things up with his mom. That after I get Khalid and get back home, I can fix this tear between us.

"Yeah," Maddox says, his voice cheery. "Having a little girl, according to Ma. She's thirteen weeks along."

I damn near run over Rudy at that. He's standing on the side of our drive, right before we hit the road, waiting for me to pick him up. I jerked the wheel at the word "girl," and now I'm careening straight for him. Luckily, he has the good sense to shift into his shadow because despite how quickly I turn to get us back onto the drive, I absolutely would have hit him.

"Rudy says, 'What the fuck?'" Maddox says a second later as our brother appears in the back seat, forming out of his shadows.

Leno laughs. "Varius is going to be a father," he shouts in excitement.

Rudy leans forward and squeezes my shoulder.

"Wait. Hold up." Leno immediately stops laughing, then twists in his seat to look at Maddox. "You tortured Micha while she was *pregnant?*" Leno shakes his head. "Dude, you are so going to Hel."

My fingers tighten on the wheel.

"Nah, that's equality, bruh," Maddox says. "That's totally heaven worthy." He pauses. "Oh, shit, yeah. You were out fixing the wards when Talon got back."

As he fills Rudy in about Talon accusing Micha, only to turn out to be the traitor himself, I tune them out again. And this time, knowing that not all hope is lost with my wife, that I didn't fuck up beyond all repair, I tune thoughts of her and our child out too.

My pulse settling, I enter 'the zone' as I drive up to meet Aleric.

TWENTY-FOUR

HIM

I pull into the back of the museum Aleric wants to meet us at. It's far enough away from the tower that the wolves won't be able to smell us. With this being a rescue first and an attack second, we don't want to reveal the fact that we're working with the Blood Fangs. So they'll be staying here unless there's a certainty of us killing Antonio; then they'll phase in and help us ambush the fucker.

As we step out, Aleric and six of his soldiers – two men, four women glide out of the shadows. His normally gray eyes are blood red now, and they reflect strongly in the night. As do the silver and black piercings he has in his eyebrow, nose, and ears.

"Look at this," Aleric says as he stops in front of me, damn near bouncing on his toes. He holds up his phone. There's a text chat on his screen between him and Antonio.

Aleric: *I see you're entering your villain era.*

Aleric: *May I suggest getting a costume? I think you'd* *look hot in spandex.*

Aleric: *Just no cape. No cape!*

"I don't have time –" I start.

"Read from the bottom. That's the latest text," he says as if he's the one who's exasperated with this conversation.

I glance at the most recent message.

"If I let you tie me up and call you daddy," Maddox reads over my shoulder, "will that get the stick out of your ass? I'll even let you use it to whip me. Kisses and licks and bites on that pretty little cock of yours."

Aleric turns his phone to him. "LOL. I must have scrolled up on accident." The fuck he did. Otherwise, he wouldn't have asked us to read it.

He swipes the chat down, then angles it at me again.

"Holy fuck!" Maddox says. "Leno, look at this."

Krypto cocks his head to the side, wagging his tail, and Aleric points the phone at him.

"Holy fuck!" Leno grabs his dog by the scruff of the neck and hauls him away from the screen. "You're an asshole," he snaps as he shoves Maddox in the shoulder. Krypto barks.

"No, *that's* an asshole," our youngest brother cackles, his arms wrapped around his sides.

The image Aleric has just shown us is of a woman on her knees with her ass in the air. Her hole's been stretched to the point of bleeding.

"She looks like Siome, Antonio's dead wife," Vlad says, no doubt seeing I am an inch away from shooting his boss in the fucking groin. "He sent that last night, and Antonio hasn't retaliated."

I glance at the bottom right of the screen. Two ticks tell me he's seen it.

"So he's planning something big for you. Got no time for me," Aleric says as he slips the phone into his pocket. "You go in tonight, and you might not come back out."

"Worried about us?" I ask dryly.

"I only need one of you to live to honor the treaty."

I stare at him for a moment, then I turn to Rudy.

He shakes his head. "I'm the strongest –"

"Which is exactly why we need you to be the calvary," I sign to him. "If it all goes to shit, you can get us out."

He doesn't look happy, but he nods.

"None of Antonio's other bases around here are missing soldiers," Vlad says as I turn back to face them, meaning the building isn't packed with an army of wolves. "And unless he has a witch with him to hide their heartbeats, there are only four humans inside."

My stomach crawls. Antonio would've expected all of us to come get our brother back. And even though he knows we won't call in any soldiers of our own as we're unsure of who is on Talon's side and who isn't, Rudy could take out his entire pack on his own if push came to shove. So if this is a trap, it's a shit one.

Unless Khalid isn't here at all. Or if he's already dead, and those four heartbeats all are wolves.

"What humans are they?" I demand.

Vampires have another sense, allowing them to detect the heartbeats of their prey. Given all our rates are different (werewolves being the slowest, with their resting rate at thirty to forty beats a minute. An average Earth human's is from sixty to eighty, but athletes can get theirs lower than forty. Witches have slightly lower rates than humans but not by much), I know he can tell us if the four in there are all our enemies or not.

"A witch, Earther, and a werewolf are on the eighth floor." That'll be Khalid, his girl, and Antonio. "And there's another wolf on the first floor, but it's fucking fast. It's racing around like it's hyped up on something," Vlad says.

Shit. This isn't a trap; it's a fucking experiment. Antonio has one of his super werewolves waiting for us, and he wants to see what it can do.

Vlad's jaw tightens. "Khalid's control has just snapped. His heart rate's all over the place."

"Fuck," Leno curses as I open my car door to get in.

"We'll be in the next building," Aleric says. "Once Antie knows Maddox is in the building, he's most likely going to bolt, but if he doesn't, call me, boo."

"What about Enoch and Ez?" Maddox asks as he climbs in behind me. My phone buzzed while Vlad was briefing us. I pull it out now.

"They're five minutes out. We'll meet them there."

Rudy stops beside my door as I start the engine. "Call me as soon as you need me. Don't make me clean up your bodies," he signs.

"Grim, bruh," Maddox says from the back.

"I'll call if you can help," I sign.

He starts to protest, but I put the car into reverse and leave him with the vampires. There's no point him coming in to die alongside us. Antonio chose one wolf to take us all on. Either that wolf is actually capable of killing us all, or he wants us to survive the night. If we don't make it, I trust Rudy to watch over Micha and my daughter.

If she survives the war long enough to give birth.

I push those worries down, keeping my focus purely in the moment. Distractions will get us killed.

"Khalid and his girl are the priorities," I say as I drive over the bridge. "Antonio's second. Maddox, get upstairs as fast as you can. The rest of us will buy you time. Leno, keep an eye on the house, and if you need to step out of this fight, you step out."

He nods as he scratches Krypto between the ears. His arms are caked in dirt all the way up to his elbows, keeping him tied to the plants back home. If Antonio decides to double back and attack the women while we're all out, Leno will rip them to shreds. On their own, the plants are brutal, but when controlled by Leno, they are a hundred percent lethal.

"And you, Krypto," Leno says in a cute voice. "You are not going to get involved in this fight. No, you are not. Nuh uh. You're going to sit in a nice tree outside until it's safe to come out. Yes, you are. Oh yes, you are. Who's a good boy?"

Krypto woofs, then pants happily in expectation as my brother pulls out a box of chicken nuggets from inside his bag. "Only one," he says as he opens it and holds it out to his dog. Krypto looks at him, then at the entire box, his thoughts clear on his doggie face.

"Only one, boy," Leno says in the same tone, not wanting to teach Krypto to only respond to a harsher voice. He's constantly reinforcing his dog's training, constantly testing him to make sure that when he's given an order, any order, he'll obey. As much as Leno tries to keep Krypto away from the more dangerous situations, mistakes happen, and it will only take one refusal to come back or stay down or leave the food someone else is offering him for something bad to happen.

Leaning his head into the box, Krypto licks one up.

"Good boy!" But even as Leno coos over his dog, worry trickles from him. If the werewolf waiting for us moves as fast as Antonio does, he might be able to get past us and to Krypto before Leno or his tree can save him.

"There it is," Maddox says as he leans between the seats and points to a sky-rise that doesn't look any different to any of the others. White stone. Glass floors. Nothing about it stands out. There isn't even a construction zone around it to block it off to the public.

"Why'd he bring Khalid here?" I ask, a knot of unease growing in my stomach. We're missing something, and that might just get us killed.

As he pulls up a shield around the car, Maddox jokes, "Maybe he's compensating for something?"

"That would only work if he owned it," Leno says.

"That's what I just said, bruh."

I glance up at the building as I park the car on the other side of the lot. Although from the door to us is a distance a werewolf can easily cover in a second, a second can make all the difference when it comes to casting spells.

"Do we know anything about Morn Industries?" I ask as I open my door.

"Nope, but if we survive this, I'll check it out," Maddox says.

We step out of the car, and Maddox expands the shield with us. I inhale, searching for the scent of our prey. In the mix of human odors, I catch two wolves, one of which is... off in some way. There's also Talon's but not Khalid's or his girl's.

Talon must've delivered them here through his shadows, meaning Khalid's girl might be close to dead. The monsters that lurk in that plane can't hurt us but nor can we use our magic there, so he would've been hard-pressed to protect her. If she dies tonight, so will he. His love for her runs too deep.

"You'll never know real love." Not like Khalid clearly can.

Shoving that envy down, I glance at Leno as he uses his magic to get a tree to bend its branches down to the ground. He taps them with his hand twice, and his dog walks up them, then sits down. The branches curl around him, giving him a perch while protecting him from being seen by any humans still walking and driving about. The last thing we need is someone trying to rescue him and them still being here when we come out all bloody and bruised.

He crushes a handful of leaves he takes from the tree, then smears them across his bicep, leaving a green streak that connects him to the tree. He nods to tell us he's ready. Maddox gives a similar nod, having just finished cloaking the lower eight levels of the building in a silence ward.

As one, we head for the double glass doors. I raise my

gun as I enter and cast out my senses. The scent of the wolf is a lot stronger now that we're inside, but it's everywhere, making it hard to pinpoint its current location. I turn my head left and right, trying to get a lock on it as my eyes are in constant motion. They shift around the large white-and-gold marble lobby, scanning for any sign of our enemy. The metal of the gun is felt on every ridge of my fingertips, the nerves tingling over the slightest shift of weight in my hands.

But nothing darts around the four pillars spread out between us and the far wall. Nothing crosses the Morn logo, an angled L, that's inlaid in red (the top of the L) and black (the bottom) stone in front of the reception desk. Nothing even drops from the ceiling that is towering so high above us that it is cloaked in perpetual shadow.

I breathe in deep and slow, dissecting the smells that come to me. The wolf went off to the right, and as I glance that way, I see a sign pointing towards the stairs. I gesture towards it, and we move together. Leno's heart rate starts to pick up, and Maddox's follows once we're in sight of the door. It's completely solid. No window to peek through to see what's waiting inside.

The hairs on my neck and arms rising, I reach out for the handle. Just as my fingers graze it, a loud crash sounds from the next floor up above, followed by a bone-chilling howl. It isn't close, but it's about to be.

I yank the door open. "Move!"

Maddox darts inside, and Leno's next, with me bringing up the rear. If we can make it past the floor the beast is on, then we can fight it off on the stairs, with the advantage of a higher position. If we can't, we'll have to retreat and find a different stairwell for Maddox to climb – while a supped up wolf hunts us down from behind.

"Fuck!" Maddox twists as he reaches the landing of the first floor, throwing his arms out towards the door. A blue shield erects around him just as the door comes flying off its hinges. It hits his shield and tosses him into the wall. Leno stops abruptly on the steps below, right above me, as a massive gray werewolf charges onto the landing. Maddox's scream is cut off as it rams its shoulder into the door still pressed up against him, crushing him further into the wall. His shield wavers. The wolf snarls, and I aim past Leno to open fire.

Darting to the side to give me space, Leno jerks one hand forward, and the vines in his bag come shooting out. One moment, the wolf is on the landing, half a staircase above, and the next instant, Leno is gone and the wolf is on me, his claws wrapping around my gun to crush it in his grip. He howls in pain as his hand's blown apart, but he doesn't stop in his attack and manages to rip the rifle off me. My finger snaps backwards as it gets caught in the trigger. Letting myself drop like a rock rather than try to scramble back, I manage to keep my head as his claws swipe the air where I just was.

Leno's vines shoot above me, wrapping around the furry arm. The wolf snarls as it tries to rip its limb free, but Leno's magic pulses down the plant, making it stronger than chain. Deciding my brother's the weakest link, the wolf lunges over me, but I jerk a silver blade free of its sheath and imbed it in its stomach as it leaps.

It howls as my blade rips a line from its belly to its dick. Blood rains down on my face, and I hold my breath as a rich stench burns my nose. It's sickly, the smell of disease, and I am assaulted by the memory of a vampire we found after he was dumped by the Death Hunt. His skin was all boiling and sliding off him, the insides of his cheeks slipping down his throat, his eyes melting down his lips. The wolves poisoned him with their fluids, and for a moment, I fear it's infected me.

But if I'm to die, I'm taking this fucker with me.

As his momentum carries him past me, I release the knife. Wrapping my arms around one of his back legs, I lunge forward with all my strength and speed. My brother's vines keep hold of him even as I propel him back, and for a second, there is a split bite of resistance as the wolf is pulled in two separate directions.

Then there is a *snap!*

The smell of blood rushes down my nostrils, tickling my tongue with the taste of copper. The wolf howls in pain as his body whips backwards to join the direction of his leg, which *cracks* as it hits the edge of the stairs. The arm Leno grabbed hold of with his vines has been ripped off, and his shoulder's a mess of torn tendons and ligaments, his arteries spraying the walls in long pulsing jets.

I chance a look at the landing above me, checking to see if Maddox is back on his feet. But the boy is gone, having hopefully raced up the stairs to get Khalid. I return my gaze to the wolf just in time to catch his foot in my chest. Pain lances across my ribs as I'm tossed back through the air. I try to twist to catch myself, but my face hits Leno, and we both topple down the stairs.

He groans beside me as we land at the half landing, and the breath is knocked from my lungs. I try to stand, but my head refuses to control my limbs, and I fall back to one knee. Blood drips into my eyes from a cut on my head, and I lift one hand up to wipe it away. The other grabs another silver knife free from its sheath. I look up to try to focus on the wolf. But one moment, he's there; the next he's right in front of me, his mouth open to latch around my skull. Fuck! He's moving too fast even with my previous blade of silver still inside him.

I try to fall to the side, to have gravity help me get out of the way, but I'm too slow. If it wasn't for the shield Leno manages to throw up just in time, his teeth would be around my head. A second later, they'd be severing it completely.

As the wolf snarls against the shield it can't penetrate, I swivel my legs beneath me so I'm on my feet rather than my knees. My muscles tense, ready to spring, as two arms of vines wrap around the wolf's head and shoulder. The pale blue shield drops. The vines wrench the head one way and the shoulder the other, and I lash out with my knife to sever the carotid artery.

Blood sprays in a beautiful fountain up the wall, but the vines keep pulling until the head is completely ripped from the wolf's shoulders, then slammed into the wall.

Falling back on my ass, I breathe heavily. Leno is sitting up against the wall on the other side of the small landing. He stares at me, one eye swollen shut, his pulse beating wildly.

"Holy fuck," he wheezes. "And that was inside a stairway so it couldn't really move."

"And with silver inside him," I add.

"Fuck."

I inhale, holding that sickly odor in my lungs a second before releasing it, but there's no mistaking it now. That's the smell of death in the form of disease. The fucking wolf was already on death's door. *Shit.*

"I got to Khalid," Maddox shouts down the stairs. "You two still alive?"

Leno is just about to answer when the stairway door below us is ripped off its hinges. Pivoting on the landing, I instinctively raise my knife to face the new threat.

"Fucking hel, you two look like shit," Enoch says as he steps in.

"Smell like it too," Ezriel adds.

"Fucking took you long enough!" Leno shouts. "You're a bit late, as always, fucking useless."

Enoch shrugs. "Had to stop for a piss."

As they're bickering, I drink a healing potion and feel the warmth of it flow through me, restitching flesh and healing bruised ribs. It's a miracle I didn't break anything other than my trigger finger. Our three brothers join us on the landing, their attention shifting to the dead wolf taking up most of the space.

"Can you copy its DNA?" I ask Maddox. Having that beast in his arsenal would be amazing, but I know the answer before he shakes his head. Antonio wouldn't have left an experiment in our hands if we could use it.

"Nah, bruh," Maddox says. "It's too riddled with disease. If I try to change into that, it might kill me."

"You're telling me we fought it half dead?" Leno shouts.

"You killed it in a few minutes; it couldn't have been that hard to fight," Maddox says.

"We got fucking lucky. It just so happened to run into my vines at one point. I couldn't sense the fucker moving. I'd hate to have to fight it in an open area."

"Where's Khalid?" I ask Maddox.

"Upstairs with his girl. He tried to fight Antonio, but the coward jumped out the window." He grins. "Antonio, not Khalid, though I can see how that would be confusing."

"Did Khalid get any DNA off him?"

He shakes his head.

"Call Rudy and get him to come clean up. I need to call Aleric."

"Real masochist, huh?" Leno teases as he stands. "I'm going to go get Krypto."

The twins move to the side so he can pass, then they follow him. "So was it really Talon?" Enoch asks, pained.

"Yeah..."

As they leave, I pull out my phone and call the Boss of the Blood Fangs. He answers on the first ring.

"I have a body here," I say. "One of the super werewol–"

He hangs up on me, but a moment later, he's here in the stairway, as is his other soldiers minus Vlad. "Oh, goodie," he says as he squats down beside the wolf's legs. "This is one fine specimen."

"It had a disease that was killing it," I say. "If Cara Jervis can replicate it, then we might be able to use it against the rest of them."

"Mmm," he says. "Yeah... I'm probably just going to fuck it."

Dear gods. How the fuck do we share any DNA?

He flashes me a smile and then he and his soldiers are gone. Alone in the hallway with just Maddox, I turn to him. "How are you?"

He rotates his shoulder and cracks his neck. "Bit sore, but I'll survive."

"And Khalid?"

"Good. No wounds a healing potion didn't fix."

I nod, relief flowing across my chest. But I don't get to stop and enjoy it, don't get to take a moment just to breathe it in. Instead, I have to send out an email to all my capos. As my fingers tap away on my phone, I tell them about Talon's betrayal and how there is a reward for anyone who finds him and reports back. Double if they grab him, but I want him alive so I can fucking torture him myself.

Slipping my phone into my pocket, I head down the stairs, Maddox following. We spot our brothers through a glass door in front of the elevators, leading outside into the parking lot. Enoch raises his hand and opens it with his magic, allowing us to bypass having to go back through the lobby. The hot night air presses on my skin as we join them.

"I don't understand why Talon would do this," Leno says sadly, his arms folded across his chest. Krypto is off sniffing the trees. "To turn on us all like that?"

"Maybe he just hates Khalid?" Ezriel offers. "It's him he kidnapped." There is a moment of heavy silence, where a weight is felt. Khalid is the reaper, and as much as he is their brother, he is not fully loved by them, not fully trusted due to being able to kill them all so easily.

My jaw locks as the silence stretches, that *understanding* of why Talon might have done what he did permeating the air. Khalid has given his life to this fucking family, taken on all the shit they are too weak to do, and this is what they truly think of him?

Maddox glances at me, and there is a look in his eyes. *We are here*, it says. We risked our lives to come for him.

So I bite back my rising anger and paranoia. As much as they might fear the reaper in the dark depths of their mind, not one of them hesitated to come here tonight.

"Maybe it's not Khalid Talon wanted gone," Enoch says slowly. He looks at me apologetically. "You did kill his best friend."

"Khalid killed him," Maddox says.

"He gave the order."

"Because the guy was a nut job who wanted to –"

"It doesn't matter why Talon has turned traitor," I cut in. "He set Micha up as his patsy and nearly got Mother killed. His reasons will not save him."

A grim silence settles over us, filled with grief from my brothers, filled with anger from me. As much as I want to direct that all at Talon though, I can't. I was the one who decided to hurt Micha like I did.

I could have called Aleric.

I could have questioned Zita.

Instead, I hammered a screw into her hands over and over again and shaved off her fingers chunk by chunk. Her screams are on repeat inside my skull, and I fear there is nothing I can do to fix what I have done.

But by the gods, I will spend my whole life trying.

Just as soon as I can get back home.

Where the fuck are you, Khalid?

TWENTY-FIVE

HER

Sitting in my room, I stare at my hands, not able to see a single mark on them. Sau even rebuilt my severed fingers using dark magic. She numbed an area of my thigh, then cut off a small chunk of extra fat – a cut she matched on the other leg. She could have used the meat in the fridge, but I didn't like the idea of being part pig or cow or alligator. And after what Varius did to me...two more cuts were nothing.

But despite how right my hands look, despite how well she fixed them, assuring me that they are completely healed now, there is something *wrong.*

Because I've been trying for the last hour to call a flame to my fingers, but there's no heat, no fire. No flicker of light.

I can feel the magic burning away inside of me, coiled tight in my chest, but no matter how much I demand it, how much I beg it, it *will not come.*

So I'm starting to hyperventilate.

Starting to panic just as badly as I was when I thought I

was losing our child.

"Come on," I mutter, willing my fingers to burn. "Come on...*come on!*"

But there is nothing.

Just a collapsing chest as reality starts to press in on me.

"No," I growl, the denial ragged and raw. "*No.*"

Tears burn my eyes, but they're not the same ones I cried when strapped to the fucking chair I'm sitting in again, my clothes still stained red but my hands unbound. They're not sad tears. Not ones of panic or fear or grief for the loss of what Varius and I had.

They are tears of furious anger. Of righteous fury. Of all the fucking synonyms for *fucking pissed off.*

Varius didn't just torture me in this godsdamn chair. He didn't just ignore my cries for far too long while I told him our child was dying. To get help. To believe me.

He fucking *took my magic from me*.

"No! Fucking come on!" I screech as I open myself up, let the fire rip free.

And it does.

Wildly.

Out of control.

The flames shoot up to my face, hungry and greedy. I shove back in the chair, caught off guard, my heart in my throat as the chair starts to fall. But I keep my focus on my flames, on trying to control them so I don't set this whole damn house on fire.

They grow bigger.

They get hotter.

Starting to panic, I swirl my hands around in familiar patterns, shaping the flames into what I want them to be. But they are not listening. And the ground is whooshing up behind me. And the knowledge that once I touch it, once my arms drop from their raised position and close the distance to another object, they will jump free.

Then they will rage with no one able to stop them.

So, screaming, I close my hands into fists, snuffing out the magic that should come so easily to me. That is a part of me, another fucking limb, and yet one I can no longer control.

The chair slams into the ground.

My back shudders from the impact, and the tears I was crying in anger come flooding out even faster.

"*No*," I growl. "I can fucking *do* this."

So I open myself up again. Not to my flames, but magic itself. To one of the first spells I learned. A simple one any witch child can do with a five-minute lesson. But instead of getting the small flickers of red energy I wanted, the magic explodes in my hands.

I scream as the heat burns my palms and fingers. I try to snuff it out, but like my flames, it doesn't listen. Terrified, I aim my hands away from me, and the magic shoots from them and slams into the bed frame. There is a large groan right before the thing cracks in two; if that had hit me, I would not have survived. As the two halves of the bed drop to the ground with a *thud*, I roll out of the chair and scream.

Ignoring the pain in my hands, needing to just let my anger out, I lift the chair up and throw it across the room. The impact of it hitting matches the blows being dealt to my heart.

He fucking took my magic from me.

He made me a fucking *freak*.

Like him.

Tears burn my eyes, and these ones are sad as well as angry because I don't think he is a freak. Don't think he is lesser due to his inability to use magic. Those words came from a place of pain, from a want to hurt him like he's hurt me.

I fucking loved him.

And he *broke* us.

With a roar, I lunge across the room to a picture I have of me and Dayne. It hangs on the wall, and I rip it off its hook, then launch it at the radiator, where Maddox's two arms still lay. The sound of the shattered glass pleases a broken shard inside of me, but the high doesn't last, and I pick up another thing to throw. To experience that release. To let at least a *little* bit of my rage free.

The bedside table holding the lamp and another picture goes flying.

Then I throw out every drawer in my dresser.

Tip all their contents out on the floor.

Rip my dresses off their hangers.

Tear them apart in my hands, shredding one after the other until I'm standing in a chaotic mess that mimics what I'm feeling.

"Fuck!" I roar as I continue to destroy it all. Destroy it like I've been destroyed by the man I love. Make it look like *me*.

I knock holes in my walls.

Throw things at the ceiling fan until it's hanging limp in all its fractures.

Smash the light in the middle of it.

I even toss the covers and pillows off my bed, wanting no sign of order, no semblance of peace.

My chest heaving, my rage still unsatisfied, I use broken shards of glass to dig great, big gashes into my mattress. Then I fill those holes with splinters.

With hatred and pain.

And love.

So much fucking love, it hurts.

He did this to me.

He fucking did this to me.

And then he left without a word. No apology. No text.

He did this, and he didn't fucking care.

And yet, I still care. I still want him to come through my

door and gather me up in his arms and tell me he's sorry, that he'll never hurt me again, that he'll keep me safe even from the monster inside himself.

And I hate that I want that.

That I *need* that in this moment.

Dropping to my knees on the carpeted floor, I scream out my fucking soul.

TWENTY-SIX

HER

He comes. Eventually.

When it's too late.

When my rage has turned cold enough for me to think again.

When I've convinced myself I hate him.

That I don't need him.

That he can rot in fucking Hel.

I don't even turn towards him as he enters my room. I'm sitting in the middle of the mess I've made, my legs curled up under me, my hands on my lap, my eyes on them. *Can I sacrifice him to get my magic back?*

"Micha!" The concern in his voice might've patched up a small broken part of me if he hadn't closed the door first. If he had reacted purely on emotions for *me*, but no, he always has to play the fucking game. Can't let his brothers know he wants to fix things. Can't let them hear me yelling at him. Can't be seen to be *weak*, as someone who would fight for his girl despite the evidence against her.

Tears burn my eyes.

I would have fought for him.

If Dayne, the person I love most in the world – *fuck you, Varius*– was missing and all the evidence I found pointed to Varius having taken him, I still wouldn't have tortured him for a location.

I would have trusted him.

Believed in him.

Believed in *us*.

When he kneels down in front of me, his hands reaching for mine, I snatch them away. What the fuck does he think he's doing? He doesn't get to *touch* me.

All of the women in his gang might be disciplined into being 'good and proper' little breedmares regardless of what their husbands do to them.

But I'm not a fucking Shadow.

I'm a godsdamn Black.

My head comes up as I sneer, "Get the fuck away from me."

He stands, then turns away from me, and I stare at him in shock and pain and *rage*. Now, a logical part is telling me that he's doing exactly what I asked him to do. But that cold anger I was feeling, that logical fury, has just been dropped into a fucking volcano.

Grabbing the nearest item to my right – a broken piece of the chair he tortured me in, I throw it at the back of his head.

He twists to the side at the last second, and the thing flies past his face. It doesn't even graze his nose. Fucking *bastard*.

Growling, I grab another item and throw it at him. He ducks this time. I throw it at his feet. He jumps. My rage builds to the point I'm ready to throw magic at him and damn us all, but by then, he's in the bathroom and opening the cabinet below the sink.

I freeze as I watch him squat down to grab the healing wand from inside it. My throat clogs up at his desire to care for me. But then bitterness opens it back up again.

Fuck him.

"I'm not using that," I say, refusing to do anything he wants me to.

"You're hurt."

A mad cackle comes out of me as I clench my burned flesh into fists. The pain that erupts there is fucking terrible, but it's a lot more manageable than the agony inside my chest. "I'm hurt?" I laugh again. "That's fucking golden."

"Micha –" he says.

"You tortured me!" I yell, jumping to my feet as he walks towards me. "I told you I didn't do it, and you hurt me so badly, I –" My throat clenches tight, cutting off my words. But I force them out. Force him to know exactly what he took from me. "I can't use my magic anymore," I say, raising my hands and opening them, letting him look at the mess I made of my palms. "I tried to do a simple spell – Something a *child* can do… And I nearly killed myself."

Grabbing my wrist, he hauls me to him. There's darkness in his eyes – a primal, feral challenge that sends shivers down my spine. I start to tell him to get the fuck off me and never touch me again when he growls, "You're not allowed to die."

I blink, and my brain stops to try to figure out what the fuck that means, but my mouth doesn't care. It just runs, fueled by all the pain and anger inside of me. Except when I start to tell him he can go fuck himself with his orders, his mouth crashes down on mine.

I freeze for a split second.

Then I knee him. Right in the fucking balls.

Impact.

He grunts against my lips and sags a bit, but he doesn't

release me. Doesn't stop kissing me. His hands are cupping my face, and his tongue is pushing inside my open mouth. Giving me the comfort I've been craving. Then his hands are on my ass, lifting me up so he can straighten, and mine are on his chest.

To push him off.

To pull him to me.

He strides over to the bed but only takes a few steps before he pivots and heads back into the ensuite – the only place I haven't touched in my rage.

"I'm not fucking you," I say against his lips.

"You're my wife."

My heart stutters over that, but he's never had an issue with claiming me in the dark, in the shadows where no one can see or hear or *know*.

"I'm not marrying you."

"The fuck you aren't," he growls, and I can't even repeat my words because they're too empty. Even though I hate him so fucking much right now, that doesn't change the fact that he purchased me.

He has a signed contract from my father saying that if I run, my own damn Family will hunt me down and kill me.

I am his property.

His breedmare to take whenever he wants.

And now that I am with child, that contract is forever binding; the back-out clause concerning my infertility has officially closed.

"You'll kill us," I whisper as he sets me down on the sink and grabs at the skirt of my dress. He pulls it up past my knees before he stops. Lifting his lips off me, he presses his forehead to mine.

"Is there anything left to kill?" he whispers, and there is so much pain there, so much godsdamn hope that there is something left, some small tether that is still tying me to him, that I want to cry for what we have lost, for what he broke by hammering a screw into my hands.

For being able to keep going despite my screams.

My pain.

Heartless and cruel.

"I don't know," I whisper. "I don't know."

Exhaling hard, he steps back, then offers me the wand he tucked into his waistband. "Heal yourself, Micha. Then I'm taking you to bed."

"I don't want to sleep with you," I mumble.

"Sleep or fuck?"

I stay silent. I don't want to admit that I want his arms around me. That I want him to try to fix what he has broken even though I have no idea how he possibly can. Perhaps I just want him to try and fail. To feel so damn desperate to change something, like I was in that chair, yet never be able to.

Grabbing my wrist, he places the wand gently in my palm. "Heal yourself, Micha. I don't like seeing..." He stops as I snort.

"Fuck you," I say.

"I thought you were a traitor. All the evidence –"

"Fuck. You."

"Fine. Be angry with me," he says, his voice flattening. "But fucking heal yourself. That's an order."

My eyes narrow, and if my hands didn't hurt so badly, I'd punch him. "Fuck you."

His jaw tics, his patience clearly wearing thin. But fuck him and his patience. I've been so godsdamn patient with him over these last four months. I have been understanding of all his paranoia and pain. Fuck, I can still understand him now. Can still understand the choice he was forced to make as the clock was ticking down on his brother's life. But I don't care anymore. I don't give a fucking shit about why he hurt me. He *hurt* me.

And he didn't stop.

He didn't fucking stop while I was screaming in pain.

No *reason* is good enough to make up for that.

"How is Maddox?" I ask as I stare at the wand, genuinely wondering how he is. He was the one who saved me, and now he's just risked his life to save his brother. I want to know that he's okay.

"Don't ask about him." There is a warning in his tone, a dark jealousy amplified by my rejection of him.

"Why not?" I challenge, my head snapping up. "I care about him. *He* actually trusted me. *He* actually tried to stop you, and *he* was the one to get Sau. He saved your fucking child." A bitter laugh leaves my lips. "A child you haven't once asked about."

"I know she lives."

"*You know she lives*?" I shake my head. "Fuck you."

"You want to know why I haven't asked about her?" he growls as he places his hands on my knees and shoves them apart. I try to keep my legs closed, but he steps between them, then hauls me forward by the hips until my pussy rubs against his cock. I try to squirm back, but his fingers dig into me, clamps that refuse to let me go. "Because all I fucking care about right now is how *you* are. Yes, I fucked up, and I'm sorry. I'm so fucking sorry that I believed the evidence instead of my feelings for you. I wanted to punish you for kissing Antonio –"

"He forced –"

"I *didn't care*," he admits, his words heavy and dark and twisted. "I didn't fucking care if you wanted it or not. You are *mine*, Micha. And he got to taste you." His eyes dip to my lips. "I wanted to skin his fucking touch off you."

"Well, thank you for not doing that," I say sarcastically, using the words as a shield to cover the pounding of my heart. Because no. No, I'm not going to accept his apology just because my fucking neanderthal says, "Grrr."

"I know you hate me," he continues as he cups the back

of my neck, his hold firm and possessive. "You hate me for the rest of your life if you need to, little monster. Wake up and plan how to make me miserable every day if you must, but just fucking wake up *here*. Beside me." His head touches mine, and the sorrow pours from him, but I pull back and cross my arms.

"Oh, so you'd rather just let me hate you than fix what you broke?"

"Of course not." He shakes his head, a flash of irritation in his eyes. He's tired. I'm tired, and we're both running ragged on emotions that have broken us, but I don't want to be *understanding* right now. I don't want to put in the effort of just 'getting what he means' so he doesn't have to put in the effort of saying it.

"Just tell me how to fix this –" he starts, and I explode.

"Fuck you! You do not get to fucking *break* us and then ask *me* to fix it. This is on you. *You* created this mess. *You*. Hurt. *Me*." I shake my head, my blood so fucking hot, I'm resisting the urge to throw my fire in his face.

"But if you just tell me, then you can stop hurting soon–"

"Fuck you!" I scream as I shove at his chest, mine so fucking tight it feels like I'm choking. And I know what it's like to be choked. Thanks to fucking him.

But I don't want to tell him. I want him to care enough to figure it out, to think about what he's done and how he can prove to me that he won't do it again. I want him to learn who I am and what I need and put in as much effort to fix us as what it took for him to *break* us.

Because he already told me he cared about me.

He already made me feel special.

Already made me believe in him, in *us* with his fucking, "Let's blood bond and be tied together forever" shit.

And because I understood his paranoia and his station and his fears and all the experiences wrought on him, I let him get away with bringing the bare minimum into this relationship. I let him just talk the talk, to fool me with his words that were only ever said behind closed doors.

And look where that got me – strapped down to a chair and tortured.

So I can't trust just his words. Can't trust him at all if he doesn't put any effort in to soothe my worries when he's the one who created them in the first place.

"Fine," he snaps. "Heal your fucking hands."

I open my mouth, but he cuts in, "Don't you want to see if it'll work? If you can still use magic through a wand?"

My heart jumps into my skull, pounding hard as I glance at the thin tapered piece of wood in my hand. A part of me desperately wants to try, to believe that he hasn't stolen all of it from me, but the other half is terrified of the answer. If I try to use the wand and it does nothing, then what am I?

A freak.

I wince.

An abomination.

I glance up at him, and he must see the guilt in my eyes, the direction my thoughts took me because his walls come up, shutting me out. He's been called an abomination all his life for his lack of magic.

A cold, bitter laugh breaks through my lips. "We could be matching abominations."

He doesn't say anything, and a part of me hopes I hit a fucking nerve there, that I hurt him just a little. But a bigger part of me already regrets the words.

What a fucking fool I am.

He can torture me as I scream, but I flinch when he looks hurt. Pathetic.

Shaking my head, I aim the wand at my hand. "Iactus," I say softly, then hold my breath. For one second, t–

White light glows from the tip of the wood, and I exhale harshly. The burn fades under new skin. As soon as I heal both hands, Varius grabs the wand and chucks it away, then bends down to place his shoulder in the middle of my chest. His arms come around me, and he lifts me up, carrying me like a fucking *neanderthal*. He slaps my ass when I try to wiggle off him as he heads for the door.

"What the fuck are you doing?" I ask as I resist the urge to bite him. He likes it when I do that.

"I'm tired, so I'm going to bed."

"Not with me you're not."

He shrugs. "You don't want to tell me what you want me to do, so I'm just going to do what I want with you."

"You're a fucking neanderthal!"

"Says the one hissing at me like a feral cat."

"Fuck you! In what fucking world would I not be pissed after you *tortured* me! You do not get to piss me off by hurting me and then get pissed that I'm hurt and pissed off! That isn't unreasonable of me – of fucking anyone, you fucking turdstain. The only *unreasonable* thing I've done is not pack my bags and left before you even got –"

He swings me off his shoulder, then pivots and pins me against the wall. His eyes narrow as he ducks his head and growls, "You even *think* about leaving me, little monster, and I'll kill everyone who hides you, everyone who saw you, just the tiniest fucking glimpse, and didn't report back to me about where you were."

I snort. "You can't know who saw me if they didn't tell you."

"Then I will kill everyone in every city you pass through."

"You're delusional."

His forehead presses against mine, and I am suddenly aware that we're on the stairs leading up to the second floor. It's dark, well into the night, and no one seems to be out, but we're not hidden away in a room. We're not protected from the eyes of his brothers. My eyes flicker back and forth across his, trying to see what this means, but then I stop. Look away.

I can't keep searching for things that aren't there. Can't keep fooling myself into thinking he cares about me, seeing the little signs that mean he does. *Fool me once...and I end up strapped to a chair and my magic ripped from me. Fool me twice...*

"I fucked up, Micha," he says softly. "When Talon told me you were the one who helped Antonio take Khalid, I didn't believe him. So I forced Leno to wake Mother up from her coma."

I swallow, remembering how badly her body was ripped apart by the werewolf alpha. She must have used so much magic to heal herself, used so much more to heal me. I saw the toil it was taking on her as she kept our child from bleeding out between my thighs. The more magic a witch uses, the more exhausted they become. And when they get too tired to protect themselves from the backlash of magic that occurs with every spell, then it starts to destroy their organs.

She could barely stand after healing me. She must have lost at least a kidney, maybe more. They'll regrow in time, but every bit of magic she uses before that happens, the more organs she will lose. Use too much, and it'll kill her. Then, of course, there's her curse. How many years has she lost in the past twenty-four hours? Will she even live long enough to see her grandchild?

"She told me you kissed Antonio," he continues tightly. "And I fucking lost it. I'm sorry."

My throat works wordlessly before I push out the words, "Sorry isn't good enough."

"So tell me what is," he demands as he steps away from the wall, and my hackles start rising all over again.

"I told you I'm not telling you shit."

"But if you know what I can do," he says, frustration bleeding into his words, "then why not tell me so I can do it?"

"Because that's just me fixing it! That's me cleaning up your mess. Making things right. Putting in the effort –"

"I'll be putting in the effort. I'll be doing them! You need me to bring you flowers and chocolate, just tell me what kind and I'll –"

"Flowers and chocolate?" I screech as he opens his door and steps inside. Then he kicks it shut behind him. "That's what you think I need to forgive you for taking my magic from me? For looking me in the eyes while you stabbed me over and over again? Flowers and chocolate!"

"I don't know because I've never apologized before!" he roars. "I am running fucking blind here, little monster, and I've had a long day –"

"*You've* had a long day? I had a nine hour fucking drive. Then I fought a monster – a legit, bonafide fucking snake, bat thing that your mother sicced on me because she thought I took down the wards because your asshole of a brother lured me back here to be his fall guy! Khalid's girl tried to kill me, but I still saved her. Then I got punched in the stomach and learned I was pregnant! That is not the time to learn you're fucking pregnant! That is the most stressful fucking time to learn you're pregnant!

"And then you!" I yell, smacking at his chest as he holds me over his bed. "You torture me! You damn near cause a miscarriage and then you leave!" My voice breaks. Cracks. Fucking splits apart like my heart is right now. "You left me. You left me all alone when I was hurting so fucking badly, and then you come back... You come back and you yell at me."

Tears burn my eyes, and I duck my head so he can't see them. I am so fucking *done* crying over him.

"Fuck, monster," he says, his voice softening. "I'm sorry."

"I'm sorry. I'm sorry. That's all you fucking say. I don't care that you're sorry. I care that you did it."

"Well, what do you want me to say then?" he asks in

exasperation. "Do you want me to not say sorry?"

"Of course I want you to say sorry! But I want you to do other things too!"

"Like what?"

I flounder, not sure. What could he possibly do to prove I can trust him not to hurt me?

"Fucking hel, Micha. Just *tell* me."

Just time, I realize. It's just going to take time, constant little actions that show me he loves me. That he'll choose me over his traitorous brothers and scheming mother and just trust me not to hurt him so he doesn't hurt me. *Ha!* My heart breaks. Varius trusting someone. That's never going to happen.

"Oh, for fuck's sake, Micha. Stop acting crazy and just tell me what you need so I can fix this," he growls, his voice low, not yelling but yelling all the same.

My eyes widen.

"Crazy!" I screech. "You want to see me crazy!" Twisting in his arms, I bite him hard on the shoulder. The taste of blood explodes on my tongue. I jerk my head up. "How's that for crazy! Or maybe this!" I grab at his waistband, knowing he has knives somewhere. Finding a handle, I pull the blade out of its sheath. "Let me cut off your dick and see how *reasonable* you are afterwards!"

He grabs for my wrist as I wave the knife around. I wave it more erratically to keep it out of his reach. The longer I manage, the more his frustration mounts, and the angrier he becomes. As his eyes darken to a cold steel, my heart slams around my rib cage, and I am hit with the memory of him standing in front of me while I was strapped to that chair.

Panic grabs hold of me, sinking its razor-sharp claws into my limbs, into my mind, and I am fully transported back to the moment I was there. When I begged him to stop hurting me. When I feared for my life and that of my child.

Lifting the knife up rather than out, I aim for the base of

his shoulder. A part of me is screaming that the only way I can live is if he dies. If I stab him and rip myself free of my bindings. My vision blurs, but I can still see his damn eyes, haunting me in their cruelty.

One of his arms comes up to block me, his forearm crossing with mine. The other grabs my wrist and bends it back. I cry out, and he releases me. But the pain is done. The damage. The memory of how easily he can hurt me. How willing he is to do so.

I ram my head forward to crack his nose. He twists as he throws me down. I hit his bed on my back, and he jumps on top of me to pin me down. My arm comes up, instinctive and quick while he's in mid-air. My breath whooshes out of my lungs as two-hundred-and-forty-odd pounds lands on me, crushing my fist into my chest and I gasp in pain, my eyes bugging wide. Fuck. I didn't expect his full weight. I thought he would hold himself up to protect me, thought he would at least try not to hurt me again.

Tears burn my eyes as my rage suddenly dies, and all I want to do is curl up into a self-pity party, knowing that we are never coming back from this. I can't see him outside of the man who tortured me. Who was okay with listening to my screams. And if I can't trust him when he's angry, how can I trust him when he's not?

As a sob builds in my chest, I try to tell him to get off me, that he's making it hard for me to breathe, that he's hurting the baby, that I don't want him touching me, that I want to be alone. My words come out as a jumbled mix of all those things though, and none of it makes sense.

But he doesn't move, doesn't say a single word, and that is such a strange reaction from him that it cuts through my sorrow just enough for me to feel it.

The wetness on my chest.

The knife that's still in my fist.

Which is stuck between me and him.

My eyes widen.

His full weight is on me!

On the blade that's poised right below his heart.

"Varius!" I shout, panic making my voice squeak. I didn't want this. Not really. I just wanted him to stop hurting me. "Varius! Varius, get off me. I can't –" I try to wiggle out from beneath his bulk, but I'm terrified of jerking the knife, of making the hole bigger. And he's just too damn heavy for me to get free.

"Help! Someone help!" I scream.

I don't care if the reaper is the one to come in. Don't care if I'm charged with treason after. I just want Varius to live. He has to live. He's my fucking neanderthal even if I hate him so much it hurts.

"*Heeeelp*!" I screech, but then I remember he kicked the door shut. The silence rune has been activated, and no one can hear me scream. No one is coming to help.

Jerking my hands out from between our bodies, I cup his face. He doesn't turn his lips into my palm. Doesn't move at all.

"No. No, no, no, no. Varius, please," I cry as I look into his open eyes.

Open but empty.

Unseeing.

"Varius, *please*. Please stay with me. I'm sorry. Don't go. Don't go. Stay with me."

Fuck!

I'm not a healer.

I can't even control my magic anymore. But the knife is still in his chest, a natural blockade. I have a chance to save him. He has a chance to live. I just need to get out from under him.

I just need to get out and open the door and get Sau.

Simple steps.

Simple fucking steps.

I can do this.

Tears burning my eyes, I try once more to shove him off me.

But I'm a hundred-and-ten pounds. And he's over twice my weight and nearly twice my size, and the torture and then my rage-fueled destruction of my room took so much strength out of my limbs. My arms shake as they shove.

He doesn't move.

"Varius, please," I beg. "Please don't leave me to raise our girl alone. Please don't –"

I scream as his head suddenly jerks up. Red eyes, sharp fangs – that's all I have time to see before he grabs me and sinks his teeth deep into my neck.

TWENTY-SEVEN

HIM

I growl against her throat as I swallow down her life, the very essence of who she is. With every gulp, I crave more, the hunger in my belly urging me on. My cock hardens to the point of pain. I bite deeper, swallow faster. Every part of me is craving every bit of her.

This isn't like the last woman I fed on – mere subsistence needed to keep me alive.

The woman beneath me is the steak tossed to a starving dog. A piece of bread offered to an escaped prisoner of war.

When I say I crave every part of her, I don't just mean the blood flowing past my lips.

I crave the touch of her hands even as they try to fight me off.

I crave the sharp stab of the knife as she bucks beneath me, keeping me poised on this edge of death, this moment where my vampirism is allowed out.

Where I can smell every pheromone pouring off her skin,

my senses heightened to their full potential.

Where I can feel how puny she is in my arms, how weak she is against my strength.

I crave the touch of her lips.

The feel of her hips.

The tightness of her pussy as she takes me.

Pulling my knees up so I'm crouching above her, I tug at the waistband of my pants. Snap open the button. Pull down the zipper.

"I need to be inside you," I rasp against her neck.

Need to know how she feels when I can feel everything, my every nerve endings so fucking *alive.*

How it'll feel when I come inside her, filling her with my cum.

How her pussy will taste when I lick her afterwards.

"No! Stop!"

Groaning, I pull out my cock and hike up her dress. I rip out the knife and toss it away. It tumbles across the floor. She tries to bring her knees up to stop me from getting close enough to slide in, but I just rock back on my heels, grab her hips, and haul her onto me with one strong thrust.

"Don't do this –"

She cries out, her back arching, and I damn near fucking come at the explosion of sensations flooding through me. The sound of her screams. The spasming of her pussy as she takes me so godsdamn deep. The smell of her arousal as it mixes with her adrenaline, her fear.

"Fuck, Micha," I growl as my fingers dig into her hips, my cock pulsing inside her but not moving. "You feel too damn good. I'm going to come before I even – *fuck.*"

"Stop. You're killing us," she says, trying to kick me off her. But I can't stop, can't help myself. Not when she feels this fucking *good.*

Grabbing her ankles, I force her legs up into the air and then wide apart, keeping them out of my way. Then I pull out of her so I can look down at her pussy.

"Fuck, baby, look how good you're hugging me. You're so godsdamn beautiful with your pussy wrapped around the head of my cock. Now show me how deep you can take me."

"Varius, please –"

I shove in, and she screams.

But I can smell the increase of her arousal, feel the flood of wetness seeping down my balls.

Growling, I ram into her again. Rub my cheek along her leg, kiss the smooth skin there. Lick it. I love the taste of her sweat spreading along every tastebud on my tongue.

Groaning, I fuck her faster.

My balls tighten.

An overwhelming heat grips my cock.

"*Fuck*, baby. I'm going to come if you keep squeezing me like this."

I growl.

She whimpers.

And godsdamn it, I crave the taste of those too. I want to feel those vibrations against my lips as she moans into my mouth.

So I lean down and take what I want, my cock sliding free of her pussy for just a moment.

My lips rub against hers. My tongue slips between them.

I rub my hands up and down her legs as they hang over my shoulders.

Fuck. I can't get enough of her.

"I need you to come for me, baby," I growl as I guide my cock back inside her hot, wet pussy. "I'm not going to last with you feeling this fucking good."

I grab her hand. She tries to pull away from me, but she's not strong enough to stop me, and I press her fingers over her pussy.

"Ride your hand for me, baby. Let me feel you come."

My pulse spikes as I force her fingers to move even as I

force my cock to stop. I am one thrust away from coming inside her. Fucking hel. "Come for me," I beg, squeezing my eyes shut as I feel my senses starting to dull. My life is no longer on the line, the wound in my chest having been healed by the magic in her blood. The vampirism is falling back under the curse. In a moment, I won't even remember what she feels like, this heaven on Earth, this irresistible temptation.

No!

I need to feel her come on my cock.

Pulling out of her, I drag her over to the edge of the bed. She still fights me, but her blows are weak, and I easily flip her over. Her feet are on the floor. I'm now standing behind her, one hand on her back, keeping her pinned. Dragging her dress up with my other hand, I bunch it around her waist.

"Get off me!" she says as she turns her head. "Stop!"

But I can't.

And I know she doesn't really want me to.

I can smell how wet she is.

Feel the goosebumps along her skin.

Wrapping my hand around my cock, I guide it into her soaking wet pussy.

I groan as I throw my head back. My knees are so damn weak, I can barely stand. Her pussy grips me. My cock jerks and pulses and threatens to come so damn quick. But I need to feel her orgasm first.

So I grab her hips and force her to rub her pussy on the edge of the bed, knowing outside pressure gets her off the quickest.

"Sto– ahhh."

Her protests turn into moans.

Her hands fist the sheets.

My whole body shakes as I watch her squirm. I'm trying so damn hard to fight my own release.

"Come for me, baby. *Please*. I will give you anything; just come for me."

I wrap one hand around her throat and arch her back so I can reach around with the other to play with her breasts. I pinch her nipples, alternating between them. Drawing her close to her O. Her glaring eyes drift shut as I fuck her slow and hard and deep while getting her pussy to grind against the mattress. Her lips part as she moans.

Leaning over her, I spit into her open mouth.

Watch her take me into both ends of her.

Her eyes pop open and find mine.

"Swallow," I growl, my hand massaging her throat.

Defiance sharpens her gaze, cuts through the haziness of her arousal, and my little monster spits it back at me.

Keeping my eyes on her, I open my mouth and catch the gift she's given me.

She cries out, her eyes hot on mine.

I tilt my head back and swallow, letting her see how it goes down my throat like a good boy.

A sudden thought rams into me. Her giving me orders like she did in the gym so many months ago. But instead of telling me to sit and hold out my hands for her to heal them, she's telling me to open my mouth and hold out my tongue so she can ride my face into oblivion.

Groaning, I come inside her *hard*, my balls drawing tight, my back arching, my godsdamn toes curling. I paw at her breasts, my hands just needing to *move* as the overload of sensations ram into me. Every nerve is so damn sensitive, and still I crave more.

Every part of her.

Over and over and over again.

Releasing her neck, I drop my hand to her pussy and rub her just like she likes.

She jerks in my arms, nearly as sensitive as I am.

"Stop – I – ahhh!"

And now she's threading a hand around the back of my neck, lifting a leg onto the bed, and riding my hand like she needs it to breathe.

Whimpering and crying, she screams, "I hate you."

The words come a bit more broken now. "I hate you."

But all I can concentrate on is how good she feels pinned between my cock and hand.

"Good girl," I growl as I turn my head so I can kiss the inside of her arm. "Ride me like I'm your whore."

She cries out, her other hand grabbing the one I have on her pussy. She spasms so hard, she jerks off me. My cock slides out, soaking wet and throbbing so hard it's painful.

Not wasting any time, craving the taste of her before my senses fade, I drop to my knees, spread apart her cheeks, and shove my face into her pussy as I inhale deep.

Fucking.

Heaven.

She cries out. Tries to crawl away from me as she jerks beneath my tongue.

But I just follow her.

I'll always follow her.

Anywhere she fucking goes.

Because she's mine.

My wife.

My mate.

My fucking craving.

TWENTY-EIGHT

HER

I scream as his teeth dig into my thigh. The bite of a vampire triggers a dopamine release in their prey so they're less likely to fight back. Like a mosquito numbing the area as they feed. But I don't feel good about this. I don't feel pleasure despite the orgasm still ripping through me. It's too much, too intense, all the rage and pain and fear of the last few hours pouring out of me like an open dam. Dear gods, I do not want this. Don't want him.

I want him to stop. To listen to me. To show me he cares enough to want to listen.

But once again, he is ignoring my screams.

Just like he did when I was strapped to that chair.

His arms are around my waist, holding me down as he spreads my cheeks open, and his tongue is lapping from my pussy to my ass, then burying itself deep in one hole and then the other. I cry out as I struggle to get away, crawling across the bed on my stomach. But he's too strong for me to stop without my magic.

My chest heaving, I sob, "You're hurting me." The words are broken, barely discernible even to me. But the truth of them resonates in my soul. I needed time to think, to stop feeling so damn raw before he fucked me. But he couldn't even give me that. He doesn't care enough to respect my pain, my boundaries. He's simply taking what he wants without any thought to me.

My mouth pressing into the sheets, I whisper, "You're breaking us, Varius."

Breaking me all over again.

Breaking my heart.

My will to fix this. Us.

And yet he does not stop.

He actually groans as he crawls after me as I try to get away. He rims my ass with a finger as he removes his fangs from me to tongue my pussy. I cry out as he fills my ass with one slow stroke of his hand.

"I'm going to fuck you with my fingers up your ass," he says as he wraps his other arm around my waist and lifts me up onto my knees. I tremble as I try to get away, my limbs weak and sluggish from blood loss, but one strong hand on the lower part of my back keeps me exactly where he wants me.

"Varius, *please*," I beg. "Just stop...please just stop."

He lines his cock up with my pussy, and on a long groan that I feel all the way between my thighs, he pushes in deep.

"That's it," he grunts as he thrusts inside me. "This is exactly where I want to be. Nestled inside your pussy and ass." His finger works its way in deeper, moving in rhythm to his hips.

I gasp at how much he's stretching me.

"You're so godsdamn wet," he groans. Pulling out, he grabs a fistful of the sheet between my legs and wipes it across my pussy, making me clench. Then his dick's pushing back in, filling me even more so than before.

"Fuck, yeah. That's it, baby. Squeeze me just like that."

His hand lands on my ass.

I yelp.

He smacks me again, and tears blister my eyes as it feels like he just wants to hurt me. Just wants to punish me like he did when I was strapped to that chair.

"Varius, please don't –"

Ignoring me, he starts to move his fingers once more. He presses my face into the sheets, and I gasp hard and fast as the pain in my ass is matched only by the pain in my heart.

I want him to stop.

I just want him to stop.

He groans. "That's it, baby. You're taking my cock and finger so well. Can you take another one?"

I shake my head. "Don't."

"I bet you can," he says as he pulls his finger out of my ass. Then two tips push up against it. "I bet you're such a good girl that you can take three of my fingers while my cock is stretching this beautiful pussy of yours."

I whimper.

Try to crawl away.

He slaps my ass again, then pushes down on my upper back, forcing me to stay still. He pulls his cock out. Another tip of a finger joins the other two already there and then all three digits spear their way inside of me.

I cry out as he stretches my ass. "It's too much! Varius, stop."

"No, baby. You've got this. Just relax and let me in."

His fingers push in deeper. His voice turns more ragged. "That's a good girl. Take me in just like that. Fuck, baby. Yeah, just like that."

"I don't want to. I want you to stop."

He starts to thrust them inside of me, his palm hitting my ass, he goes so deep. I close my eyes, fighting back the tears I'm tired of giving him. Burying his fingers deep, he lines his cock back up with my pussy.

I tense, knowing there's no way he is going to fit without tearing me.

"That's a good girl," he groans as he slowly starts to fill my pussy with his cock. "Fuck, if I could make a duplicate of myself, I'd be licking this pretty pussy at the same time."

Despite myself, I whimper, imagining his head there, his tongue stroking me while I'm filled with his cock. His free hand comes around and wraps around my face, cupping my cheek. His fingers push against my lips. I try to turn my head, but his grip is too solid, and he slips his fingers inside, now fucking me in every hole.

He grunts and groans as I squeeze my eyes tighter still. "Fuck, baby. I'm going to come. I'm going to fill this hot, wet pussy of yours and make you pregnant."

He thrusts into me, smacking our hips together as he fingers me in my other holes. I try to stop the orgasm from building, the heat from growing in my stomach and making my toes curl. I don't want this. I don't want –

I cry out as it splashes over me, spreading out from my pussy to set off every nerve in my body. I jerk and scream and come so damn hard, I forget how to breathe. I can only pant, only drag in great big lungfuls of air that come out as harsh little whispers that leave me light-headed. My eyes close as the orgasm shakes me, even stronger than the last one. He thrusts inside my ass and pussy and mouth a few more times and then comes inside me on a roar.

"Can you feel that, baby?" he pants. "Can you feel my cum filling you up?" He tenses his cock, making me feel it, making me jump.

I whimper as I nod frantically, tears flowing down my cheeks. The release is too damn intense, breaking me apart as all the emotions that have been beating me down for the last few hours come spilling out.

The rage and pain over my torture.

The fear of losing our child after having just learned of her existence.

The agony when he left me broken for hours.

The anger over his thick-headed stupidity when he got back and called me crazy.

The heart-wrenching sorrow over thinking I killed him when I stabbed him in the chest.

The fear when he bit me.

The anger when he ignored my pleas.

The pain where he broke us all over again.

There is also the unwanted lust and the confusion about what is happening, about what he is, and how I feel. And dear gods, I don't know how I feel.

My hatred of him is clashing with my love. My disgust of him touching me is going to war with my desperation to be held by him, soothed by him. I'm terrified that his treatment of me in that chair was not a one time thing, but I don't know if I have the strength to walk away. Don't know if leaving him will hurt more than staying.

All those things get tossed into a massive pot behind my eyes, and it boils over down my cheeks. I cry with my head pressed to the sheets and my ass in the air, sobbing out my heart and all the emotions that are leaving me wrecked.

And fuck, I'm so confused.

So godsdamn confused about what is happening.

He falls to the side, his cock and fingers slipping out of me. There is a soft *thump* as he hits the mattress.

I don't look at him.

Can't look at him.

I'm just consumed by my tears, by the overwhelming emotions that are crippling me.

Hurting me.

Breaking me.

I told him to stop, and yet again, he did not.

How can we ever come back from this?

We can't.

We just fucking can't.

Bawling my eyes out, I wrap my arms around myself, giving me the comfort he does not.

TWENTY-NINE

HER

By the time morning comes, I'm all cried out. I have no more emotions left inside of me, but I've had time to think. To process what has happened.

And now I know three things.

One, Varius is not a zombie. Zombies don't breathe. They don't mumble in their sleep, and their wounds don't heal overnight. So he's something else. I would think he is a hybrid, but hybrids are infertile. So he has to be a monster Sau adopted from the Plane of Monsters or something. A creature that looks human that she decided to keep and raise as her own.

Two, I don't want anything to do with Varius fucking Shadow anymore. He tortured me. Then he raped me. And perhaps it wasn't violent, perhaps it wasn't cruel, but it was a violation of my trust. I asked him to stop, begged him to because I wasn't ready to be touched by the man who'd hurt me. I *told* him he was breaking us… and he did not care.

And three, I can't leave him. My father won't care what Varius is. He could be an actual slug, and Stefaan would still force me to honor the marriage contract drawn up between us due to all the perks it gives him. The connections. The money. The fucking prestige he has always been after. But even if he was willing to hide me, even if he cared about my happiness, I can't go to him. Can't go to anyone because I absolutely believe Varius' words when he said he would kill anyone who helped hide me.

So I am stuck with him in this life.

But that doesn't mean I have to be stuck with him in all the others.

I took his blood into me again last night. And he took more of mine. The bond has strengthened considerably, and I know if I just look inside it, I can feel all the love he has for me. The guilt over what he's done. The stuff he doesn't know how to say or show. Parts of it flickered into my fitful, sleepless dreams. But I don't want to look.

I don't want to forgive him.

I don't want to fix this anymore.

So here I am, sitting in the quiet of his room, with my back to the wall and the knife I used to stab him hanging loose in my hands. I cut away the front of my skirt and look down at my pussy. It smells of him, and I breathe that scent in, use it to give me the anger, the fuel for what I'm about to do.

Lowering the knife in my hands, I trace its tip along the tattoo on my pussy. **Property of Varius Shadow**

But he does not own me anymore. He might be able to force me to his bed and force me into being his bride, but I am no longer his.

So I breathe in deep and pick up the dildo I pulled out of the drawer. I put it in between my teeth, clenching it tight in preparation for the pain. My nostrils flare as my hand shakes, so I keep breathing until it calms. Until it steadies.

Once it does, I start cutting off the layers of skin that mark me as his.

Taking my power back, making myself *mine* again.

Tears burn my eyes as the agony rips through me. My teeth sink into the bright pink silicone, stopping at the rigid core inside it. Grunting, I force the knife to keep going, to keep peeling his name off me even as the pain builds.

Property of is gone.

Then **Varius**

Then fucking **Shadow**

Dropping my head back against the wall, I pant heavily as I close my eyes. I remove the dildo from between my teeth with a shaky hand. Then I grope for the healing wand that I took from the ensuite and point it at the bleeding patch of missing skin.

"Iactus," I mutter, breathing out harshly as the white light soothes the pain on my pussy. If only it could fix the shit inside.

I swallow hard as I sit here without his name on me. I feel both heavier and lighter at the same time. Happier and sadder. But less broken. I'm taking back the strength he took from me. I'm making it so no one else can hurt me but me. My own body. My own heart. Nothing about me is *his* any longer.

Now comes the second part of my plan – a part I'm not entirely sure will work. I don't want to die, don't want to leave Dayne all on his own, knowing the spiral he will fall into in my absence, but nor can I live like this. Knowing that death will not relieve me from Varius' shackles. So I flick off the tattooed piece of skin still stuck to the knife and then lift the blade to my wrist.

Once a blood bond is started, it must be paid for in one way or another.

We shared a lot of blood last night – way more than the few drops needed for the ritual to be sated. So maybe I have already paid most of the blood due. But...

I have also lost a lot between the fighting and the torture and Varius feeding from me. If it needs more than I have...

I shift the knife in my grip.

The blade skims across my skin, leaving goosebumps in its wake.

I don't want to die.

But I don't want to live like this either.

So I take a deep breath and close my eyes.

Then I slide the knife quickly across my skin.

THIRTY

HIM

"Are you fucking insane?" I rip the knife up as she slides it down her arm, my heart beating so damn loud that I can barely hear the words I'm screaming at her. My eyes go to where she cut, and relief hits me when I see I made it in time. The slice is barely more than a graze.

I throw the knife across the room, but she doesn't say a word. I pick up the healing wand beside her and shove it into her other hand. "Heal yourself," I snap, trying to get a rise out of her with the harshness of my tone because I'd rather take her fire, her fucking fury at me than seeing her like this.

Empty.

Emotionless.

Fucking suicidal.

"I told you you can't leave me," I snarl as I haul her to my chest. She lets me pull her without any resistance, without any of the 'fuck yous' she was all too happy to scream last night, and that is making me fucking *panic.*

Last I remember, she seemed fine. We talked in her room. I apologized for torturing her. I carried her up to my bed. She had her legs wrapped around my waist. Yeah, she was not happy with me, but she wasn't like *this.* She was angry with me, ready to make me pay and beg for forgiveness, but she wanted me to fix us. And I was willing. I told her that, didn't I?

"Talk to me," I demand. "Tell me why the fuck you just tried to kill yourself."

"I didn't," she says.

"You had a knife to your wrist!

"I wasn't trying to kill myself."

I clench my jaw, force my rage down so I can talk to her without screaming. "What were you doing then?"

She shrugs.

"Micha. What were you fucking doing?"

"I was trying to remove the blood bond."

"Remove –" I stop as I move away from her, holding her at arm's length so I can see her face. "We're bonded?"

"Unfortunately."

"When?"

She blinks, and there is a bit of soul back in her eyes that I could almost weep over. "What do you mean 'when?'"

"When did we bond?"

She looks at me like I'm crazy, and it's the most beautiful look in the world. She's coming back to me. Has a bit more fire in her veins. "When you asked me to bond with you," she says.

"No, we didn't. It didn't work." The words hurt like hel, but I'm fucking glad of that truth if it means she won't try to kill herself to try to remove it.

She blinks at me. And there's no mistaking the fire in her eyes now. "Oh, is that what you're going for now? Pretend like you couldn't fucking feel what I was going through as you tortured me? Or when you raped me last night? Did you not just focus on the pleasure so you could –"

My skin feels tight across my chest. "When did I rape –"

"When I said no and you didn't stop!" she screams before she clenches her fists and gets her anger back under control, shoved down in a deep dark depth where nothing can touch her. "I don't want to talk to you anymore," she says flatly.

"Micha, I swear to you, I don't know what you're talking about. I came home last night, you said no, and I stopped. Then we went to bed."

She doesn't say anything.

"Micha," I say, stepping closer to her, lifting her chin up to look at me. But her eyes are blank, not focused on me at all. A sickness pooling in my stomach, I look down at my chest. There's a hole and bloodstain right over my heart, and I stagger back as the realization of what happened hits me.

She fucking killed me.

My little monster.

She's nothing but a traitor like all the others.

My hands curl into fists as I am consumed with a need to hit something. To break it. To fucking *destroy* it like she's done to me. I've never thrown a tantrum before, never lost control even as a child. I've always thought people who did were weak and pathetic, but I fucking get it now. I get why her room looked how it did last night – how she just needed to get what was inside *out.*

Pivoting to the side, I grab hold of the dresser full of toys that I bought for us so we could experience all the firsts together, and I launch it across the room, straight through the door of the ensuite. She doesn't move, doesn't react, her assassin training keeping her poised, but I can smell her fear. Hear the rapid beat of her heart.

And I hate it.

I hate that I've made her scared of me.

But I can't stop the rage inside. Can't control it this time. If she was anyone else, she'd be dead on the floor already, bleeding out for her sins.

But she is mine.

Even in her fucking betrayal, she.

Is.

Mine.

Grabbing the top of the dresser, sticking my hands where the drawer no longer is, I lift the entire thing and throw that too. Then I grab her biceps and haul her to the feet, pulling her into the middle of the room. I clutch the top of her dress and rip it down the middle before she can even gasp.

"Get off me!" she screams, and there is panic there that cuts me down to my soul. Is this how she yelled at me last night? Frantic and terrified and helpless to stop me?

I can't fucking remember.

I can't remember an event that hurt her so deeply, and I am so pissed off at myself for that and at Mother for making that damn clause in the first place. I don't even know if it's me when the vampirism hits, or if I am fully consumed by a hunger I can't contain. If I black out and a primal beast remains, a vampire who's starving and living off the crumbs of life he gets to experience, or if I am aware the whole time. I want to believe that it's the former, that I didn't fucking *choose* to hurt what's mine, but I can't remember a godsdamn thing about it.

And in the end, it doesn't matter.

Because *she* remembers all of it. I can see it in her eyes. I can smell it in the pheromones coming off her, and it makes me want to destroy more shit.

But I can't right now because I need to check her over.

If I'm alive, then I must have fed from her. Micha's a strong witch; her magic must have healed me faster than that woman in the alley did – the first person I killed when my vampirism was activated.

I tear her dress from her and step back. Her arms go up to cover herself, but I'm looking at her neck, her arms, her chest, anywhere I might have bit her or simply grabbed her too hard in my desperation to feed. There are bruises. A lot of them. In the shape of my fingers.

My jaw locked, I say, "Turn around."

"Fuck you."

I dart behind her, using my enhanced speed now that she already knows I'm not a witch. She tries to turn, but I'm much faster, and I glance her body over. Red hand prints mar her ass. More bruises dot along her body, but there isn't anything outside of love bites and grabs. Whatever I did last night, at least it wasn't overly violent. Wherever I bit her, I must have healed with the powers of my vampire side.

"How many secrets are you fucking hiding?" she asks as she spins back to face me, but I don't answer because my eyes have caught sight of her pussy.

She's fucking cut a patch away. And my heart breaks at the bareness of her skin, at the lack of the ink that I put there. The physical rejection of my claim.

Wails ricochet inside my skull, growing in pitch until they become banshees that wash out all other noise. My heart slams itself against its cage over and over in a desire to get out, to touch her and be certain, but she told me not to do that. So all I can do is look.

And break in utter silence.

"You cut my name off?" I rasp out, my fingers clenching into fists.

She lifts her chin stubbornly. "I'm not yours anymore."

"The fuck you aren't," I snap as I reach for the back of her neck before dropping my hand and striding towards her instead. She takes a step back for every one I make until she bumps into the wall. Her pulse quickens, but she doesn't cower, doesn't recede back inside her walls. She lifts her chin, daring me to do my worst.

Pressing both hands on the wall beside her face, I lean in and duck my head. "Whether we're blood bonded or not, little monster, you are *mine*. I will find you in the afterlife. I will find you in the next life. You will never be fucking rid of me." *And I will make you fall in love with me again. I will spend the rest of all my lives following you around until you fucking come to remember that I. Am.* Yours.

My heart pounds, those words stuck in my throat, but I can't bring myself to say them, to put them in the air for her to reject when I'm this raw.

So I turn away from her. Removing my blood-stained clothes, I pull on a pair of shorts, then head for the door so I can go find a fucking brother to spar with.

Except I stop when I catch sight of her patch of skin. A clean cut. One piece with everything on it. Bending down, I pick it up with a shaky hand, then walk over to grab the knife so she can't cut herself again in my absence.

Striding across the room, I make my way to the door. I hesitate before stepping through it, wishing I knew how to cross the divide I've made between us. I turn to look at her. She isn't looking at me. Isn't looking at anything, back in that void inside her mind.

My knuckles tight, I step out into the hall before the sun is even up, then shut it softly behind me.

THIRTY-ONE

HIM

"Are you sure you're okay?" Enoch asks as he stares up at me from the floor of the gym, nursing his swollen jaw.

"Fine," I say as I kick his sword back at him. "You need to get better at hand-to-hand. You rely too strongly on your magic. What happens if you lose it?"

Blowing out a breath, he works his jaw, then grabs his sword and climbs back to his feet.

"I'd get into the habit of carrying a gun," he says. "What I wouldn't do is use a sword." He scoffs. "I don't know why all the fantasy books keep to medieval shit. So many natural things burn so well. Did they just get rid of all of that, as well as teenage boys just wanting to fuck about with shit when they were world building? Like, seriously? Do you know what gunpowder was originally used for? Trying to make an immortal elixir. You're telling me, no one in all the fantasy worlds ever decided to fuck around with materials just to see what they did? It doesn't make *any sense*."

He's talking shit just to stall, and the irritation I have is growing. "Would you rather we lose the swords?"

He looks at me warily. He knows I'm holding back. He's a shit swordsman, so I'm not hacking at him like he's Khalid or Maddox. Hel, even Krypto's footwork is better than his.

But Khalid is in bed with his girl, well deserved after the shit they went through. Antonio forced him to beat her while he touched himself. Khalid then cut off his own hand, the one he used to hit her, unable to bear having it attached to him. For hurting his girl is an unforgivable sin.

And Maddox is out hunting, rebuilding his stash of dead bodies, and Leno refuses to let me spar with his dog. Says it gives him too much anxiety.

So I'm stuck with the bottom-of-the-barrel Enoch.

"No," my brother groans as he hacks his sword through the air at his feet. "I don't need you kicking me in the balls this morning."

"You ever planning on using them?"

"I use them all the time –"

"Not your dick. Your balls."

He looks at me warily as I shift into a fool's guard position, the blade pointed at the ground in front of me and off to the side as I bend my knees, ready to move forward or back as needed. He holds his up in a roof guard, his blade pointed back, with his hands up by his head, reminiscent of a baseball bat.

"Is this a very weird way of asking if I'm planning on having kids?" he asks as he darts forward and swings for my head.

I bring my sword up to parry. His blade slides off the tip of mine as he completes his arc. He swivels his wrists, swinging it around over his head, continuing to carry that momentum for a second blow. I raise my sword once more as I shift to the side. The clink of the metal resonates around the gym, cut by the heavy beat of his feet as he barrels past me. I lunge forward as he tries to stop and turn, and my sword raps him on the shoulder. That hand drops as he shakes it out with a small yelp.

"You are pathetic," I say.

His sword slips from his other hand as he holds it palm out and shouts, "No, I am your – ow!"

The pommel of my sword knocks him in the head even as I'm tossed backwards by his telekinesis. The fucker is too predictable, and I threw my blade at him before he managed to fire off his shot.

"Why the fuck aren't we wearing face masks?" he yells as his magic releases me. He's backpedaling, one hand to his forehead, and I twist in the air so I'm facing the ground and extend my arms out in front of me with my elbows slightly bent. I roll over my head as I hit the ground, push off, pivot, then charge at him as he still has his hand over his face, blocking his vision.

He lowers his arm just as I slide on my knees and wrap both of my arms around his right leg. I pivot around him, bringing up a foot to plant behind him. My left arm rises up between his legs, slamming up into his crotch as the other wraps around his waist.

He gasps, then creaks, "Oh, come –" as I arch backwards, flipping his body over mine and slamming him onto the mat.

"*Ooooonnn...*"

I roll onto my feet.

"I swear...if you kick me while I'm down," he says as he lies there wheezing at the ceiling. "I won't marry whoever the fuck you want me to marry."

"Stormie Green." His childhood crush. We need to forge alliances and *now*. Antonio was playing with us last night, testing his experiment in the field while trying to psyche us out, showing us what we'll be up against if we go against him. The wolf was sick, probably already dying. How long until he perfects his craft and manages to create a whole army of them?

Whereas my thoughts take a darker turn, Enoch's clearly doesn't. He sits up, a blush spreading across his cheeks. He rubs a hand over his head, and the tired gecko mohawk he has gets a second life as he uses his telekinesis to put all the strands back in place.

I look at him dryly; what a waste of magic. "She isn't even here," I say.

"When she coming?"

"Few weeks if you acc–"

"I accept."

I frown. *I bet I could've kicked him in the balls. Got out a bit more of my rage.*

His eyes narrow slightly as he studies me. "You don't look happy about it."

"I'm fine."

"How are you and Mi–"

"Get up," I say as I pick up my sword. "I want to go another round."

He snorts. "Ain't happening. I've let you hit me for over an hour. I'm starving. I haven't even had breakfast yet, and I don't want to risk a blow to my balls when we're all fucking Khalid's girl later. I have to last as long as Ez, or he's never going to let it go."

My fingers tighten on my sword. Yet another reason why I want to go another round. After we got home last night, Khalid told me about what he needed to complete the bond.

"I need you...and the rest of our brothers..." Khalid's jaw clenches, the words heavily strained. His dark eyes flash with a desire to kill everything around him, but this is the price of a blood bond. The djinnis who gifted us the ability to choose our own mates didn't do so out of kindness. They wanted entertainment, and nothing makes them happier than seeing witches tear each other apart by hurting those

they love.

"What?" I press, itching to leave this conversation and get back to my girl. I need to make sure she's okay. I need to fucking apologize for what I did to her.

He glances away. Breathes out, battling with his anger before looking back at me. "I need you all to fuck her and come inside her at the same time she does."

My lungs stop as the very soul of me freezes. I can't do that to Micha. I don't want to do this. She's the first person I've been with, and I want her to be the last.

"Are there any other options?"

"No."

Fuck. I want to tell him I'm not going to do it, but he's already started the blood bond. If he doesn't complete it, it will kill him. Unless I killed his girl.

And dear fucking gods am I tempted to go that route. To choose mine over his.

"So will you do it?" Khalid asks softly.

My jaw clenching, I turn and head over to the weapons rack and place my sword down. The thought of doing it is making me sick, but if I don't participate, then Khalid dies.

It's the same fucking scenario all over again: Khalid or Micha. Which one do I hurt?

She hates me enough to risk killing herself; I doubt she'll care if I fuck another. The only person who does is me.

"I'm going for a run," I say. "I'll be inside the wards if Khalid asks."

"Do you want company?"

"You asking?" I call over my shoulder.

"Yeah. I'm up for talking bring as long as you ain't hitting me."

Deciding I want to be alone so I can push myself as fast as I can go, I say, "I'll pass." As the door swings shut behind me, I hear a soft, "Thank gods."

The house is still quiet. No one else is awake yet. Mother is normally up at this time to make us all breakfast, but the kitchen is empty. She undoubtedly needs her rest after what was done to her, but I'm of half a mind to drag her out of bed like I did Enoch. The bitch's curse made me hurt my wife. No. *I* hurt my wife.

I just can't remember how because of her.

But as mad as I am at her, most of my anger is directed at me, and waking her up won't do anything to help with that. So I head outside, dressed only in a pair of shorts. Despite the early hour, the Floridian day's already packing heat.

The door closes behind me, and I take off in a jog, but as soon as I'm under the cover of the trees, I push myself as fast as I can go, riding myself hard, wanting to feel the burn of my lungs and the ache of my muscles. It's a poor attempt at a distraction. My thoughts are all too easily keeping up.

She cut off her fucking tattoo.

Removed my mark from her skin and threw it away like it was nothing. *Almost as if she's given up on us.*

Snarling, I pivot to the right, heading towards the edge of our property. The ward shimmers up ahead, crackling with blue energy. Rudy didn't have any issues putting it back up. Talon didn't use brute force to break it. He simply gave it the command to go down, which makes me think he has not turned against the Family. He's just turned against me.

Because I killed his best friend?

My chest tightens.

Or because he knows I'm a hybrid?

Either way, I will not hesitate to put him down. I never do. Never give mercy.

Except when it comes to *her.*

My teeth grind together as my legs pump harder. What the fuck am I going to do with her now? If the reaper learns she tried to kill me, he'll kill her regardless of my wishes. Her rage is a threat to this Family, and with us going to war, we cannot afford to be tearing each other apart from the inside. We won't survive.

If she wasn't pregnant, I might take Maddox up on his offer to help me break her and remold her, but his methods might trigger a miscarriage. So I only have two options.

Make her fall back in love with me – something I'm not certain I can do.

Or make her fall in love with this Family so she'll never betray it.

She already likes Maddox. My eyes narrow as my chest burns with jealousy. But I force my thoughts to keep going, to form a plan –however much it fucking hurts– to get her loyalty to this Family. Despite being a little shit most of the time, my youngest brother can be charming if he wants to. He sweeps women off their feet, lures them into his trap so he can butcher them and throw their bodies into the cooler he has in his shadows. He needs their meat to be able to shapeshift into bigger bodies as magic still obeys the law of nature, and mass doesn't come from nothing.

If I get him to put on the charm, to make her *like* him more... My nostrils flare as I think about her laughing with him when she won't even look at me. Talking to him when she won't even tell me hello. The fucking little shit. I'm going to kill him.

The ward bites into my skin – a dozen bolts of electricity arcing through my body, forcing my legs to lock, my body to freeze as it captures me. My muscles tense as the pain intensifies until I can't breathe, my lungs twisting inside my chest, spasming so godsdamn tight not even air can get through them.

And then I'm released, the ward deciding that I am, in fact, enough of a witch for it to allow me through.

I stagger forward, my hands on my knees, sweat beading across my face and neck as I swallow in great big gulps of air. Mother *fucker* that hurt. I squeeze my eyes shut for just a moment, using the pain to finish my thoughts.

I need to get Maddox to charm her, to make her want to

stay for him rather than for me. I need to get my other brothers to do the same. She didn't have a great family life growing up, and I know she secretly craves one. And then I need to figure out a fucking way not to kill them all in my jealousy when they have her full attention and I'm still begging for crumbs.

"Fuck!"

Lunging to my right, I slam my fist into a tree. The wood groans and creaks as the branches sway. The burst of energy explodes up my arm as my knuckles protest my idiocy of trying to take on a fucking hundred-plus-year-old elm. And yet, I try again, swinging my other fist into it, bruising the knuckles in that hand too. Making them swollen. Bruised and scraped. Perhaps even broken. But I relish the pain; it's so much nicer than the shit in my chest.

Collapsing to my knees, I breathe out heavily and close my eyes again. My teeth clench, my jaw locked so tight that pain radiates down my neck.

Fucking hel. I've fucked up.

But I'm going to fix this.

I'm going to make her love my brothers too much not to hurt them. And as a trump card, I'm also going to bring her best friend into this Family. If Dayne's a part of it, there's no way she'd turn against it. And I'll make her see that I'm the best one to lead – that Leno is too fucking soft, that Khalid does not want the position, that Enoch and Ezriel aren't smart enough to play the game, that Maddox is too feared by our allies, and that Rudy is too sweet. She might still want to kill me after all is said and done, but she won't if she knows that will most likely mean everyone else she loves will die too.

She also has a sister she loves, my brain points out.

Then I'll bring her into the Family as well. She's sixteen, too young to get married for my tastes despite it being legal in many states, but she can get engaged to Maddox. Stefaan might wish to save her to sell to another Family, to build ties outside of just ours, but everyone has a price, and I will pay whatever it takes to have her and Dayne.

With a plan forming, my panic-fueled rage calms enough for me to stand. My hands ache, but I wiggle my fingers, and none of them seem to be broken. Turning on the spot, I head back through the ward, clenching my teeth when it zaps me, though not as strongly as before, and then make my way towards the house so I can grab my phone.

THIRTY-TWO

HIM

As I reach the drive, I catch the hum of an engine. I turn my head to see Maddox coming up behind me. He parks by the house and steps out as I wait for him.

"You look like shit," he says with a grin. "I take it Micha didn't just accept you back like a good little breedmare?"

I take a step towards him, my eyes narrowing, and he backpedals around to the trunk of the car, still grinning like a fool. Grabbing the latch, he says, "Maybe this will cheer you up," then pops it open before I can get to him.

I stop at the smell of a werewolf.

My eyes drop to see Zita hogtied in the trunk of the car. Her violet eyes are full of pain, the silver chains around her seeping poison into her veins. They're not made out of the silver from Earth – a soft material that does nothing. The chain, just like my silver knives, is from Blódyrió, the world werewolves and vampires originally come from – used to bind wolves on the night of the full moon and the nights on either side of them.

The Hunt there is wild and dangerous. The call of the moon can't be denied like it can be here on Earth, and it makes them crazy, feral, not of any mind other than a need to kill. Artemis, the Grecian Goddess of the Moon and Hunt, is even known to visit on the nights of the blood moons. Dressed in red garb, she's given rise to the tales of Red Riding Hood.

It is not a time for most beings to be out, let alone pups who have just hit their ascension and have shifted for the first time. So a material was made, crafted out of Artemis' moonlight itself. A wolf is bound in silver chain, their arms and legs wrapped, as is their chest. And when they're strong enough to break free, then they are strong enough to join the Hunt.

Although Zita is well past her ascension, she is young and has never been to Blódyrió, hasn't built up any sort of tolerance to its silver. Her body's spasming uncontrollably as sweat beads down her face and back. She looks pale, a touch away from death, but there is still defiance in her eyes. Still a desire to stab us both.

"I bet she knows a lot about what Antonio's been doing," Maddox says with pride.

She laughs, a broken chuckle that's twisted in agony. I glance down at her, and she holds my gaze with foggy eyes. "You idiot," she rasps. "I'm the damn...omega." The most hated wolf in the pack. The one whose entire purpose is to be a stress-relief punching bag, and because of that, they are killed all too often. "They don't tell me..."

I reach forward and grab the trunk of the car, then slam it shut.

"She can't be the omega," Maddox sputters, but I don't give a shit. "She's too pretty to be the omega."

"You were supposed to be hunting," I snap. "You said you didn't have enough bodies –"

He blinks as his mind shifts gears. "Don't worry. I got them."

"How many?"

"Three."

My jaw tics. "You need more than that –"

"And I'll go out again tonight," he says calmly.

"You're not going out again until Dayne gets here."

He blinks again, but this time, his brain doesn't catch up.

"I need bodies," he says.

"Which you were supposed to get last night. If you were not too busy chasing a useless bitch –"

"That better have been the word for a female wolf," he says softly.

"Are you claiming her?"

"I don't have to claim her to be a gentleman."

I snort. "You might be able to change into Khalid, but you can't pull him off."

A small smile twitches at his lips. "Tell me what's really bothering you. Because I have more than enough bodies for now, and Rudy can easily pick up some more for me."

"You're fussy."

"I'll give him a list of requirements. Now tell me at what angle do I need to pull to get that stick out of your ass."

My eyes narrow.

But he holds my glare, never wavering. *"Because I care about you. You know you're not alone, right?"* The words he said as he tried to stop me from torturing Micha come back to me, and I blow out a heavy breath.

"Micha tried to kill herself this morning," I say tightly.

His eyes widen, calculating and confused, and I can see his gears shifting. Micha isn't the type to commit suicide over a bit of pain. She's the sort to bide her time until she can kill the fucker who hurt her.

"What did you do?" Maddox asks softly.

"I took her magic. She can't control it anymore."

"But Mom healed her."

"Not well enough."

"Shit." He turns to the house. "You think the fault is with Mom?"

"I don't give a fuck about her right now."

Maddox spins back around to face me. "Think about how much magic she used, bruh. She could be dying."

There is a flash of hope inside me, that Micha can get her magic back if I find her a better healer. That I can fix at least one part of what I've broken. And right on the heels of that is choking concern for the woman who's done everything she could to protect this family.

Fuck. Today is going to be one of those fucking days.

Feeling a headache coming on, I head for the door. "I'll talk to her. Tell Rudy what you need and get rid of Zita. She is of no use to us as an omega."

"She can still –"

"Get rid of her Maddox. You'll be marrying Lou Black as soon as I can arrange it with her father."

"What the fuck –"

I shut the door on him and head towards Mother's room, but I detour at the sound of someone singing in the kitchen. A dark country song with long drawn out words and deep vocals.

"The sun iiiiis...only rising,
The dew's noooooot...even burned,
The coloooooooors...are all enticing,
But, Mamaaaaaaaa...I'm ready to come home.

Oh, my daaaaays.

Coming hooooome.

I sit by a laaaaaake...in the mountaaaaaaains

Throwing in coiiiiiins...to cross the black,
I daaaaaance...in the aaaaaarms...of my loveeeeer
Feeling her chill across my back."

I find Mother standing at the counter, both of her hands on it, a walking cane lying across the wood in front of her. Her eyes are closed as she continues to sing. Our monster sister ripples beneath her hands, the zebrano wood shifting, the knots in it racing up and down in movement to her tone. I lean against the threshold of the door, studying her, seeing if she looks too pale, if there is too little strength in her limbs, too much waver in the pitch of her voice.

"The Devil's come a'knockiiiing
And I am opening up my dooooor
Offering her a beer
Then grabbing up my coat

And though I untiiiiie...my shoes
The laceeeeees...are still used.

Oh, my daaaaays.

Oh, my daaaaays.

Oh, Mamaaaaa,

I'm coming hooooome."

"You're singing that with a lot of passion," I say as I step inside. "Thinking of seeing Hel soon?"

She looks at me as she runs her hands across the wood, a slow pat before she hobbles towards me. I look pointedly at her cane. She does not pick it up.

"Mother," I say, my voice low.

"I'm not dying yet."

"The cane doesn't help if you don't use it."

She waves a hand. "The cane is there to whack you boys upside the head." She arches a perfect eyebrow. "Do I need it now?"

My eyes narrow. "You tell me," I say softly, my anger at her building again now that I know she isn't about to die on us. "Did you purposely not heal Micha's hands all the way?"

Her eyebrow drops. "Of course not. What's wrong?"

"She can't use her magic."

She purses her lips. "I thought this might happen. When one suffers a great amount of trauma like she did, they can create a mental block."

"Are you saying it's all in her head?" I demand.

"I'm saying I fixed her hands."

I stare at her, looking for secrets she's hiding. "If you're lying to me –"

"I have no reason to split you two apart," she says. "You have caused a bigger divide than I ever could have."

My entire body fucking stills, but I can't refute the truth of her words. I start to turn, to head upstairs to let Micha know her magic isn't gone, but then I stop and twist around to face her again. I push my senses out, my ears and nose twitching to make sure no one else is nearby. Still, I lower my voice. "The blood bond," I say. "Is there a reason I would not be able to feel it?"

She stares at me for a moment, thinking it over. Then she says, "Only if she lied about –"

I take a step towards her. "Don't you dare try to make me paranoid about her again."

She lifts her chin. "I didn't realize I raised a fool. You can't blindly trust her now, not after what you –"

"We bonded before that," I say. "But try to come between us again, no matter how minuscule, or speak a single bad word about her, and I will sell you to Aleric."

Fire blazes at me behind her eyes, and the counter shifts with a cold crawl. But I don't give a damn. "We need the alliance," I say softly. "Anything to protect the family, right Mother?"

The fire in her eyes grows hotter, but she jerks her head. "How much blood have you exchanged?"

"Enough." I don't tell her I must've drunk enough to heal a lethal stab wound. If she knows Micha doesn't just *want* to kill me, but has tried, she will risk being married to Aleric to save me. There's nothing she won't do to protect us; the only reason she didn't sense what happened last night is due to her current exhaustion. A part of me aches over the fact that I am about to cause her the most pain she has felt in decades when I kill Talon. Or rather, when Khalid kills him. As much as I want his death to be at my hands for setting up Micha, Khalid is the reaper, and he is absolutely playing that card on this for what he was forced to do to his girl.

"Are you sure?" she asks.

"She can feel me," I say.

"Then you should be able to feel her. Curses don't affect so–" She stops. Frowns.

"What?"

"I need to get breakfast started."

"Mother," I warn.

"I have a suspicion. If it turns out to be anything, then I'll let you know. Now either help cook or get out." She turns from me, and only the frailty of her walk has me stopping from demanding she tells me now.

My shoulders tense, I head upstairs to my office. I dig out the piece of Micha's skin from my pocket as I enter. My chest tightens as I lay it gently on my desk. I lick my thumb, then use it to wipe away the blood covering my name.

Fucking hel.

She hates me so much, she skinned herself.

Tearing my eyes away from it, I grab one of the spare phones I have in my desk and key in Stefaan's number. I pace as we talk about purchase prices for his daughter. He starts off with a much lower dowry offer for Lou than he did Micha on the basis that he will be losing out on cementing any ties with other Families.

"Our territory covers nearly a sixth of America," I reply.

"And you've just gone to war," he counters.

"You think we'll lose?"

"I think it's too early to say."

A humorless smile curls a corner of my lips. "Fine, then I accept your offer as a down payment, but *when* we win this war, I will see the rest of it."

He laughs. "Agreed."

"Now about Dayne…"

"I'll throw him in for free if you promise me the first kid of Lou's that comes out as a shapeshifter."

I don't say anything for a moment. It is my right to sell any member of this Family, but I am banking on Maddox's help with Micha. Then again, he doesn't need to know until all is said and done, and once Lou and Dayne get here, I will not need his help any longer. He might be my brother, but I chose blood over Micha once already and I will do so again later today when I help Khalid complete his blood bond, but that will be the last time.

She needs to learn she can trust me, that I won't ever put her back in that chair. So I will prove it over and over again. For the rest of my life if that is what it takes. No one else will ever come above her again.

"You have a deal then. I expect them both to be here tomorrow."

"Tomorrow won't work. Dayne is on a job in Europe, and Lou is my baby girl. Give me at least a week with her."

"You've had sixteen years."

"I've had two weeks since I got my head out of my ass

thanks to your fiancee. I'm trying to make up for those sixteen years."

"Then you shouldn't have sold her."

"A week," he cuts in just as I'm about to hang up. "Or she doesn't go at all."

Annoyance flares through me. "Then give Dayne's job to another and send him here as soon as he's back." I click end call, then pull up a contact called Quinton. He's the same guy I've had on Dayne since the beginning, protecting him from the shadows. The same guy who got caught out and tortured by his charge too, but during that time, he learned things about the two of them that he would not have otherwise; people aren't as careful with what they say when they think they're talking to a dead person.

So I know details about the network they have in place if they ever need to go on the run. A network I'll tear apart piece by piece if she tries to fucking use it. Texting Quinton, I ask: *You still on Dayne?*

Quinton: *Yes. We're in France. Need me to drag him back?*

Varius: *No, but escort him straight here as soon as he lands. If you lose him, you die. If he dies, you die.*

Quinton: *Understood.*

Tossing my phone onto my desk, I bite back a curse. But with the smell of omelets wafting up from the kitchen, I know I can't put this off for any longer. Khalid wants to do the ritual right after breakfast.

So I leave my office and head into my room. Micha is sitting against the wall where I found her this morning, and my heart trips in my chest at the thought that she managed it this time. But there's no blood around her, and her chest still moves.

Swallowing hard, I walk over to her and squat down in front of her. "I talked to Mother," I say.

She doesn't respond.

"She says it's a mental block that's stopping your magic."

Her eyes stay distant, like she cannot see me at all. My stomach twists, hating this side of her.

"Micha. Did you hear me?" Of course she fucking heard me. I'm only a few inches away from her ear. "I didn't take your magic."

Her eyes don't move, but there is a flicker of heat inside them. Anger, absolutely. I am wording things as an utter bastard just to get a rise out of her, to break through this terrifying wall she's erecting. "The issue's all in your head." I reach out and touch her arm. "If you'd just –"

Her head snaps forward, nearly cracking with my nose, then her right hook follows it immediately. I dodge out of the way, not wanting her to hurt her hands.

"Don't you fucking touch me," she snaps. "You purchased me for a womb, not a wife. I will suffer this life with you, I will bear your heirs and marry you if this baby survives to term, and I will be the perfect wife you want in public, but behind closed doors, you will stay the *fuck* away from me."

"Micha –"

But she's already falling back inside her walls.

My jaw tics. "Khalid needs us all to fuck his girl for his blood bond. We're doing it after breakfast."

Her eyes harden, but there's not a single flicker of care in them. "Have fun," she sneers. "Because I'm already pregnant and I'm not fucking you for another six months."

"I'm not going six months without sex," I say irritably.

"Then get a whore."

"I don't need a whore when I have a –"

"You have *nothing*," she snaps, and if looks could kill, I'd be wearing my intestines as a necklace. "Now go get your fucking dick wet and leave me the fuck alone."

Standing abruptly, I grab a shirt and storm out, getting dressed when I get in the hall. My brothers are all already at the table, talking shit. Khalid's girl is helping Mother lay the plates out, and I take my seat in silence.

Maddox glances at me, worry in his eyes, but I ignore him. Stabbing at my food, I don't say a word throughout the entire meal, and as soon as we're all done, I stand. I want to get this damn blood bond done with.

Khalid's eyes find mine, and there is a calculation there I don't like. I keep my face schooled, all thoughts of Micha drowned out by the duty I must do.

To protect my brother.

So his life isn't taken as payment by the blood bond.

So my torture of Micha to save him in the first place wasn't for nothing.

Even still, he approaches me in the hall as the rest of our brothers put on their blindfolds.

"Is Micha okay with this?" he asks softly. "I know you started to care about –"

"It doesn't bother her." And that just fucking hurts to say out loud.

"Are *you* okay with this? You didn't take a single bite of breakfast."

I'm so tempted to tell him I claimed Micha, then tortured her just to get him to hit me. To punish me for what I did to her, but I don't. Because I don't trust the words I spew to stop then, don't trust the emotional dam leaking inside of me. And if he finds out just how much she means to me, Khalid might stop me from taking part in the blood bond. To him, it is an unforgivable sin if a man cheats on his partner. If Micha is okay with this, then that is different. He accepts that open relationships exist.

But he'd rather die than help me hurt the woman I have claimed. Or he normally would.

In this instance, I don't know what he would do. If he would force me as reaper – for the good of the Family, so he could bond with his *kira* and find her in the next life. Or if he would still refuse to let me hurt the one I love.

And I can't take that risk. I would rather suffer than lose him. After all the shit he's been through, he deserves to be happy.

So I say, "I'm fine."

"Varius —"

"I'm fine." Dismissing him, I put on my black blindfold. Khalid might need us to fuck his girl, but he does not want any of us to see her naked. To see her face as she comes. Not wanting to see her either, to see anyone but my damn wife, I tie it tight. Then I wait in the hall with all my other brothers as Khalid and his girl go into their room.

Nearly an hour later, Khalid comes out.

And then it's our turn, one by one, to go in.

THIRTY-THREE

HER

As much as I'm trying not to think about what Varius is doing in this moment, I can still see him fucking her. He has his hands in her long gorgeous hair as he's railing her from above, grunting and groaning and talking to her like she's fucking special. He holds eye contact until he leans down to suck her giant titties into his mouth. Then he's coaxing her into an orgasm, talking her through the tight fit of his cock.

"That's it, baby. Just relax for me. Gods, you feel so good around my cock. Much better than Micha. Fuck, baby, you are taking me so well. Squeeze me just like that."

Screaming, I jump to my feet and slam a fist in the wall. Then I clutch my head in both my hands and curl inwards on another scream.

I only have myself to blame for this. I told him to go get his dick wet, but I was pissed off and hurt, and at the time, it seemed like a good idea to give myself another reason to hate him. Another sin to remember so I don't give in to his attentions, no matter how intense they get.

"I don't want him back," I rasp as I squeeze my head in my hands. "I don't care what he does with her."

Tears burn my throat, calling me a fucking liar.

So I press my hand to my neck and think about how he raped me last night. How he bit me, nearly killed me. How I lay in his arms, bleeding out, feeling like a lamb to be killed for his substance. My life under his.

Not an equal.

Just a breedmare to be used and discarded.

I hold on to those feelings, use them to regain control of my breathing, to grab both sides of my heart and stop it from ripping apart completely. I can do this. I can survive this marriage. I can watch him take mistress after mistress so he doesn't go without sex, and I can learn not to give a damn. It'll take time for the pain to stop, but eventually it will.

His cock slides into her hot, wet pussy. He's groaning in her ear. "Fuck, baby. You feel so damn good."

Digging my nails into my neck, I force those thoughts to keep going. To sear those images in my mind so I will never forgive him. Never waver even when he looks at me like my silence is killing him. When I can feel his pain ricocheting inside me, making it hard to breathe as it comes down the bond I don't want.

A bond, that for some reason, he doesn't believe in.

That thought cuts through my pain, a question that needs an answer, and I swallow hard as it rides to the forefront of my mind. My hand presses to my stomach as I breathe.

Why can't Varius feel it? Is it because of what he is?

A monster from the Shadow Domain.

My mind flickers to the bat-snake Sau pulled out of her shadows. Is he the same species? Or something different? Does he have another form he can change into? My heart plummets into my stomach. Or did Sau change him in order to keep him as her son? To pass him off as Caden's? Is that why their father cursed her with his dying breath?

That knot grows. As does that feeling of sickness as so many things start to make sense. The story about her saving Varius as a child... Was part of it true? But instead of his father having hurt their firstborn, was it her? After waking up from a nightmare, did she accidentally kill him, then in her grief, replace him with a monster she spelled to look like their child so no one would know?

Does Varius even know?

He said he didn't remember a thing about what he did to me last night, and I felt his anger, his horror. I believe him, so is it part of his curse? Keep him in the dark so he doesn't ask questions, doesn't feel like the monster he is?

Acid burning my throat, I press a hand to my stomach.

Is the thing inside me like *him*?

Oh my gods. Is it going to pop out of my stomach like in *Aliens*? Or worse in *Space Balls?*

Shit. Am I going to have to drink blood?

My breath catching, I try to keep control of my rising panic. But I don't want to drink blood! I like my steaks well done. And I especially don't want a fucking monster baby popping out of my uterus and dancing as it sings "Hello, My Baby" while I'm lying in my own intestines!

Fuck. Micha. Breathe.

Fuck breathing! I need answers!

Jerking my head towards the door, I run out of it, seeking Sau. I find her in the hall where I fought her monster. She's sitting with it, one hand on its scaly hide, right below where its head used to be before I turned it into a pile of ash. She's singing softly to it, her voice so godsdamn raw, and for a moment, I hesitate.

Despite all the shit she's put me through, she is clearly grieving. A mother who's lost a child. Pain etched in every crease of her face. In the sagging of her shoulders. In the tiredness of her aura. She is in agony as she says goodbye. I killed her baby, and she saved mine.

My heart in my throat, I shift awkwardly on my feet. "It fought well," I finally say as I approach.

"She shouldn't have died," she replies softly, not looking at me, her hand stroking the blackened scales.

"I –"

She shakes her head. "I shouldn't have brought her out to fight you. When the wards came down... I assumed it was you. You were back early. Not part of the family... I did not think one of my own boys... That Talon might have set a trigger for the wards to come down when you returned. I am sorry, Micha." She looks up at me now, her eyes dry but still so full of pain. "And I am sorry that my interpretation of what I saw led to your torture."

I swallow hard as I force a flippant shrug. I don't know if I want to accept her apology just yet. She acted exactly how I would have. You don't talk to a strong opponent; you hit hard and fast and hope like hel you catch them off guard. She didn't have time to ask questions when the wolves were closing in on us. If I was the traitor, and she tried, I would have killed her. But still...she's the bitch who caused Varius to mistrust me.

Looking at the dead beast, I focus on why I'm here. "Was the..." 'Thing,' though, seems rude to say. As does 'monster,' so I gesture at the snake-bat instead.

"Monmon," she says as her eyes dip back to the creature.

"Was it a pet?"

"You cannot own a creature from the Plane of Monsters," she says. "Even Olivia, who lives in the kitchen counter now that her body is gone, is not a pet."

I blink. Oh my gods, that makes so much sense. "You used dark magic to trap a monster in your counter?"

"To save her," she corrects. "She got infected from the poison of a kelorara."

"What is she?"

"An echnida."

"Wait, what?"

She smiles wryly. "Not the tiny animals you're thinking of. Olivia is the offspring of Echidna herself."

My jaw drops. "The Mother of Monsters?"

She nods.

"Shit. So is that what she looks like? Half human, half snake?" I hesitate a second, then ask, "Is she a human?" A creature that can take a full humanoid shape regardless of its origins.

She shakes her head. "No. She looks more like a praying mantis mixed with a xenomorph. And she has a humanoid shape, but she isn't human."

My heart stops at the word 'xenomoph.' Is that what Varius is? "Can I see her?" I ask nervously.

"She isn't a thing to be brought out for our amusement."

"Shit. Of course not. I was just..." *Wondering what I can expect when the baby pops out of my stomach.* "So why is she not considered a human if she has a humanoid shape?" I ask instead. "Isn't that the definition of what a human is? Anything created in the image of a god?"

"It's the layman's definition, yes. But humans are given a humanoid shape first and another form second. Monsters are beasts, created to be wild and untamed. There are a few cases, though, of them pleasing the gods enough to be gifted a humanoid shape. But that is not who they are."

"By 'pleasing,' do you mean by pleasing Zeus?" I can't help but ask.

She smiles wryly. "I would not be surprised if that were the case with some." She cocks her head. "Then again, I do not think he has any issues with fucking things that aren't human."

My cheeks burn as I glance at the monmon – a name that is way too cute for it. *Where would Zeus even put his dick in that?*

I shake my head to get myself back on track. "So do they give birth to humanoid shapes then," I try hopefully, "or..."

"No." She pauses for a moment, her eyes piercing. Slowly, she says, "I'll be training some monsters later today if you would like to join me."

I match her stare. "Are you fit to do that?" I might not be ready to forgive her for all the shit she's pulled, but she is the best healer on this side of the Atlantic, perhaps even in the world, and I'm pregnant. With a potential monster baby. I am not being dumb enough to risk her life.

She smiles. "We're at war. If we all waited until we were well-rested, we would lose. Now. Stand back. I need space to put Hoo-hoo to rest."

Okay, what the fuck? That thing is not a Hoo-hoo. It's a Regina. But I keep my thoughts to myself as I step back, and her shadows swirl out of her hands.

She starts to sing again, a dark country song that speaks to me all too well right now.

My throat working, I ask once Hoo-hoo is gone from this world, "Who's that by?"

"Ryo Shadow."

My lips part in a soundless gasp, but then I quickly close them again, an insensitive question on my tongue. About whether he did what the person in the song did – suffered from depression until he committed suicide.

"It's a beautiful song," I say instead. "Did he write many of them?"

"A few, but that's the only one I remember." She stands, and the sadness in her eyes is beaten back by an explosion of cold anger. "Antonio killed him on his wedding day while I was trapped in the Plane of Monsters. I never got to bury him. I didn't get to bury my only grandchild either because I ran off to go kill Aleric, half-cocked and full of rage." Her eyes dart to my stomach. "And I almost aided in killing my next one." Her gaze lifts, holding mine. "I cannot tell you how sorry I am, Micha –"

"You can fucking try."

She stops with a small smile, a bit of pride in old green eyes. "I am sorry I attacked you. I misjudged your love for my son and for my family. I have tried to enjoy the peace of the last three decades, but the paranoia I developed in the time before, when we were at war with the Death Hunt and the Blood Fangs, when I lost child after child, with parts of them mailed back to me in boxes... I learned to trust no one but my family, and I raised my firstborn to value that same paranoia, thinking it would save him." She shakes her head sadly. "But instead it is killing him."

I still, my anger rising from the embers it's been sizzling at. "He isn't fucking dying over thi–"

"He threatened me this morning," she cuts in. "Said if I ever said another negative thing about you, he'd sell me to Aleric. The same fucking Aleric who butchered over half my children, who raped me repeatedly, and stabbed me multiple times in the stomach after killing three of my kids damn well in front of me." The fire in her eyes burns hot enough to compete with my flames. But then it cools as she looks at me softly. "Varius cares about you, Micha. He just made a mistake, and he's paying for it."

"No, *I'm* paying for it. Varius didn't pray to the gods, begging them to take his life or his magic, anything they wanted as long as they would save our child." I raise my hands, forcing her to look at them. "It isn't a mental block that's stopping me. It was a trade Varius forced on me, and I will never be able to control magic on my own again." I feel that truth in my fucking soul, and I clench my teeth shut to stop the pain that wants to escape on a scream. "So I don't give a damn if he made a *mistake*," I continue. "His choice will affect me for the rest of my life, and there is *nothing* he can pay that will measure up to that."

"Not even if he suffers for the rest of his?"

"He won't." It's been one day, and he's already getting his dick wet. He'll forget about me in a week. I never gave him any peace of mind, never gave him anything that he didn't already have other than a vagina to hit anytime he wanted. Our relationship was too new. He was just getting comfortable with me. So he hasn't lost anything but a toy to play with, and he will easily replace me with another.

Sau looks at me like I'm an idiot. "Do you know how hard it is for him to trust someone, Micha? For him to love anyone?"

"He doesn't know what love is."

"No, and he never will because he is firstborn. But your child will also be firstborn, and you will end up having this same conversation with her fiance. So will you tell him to hold on to his misery like you're doing now, or will you try to convince him your daughter loves him as much as she is capable?"

"I will teach her what love is."

"*You* don't know what love is. Otherwise, you wouldn't be shutting him out after one mistake."

"He tortured me. That's not something like forgetting our anniversary."

"Talon lured you back on a day you weren't supposed to be here, a day when all the boys were out. He wasn't here when he brought down the wards, and none of us knew they could be lowered from afar. The suspects were either me or you, and you were the one kissing Antonio."

"He forced me."

"It didn't look like it from where I was."

"He took me by surprise! By the time I could even think to move, he was gone."

"You could have shoved him away and thrown fire at his face, and I still would have thought you were with him. You would not be the first girl having a tat with her lover. The ward came down. The wolves attacked, and I know I was not the one who did it. You were the only other one there. And then Talon came back, and he told everyone you were the one to help Antonio take Khalid."

"He punched a hole in my stomach."

"Talon told us Khalid did it, and Varius thought he was about to lose not just a brother or the reaper but the last person he could trust." She shakes her head. "I betrayed his trust by blackmailing you. He thought you did by being a mole for Antonio. Khalid was all he had left, and he did what he thought he had to do to save him."

Not wanting to listen to her fucking logic, I snap, "Why *did* you blackmail me?"

An ironic smile curls her lips. "Because I didn't want him to trust you."

"You bitch." I swing for her jaw. She twists her torso, moving the barest amount needed to get out of the way. I feel the heat of her skin as my fist passes but never touches. Hammering my arm to the side, I twist it at the same time so my knuckles will connect with her face.

She simply ducks and moves to the side.

Then rises again. Her foot kicks out to connect with my chest, but it stops an inch before contact. She poises on her other leg in perfect balance. "I'm not going to fight –"

I try to grab her leg so I can haul her to me with one hand and pummel her face in with the other. But she moves it out of the way, swinging it down and sideways, then up in a perfect arc to connect with my face.

I turn my entire body, pivoting wildly, expecting the pain and wanting to transfer the energy into a spin rather than taking it all as a solid block to my jaw. But it never hits, and I complete my three-sixty to face her again, my arms up, my heart pumping. Her leg is still in the air. Perfectly held to where my head just was.

"Your hand-to-hand needs work," she says. "I can tea–"

She ducks and dodges as I swing for her. Rapid punches that never hit. And I'm getting exhausted all too quickly, the blood Varius drank from me heavily felt in its absence. As the last of my energy starts to go, I lunge at her, no thought, no technique, just primal fury to catch her off guard.

My arms wrap around her waist as I tackle her to the ground. There is a soft tap on the back of my head right before we hit, and I know the bitch's telling me she could've just ended me. But I don't care. There's no such thing as a dirty fight, and just because she refuses to hurt me doesn't mean I'm going to hold back when I beat the shit out of her.

So I shuffle up her body to straddle her chest with my legs. Fisting her hair at the back of her head with one hand, I punch her in the face with the other. Blood sprays from her lips and nose, and her eye becomes swollen as she lies there and lets me hit her. But if she thinks not putting up a fight will make me stop sooner, she's wrong. I do not care if she doesn't fight back. Don't care if that means I have no honor. She tried to come between me and Varius; she helped break what we could have been, and for that, I will hit her until she passes out.

The utter fucking *bitch*.

But before I can give her a concussion, I'm hauled off her by two strong arms, then held against a chest I know all too well. The fact that I'm holding a huge bloody chunk of her hair and that Varius doesn't go to see how she is pleases me a little, but then I recall how fast she heals. She's probably already sitting up, not even nursing a bruised jaw.

"Get off me," I snap as he carries me away.

"This isn't good for the baby."

"This is terrific for the baby! She's learning what to do when some utter *bitch*," I yell over his shoulder, "tries to –" I stop suddenly, swallowing down the words, *get between her and her man.* Varius isn't my man. I can even smell another fucking woman on him. His dick must be soaked in it. Or did he eat her out, and it's his godsdamn breath that I'm smelling?

"What did she do?" he demands as he climbs the stairs to the second floor.

"None of your fucking business."

"Did she hurt you?"

"Fuck off. I'm not yours to protect anymore."

He swings me off him and pushes my back against the wall, then lifts me up until I'm staring into his eyes. "You'll always be mine to protect, little monster."

And fuck, his gaze is too damn intense.

So I inhale deeply, holding the scent of another woman's pussy in my nose.

Leaning back, he opens his office door and enters with me still in his arms. The door shuts behind us, and I bite my tongue before I can ask him what I'm doing here. I don't want to give him anything when he still smells like a hoe.

"You stink," I say, trying not to sound like it's bothering me, like I'm just stating a simple fact.

He growls low, then says, "I was about to shower when I smelled your blood."

I glance down at my hands. "It's Sau's."

"I know the difference, and it's yours."

He sets me down on his desk, then grabs one of my hands. I try to jerk away, but he holds me firmly. Then he licks his thumb on his other hand and wipes it across one of my knuckles. Sau's blood comes away, and beneath it is split skin.

"You couldn't possibly smell that," I say.

"I have enhanced senses."

"What are you?"

"Don't you know?" he asks softly.

My eyes narrow. "If you make me do a *Twilight* scene, I will beat you better than I did your mom."

A small, humorless smile flicks at his lips. Then he drops

his hand and steps back. Crossing to the door, he pushes on it to make sure it's shut and the silence rune is activated. Then he locks the door, and my heart jumps into my throat at that *click*.

He turns slowly.

Walks back towards me.

My pulse gets faster and faster with every step he takes.

"That scene would be half-right," he says softly, his gaze sharp and intense. Every inch the predator eying up its prey. "But I'm not just a vampire, Micha."

Not just... My eyes widen.

"I'm a hybrid."

My mind blanks as I stare at him.

Then it all fucking slides into place, and utter terror and disgust fill my mind. Screaming, I twist to grab the nearest thing beside me, and I sling it at his face.

THIRTY-FOUR

HIM

I grab the laptop before it breaks across my face, then twist it out of her hands, but the damage is still too fucking crippling. I hoped that at the very least, my little monster would be able to accept me for *me*. That when she said she loved me, she fucking meant it.

But all she sees is the hybrid.

The abomination.

The monster.

I can see it in her eyes as she glares at me from the other side of the desk. She wants to rip out my organs, to go back in time and kill me as a baby while I was still in Mother's womb. She wishes she sided with Talon.

Fighting back the urge to throw the laptop I just saved at the wall, I toss it gently onto the sofa.

"I should have fucking killed you!" she spits as she picks up the chair and launches it at me. I dart out of the way, and a loud *bang* smashes across the wall behind. "I am going to kill you!" She yanks open a drawer and grabs a stapler, a box of pens, a pair of scissors. Anything she can throw in the time it takes me to dart out of the way. "Fuck you and fuck this family, and dear fucking gods –"

I launch over the desk just as she opens the drawer where I keep my knives. I must have nearly drained her last night. She won't survive another feeding this soon if I can't control myself.

But she doesn't grab a knife for some reason. Instead, she yanks so hard, she tugs the whole thing free. As I'm in the air, she swings the wooden box at my face like it's a purse of rocks. "– fuck Maddox, the fucking *pervert!*"

I throw up my arms just in time for the drawer to smash into them, splinters breaking off in all directions. I twist as I am knocked to the side. I hit the edge of the desk, then roll off it.

She storms over to me, but before she can kick me in the stomach, I wrap an arm around the back of her leg and roll away from the desk. She falls on top of me, and I keep going until she's beneath me. She tries to slam her elbow in my face, but I catch it in my hand and shove it back, pinning it to the ground. I do the same with the other one, but she just leans up and tries to bite my nose.

I jerk my head back, and thank gods, my arms are longer than her reach. She hisses at me, her eyes hot with rage. "How many times did he fuck me?"

My head spins. "Who the fuck is *he*?"

"Maddox."

"*Maddox*?" I'm going to kill the little shit.

"Yeah, you fucking pervert. I figured it out! So which times was it him, huh? Which times did you allow your pervert of a brother to shapeshift into you and take your place between my legs? Dear fucking gods, Varius, I am going to kill –"

Wait. What? "Micha, shut up," I snap so I can think.

"You did not just tell me to –"

I cup her mouth with one hand, and she screams muffled curses into my palm as she twists her head side to side. But I keep my hand locked firmly on her as I try to make sense of what she's saying.

"Are you telling me," I say slowly, "that Maddox has been shapeshifting into me to rape you?"

She growls in my hand, and I remove it so I can hear her. "You tell me," she snaps. "I'm assuming it was your idea."

When I don't say anything, she cackles. "Oh my gods, it was your mother's and you didn't know. What a fucking idiot. Bet you wish you let me beat the shit out of her now."

"What are you talking about?" I ask, each word pulled through gritted teeth.

"The baby isn't yours, you damn neanderthal. It's your brother's."

"The hel it is," I growl, my tone ice to her fire.

She laughs wildly. "Think about it. Hybrids are infertile."

"I'm not."

"Oh, no? Let me guess, your mother told you that, and she isn't known for lying at all."

I stare at her.

She stares at me.

And then I'm on my feet and pulling out my phone to tell Mother to get up here. *Now.* If I leave this office to go get her myself and run into Maddox, I'm liable to fucking kill him before I even know if this fucked up theory is true.

It better not be.

But I can't help but remember how concerned he was for her when Talon called her a traitor. How he tried to stop me from hurting her. How he chewed through his own arms to escape the witch's snare. For *her.* You don't fucking do that for someone you don't love.

My fingers tightening on my phone, I toss it onto the desk, then turn to look at my wife. My eyes drop to her stomach. "If she's his," I say. The words are tight, choking me, but I have to get them out. I have to *know*. "Will you keep her?"

She stares at me, now on her feet. Then she scoffs. "As if I think you'd let me. You can't try for an heir if I'm already pregnant."

I step towards her, my heart in my gaze. "It is your body, Micha. The decision will be yours and yours alone. If you decide to keep her, I will claim her as mine."

She blinks, then nods like she gets it. "Maddox changes his whole DNA when he shifts, doesn't he? So I guess from a biological standpoint –"

"She will be mine because she is *yours*. And everything about you is *mine*."

She stares at me, her jaw slack. Then she shakes her head and mutters, "You're such a fucking neanderthal."

But there's a wistfulness to her tone, a remembrance of the time before, when she used to say that with love, and my chest tightens with the hope that I can fix this. That she has not completely given up on us despite what she said.

"So will –"

A knock on the door cuts me off. Her eyes drift from mine, dismissing me so easily, like I mean nothing to her, and for a moment I am tempted to sell Mother to Aleric just for her interruption. Instead, I step towards my wife and finish the question whose answer I need to know. "Will you keep her?"

She doesn't look at me.

"*Micha*."

Her eyes drift over to mine. "No."

My chest expands even though she does not. She doesn't tell me her decision stems from the child not being mine, but I let myself believe it. Let myself hope for one moment that she still wants me and me alone.

Then I turn to face the door. I want to know the answer

to the question Micha raised. If the child is mine. If Mother has lied to me yet again. If Maddox is fucking in on it. Fuck. If the child is his, it doesn't matter if she decides to keep her or not. I will *kill him*.

"Come in," I say.

Mother enters gracefully, no fear rolling off her. Not even a twinge of worry. She steps over the broken chair as if it's a natural part of the landscape, then stops in front of me and waits.

"Sit down." My words are tightly controlled, utterly flat, and there is the first flicker of concern. She knows me well enough to know this is the state I fall into when I leave my humanity behind. If she has had any part in Micha being raped, I will cut out her eyes and pour helfire down the two holes so they never reform before I sell her to Aleric.

She sits down on the sofa, her ankles crossed, her hands in her lap, her chin lifted. "What is this about?" she asks.

"I will ask you each question once," I say as I pick up my phone and click on Aleric's name. "If I even think you are lying, you will never see any of your children again and you will never meet your grandkids."

Her back goes ramrod straight.

"Now." I place the phone down on the arm of the couch so she can see the screen. Her eyes dart to it, then to Micha, then me. Holding her gaze, I press the call button. "Am I infertile?"

The phone rings.

"No."

"Did you tell Maddox to shapeshift into me and fuck my wife?"

Her eyes widen. "Of course not!"

"Why can't I feel the blood bond?"

She presses her lips together.

The phone rings again.

And again.

On the third ring, her eyes dart to it.

But I'm not asking again. If Aleric answers, she's sold.

The ring gets cut off as the line starts to connect. "I think you're starving," she blurts, and I end the call, but my finger does not leave the screen, telling her she better keep talking.

She glances at Micha.

"I told her I'm a hybrid."

She breathes out slowly as she looks back at me. "A born vampire can eat just like we can, so when I cursed you, I also bound your bloodlust. You don't need it to survive, but I guess part of you must still crave it, and it's consuming her blood too fast."

I stare at her, wondering why that explanation caused her pause, urging her with my silence to fill in the gaps. Her lips purse together. She doesn't say anything for a while, but then she says, "I might've made it..." She clenches her jaw and looks away. Then breathes in deeply and holds it. After letting it go, she continues, "You might always be under the influence of the Craving when you change."

Fuck. The Craving is when werewolves or vampires lose all sense of themselves. They react instinctively, primitively, driven by nothing but the hunger. They feed until they kill, ripping apart their prey like a pack of starving dogs. No control. No thoughts. They are the closest things to zombies we have, albeit much faster, much stronger, and much more dangerous. Knowing that is what I become sickens me. That loss of control goes against every value I hold myself to.

But it also means I wasn't responsible for what I did to –

I stop.

Clench my teeth.

Because I am fucking responsible. Under the Craving or not, I *hurt* her. And I will have to live with that for the rest of my life.

Disgusted by all the shit that's unraveling, I want to kick Mother from my office, from this damn house, but I have another question I need to know. "Will I be able to feel her after we're fully bonded?" I ask.

"I don't know."

My finger hovers over the call button.

"I don't see why you shouldn't," she says. "Before the bond is finished, the blood you share is the only tie between you. Afterwards, your souls are tied. Your vampirism can't eat that."

I stare at her, searching her face before asking over my shoulder. "Any other questions you want to ask, Micha?"

"Am I pregnant with a hybrid?"

I still, my stomach dropping as I wonder if she will cut it from her belly like too many mothers do when they find out they have an abomination inside them.

"No," Mother says. Then, "I don't know. I bound Varius' true nature with dark magic. I think I did it right, but we won't know until she's born."

Micha's silent for a long moment, holding my breath in the palm of her hand. Then she asks, "How do you break a blood bond?"

"Get out." Mother starts to leave, but so does Micha. I spin towards her and grab her wrist. "You know damn well I wasn't talking to you."

She tries to tug her arm away but can't. As Mother slips through the door, Micha glares at me. "Stop touching me."

"No –"

She laughs coldly. "Of course you won't listen to what I want. Surprise, surprise."

I grit my teeth, torn between letting her go and watching her walk out of my life and keeping hold of her, which will break us further. My heart pounding, I drop her arm, then dart in front of the door, blocking her from leaving. I cross my arms. She glares at me.

"We need to talk."

"I don't have shit to say to you."

"Are you going to keep the baby?" Or will she abort her now that there's a chance our child's a hybrid?

"Fucking hel, Varius. You don't know me at all."

"Micha –"

"Yes, I'm fucking keeping her." Her eyes go cold. "Even if she is a rapist's baby."

I flinch. "I was under the Craving, Micha. The fact that I didn't kill you –"

"Oh, wow! What a high fucking bar." She claps slowly, her face so damn sarcastic. "Give my fiance a golden ribbon. He didn't fucking *kill* me when he could have."

"Not could have," I say in frustration. "The Craving isn't something you can control. I *should* have killed you, but I didn't because I –" *Love you. Don't you see? My feelings for you cut through even the mindlessness the Craving causes. I fucking love you, Micha.*

But I don't get a chance to say those words because her gaze softens into that sickly indifference, and they stick in my throat in utter terror.

"Let me go, Varius," she says flatly.

"No." My voice fractures, fucking *breaks*.

If she leaves, she isn't coming back. Physically, yes. I will drag her back here from wherever she goes, and she knows it. But emotionally? Never. I can see it in her eyes, in that utter blankness that is squeezing all the air from my lungs.

"You know..." she says in a monotone, each word a stab to my chest, "as much as I didn't want to be raped by your brother, I hoped the baby was his. Then I wouldn't have to have any part of you inside me for the next six months."

The strength goes out of my legs, and I sag back against the door. "Monster..." I say, my voice breaking. "You don't mean that."

She doesn't say a word.

I stare at her, my heart pounding, wondering how I can fix this. "Just tell me what you need from me," I beg. "Please.

I will do it, Micha. Just please. I am sorry for hurting you and for…raping you." The word burns across my throat, the absolute fucking fury and disgust I feel for myself twisting in my stomach. "I am sorry I didn't stop when you asked me to. That I didn't trust you. I'm sorry. I'm so fucking sorry."

She stares at me in silence. Not a flicker of emotion. No reaction to what I'm saying.

My throat closes.

My eyes burn.

"I will fix this," I say desperately, willing those words to be true. "I will get you to fall back in love with me. Just let me try, Micha. Please. Just stay and let me try."

She stares blankly ahead, not saying one damn word.

But she doesn't try to leave. Doesn't move at all, but I'm focusing on the former, ignoring the weight of the latter. As long as she is here, I have a chance.

I have a chance.

And with it, I will make Micha Shadow remember that she is mine.

No.

I will make her remember that she wants to *be* mine.

THIRTY-FIVE

HER

The fucker still smells like a whore.

It doesn't matter how many showers he has, I can still smell That Bitch on him. He must have buried himself so deep inside her, made her squirt all over his cock so fucking hard that it seeped into his skin.

And I hate that that is what I am focused on more than the fact that he tortured me, then raped me. But every time he glances at her as we sit at the kitchen table eating dinner, four days after he fucked her, I want to stab her in the face, then him. Every time she tries to talk to me, I want to shoot her in the throat, then him. Every time she fucking *breathes*, I want to shove her godsdamn head into a shit-clogged toilet and drown her in it. Then. Fucking. Him.

It's only the fact that Khalid is beside her that I don't. He might be missing one hand, but he can still kill me easily, especially given I can't use any magic now. But dear gods, if I get one second alone with her... I will end her. I don't care if it was Khalid's payment that led to Varius having to fuck her; she knows what my husband's dick feels like, and I –

I stop those traitorous thoughts.

Although he will be my husband in a few months' time, once the baby is certain to survive, he will never be my *husband*. I don't want anything to do with him outside of the terms of our contract unless it's making plans for his funeral.

"Careful," Maddox murmurs as he leans in towards me from my left. "You're starting to show some emotion."

The muscles on my face relax instantly, and he chuckles softly. "You're really making him work for it, huh?"

"I'm not making him work for anything," I growl as I try not to breathe in the smell of the French fries in front of me. The fried smell is making me nauseous, but I don't exactly have an appetite anyways. "I'm dealing with my own shit. If he suffers, that's just a benefit."

He chuckles. "The gods help us if you two ever make up."

I glare at him side-eye as he chews on his burger. We've been having different types of them for the last few days – another attempt by Varius to show me he loves me. My chest tightens from the memory of our first meet, then our first date. *I like burgers.*

It came to mean: *I love you.*

I blink away those memories, but the pain in my chest stays.

"What?" he asks after he swallows. "You can't tell me you don't daydream about how badass you two'll be ruling this Family together?"

"It'll never be *together.* I'm just a breedmare."

He gives me a pointed look. "Of course you would rule together because the thing about the men in this family," he says, his voice lowered, "is that when we love, we love *hard.*" He nods at Enoch before I can tell him Varius doesn't know what love is.

"He's been in love with Stormie Green since she punched him in the nose for pulling on her hair in the first grade," he says. "Oh, he's dated a couple times. Tried to move on given she's never given him the time of day, but the only time he has sex is when Ezriel drags him into a threesome." He nods at Leno. "He lost his eyes to a wolf when he was thirteen. You know what he said when he finally found his way home, and Mom asked him what had happened, freaking out, mind you, because he'd taken so damn long to get back that even she couldn't heal him by then?"

I shake my head.

"The fucker grinned like a fool and said, 'I found the girl I'm going to marry.' He's been looking for her ever since. And Khalid," he says as he nods at the reaper, who is talking to his whore. "He cut off his own fucking hand for her. He absolutely worships the ground she walks on, even calls her 'master' in Drazic. And Varius…"

A lump suddenly forms in my throat as my eyes shift to him. He looks miserable, his cheeks sunken, his eyes dark and bagged. He's barely eaten these past few days, his plates even more untouched than mine. And I know he hasn't been sleeping well. When he carried me back to his room that day I destroyed his office, he told me to pick a side of the bed. So I chose the upper half as I'm small enough to sleep sideways across it. He's over a foot taller than me and has to curl up awkwardly to fit.

His eyes hold mine, and I'm sucked so deep inside them that I almost miss what Maddox says.

"…marry her sister."

"What?" I blink, then break Varius' gaze to look at his brother.

"I said Varius is so desperate to fix things with his girl that he's forcing his little brother to marry her sister so she can come live with us."

My mouth falls open. "Wait, what? Lou's coming here?"

Before he can say anything, I give him my best 'touch her and die' glare. "Maddox..." I growl.

He holds up his hands. "You want to stop it, you're going to have to talk to him. Trust me. I've tried to get out of it."

"You little shit."

He shrugs, not looking embarrassed in the slightest about being caught. "Desperate times call for blatant manipulation of your sister-in-law and all that. So will you talk to him for me? If it helps, I have a side piece I'm in love with. Varius told me to kill her, but honestly, I've just been keeping her hidden in a cage in my shadows."

My eyes widen. "In the Plane of Monsters?"

"Yep. And let me tell you, she is both extremely pleased and extremely pissed to see me every time I pull her out. She fucks me like she wants to kill me. The girl is giving me some really mixed signals." His eyes widen as he shakes his head slowly.

"You're crazy, and that does not sound like you are in love."

His eyes twinkle. "Yeah, I know. But she is sure fun to play with." He laughs as I just stare at him like the mental nutcase he is.

"But I'm sure I'll fall hard too if it ever happens for real," he says with a wink. "I'm too much of a hopeless romantic."

I snort as I pick at my fries.

"Hey. Wounded."

I laugh.

He smiles at me.

Dark jealousy jolts through me, and I can feel Varius' glare. But if he's mad at me, he isn't looking at That Bitch, so I deliberately laugh some more.

Maddox leans over, bumping my shoulder with his. "So what do you say? Will you talk to him for me? Save your little baby sister from the cruel fate of being my bride?"

"For her, not you."

"Of course."

But he looks way too fucking pleased with himself.

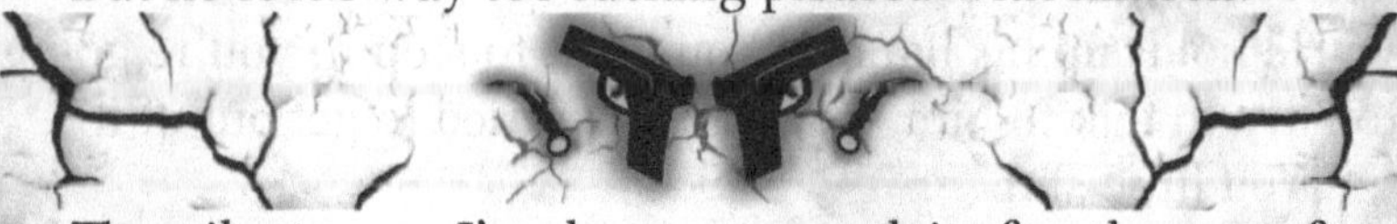

The silent rage I've been wrapped in for the past four days is now itching to explode. Varius damn well knows I have been trying to keep my baby sister out of this life. She wants to go to college for an art degree, travel the world, see new things. And she's shit with any weapon that has ever been invented. Including poison. She once forgot which cup she put it in during training and nearly drank it herself. She is the worst person to pull into this life.

So by the time dinner is over, and I'm in my room, pacing back and forth as I wait for Varius to get here and drag me upstairs – something he has done for the past two nights (the first night, I was dragged from his office), I am ready to go six rounds with him. Bare knuckled. To the knock-out.

But not to the death.

As angry as I am with him, I never want to see him dead. That glossy-eyed look he pinned me with as he lay above me bleeding out... It haunts my fucking dreams. I absolutely hate that I was the one who did that to him. That in my panic and rage and *pain*, I was capable of killing the man I love. I don't ever want to be that kind of person, don't want to turn into someone who is such a slave to their emotions that they can't control them. And that is one of the main reasons I've refused to talk to him these past four days, why I've given up trying to fix this. I fear the person he could turn me into. The miserable bitch who just wants to hurt him for the sake of hurting him.

But I don't have a choice anymore. Not if I want to save my baby sister from marrying Maddox.

As the door to my room opens, I clench my fists as I

stand, waiting for him. There is nowhere for me to sit in here. He hasn't bought any new furniture, and I've been too stubborn to ask for more.

"How dare you buy her," I growl, and he stops just inside the room, shock on his face that I'm talking to him. But then it turns into relief, a small smile in his eyes as he shuts the door, and that just pisses me off.

"If I didn't, someone else would've. And you were upset you didn't get to see her the last time you were home. So I thought you'd like it if she lived closer."

I glare at him, hating that he's noticed how much I have been missing her. "I'd like her to go to fucking college," I say irritably.

"Maddox went to college."

"That's not the same thing."

"She's the daughter of Stefaan Black and the sister of my wife. She's never going to live an ordinary life. If she's here, we can protect her."

"Oh? Like you protected us from Antonio?" I snap.

"We've changed the wards. If Talon wants to bring them down, he'll have to use brute force."

"And what if there's another Talon? Lou's utterly useless. She can't use a weapon to save her life."

"We're adding more defenses to the house. Hence all the plants that are now everywhere. There are multiple wards around the safe room now."

"I broke the old one easily."

"Your magic is special."

"Was," I spit.

"*Is*." He crosses the distance between us. "You still have it; you just need to relearn how to control it."

"Fuck you."

"No, you're fucking yourself," he says flatly. "You can be pissy about it, little monster. Or you can learn to remaster it."

I open my mouth to tell him to go fuck himself again, but then I stop. Because damn him, he's right. I've been seeing this as a disability rather than just a new challenge, a new way of life, and I've let it define me. But it isn't who I am. It is not who I want to be. "Will you buy me a fucking wand then?" I ask, each word pulled through gritted teeth.

"There's already one in my room. It arrived yesterday."

My eyes widen. "Why didn't you tell me?"

"Because you needed to reach this decision on your own. The healing process only works if you stop fighting it."

I breathe out on a huff, but there's nothing I can say to that either without sounding argumentative. And as much as he might think I'm just doing things to piss him off, just being silent to hurt him, all I've been doing is trying to heal myself. I've simply stopped putting his feelings before mine, stopped caring if what I need clashes with what he wants from me.

"Well, fucking thank you then," I snap. "But I'm still not happy about Maddox. He's the worst choice for her!"

"I thought you liked Maddox." There's a flatness to those words, a deadly jealousy that lingers beneath the surface. A part of me wants to keep poking the bear, but I know he'll kill his brother if I do.

So I take a step back and cross my arms as I glare at him. "Not for my sister!"

"Then who?"

My jaw clenches. *No one.*

"Pick," he says, "and she'll marry him."

"I don't want her to marry at all. She's *sixteen*. Maddox is the youngest, and he's six years older than her."

"I won't have her marry until she's twenty-two."

"And she'll go to college?" I press.

"Yes." He pauses. "And if you want, we can tell your father she's infertile. She only needs to marry in name."

"You'd do that?" I ask in shock. Lying to another Boss is

grounds for war.

"I'd do anything for you, Micha. All you need to do is ask."

I exhale through my nose, slightly irritated that he's being too damn nice. "Fine. Rudy then." He's the sweetest.

"Done."

"Where is she going to stay?" I snap, still wanting to fight. "She isn't sharing a room with him."

"Here."

"This is my room."

"Your room's upstairs."

My jaw clenches. "That's your –"

"It's our room, Micha, and you fucking know it."

"No one else does!" I snap before I can even think the words.

His eyes narrow in speculation. "Is that what you need from me? To tell everyone you're mine?"

"No." *Yes. No. Fuck. I don't know.* "I'm not yours," I say bitterly. "I cut it off, remember?"

"How could I forget?" he growls. "Your patch's sitting on my bedside table." Pickled and in a glass container.

I shift uncomfortably, my skin feeling too hot. I didn't expect him to keep it. Didn't expect him to be so fucking obsessed and hurt by what I'd done. But I needed to do it, and I would do it again in this moment. Giving Varius any sort of control over me right now is a bad thing; then it'd be way too easy to give in to my desire to forgive him. To go back to what we were. To when I loved him and thought he might even love me. To when I found comfort in his arms rather than pain – a comfort I crave.

But I can't go back to that.

That time, that *person* doesn't exist anymore.

So I take another step back – a physical distance on top of the emotional.

"When's she supposed to arrive?" I push out.

"In a couple days."

Excitement and happiness war with the annoyance in my chest. I haven't seen my sister in over four months. When I went back home three weeks ago, she was out camping with friends, so I missed her. I chew the inside of my bottom lip for a moment before begrudgingly saying, "Fine."

"Good. Shall we go upstairs now?"

I don't answer him as I fall back into my state of silence. Now that my sister is safe, I have no desire to talk to him. I feel empty. Hollow.

Pain and panic flash across his eyes. "Micha, please don't shut me out again," he begs.

But I'm not shutting him out.

"Just talk to me."

I'm shutting me in. I need the space he's refusing to give me.

He stares at me, willing me to speak, but when I don't for several minutes, he closes his eyes briefly. Then he steps forward, kisses me on the forehead, and picks me up in his arms. I don't fight him as he carries me up to his room. I don't move at all.

But gods do I want to.

Because with my head against his chest, I can still smell that fucking *bitch*.

THIRTY-SIX

HIM

As soon as I step from the shower, my phone rings. It's sitting on the sink, and I grab a towel to rub over my head before glancing at it. Seeing it's Aleric, I answer it as I continue to dry my hair.

"What is it?" I ask.

"This? It's a phone call. It's what happens when you –"

"*Aleric.*"

"Oh, that. He's a vampire with a tiny, tiny cock, but gods, does he know how to use it. Just ask your –"

I hang up, take a deep breath, and do my best to calm down while I wait for him to call back. But it's not even six o'clock in the fucking morning. I'm tired. I'm hungry. I am a fucking mess because Micha gave me a sliver of hope that we were healing last night, only for her to shut me out again.

As I look at my haggard eyes in the mirror, I tell myself it's still progress though. She talked to me, and she only yelled a little. We even managed to find a middle ground. So eventually, we'll get through this. *We have to.*

I finish toweling myself off. Aleric still hasn't rung back, but as much as I want to believe he's just being a massive jackass because that's who he is, I know he isn't. There's always a method to his madness. So I snatch up my phone and call him back despite knowing that's what he wants. The action seems weak, almost like an apology, and it irritates every inch of my body to do it, but he either has news about Antonio or Talon, and I want to know both.

"What news do you have for me?" I ask, my voice calm and flat.

"Oh my gods!" Aleric says as if he's a New Jerseyan gossiping at a hair salon he often visits. I put the phone on speaker and half-zone him out while I brush my teeth. "So Vlad finally went on a date last night, but not, like, with one of the vaginas I keep trying to set him up with. So obviously I wanted to know who the fuck he was seeing and why Margo from the cemetery or Daisy from the pound wasn't good enough for him. Like, those bitches are so right for him. So obviously I, like, followed him, but he caught me and threw me against the wall and told me to mind my own business. Which is rude, right? But also, like, really fucking hot. I'm not gonna lie. I got rock hard. But then he phased away, and I lost him. Buuuuut I still did manage to come, so I guess it wasn't a terrible waste of a night."

I frown, wondering if it was Rudy he was meeting. My brother did go out last night, but he came back around ten o'clock. Bit early for a secret fling...

"And then there's Cara Jervis. I've been trying to set that boo up for a while too because she has terrible taste in men. Like, Leno is ew."

Leno?

I perk up at that. If I offer her a marriage with him, can I steal her from Aleric? She'd be a great asset to this Family, and she has to be fucking tired of working with him.

I spit and rinse my toothbrush.

"I mean, don't get me wrong. He's kind of hot with those scars across his face, and yeah, the tall, chiseled, dark haired guy is all the rage at the moment, *I guess,* but like, he uses a dog to see. Can you imagine him giving oral?"

"I'd rather not." I flick my toothbrush and then put it away.

"Like, whose head is between her legs, you know?"

"I don't think it works like that," I say as I start to get dressed.

"So you *have* thought about this?"

Irritated, I ask, "What do you want?"

"Oooh, you buying me presents already? In that case, I'm going to email you my TBR. One sec."

I breathe out heavily as actual hold music comes on the line. After shoving my legs into a pair of shorts, I leave the bathroom with my phone in my hand.

Micha is still asleep, lying horizontally on the top of the bed. I stretch my back as I watch her, a weightless feeling expanding across my chest.

At least in her dreams, she doesn't look so miserable.

Heading over to the bedside table, I pick up the empty glass and fill it with water from the bathroom sink. Then I grab a bar of chocolate from my stash and place it beside it before walking downstairs to get her an orange. I never see her eat them, but sometimes I find the wrappers and peel in the trash can.

After I place the orange down on the table, I stroke my fingers across her shoulder. She moves away from me, and I pull back, my throat tightening. Leaving her, I head for my office so I don't disturb her sleep.

"Okay. Sent," Aleric says just as I sit down in my new desk chair. "And like, I *know* there are thousands on there, but I *swear* I'm going to get to them all one day."

My phone beeps with a new email alert. I swipe away the notification without opening it.

"So anyway," Aleric says, his voice changing to a more serious note. "I need to go take a shit."

My jaw clenches.

"So I'm going to make this quick. Talon's been spotted in Alaska, working at a bar."

"Where in –"

The line goes dead.

I breathe in slowly, then out. Going through my contacts, I call Quinton. Dayne was supposed to be here a few days ago, but someone took out a hit on him. If Quinton wasn't watching over him, he would have died in France. They've been on the run for the last couple days, but I got a text last night to tell me they have dealt with the team chasing them and would be here later today.

"Yes, sir?" Quinton answers, not a slick of tiredness in his voice despite the early hour.

"Where are you?"

"New York."

"I need you to head to Alaska and figure out where Talon has been spotted. I've been told he's in a bar."

There's a moment of silence. Then, "Did you ask them which bar?"

"Yes."

"And?"

"He didn't say."

"That seems –" He stops. "Ah. You talked to Aleric. Yeah, that checks. Do you want me to call Vlad?"

If he knows, it would save us a lot of time. "You think he'll tell us?"

"He won't tell you if Aleric's told him not to, but he owes me a favor."

"Then do so."

"Yes, sir. I'll do it now."

He hangs up, and a few hours later, as I'm researching more ways to apologize to Micha, I get a text from him with an address in Nome. The town has an airport, but if the reaper books a plane, Talon will know about it. There aren't any roads leading into it either, and I am certain he has eyes on any boats coming in. It's going to be an utter bitch for Khalid to get there and take a lot of time too. We can't spare him for that long. With every day that passes, there's a bigger chance that Antonio has finally perfected whatever drug he gave to that wolf to turn him into a super soldier.

According to Aleric, Cara Jervis still hasn't managed to crack the disease. Everything she's made out of it has either been too unstable or far too dangerous to let loose in the world. Over a hundred years ago, when she was young and bold, she wouldn't have cared, believing herself capable of controlling whatever she created. But then a war between her and Terra Harrison, another witch progeny with the innate power of disease, broke out, and she created the Spanish Flu. Nearly a third of the population in the entire world – five hundred million people, were infected within a single year. Fifty million of them died, including Terra and two of Mother's children. Since then, Cara has been more cautious about what she creates.

Glancing back at my computer, I skim the article I have up. *Twenty Ways to Apologize After Hurting Her.* 1. Buy her flowers – she doesn't want any. 2. Bring her breakfast in bed – she isn't eating. 3. Redo a date you've done before to rekindle old feelings – that date ended with me tattooing my name on her, which she's since skinned off. I don't think that would be a good idea. 4. Genuinely say sorry – I have, and it isn't enough. *Fuck.*

My lips tight, I close the laptop, then stand. Grabbing my phone, I leave the office, texting as I go.

Varius: *I need someone who can phase. Talon's holed up in a town without roads.*

Aleric: *You are asking a lot of favors. I'm starting to feel used. The sex ain't even good.*

Varius: *The benefit comes when we kill the Death Hunt together.*

Aleric: *Ugh. Fiiiine. I'll send Vlad over. Text him when you sort the ward for him, and he'll come quicker than a girl on my fingers with a werewolf breathing down her neck.*

My eyes narrow on the text, but I don't ask him to clarify what timescale that is. Opening up that can of worms will surely lead to me bleaching my brain.

Slipping my phone away, I open the door to my room and step inside. Micha's found the wand I purchased for her and is sitting on the bed, holding it in both her hands. Her eyes are wide, and I know she can feel the power radiating from it.

The wand is pitch black with bright purple lines running through it like cracked lava with the tip brighter than the bottom. It isn't made of wood but from the shed horn of a kezja alicorn – a pegasus-hellhound-unicorn mix, with lava-like veins beneath its feathers. The wand's handle is plain and smooth to make for a comfortable hold, but its length is carved so intricately as to mimic a line of fire with various creatures dancing inside its flames.

"This isn't from Earth," she eventually says as she looks up at me.

"No."

"Blódyrió?"

"Gaera, with the antler coming from Halzaja." The plane of the angels and demons. Kezja alicorns spend their entire life in the air, so when their horn falls off after the mating season, they're incredibly rare to find due to not having any way to track the creatures down – and that's if they end up on land. With the majority of that world covered by water, with only one major landmass surrounded by a few dozen islands, most of the horns fall into the sea. Only one horn is found maybe every hundred years or so. There are boats that try to follow the alicorns around during mating season, but the seas are rough and dangerous and full of monsters looking for their next meal. Some people try to chase them from the air, but that is the territory of the angels, and they do not take kindly to trespassers.

Her eyes widen. "Holy shit. How much does this cost?"

Well over seven figures, and that was before the shipping and smuggling costs. "Less than the value of you talking to me," I murmur.

Her mouth closes tightly as she looks away. She puts the wand down, her body language closing up.

"Shit. That came out wrong. It's not a trade, Micha. You don't have to talk to me to use it. It's yours."

She doesn't say anything for a long moment. Then she picks up the wand again, and as she turns it over in her hands, she says, "Thank you."

"Don't thank me, Micha. I took your magic. This is my apology to you." The silence that stretches is uncomfortable and heavy, and I fish around for something to say before I remember what I came in here for in the first place. "We found Talon," I tell her.

Her entire body stills like the poise of a snake about to strike. She slowly raises her head, her eyes burning with rage. "I want to be the one to kill him."

I shake my head. "He's up in Alaska, and you haven't even used the wand yet."

"I'm a fast learner."

"The town doesn't have any roads, and we can't fly in without Talon running. Khalid's going to have to phase with Vlad to get there, and he can't jump that distance in one go."

Her jaw tics, as does the pulse at her temple. "He blamed me, Varius. He fucking set me up for you to torture."

"I know."

"And you're telling me I can't even kill him?"

"If he was here, Micha, I'd let you, but you can't phase while pregnant. We almost already lost the baby once –"

"Because of you! Because of him!"

"I know –"

"Do you? Because you don't seem to fucking give a shit." She jumps to her feet, the wand pointed down at her side. The purple lines glow, the magic in it feeding off her rage. "You don't even want to go after him yourself!"

"Of course I do," I say tightly. "But some of the capos are already wondering if he's even guilty. They want any excuse to turn against me and put Leno on the throne. If I go after him, it will tear this Family apart. We cannot survive a coup when we're at war, and I will not risk your life and that of our daughter's for one moment of revenge."

She grits her teeth. Her lip wobbles as she glares off in the distance, but she does not argue with me. She doesn't say anything at all, and I exhale harshly. Knowing she can feel the bond even if she doesn't want it, I push as much love down it as I can.

"Micha, I care for you. More than anything –"

"Except for this Family," she says bitterly.

"I have a duty to this Fam–"

"What about your duty to me?" she shouts, her voice raw as she turns back to me. "You say you will kill anyone who makes me wet. You called a waiter who gave me his number and fucked me on the line so he could listen to my screams as you had your men cut off his balls and force him to eat them. You tattoo me, say I am yours to protect and care for and all that shit, but you won't kill the man who caused you to torture me? What the fuck kind of bullshit is that!"

It's my turn to grit my teeth. Because I want to kill Talon slowly for her. I want to carve off every inch of his skin and make him eat it as I go, using magic to keep him alive. But I can't be the one to kill him when he was loved by all the other capos and was the one the soldiers went to when they had a problem. He might not have been my Underboss, but he had the people's ear. His absence has already increased tensions, and his death will twist that even more. I cannot be the one to kill him.

Breathing out heavily, I hold her gaze. "Talon will die," I say. "That has to be enough for you."

Then I turn and leave the room to go find the reaper because I know that if I stare into those pain-filled eyes any longer, I will do something stupid, like kill the man whose death will start a coup.

THIRTY-SEVEN

HIM

I storm out of the house not long after Khalid leaves with Vlad to go kill our brother – something I should be doing to please my wife. I know she isn't an irrational woman, that even though I've called her crazy a couple of times when I have been pushed to my limit of frustration, she isn't the type to risk everything for a moment of revenge.

Which means this is about more than just either of us killing Talon. If I can figure that out, maybe I can soothe the pain I saw in her eyes.

Because, fuck, that damn near crippled me. She looked as if I was torturing her all over again.

As I move away from the house, the screams she made in that chair ring inside my skull. If I thought they were hard to bear then, they're damn near impossible to handle now. My stomach churns at the sound of her cries. She fucking begged me to stop, to listen to her, to believe that she loved me, and I fucking ignored her every time. I took out my rage on her. My jealousy that she kissed Antonio. My agony that she betrayed me. I looked her in the eye, and I hurt her over and over again.

"You say I'm yours, but you don't even protect me! What kind of bullshit is that?"

My jaw clenches as my strides lengthen into a run. The need to move has me blitzing through the trees as her voice haunts me.

"What about your duty to me*?"*

The rawness she screamed that with echoes inside my skull. My feet trip over nothing but guilt, and pain flashes up my ankle as it twists. But I don't stop running, don't stop chasing that burn in my muscles and lungs.

Fuck!

No wonder my little monster skinned off my name from her pussy.

I gave her a promise. But it was fucking hollow.

She saw no meaning in it. No meaning in *us*. And she's fucking right.

I claimed her in the moments where it was easy. I killed people who didn't make a difference. Told her words in the dark of the night, in the shadows where no one else could hear. She might have said she didn't care about me publicly claiming her, but I fucking care. I might not be able to kill Talon for her still, but I can damn well do this.

Storming through the house, I find her in the gym with her new wand. She's aiming at a target on the other side of the room, her face scrunched up in concentration. Her spine stiffens as I approach, but she doesn't turn to me. Keeping her focus on her target, she jerks her wand up, then waves it in a quick pattern.

With premade wands, you just point and shoot. They've been made to work for anyone. But with custom wands like this, you have to get them finely tuned into you. Magic is not a rigid science with steps to follow to get it to work how you want it. It is a fluid dance with an ever changing beat. The wand needs to learn her movements, and she needs to feel its soul. So she moves without firing it. Her wrist flicks in rhythm to the emotions inside of her, but the movements are clumsy and have too much thought in them.

Until the wand becomes an extension of her, it'll be too dangerous for her to use. If a premade wand is like a gun, a custom is like a stick of dynamite that's been left to weep nitroglycerin. It will give you the power to create what you want, to form the magic inside of you into the mold you wish it to take, but it will not control it after it leaves its tip. Custom wands are not meant for witches who don't know how to use magic. They are merely a more powerful, more capable alternative to the runes we tattoo on our skin. The reason they are not the norm is that they get lost or stolen, and if that happens to a witch who has relied too heavily upon it, then you might as well have broken their hands, leaving them defenseless.

The average person will take five to six weeks to learn a wand enough to not blow their face up while using it, but it takes one to two years to really connect with it, and that connection is ever shifting. With the properties of this wand mimicking the wild, powerful nature of a kezja alicorn... I don't expect Micha to master it for nearly half a decade, if not more. But when she does, the world will quake at her feet. A kezja alicorn is a master of fire, and Micha's flames are hot enough to consume the entire world.

Feeling her frustration as I cross over to her, I ignore what I originally came here for and focus instead on what I can do to help her. "Have you ever danced, Micha?"

She ignores me, but I keep talking.

"A high quality wand isn't like the ones kids get to help them during their ascensions. You can't just jab it in the air."

"How would you know?" she snaps. "You've never had magic."

"No, but I practiced for hours every day with one from when I was twelve until I was twenty-two. I thought if I just connected with one strongly enough, it would work. It was a hel of a motivator."

"But it didn't work, did it? So what do you know?"

"I know you need to let it talk to you and let it feel you. Wands hold properties from both their creator and the item they were crafted from. What do you know about Suzanne Ledford or a kezja alicorn?"

She jabs the air a few more times before angrily turning towards me. She doesn't say anything, but I can see the desire to know in her eyes.

"Suzanne Ledford is a romantic and a perfectionist," I say. "Extremely skilled. Very powerful. If she ever had the motivation to take over the Seven Planes, she could make one hel of a run, but she prefers a quiet life of travel. One that brings her into harmony with the worlds around her."

I reach for Micha's wrist and hold it up so the wand lies horizontally between us. I glance at it as I talk. "She did not find the shed horn she used to make this wand. She found an orphaned colt in the Chisiho Desert, only a few days old. Starving, half-dead. His mother had been shot down by poachers, and the last thing she did was give birth to their son. His father lay underneath her, having used himself to cushion her fall."

She sucks in a breath as her grip on the wand shakes.

"Now, anyone else would've stripped the two adult kezjic of all their fur and bones and horns, then either killed the colt for the same or kept it in captivity, but Suzanne Ledford shapeshifted into a kezja alicorn, then raised it as her own. And when it grew old enough to want to mate, she sent it out into the skies above, never trying to take one thing from it. Not the feathers it molted. Not the embers it left. She cleared it all, hiding it beneath the sands."

I look up at Micha, and she is staring at the wand in

captivation.

"So is this hers from when she shapeshifted?" she asks.

"No. That colt she raised found her after mating season and gifted her his first horn."

Her eyes widen in wonder. I let her stare at it for a bit, the silence between us this time not as heavy as it's been for the past few days. With my fingers still around her wrist, I stroke my thumb across her skin ever so slowly, trying not to draw attention to my need to touch her. My chest aches as I watch the emotions flit across her face. Gods, she's so fucking beautiful.

She glances up at me, then sucks in a breath when she catches me staring. Her cheeks heat an adorable pink as she clears her throat and quickly looks away. "You said I need to know about the kezja alicorns too?"

I spin her around by the arm, a quick pull and a sidestep so her back is pressed against my chest and my arms are wrapped around her. She stiffens.

"Kezja alicorns come together every year to find their one true mate. It is a ritual that takes place over a month in the skies of Halzaja, normally over the open ocean and out of sight. But whenever they happen to mate above land, tourists flock from all across the Seven Planes just to watch them, and celebrations are held for the entire time they're above that city.

"It is the one moment in time when angels and demons work together. The angels police the skies above, and the drazic demons take care of any ruckus on the ground. The sight is said to be one of the most beautiful things to witness in all of the Seven Planes because the kezjic dance to find their mates."

I drag her wand arm up her body, from the hip it was at to the opposite shoulder, then feather it out further until her arm is nearly outstretched but with her elbow still bent. As I guide her limb through a fluidity of motions, I move my other hand to her stomach and get her to rock her hips in rhythm to mine. "The movement starts in your wrist," I say.

I can feel her concentration in the stiffness of her limb.

"Relax. Just close your eyes, and let the wind take you."

"There's no wind in here."

"Close your eyes, Micha, and feel it under your wings."

She blows out a breath, but her eyes drift shut. I guide her wrist up and down, side to side in slow patterns, and her heartbeat starts to slow as she stops fighting me. Her hips sway from side to side as her arm moves in fluid motions I no longer control. My fingers are just on her wrist, holding her to me as she soars in the imagination of her mind, the black feathers of a kezja alicorn ruffled in the breeze, the embers of its soul imprinting on the air behind.

"Good girl," I murmur. "You're doing so well."

She stiffens for a few seconds, then relaxes again, finding that fluidity she needs. She isn't graceful; her movements aren't 'pretty,' but what they are is free.

And that is what kezjic value over everything else. The freedom to *be*.

The wand starts to glow softly; the sound of a crackling fire hums from it, and Micha opens her eyes with a small gasp. "It feels..." She struggles to find the words, and a jolt of envy hits me. I practiced for ten years, dedicated hours every day to feel the connection with my wand, and yet it never happened. But she spends one hour, and the look on her face is one of utter amazement and joy and wonder.

The longer I stare at her though, the more my envy fades. I might not have ever felt the bond of a wand, and I might not feel the blood bond yet, but I have experienced all she is feeling now. I experience it every time I look at her.

She takes my fucking breath away.

"Marry me," I blurt.

Her eyes jerk to mine. She knows we are to wed as soon as the baby is believed to make it to full term. Miscarriages are all too common in witches, and it is the last back-out clause in our marriage contract. A Shadow does not divorce.

Just like kezjic mate for life.

"I said I –" she starts, but I cut in.

"No, marry me now. Today." I spin her around and drop to one knee in front of her. I pull off one of the rings I wear, a black band I thought gave me extra power until Mother told me the truth. I wish I had an actual ring picked out, one that didn't have so many lies around it, but I don't want to wait that long to ask her. To beg her to be mine again.

"I know I fucked up, Micha. I hammered that screw into your hands, cut that knife through your fingers, and I broke the promise I made to you. That you were mine to love and protect and fucking worship. And then I raped you, didn't listen when you told me no. I ignored your boundaries for a second time, and even though I was under the effects of the Craving, I accept responsibility for that, and I am sorry. And I am so fucking sorry for the pain you are carrying and will continue to carry because of what I've done."

I grab her left hand as she stares at me with wetness in her eyes.

"Fuck, baby, I know that pain will never go away. I know that trust will never go back to how it used to be, but if you bless me with a lifetime with you, I swear I'll dedicate every moment of it forging a new trust, new memories to counter that pain.

"I need you, Micha." My voice breaks as the words spill out. "These last few days, I have been listening for any whisper of your words, watching for any smiles you give. And when you laughed at what Maddox said at dinner last night, I wanted to kill him. I wanted to kill him for getting to experience what I needed."

I shake my head, trying to remember everything I have read these past few days about how to express myself, how to turn what I feel into words so I don't fuck it up. But my chest is squeezing and my lungs are aching and my head is feeling all the pressure of research and midnight attempts at speaking to mirrors.

"I don't want you to say yes to stop my pain," I say. "Because I will carry the agony of what I did to you for the rest of my life. Shit, Micha. I'm so sorry. I'm so sorry for what I did, and I will never forgive myself for that even if you do. But I'm asking you to marry me because I love you."

I swallow down the pain of that statement, the lie that comes from the curse she doesn't know about. But I love her as much as I know how, and it's fucking terrifying.

"I love you, Micha," I say again as I squeeze her hand. My other hand shakes as I hold up the ring. "So will you please marry me?"

There is a long moment of silence as she stares at me with wet eyes. Her cheeks are dry though. Her lips wobble even as they stay tightly pursed.

My heart hammers in my chest, hitting my lungs hard enough to bruise, to knock the wind out of them so I can't breathe.

And then...

Without a word, she walks away.

Shattering me into pieces.

THIRTY-EIGHT

HER

He's on me before I get to the door. Grabbing my hips, he throws me into the air with a twist of his arms. It forces me into a spin, and as I fall, now facing him, his hands land on my hips again. With a burst of speed, he arrives at the wall, crowding me in with his body, wrapping my legs around his waist. Grabbing my wand, he yanks it out of my hand. My heart slams wildly as he swivels it around so he's holding the handle.

"If you think I will give up after one rejection," he growls, "you are mistaken. I told you you are mine, Micha. I didn't mean that only when you love me back, when you are at your best. You are mine when you hate me, when you stab me in the heart, when you fucking rip it out with your rejection.

"And I will spend the rest of my life proving that to you. So I'm going to ask you again. Will you marry me?"

"I told you I will in a few months," I bite out, mad as all

hel. "Because I don't have a fucking choice."

A war of emotions flashes in his eyes. Then they harden as he shakes his head. "Marry me because you love me."

"Fuck you."

"Please."

"Fuck. *You*," I sneer as I lean forward. "I will never marry you out of love. I will never *choose* to be your wife. I will say, 'I do,' only because you purchased me. So I hope you know that every day you have me as your wife is just a fucking lie."

I lean back against the wall, holding his gaze and hoping he's suffering. Because he's asking me to be his while still smelling like that fucking *bitch*.

And I know it is all in my head. He had four showers the first day he fucked her and two every day since. There's no way I can actually smell her, but he's forever tainted to me. I can still imagine his cock thrusting inside her and his lips on her nipples as he moans, "*That's it, baby. Fuck…you feel so good. Fuck me just like that.*"

And I know I might have given him permission to fuck her when I was hurting and didn't want us to be together, but he *did* it. He took what we had, all the first moments, the fact that we were each other's onlys, and he went and fucked her. He fucked her because he wanted to.

Even if I have his ring on my finger, I will smell her on him for the rest of my life. Especially since she is living in our godsdamn house, sitting at our godsdamn table, and smiling like she can still feel my husband's godsdamn cock as he came inside her.

So fuck him.

And fuck that bitch.

He never even apologized for doing it. And I can't help but think, is that because Varius doesn't see it as an issue? He is a Boss, and Bosses have mistresses. And the idea that he's planning on fucking all the hoes who throw themselves at him is making me feral. If I ever find one in our bed, I'll burn the entire house down, starting with the mattress with her tied to it.

"Good," he snaps.

I blink. Then narrow my eyes at him. "What do you mean 'good?'"

"You will be my wife, beside me every day, so I accept your yes."

My mouth drops open as I sputter, completely caught off guard.

"We'll marry tomorrow evening," he says.

"That is not what I meant," I snap.

"I don't care. I want to be married to you, Micha. I want everyone to know you are mine. I want *you* to know, so I'm going to accept your yes, and if you hate me for it, I will simply beg for your forgiveness later. I can add it to the list of all the other shit I've done."

"You can't just add to the list!"

"Why not? You're already mad at me; it won't change anything."

"You – you fucking neanderthal!" I sputter.

"Dayne is to arrive later this evening," he says, his eyes calculating as he ignores my protests completely. "Lou isn't supposed to get here for another two days, but I'm sure your father –"

"Dayne's coming?"

He nods. "He should be here in an hour or so."

I grit my teeth, not wanting to show him how happy I am over that. But fuck, could I use a drink and a long talk with my bestie. Except I can't drink because I'm fucking pregnant. Dammit.

"I'll need to invite my capos and Aleric so no one thinks they're being disrespected, but with Talon dead, they'll want to talk to me anyways." He nods. "They'll come."

"Well, I'm still not fucking you tomorrow," I snap.

"We'll need to consummate the marriage."

"Then you'll have to rape me."

His eyes grow heated. "I was out of control then, Micha, and I am sorry for not listening to you. But when I fuck you tomorrow, it'll be because you beg me for it."

My jaw clenches at the same time my pussy does – a bolt of desire slamming down through our bond. His nostrils flare as his eyes dip low, and I am suddenly aware that he can smell my arousal. My cheeks heat as his gaze turns hot and heavy.

"Shall we see if I can get you to beg now?" he murmurs as he lifts his eyes to mine.

"Don't you fucking touch me."

His fingers dig into my hips as he steps back, and my legs drop from around his waist. He sets me on the floor, then places his palms flat on the wall as he leans his head down to mine. My heart hammers as he stares at me with so much wicked heat.

I yank my gaze away and stare at his chest instead.

"After we marry, Micha," he says, his voice a deep purr, "I will not take you upstairs unless you ask me to. I will not touch you outside of the first dance. But I will be by your side the entire time, thinking about the feel of your pussy around my cock, how you'll taste on my tongue when you ride my face until you come."

I tremble against the wall as I try to throw a block up around our bond. But my magic no longer listens to me. Because of *him*. I try to hold on to my anger, and I manage it –I fucking manage it so damn well– but love and hate is too thin of a line. And the desire he's pushing down our link isn't one of gentle lovemaking and calming hearts. It's wild and primal – pure hate fucking at its finest. It's a release of all our pain and anger and emotions we can't name.

"You'll look at me," he growls low, "and I'll get so fucking hard imagining what those lips can do. What orders they will give me as I'm begging you to let me fuck you."

My gaze snaps to his as the image of him tied and bound at my mercy fills my mind. My lips part. I swallow hard as I force my mouth closed. But his eyes tracked the movement of my lips, and he makes a noise that causes me to shiver.

Lifting his gaze back to mine, Varius murmurs, "Will you place my cock inside a chastity cage and make me kneel between your legs, licking and fingering you until morning while never giving me the command to touch myself? Will you tie me to the bed with a witch's snare and hover your pussy right over my face as you fuck yourself with a toy, torturing me with the teasing drops of your cum as I beg for you to let me taste you? Just one fucking lick." He groans. "Just give me one lick, baby."

My lips part as I press my back hard against the wall to try to increase the distance between us. My every nerve is aware of how close he is to me, how if I just rock my hips forward the slightest inch, I can feel the hard, pulsing length of his cock. If I tilt my head up, I can taste his lips. I tremble beneath the images he is feeding me, and my breaths come out on harsh, shallow pants.

"And when you finally allow me the pleasure of taking you up to our room, I still will not touch you. I will walk behind you so everyone knows that I am yours just as much as you are mine."

I shudder on a rasp.

"But know that I will be watching your ass as I imagine burying my face in it. How I can press you against a wall, bunch up the skirt of your dress, and trail my tongue from my lips to your ass..."

His voice trails off, and I know he's imagining it now. I can hear the strain in his voice, feel the pulse of his cock even though it's not touching me. But it's just right there, not even an inch away from my body.

"Gods, I love the taste of you," he groans as he shudders.

And seeing him this tense has my hips rocking forward so I can feel just the barest touch of his tip.

He groans again, and the muscles in front of me flex hard as he struggles to keep his hands off me. "Fuck, Micha," he growls.

His breaths are hard and fast as he continues, "You will have all the toys at your disposal. And amongst them, there will be a knife."

I suck in a breath. "A knife?" I whisper, the words falling out before I can stop them.

"I love you, Micha, but if you think you can never forgive me, if you can never love me again like you said, then use the knife on me. Tie me down with the witch's snare, and when my vampirism activates, then go ahead and cut out my heart because it'll already be fucking destroyed. These last few days have been hel, but I have held on to the hope that I can fix this. That I can show you how sorry I am for hurting you, so if I can't – if there is nothing I can ever do in all the years I will be married to you, then go ahead and stab me. But at least let me die knowing you have my last name."

My breath catches as I stare at him, trapped in the heat of his gaze. His eyes dip to my lips and linger. My chest squeezes tight. He leans his head down ever so slightly, but if he tries to kiss me, I'm going to knee him in the fucking dick.

Because fuck him and his smooth words.

Fuck my body for being addicted to his touch after four months of constantly having it.

And fuck the blood bond the most. Fuck the mixing of our souls where his desires now feed into mine. Where his arousal and need fill me up and make it hard for me to resist him. I'm like a cat in heat where he controls the fucking dial. But though his emotions might be influencing mine, I am a fucking Black. I am stronger than my *desires*.

So I lift my chin, giving him that tiny bit of hope that I will give in to him.

Then I say, "Fuck you."

His head jerks back. Pain flares in his eyes. He stares at me for a moment longer, and then he's gone.

Fucking.

Asshole.

THIRTY-NINE

HER

I yank open the door to the gym, completely pissed. I'm mad at Varius for having tortured me, then tricked me into accepting his proposal before I'm ready. I'm mad at myself for *wanting* to get married to him tomorrow. I'm mad and I'm happy and I'm mad that I'm happy and I'm just – *Ugh!* I'm all over the fucking place.

A sudden craving for mint ice cream hits me, and I turn towards the kitchen. I haven't eaten much in the past week due to being too upset, but now all that hunger hits me with force. My stomach growling, I pass through the archway connecting the kitchen to the living room, then freeze.

Khalid's girl is standing at the fridge, with her back to me as she looks inside.

We are alone.

My blood chills, my anger becoming cold.

Khalid is thousands of miles away, and he doesn't have any alexandrite with him. He won't be able to kill me before

I can kill her. I might not have any magic anymore, but I am a trained assassin, and she is nothing more than a human.

I stalk up to her. My footsteps are utterly quiet. I toy with the idea of pulling out a knife as I get closer. It'll only take one precise thrust to end her life. But I need to be smart about this. I need to make it look like an accident.

Humans trip over all the time... If her head connects just so with the counter, Khalid will suspect another traitor in the house, but he won't know it's me. I can grab her by her hair, yank her head back, and then slam her temple into the counter.

My fingers itch with the need to release my anger and jealousy out on her, but she turns before I make it halfway through the room. *Dammit.*

She jumps when she sees me, dropping the eggs she took out of the fridge. A sharp gasp leaves her, and I curse inside my head. Although I can still easily kill her with her facing me, if she struggles or screams at all, it'll be a lot harder for me to make it look like an accident.

"Crap. Sorry. Let me clean this." She rushes over to the sink to grab a sponge, then kneels down to clean up the mess. "But then do you want an omelette?" she asks with a small smile in my direction. "Sau isn't cooking today as she is planning everything for the wedding, so I was going to make everyone some lunch –"

"Fuck you, you fucking whore," I growl.

She pales, her entire body freezing.

I step towards her, fire burning inside my fingers. "Do you seriously think you get to talk to me after you fucked my husband?"

She flinches and ducks her head. "I'm sorry, but I could not leave Khalid to face Talon on his own."

"He would've been fine. He's the fucking reaper."

Her head snaps up at that, and fierce anger burns in her eyes. "Fuck *you*," she snaps. "Fuck everyone who thinks that of him. He is *Khalid*. He is more than just a weapon to be used. He deserves to know what it's like to have people who love him."

"Varius loves –"

"He makes him kill those he loves! He loves Talon. He loves all his brothers so fucking much, and his job is to kill them without mercy. He is not just a weapon to be used," she repeats, agony in every word. "He is a person. He's my person."

Fuck. I hate how that gets to me. I still hate her and want to kill her, but I can understand where she is coming from. *The bitch.*

"You knew I loved him," I snarl, holding on to my rage with both hands. I clench my fists.

"I know, and I'm sorry." Steely determination fills her blue eyes. "But I couldn't leave him on his own. He's going to hurt so much after he kills Talon. I don't want him to be alone or think he's a monster."

I clench my jaw, hating how I can see myself in her and Varius in Khalid. The both of us are fighting to make our monsters feel whole.

But there is a difference that only increases my jealousy. Her monster fights to protect her. Mine tortures me.

Turning from her, I snap, "Stay the fuck away from me."

Then I spin back around, remembering I want ice cream. She scrambles out of the way as I yank open the fridge and take the whole pot with me. I stab a spoon into it and take a bite. I wrinkle my nose; it's missing something.

Turning to the fridge, ignoring the whore standing in my peripheral, I rummage around until I find it. Grabbing the jar of pickles, I open it and pour a bit into the ice cream tub. I take a bite, nod in approval, then storm out of the room to go enjoy my lunch in peace.

"Hey, bitch."

My eyes widen as I spin towards the hallway leading to

the side door of the house.

Dayne is standing there with a smile on his face and a rucksack on his back. Running towards him, I leap into his outstretched arms. He catches me with a laugh even though I spill pickle juice all over him.

"I'm so glad you're here," I say into his neck.

"I almost wasn't," he says with a dry chuckle.

Knowing that tone, I climb down from him and step back. Glaring at him, I check him over for wounds. I don't see any, but he could be hiding some under his T-shirt and shorts. "Strip."

"No." He crosses his arms.

I roll my eyes. "Fine. Then what happened?"

"I got a hit called out on me while I was in Europe."

"What! And you didn't call?" I wince, realizing that he shouldn't have had to. "Shit. I should've checked in on you." I can feel him through the magical rune I tattooed on his skin; he used to be able to feel me through a matching rune I had on my hip, but Varius made me burn it off.

Concentrating on the bond between us, I notice that Dayne's heart is beating slightly higher than normal. He's still on edge. Fuck. How close did he come to dying?

"It's fine –" he starts, seeing me frown.

"Yeah, because I saved your ass," a guy says as he steps forward and slaps Dayne's ass. My friend's jaw locks as he spins out of range of the newcomer.

My eyes widen as I recognize him. "*Torture guy*?"

With a charming smile, the guy Dayne (and sometimes I) tortured, thinking he was working for my blackmailer, tips his black cowboy hat. "Name's Quinton," he says with a western drawl.

"What were you doing in Europe with him?" My eyes widen as I glance between them. "Oh my gods, are you two fu–"

"No," Dayne says sharply. "Varius has had him watching

me since we let him go. He escorted me back from France. That's it."

"Technically, I've been watching you since well before I got tortured," he says as he shifts the two backpacks he has hanging off his shoulders. "Weren't you in the same room with me for most of that time? Somewhere I could see you? Hmmm?"

Dayne turns his head to glare at him before looking back at me. "Do you see what shit I've had to deal with these past few days?"

I roll my lips in as the pain in my chest finally starts to ease. I might not have any magic still, but just being near my bestie is picking up my spirits. Laughing, I shake my head. "I reckon my shit can outdo your shit."

Dayne snorts. "Nothing can beat the misery of being in Quinton's company."

"Hey!"

I grin. "So want something to eat or drink?" I ask. "How long was the drive? Where did you fly in?" I head for the kitchen, and I'm glad when Khalid's girl isn't in there. The urge to kill her, knowing my best friend would cover for me, would be way too tempting.

"Orlando," Dayne says as he follows me. "And just an orange juice. We got lunch on the way."

My eyebrows shooting up, I grab a knife from the block on the counter and spin around to face him. "Who are you, and what have you done to my friend?"

"Ha ha," he says dryly.

I grin. "Seriously though. You feeling okay?"

He looks at me dryly. "You can't drink while pregnant, so I'm giving it up in solidarity."

Awww. I love my bestie.

His eyes drop to my flat stomach. "Fuck. I thought you were further along," he says warily.

A smile cracks through my anger and pain. I punch him

in the shoulder. "I'm fourteen weeks. I just seem to be lucky enough to not have any symptoms."

"You always were a lucky bitch."

I shake my head and turn before he can see my smile fall. The last week hasn't felt lucky at all.

After putting the knife back, I set the tub of ice cream down too, then reach up to get him a cup. I grab one of the custom photographic dick mugs, knowing he'd appreciate the humor. Quinton seems to have left us, no doubt to go check in with his Boss, so I only pour one drink.

I turn to find Dayne warily eying the counter splitting the room in two. "It's a monster," I say before I dig into my tub of ice cream and pickles.

"What?"

"Yeah, Sau trapped it in the wood when it was dying. So it's like the bodyguard of the house."

"That's so fucking cool."

Recalling she's training monsters at the moment, I say, "If you're really nice, she might let you help feed some."

"What!?"

I laugh as I tell him about her preparations for the war. My stomach crawls as I remember why we need them in the first place. Antonio's sneering face flashes in my mind, but I do my best to block him out. I want to enjoy my bestie's company for a bit before I bring up all the shitty stuff.

Eventually, we move into the spare bedroom to talk more in private. He drops his bag on the bed. "So how are things between you and Varius?" Dayne asks coyly. The last time he and I talked, I told him I was in love with the Boss of the Shadow Domain.

Gods, that feels like forever ago.

"He is a fucking asshole," I say as I cross my arms.

He raises a brow as he glances me over, but there are no injuries for him to see. All the damage is on the inside.

"How so?"

Shit. I can't tell him Varius tortured me; if I do that, he will kill him while Khalid's away, and that's something he can absolutely pull off. Dayne might have been my spotter when we worked together, doing most of the admin rather than the killing, but that was only because I was shit at it, and one of us had to do the job.

"He fucked Khalid's girl for a stupid blood bond ritual," I grumble instead.

"The asshole," he says immediately. "Want me to help hide their bodies?"

I grin. "I love you so much."

"I love you too." He pauses, then asks, "But seriously. Are we killing –"

"No. And don't hit either of them for it either." Khalid would kill him either way. "I can take care of my own shit."

He frowns, then sighs. Then eventually promises after I wheedle him some more.

"So do you think you two can work past this then? Or do you want to run before the wedding tomorrow?"

I sigh as I flop down onto the bed beside him. As mad as I am at Varius right now, though, I'm not even tempted. I have too much tying me here. Lou is marrying in. He's the father of my baby. And we're bonded. If we don't keep exchanging blood until the ritual is finished, it'll kill me.

"I don't know if I can ever forgive him," I say truthfully, "but I can't leave him either."

"Our network –"

I shake my head. Our network is for hiding the children we pretend to assassinate. Those people aren't being looked for. If there is one truth in this world, it is that Varius will tear this world apart looking for me.

And there is one other reason I won't take Dayne's offer. "I still love the damn fool."

Dayne looks at me softly. "Okay then. But if you ever change your mind, I'll always have a bag packed."

I grin as I turn on my side to look at him. "You're the best."

"I know."

I stick my tongue out at him.

Then I sigh.

I'm going to have to tell him about the werewolf attack. We share everything, and it'll be good to get the nightmares out of my head. Reaching over to him, I hold his hand as I go into all the gritty details about what Antonio did to me, including his promise to come back.

"Fuck," Dayne says when I finish. "How are you?" He immediately shakes his head. "Dumb question. Shit, Micha. I'm sorry you went through that alone. If I'd still had the bond –"

"You'd be dead," I cut in. "Antonio left me alive to fuck with Varius. He would've had no reason to keep you alive."

"Still…" His gaze hardens. "I'm going to ask him to let me tattoo you again. If he wants to torture me to make sure I won't break –"

"No," I cut in, my heart hammering in my throat at the idea of Varius torturing my best friend. My hands tighten into fists. I remember the feel of that screw. He did that to me, someone he loved. What would he do to someone he's jealous of? Dayne might be gay, but Varius doesn't care. My best friend has a part of me he does not, and that is enough of make him feral.

"Micha –"

"No," I say sharply. "I don't want you feeling me if–" *When,* my brain corrects, remembering the wolf's promise to me. I tremble. "*If* Antonio gets to me again."

"That's exactly why –"

"You won't be able to stop him, Dayne," I say softly, my heart in my throat. As much as I want to protect him from Varius' jealousy, I also want to protect him from that. If he feels me die, he will kill himself trying to avenge me, and all

I want is for him to be happy. "So tell me about you and Quinton," I say with a false cheerfulness.

He stares at me for a moment, not wanting to change the subject. Then he sighs. "There's nothing to tell," he says.

"No? So you two haven't fucked yet?"

His eyes narrow, but he doesn't say no…

I laugh. I'm just about to tease him, but then I sit bolt upright as I remember what Quinton said when he first came in. He said it so jokingly though, that it didn't really register until now. "Wait, did he really save you?"

He looks utterly annoyed. "Don't tell him, but yeah. I got trapped between three shooters."

I suck in a breath.

"But I probably would've figured a way out of it. I always do. Quinton just happened to be the easy option." His eyes narrow. "In fact. I'm sure of it." As he starts to go off about all the different ways he could've saved himself, I struggle to breathe.

I would've lost my best friend if it wasn't for Varius.

He's been watching over Dayne all this time…

For me?

"I need to go do something real quick," I say, jumping to my feet.

He sits up. "Want me to come –"

"No. I'll be right back." I wave as I head for the door, but I don't feel relaxed at all. All my nerves are fried, and they wind tighter and tighter as I make my way up to Varius' office. I knock on the door. He doesn't answer. I knock again. Still silence. Shifting on my feet, I call, "Varius?"

"Come in."

I step inside. As I shut the door, he shuts his laptop, giving me his undivided attention.

I stand in front of his desk, confused by all the different things I'm feeling. But even if I mostly seem to hate him right now, he saved my friend. Dayne is like the other half of me. The brother I always yearned for. If I lost him, a large part of me would've died.

"Thank you for saving Dayne," I say.

His eyes soften. "He matters to you, Micha, which means he matters to me. There are no thanks needed."

"But you saved his life. I owe you –"

"You owe me nothing."

"But –"

"You don't owe debts for saving family."

"But he's not your family."

"He's yours, Micha. Which makes him mine."

I look at the painting behind his desk as I swallow hard. *Fuck.* "Well…I guess, maybe, I will marry you then."

A small smile tugs at his lips. "I would like that."

I clear my throat, then nod. "But I'm still mad at you."

"I know."

I hike a thumb over my shoulder. "And I'm going back to talk shit about you to Dayne. So I'm going to get all riled up again over what you did."

"I expected as much."

"And you still brought him here?" I ask suspiciously.

"You needed him."

My mouth drops open.

Fuck.

I really did, still do.

"I'm still mad at you," I whisper.

"I know."

Nodding, I turn and make my way back to Dayne.

But I leave a part of me in that office with the man I supposedly hate.

FORTY

HIM

Leno got in touch with all of the capos yesterday. Despite a few silent grumbles, they've all found the time to come in. They'll be here in a few hours, just in time for the wedding. I spoke to Aleric myself, Boss to Boss so the invite wasn't insulting, and the members he has in the police force are keeping the legit ones off our asses. There's been whispers of the FBI in the area, having been alarmed by the last-minute roll out of all of our capos and many of our allies. The Blacks are here, as are the Mattos twins, and numerous other higher-ups.

Leaning back in my chair, I finish my conversation with an off-world Boss through a scry Leno set up for me a few minutes ago. Given what we saw at Morn Tower, we are going to need more silver and not the useless shit from Earth. Ryker is the Boss we have been running a smuggling ring with for the past few decades, but we move people, not product.

All the portals to Earth were closed by the archangels thousands of years ago during the Great Extinction (when Sebastian the Ancient Destroyer – an ancient vampire who wanted to be worshiped like a god, and Rakian the Rise of Ragnarok – the son of Loki and the Morrighan, who was pissed off at his parents, tried to destroy the Seven Planes), so if we start bringing in items and materials that will shine a light onto the existence of another world rather than just another species, then the SCU will come here to investigate.

"I'll agree to the forty-five cut," Ryker says, his golden eyes sharp beneath his heavy brows. "Even though we have a higher risk, what with the Elv've'Norc actually being here rather than just the weak-ass SCU you have there."

Although the SCU runs with the full authority of the Elv've'Norc here on Earth, they don't have the same weight to throw around given how cut off they are and how they're made up of mostly Earth humans rather than sups who can take on the creatures they police.

My expression doesn't change. He might have the higher risk – especially since the archangels are no longer policing the portals themselves, but all he has to do is get the goods and toss them. We have to distribute it, and if we get caught bringing off-world goods here, we'll become a high priority for the Special Crimes Unit to deal with.

And though we might really need this silver and soon, a fact that would normally put us at a disadvantage during any other negotiation, Ryker doesn't know a damn thing about what happens on our end. So he thinks I'm just ready to risk smuggling goods if the price is right.

"I'll send a box with the people tomorrow," he says. "See how long that takes to move, and we'll start from there."

I nod, then run my fingers across the glass in front of me, feeling the cold 'wetness' of the magic. The image of Ryker shimmers, the scry now broken, and my own face looks back at me.

Standing, I head for the door, then down the hall. As soon as I reach the bottom of the stairs, a fresh new ward bites into my skin. Mother and Rudy erected them around the stairway to keep nosy guests out of areas they don't belong. The three wards right outside the basement door, one after the other, are warded to kill upon contact.

When Micha blasted the old one apart, she destroyed decades of magic that not even Mother or Rudy, the two strongest, can rebuild to the same level of power (it'll take them decades), so they've had to stack weaker wards. It isn't anywhere as strong as what it used to be, and Mother worries a powerful, dedicated witch might be able to get through, but Kati Vosika, Cara Jervis, and Joshua Tobler – the only three she thinks might have a chance, will be watched at all times tonight.

If any of them slip away, Maddox will shift into them, give a bit of "their" DNA to our brother, and Khalid will kill them with a soul doll. Although we do not have much alexandrite left, Antonio having stolen our main stash, we can't afford another Family thinking us weak. The Shadow Domain is dominant in the southeast of America because everyone knows we are strong and merciless. Let either of those things slip, and our allies will turn on us like vultures.

My brothers are all standing at the bottom of the stairs, dressed in three-piece suits despite the heat. Rudy traced a rune on each of us to keep our body temperatures cool an hour ago, so none of us are even sweating.

My eyes find Khalid's. I have only talked to him briefly since he arrived this morning, back from having killed T. He took our brother into his shadows, and that's making me fucking paranoid. It was because of T that Khalid's girl was violated and abused. For the reaper to have forgiven him enough to give him a proper 'burial'... What reason could T have given to warrant that much understanding?

Does he know I'm a hybrid now?

Does he think Talon was in the right, but he only killed him because he hurt the woman he loves?

Will he be the next person to try to kill me?

I search his eyes, but all I see is the reaper staring back at me.

"We in business?" Khalid asks.

I nod.

"Aw, fuck off with the shop talk," Maddox says. "Tonight is for getting drunk and forgetting we're going to get eaten by super werewolves."

Rudy grins. "If I was there, you wouldn't have got your asses kicked."

Maddox laughs. "You would've been the first to go. You would've taken one look at him and died of a heart attack."

Rudy flips him the bird, and Maddox reaches forward with all his fingers curled into an O. Then he pumps it up and down Rudy's finger. Scowling, Rudy shoves him away and wipes his violated hand on his thigh.

Maddox laughs and turns for the door. I glance at Khalid again, a silent question asking how he is.

He turns from me without an answer, and for one stupid split second, my fingers itch to shove a knife into his back. Kill him before he tries to kill me.

"Are you okay?" I ask softly as the rest of our brothers step outside, heading for the lake on our property. Rows of white chairs sit in front of it, and they're already full of people. The sound of chatter whispers on the wind, too far away to make any specific voices out. At the front, between the two columns of chairs, is an archway of flowers Leno weaved together.

The flowers around us blossom as we walk.

"Yes."

I can't smell that he's lying, but I can fucking feel it.

The skin across my shoulders tightens with the knot in my stomach. Glancing at my brother as he walks beside me,

I wonder just how long it's going to be before the man I trust the most, the one I tortured Micha for, is going to turn on me.

A week from now?

A month?

Or will he kill me and Micha tonight while we're asleep in our bed? Cut out our child in fear that she's a hybrid too?

FORTY-ONE

HER

When I step out of the house, I see him instantly. He is standing in front of the archway of flowers down by the lake, wearing a dark-red tux. He's too far for me to see his face, but even at this distance, I can still feel the intensity of his stare. He sees me, and he is waiting.

Down the bond between us comes a flood of love and desire and so much fucking happiness that I am his, that it rips all the air out of my lungs. So I tear my gaze away and try not to feel his love for me. I don't want it when only a few paces from him is the bitch he slept with a mere week ago.

I force myself to look at her as she stands so beautifully behind my sister, holding a bouquet of white flowers. Force myself to feel the pain of her presence. As long as she's living with us, I'm never going to forgive him. This last week, I've been avoiding her so I don't kill her, and it's been doing my head in.

I don't know the other three women behind her, so my eyes sweep forward. Lou, my baby sister, is next, and at the front is Dayne, my maid of honor. He's dressed in the same red dress the others are wearing. Same heels and make-up too. I wish he was the one walking me down the aisle, but my father is, unfortunately, still alive and he made it in time for the wedding.

"Micha," the devil himself says as he appears behind me, and I *hate* how I didn't notice his approach. Despite all the years he trained me, I never got anywhere near his level on any skillset outside of pure magical strength. Even then, he still managed to kick my ass in a magic-only fight. And my magic *ate* magic. I'd complain it wasn't fair, but then he'd just beat me for being whiney.

"Stefaan," I say, my words lacking all the warmth that comes so easily to my lips when I talk to Lou or Dayne.

"Micha." I can hear my sister whining in my head. She hates it when we fight. To her, Father isn't warm per say but nor is he the cold bastard I know him as. He isn't the brutal trainer who left her with fractured bones, ruptured tendons, and internal bleeding as a way to make her tougher.

But Stefaan doesn't discipline me for my lack of respect. He doesn't really react to it at all. I am no longer his charge; he sold me, so my actions are no longer a reflection of him.

They are a reflection of Varius though, of how well he can control his woman, and thus a reflection on the entire Shadow Family. I am not dumb enough to let my pride get in the way of a solid alliance between our gangs. So I force my smile to come across as more genuine, for my tongue to have less bite.

"Thank you for coming at such short notice," I say.

"One does not simply ignore an invite from the Boss of the Shadow Domain," he says, offering out his arm.

Begrudgingly, I take it.

Of course that's why he's here. Not for me. Not because

it's his daughter's fucking wedding. I hate how much that knowledge hurts, even though that shouldn't be a shock at all. He died the same time Mom did sixteen years ago; his soul simply didn't pass over into the Underworld. Instead, it grew cold and dark and empty. My two brothers were old enough to take care of themselves at that point, but Lou was a newborn and I was only eleven. That overnight rejection hurt, but I should've learned my lesson by now.

Irritated with myself, I start to stomp across the paving stones leading down to the lake, just wanting to get this over with, but Stefaan's hand tightens on my arm. Not hard enough to bruise. Just enough to gain my attention and get me to slow down, to walk like a "lady." I glance at him, and he leans in close.

"Your mother was sold to me," he says, and I turn to him fully now. "But she owned me more than I ever did her," he says softly. "And when she died giving birth to your sister... I lost a large part of myself. Too much. So much I failed you and Lou..." He trails off for a moment. "She would've been so disappointed in me." The words are a mere whisper. Then they strengthen again as he says, "But when I finally started to live again, you wanted to become an assassin, and I was terrified of learning to love you, only to feel that loss all over again. So I was never there for you, Micha. That was selfish of me. To think of only myself and my pain rather than my daughter's."

My throat closes, and dammit, I feel tears behind my eyes. I tried to get his attention all throughout my teenage years, having lost my mother when I was eleven, having seemingly lost my father too. Then when I hit sixteen, when I learned he would never love me even if I followed in his footsteps, I convinced myself I didn't need him anymore.

But fuck, a part of me has always yearned for the father I used to know. The one who tried to teach me how to whistle with a blade of grass, who picked me up and carried me inside whenever I fell asleep in the car, who would sneak into a closet and eat apples with me because he made me believe they were a 'naughty treat' like candy.

My throat feeling tight, I snort. "Have you been going to therapy or something?"

He glances away briefly. "Yes."

My jaw drops so far it bounces off my nonexistent boobs. Visiting a psychologist in our line of work is like visiting a cop. You don't do it if you don't want to end up dead. For him to reveal that to me? Does he really trust me that much despite how many times I've gone out of my way to piss him off?

"You remind me so much of your mother, you know," he says, and all I can do is stare at him in shock for a few steps.

"Lou is the one who looks like her," I finally manage to sputter.

He nods. "She might have got all her looks, but you got her fire, angel."

I turn away from him and squeeze my eyes shut to stop the tears. The last time I heard someone call me 'angel' was when mom was alive.

"She would've been so proud of you," he says.

My throat constricts until I can barely breathe. But we're getting close to the crowd now. In another few seconds, the music will start playing and everyone will turn to look at me. So I take a deep breath and lock it all down. I don't have the emotional capacity right now to deal with this. So I do what I always do. I crack a joke. "Oh, yes. She always had such dreams of me being a breedmare to a monster."

He stops abruptly, and I'm jerked to a stop with him. We are still far enough away from the back of the row that they don't notice we're here, but Varius notices. I can feel his paranoia running down our bond, his instant desire to come get me and drag me the rest of the way if he has to.

I catch his gaze and shake my head. His eyes narrow

ever so slightly, but he doesn't move even though I can feel the vibration of his energy.

Stefaan's voice is low, deadly. "Is he a monster to you?"

I snort. "You can't act like you care after selling me to him."

"I found out about your secret network and knew it was only a matter of time before some very powerful people came after you. I won't be able to protect you from them, but he can."

My eyes widen as I spin fully towards Stefaan, ripping my arm from his. Fear ruptures down my spine. Dayne and I specialized in killing kids as a cover. Any time a hit went out on one, we took it so we could pretend to assassinate them. In truth, we gave them a new face, a new identity, a new family that didn't want them dead – most hits having been taken out by siblings who didn't want to share their inheritance or step parents who didn't want kids or widows who realized they would get everything if said kids weren't alive. We were very careful to cover our tracks. "What did you –"

"I covered your tracks better," he cuts in quickly.

"Dayne..." I say, blood draining from my face. If Father can't protect me, then he can't –

"What the fuck have you said to my wife?" Varius asks softly as he comes up to us. His fingers wrap around my arm as he hauls me to him. My eyes widen at the fierce protectiveness rushing down our bond.

The sudden burst of laughter from the crowd takes me by surprise, and I glance behind Varius to see Sau in front of the crowd, playing the smooth hostess who distracts them from the shitstorm brewing in the corner. There's a slight glimmer in the air around us too, meaning someone has cast an illusion over us, perhaps showing Varius is on a call – a Boss that never stops working.

I look back at him as I try to pull away, but he doesn't let me go.

"I told her someone has taken a hit out on her," my father lies smoothly.

"Who?" Varius asks softly, every part of him poised like a snake about to strike.

"William Florsley." My blood instantly boils at the mere sound of his name. Ten years ago, the fucker paid for us to kill his son just because he suspected him of being gay. That way he could favor his 'normal' child without losing face. My five-figure fee back then was nothing compared to how much he threw at marketing to be "an ally" to the LGBTQ+ community so they would support him financially.

His public persona is so well played and he's so rich that he's too powerful to touch. He owns the majority share of the retailer Flormart, which has thousands of branches all across the US. They're terrible places to work, with low pay, long hours, no benefits, and no overtime. But if you focus on hiring the desperate, they're not going to complain about poor or illegal work conditions due to being too terrified of losing their job. After all, there's always someone else to replace them because every capitalist economy needs a sum of people unemployed and desperate for just this reason. You can't rely on firing the people who complain if there's no one else to take their place.

He's utter scum, and although I doubt he actually knows about me having not done the job he paid me to do, I am okay with him dying to protect my secret. Because that is what's going to happen. I can feel Varius' decision in the power of our bond.

"He won't touch her," he says, not giving my father any evidence to use against him. "Now come." Releasing me, he strides back to the altar to wait for us to walk down the aisle.

I breathe out slowly before looking at Father. "Does he actually know?"

"I don't know. But some PIs have been spotted at his son's college."

My lips tighten. We didn't have the means back then to give the kid a new face. We hoped moving him to the other side of the country and to a small town would be enough.

"They might not be working for William," I say.

"Perhaps not."

"They could be watching anyone at his college."

He nods. "There are thousands of students and faculty. Someone is probably just cheating on their spouse."

Most likely. But any assassin who goes off mere statistics ends up dead. My heart hammering, my eyes find Dayne. He's looking at me in concern. "If you want to make things up to me," I say, my voice cracking, "do whatever it takes to protect Dayne."

Before Father can say anything, a guitar starts to play, and the chatter of the crowd dies down. Chairs squeak and fabric rustles as everyone turns to face us. As Leno starts to sing a cover of "You Are the Reason" by Calum Scott, I walk slowly down the aisle on my father's arm, surprised at how good the man can sing.

He's standing beside all of his brothers, all of whom are dressed in crimson suits and black shirts. Rudy is first in line as his best man; Leno is last with Krypto beside him, a fancy red bow tie around his neck. But Talon's absence is heavy in the air, seen in the tight smiles and pain hidden inside a few of their eyes.

I glance at the reaper, who looks cold and empty, hoping he made Talon suffer. Only, Khalid's back too early to have done as good of a job as I would've. I would've spent days, weeks perhaps, skinning him alive. Taking his magic and making him feel fucking helpless to fight back. Making him feel weak. Broken. Like he'll never be whole again.

Reminded of all that I've lost, my eyes harden on Varius. He's watching me, his face that of indifference, perhaps even boredom. But the feelings flowing down our bond are those of guilt and pain but also happiness and joy and a fierce determination to make things right between us.

As the lyrics of the song hit me, I wonder if he chose it or if it's just coincidence that it matches us so well.

My throat tightens as Father hands me off to him.

His hand wraps around mine. His thumb feathers across my skin. And for a moment, all our problems disappear.

I love you, little monster.

Let me prove that to you for the rest of our lives.

He turns on silent promises and leads me up to the altar. My legs are weak beneath my dress, but I somehow manage not to trip over my feet.

The next twenty minutes feel surreal. Our bond has been weakening over the past week as we haven't exchanged any more blood, but today it has been so strong. So fucking clear that what this moment means to him, what *I* mean to him is more than he can find words to say.

Everything on the surface might seem cut and dry. No personalized vows. No smiles. Nothing to show a glimmer of what he's feeling inside. I look at him, then I look past him, and it hits me how alone he is. How not even Rudy, his best man, or Khalid, the one he trusts the most, knows how happy he is with me.

I squeeze his hand. He doesn't squeeze it back. Not here. Not when there are all these witnesses, these allies in wolf clothing that would not hesitate to tear him apart if given the smallest opportunity. But I feel the flare of emotions inside of him, triggered by something so simple as a squeeze of my fingers.

And fuck, do I feel loved.

Almost like I did before he ruined us, but there is still that weight in my chest, that tightness I can't push past.

He raped me.

He tortured me and took my magic.

He nearly killed our child.

And he fucked one of my bridesmaids a week before our wedding.

Fuck him, I want to say.

And yet...

I can see how much he's trying to fix what he's broken.

"Do you, Varius Sin Shadow," the celebrant eventually says, "take Micha Black to be your lawfully wedded wife?"

"I do."

"And do you, Micha Black, take Varius Sin Shadow to be your lawfully wedded husband?"

I start to say the words required of me, but the celebrant doesn't stop.

"To live together in matrimony, to respect him, serve him, honor and obey him, in both sickness and in health, in sorrow and in joy, in anger and in happiness, to have and to hold, from this day forward, til death do you part?"

My eyes narrow.

Maddox half-coughs, half-laughs into a closed fist as I grit out, "I do."

Though 'until death do us part' might be coming really fucking soon.

Rudy steps forward, his lips curled in as he tries to keep his face straight. My narrowed eyes turn to him, a trickle of paranoia hitting me as Varius stiffens. *What the fuck is about to happen now?*

But then I notice it. There isn't a ring on the pillow he's holding. It's a fucking collar. Black and studded like for a dog.

"Where are the rings?" Varius growls low so only the three of us can hear. But Rudy just grins wide, knowing his brother won't make a scene in front of this many witnesses. I narrow my eyes at the red-headed devil.

"I used to like you," I mutter.

His teeth flash white as he pulls another collar out from

inside his red jacket. This one is pale pink and has a bow on the front. For a moment, Varius and I just stare at it. Then understanding dawns. One of us is going to have to wear it. I snap my arm forward, grabbing it right before Varius does.

"Ha!" I grin wide. Rudy laughs silently as the celebrant clears his throat.

Varius slowly picks up the black collar, his lips tight. But it isn't annoyance that's coming down our bond despite what his face says. It's joy at the sight of my happiness.

When he turns to me, my smile fades, washed under the hard beating of my heart. His intense gaze on mine, he undoes the buckle. A shiver runs down my spine. The man in front of us says something, but I don't hear it. I don't hear anything other than the blood rushing through my skull.

I stand dead still as Varius reaches forward and wraps the collar around me. The leather is hard against my skin. It pulls flush as he buckles it. I swallow and feel the press of it.

A small breath leaves me.

Lifting my free hand, I touch the leather collar; the way he put it on didn't feel like the joke it started out as. It feels more permanent, more meaningful than any ring.

"You're mine, Micha."

Property of Varius fucking Shadow.

In front of all these people, you are mine.

When the celebrant clears his throat, I'm jerked back to the fact that I'm surrounded by people who are waiting on me. I blink rapidly with a small shake of my head as I drop my gaze to the collar in my hands. My hands shake slightly as I undo it. I breathe out, then reach up to place it around Varius' neck.

The air feels poised and pregnant as I struggle to do the clasp. Reaching up behind him, he closes his fingers around mine, steadying them. He stares into my eyes, and I am reminded of the night he took me to sing karaoke. The silent support he gave me when I almost got cold feet. I wet my lips, then try again when he drops his hand.

It takes a bit of feeling, but I finally manage to poke the prong through the right hole. I thread the end tip through the rest of the buckle until it lies flat.

His gaze doesn't leave mine.

The world starts to fade again...

"...I now pronounce you husband and wife. You may kiss your bride."

FORTY-TWO

HER

Varius hauls me to him, and his lips descend on mine. Hot and wild, it's not the kiss of a man who doesn't give a shit about his bride. It's a kiss of passion and desperation, a primal need to have me as his. To mark his claim for all to see.

By the time he pulls away, my knees are weak, my lips are far too sensitive, and my heart is raw and loud inside my head. A pen is shoved into my hand. I blindly sign the registrar, and then he's pulling me down the aisle as the crowd cheers on either side of us.

He walks quickly, and I stumble to keep up with him, my awkwardness hidden under the white puffy skirt of my dress.

I glance over at him. At the sight of his erection, my pulse kicks up a notch. As soon as we reach the house, he pulls me inside rather than continuing to the reception area that's been set up in the backyard. He shuts the door behind us, pivots, and pins me against it.

"Let me kiss you, Micha," he says as he looks down at me. My body trembles with need as our wedding kiss is still felt across my lips. The blood bond runs through me, urging me on.

But the words are trapped in my throat. I'm still in so much pain over what he's done to me.

He bends down so his head is level with mine. He leans in, his breath feathering across my ear and neck. He doesn't touch me. Doesn't go that last sixteenth of an inch so our skin can brush against each other, sparking an explosion of electricity. The hairs on my neck rise. The nerves all down that side of my face tingle. Electrified air making it hard to breathe.

"Let me touch you, baby," he pleads, his voice cracking, pure desperation and desire flowing through our bond. At this rate, I won't be able to feel him at all tomorrow. The strength of his emotions will consume every last drop of his blood inside of me; yet, right now, the bond is trying its best to get me to give in.

"Let me worship your body like you deserve..." He trails off as he blows a gentle breath across my ear. I shiver, and he moves his lips down, still blowing against my skin. He runs a trail down my throat to the base of my neck, then across my naked shoulder. My strapless dress doesn't get in the way, doesn't offer any sort of protection at all.

I suck in a breath (or is it a moan?) as my head tilts ever so slightly to the side, giving him more access. I stiffen near instantly, fighting it.

He groans. There's no mistaking the meaning of the deep growl reverberating inside his chest and out past his lips. "My cock is so fucking hard for you, baby," he says as he keeps his lips just off my neck. They're so close though, I can feel them touching the fine hairs there. My magicless hands clench in the fabric of my dress. I let out a shaky breath, and he moves his head to intercept it, his lips now a paper's width from mine.

"I need to kiss you, Micha. I'm begging you to let me kiss you."

"Begging means you're down on your knees."

My eyes widen as I realize what I just said. My cheeks heat in embarrassment, but he drops to his knees without hesitation. He looks up at me with eyes that are way too intense.

"Let me kiss you, Micha. *Please.*" His words are ragged and raw and needy.

My heart pounds in my throat as I'm caught up in the stare of his gaze. It consumes me, drawing me a picture of a future that could be.

Any one of our guests could peer in.

See him.

A Boss down on his knees for a breedmare.

I tremble as I think about all his promises in the dark. Only ever in the dark. But right now, he's out in the open. And there might be a door between us and our guests, but there are too many ways for people to look in. I can feel his discomfort over being caught.

But I can feel his need for me more. His willingness to risk it all.

Swallowing hard, I don't trust myself to speak. But holding his gaze, I nod.

"Fuck, baby," he groans. Grabbing the skirt of my dress in both hands, he starts to lift. "Thank you."

I stiffen as he pulls my underwear to the side, already having regrets. I expect him to take it all the way now that I've given him the slightest approval, but instead, he kisses me gently, hesitantly. Slow passes of his lips and tongue that pause on a question each time. *Do you want me to stop?*

My throat works as I stare up at the ceiling.

My body is craving his in a hard, angry, hate-filled fuck.

My mind is screaming for him to stop, that I need more time, and my heart is being pulled between the two. I just want us to go back to what we used to be. That budding of hope. That *potential* to be something so fucking powerful.

But life is never clean. It's not black and white and full of easy solutions. It is messy and raw and *broken*.

"Micha?" Varius murmurs, no longer willing to take my silence as consent.

He starts to lift his head, but I don't want to look at him. I don't want to address the feelings inside of me. I don't want to fucking *talk*.

So I grab a fistful of his hair, rock my hips up, and fill his mouth with my pussy.

If I can come while being raped without it meaning shit, then I can sure as hel use him without it meaning shit. Fuck the blood bond wanting intimacy. Fuck my heart wanting to fall into his arms and find the comfort I've been craving. I will show him how little he means to me. How even when he makes me come, he still won't own me.

He never will again.

My grip on his hair turning angry and tight, I lift a leg over his shoulder. My pussy opens up to him, and I push it against his lips. He matches me with utter need. There's no request in his kiss now, no apology. Just uncontrolled desire that breaks free. His hands grab my ass and squeeze. I cry out as his tongue delves between my lips.

Humming around my clit, he presses a finger against my back hole. I whimper as his other hand comes around to join his mouth, but his fingers stay poised, waiting. He's doing nothing but kiss me.

Damn the man.

He's going to make me ask for it.

I clench my jaw, wanting to fucking refuse.

But my body's getting hotter and hotter in its need to be penetrated. And I'm getting angrier and angrier in my need to prove to him – and me that his touch means nothing.

"Varius," I snap, but I know my tone won't be enough. I'm going to have to say what he's allowed to do. My teeth grind together as I bite out the words I need for my own release. Not a connection. Not intimacy. Just pure carnal release. "Put your damn... fingers... inside me."

I cry out as he sucks on my clit, then hums again. I buck against his face, my head falling back against the wall. His fingers slide in easily into my wet pussy and curl, hitting that spot I love. My knees buckle. His other finger presses into my ass, stretching it fully. Pleasure explodes all down my body. In another few minutes, I'm going to come.

My breaths hitch as I squeeze my eyes shut and just focus on the sensations. His front fingers curl inside my pussy. His back one pumps in and out of my ass. His tongue flicks across my clit, then presses down hard and rubs, overstimulating me.

I cry out as all my strength flows out of my legs, so I'm only held up by his shoulder. The intensity inside me builds, curling my toes, making my entire body flush. I open my mouth to scream.

But just as I'm about to come, I shout, "Aleric!"

"Oh, darling," the vampire purrs as he winks at me, "I'd love to join in."

FORTY-THREE

HER

Varius rises as he spins to face the vampire. I push down my skirt as I stand behind him. If I had my magic, I'd be sorely tempted to set the fucker on fire.

"But I really need to take a piss," Aleric says, leaning inside the archway of the kitchen as if the two of us aren't ready to kill him. "Can you show me to the bathroom?"

"It's through there, down the hall. First door on the left," Varius says.

"Oh, but I get so easily lost. You wouldn't want me to end up in Sau's room. I'd be way too tempted to come all over her toothbrush. In her bottle of lotion. On the dildos –"

"It's this way," Varius snaps, stepping forward.

"Thank you," Aleric purrs, his dark eyes dancing.

As they walk off, I don't know if I should stay here and wait for him to return or run off to find Dayne so he can talk some sense into me. I'm not ready to forgive Varius for what he's done to me, but fuck, am I ready to fuck him.

When the front door opens, the decision is made for me. Khalid steps in, and knowing his girl will be right behind him, I hurry for the stairs.

It's been absolute hel seeing her every day at the dinner table. I have managed to avoid having breakfast and lunch with her, mostly by not having an appetite, but by the time dinner comes around, I'm starving. The only saving grace is Varius only talks to her when she instigates.

Stepping into his bedroom, I shut the door behind me. I sag against it, taking a moment to breathe before striding further into the room and taking off my collar. I toss it on the bed before reaching around me to undo my corset. The lace is hard to pull through the grommets though, and in no time at all, I'm cursing the damn thing.

"Allow me," Varius says, and I freeze, half twisted with my eyes straining to see my back. I never even heard him enter the room. The hairs on my neck rise over that, and the most primal part of my brain is screaming that I'm in an enclosed space with a predator that can kill me with one blow. Will I ever be able to trust him again?

"Turn around," he says.

I hesitate for a second, but fighting in this dress will get me killed anyways. My eyes dart to the new dresser, where the wand is hidden while I turn around. Locking my knees, I force myself to stay still. I haven't bonded with the wand yet, so attempting to use it has more risk of killing me than him.

The air feels weighted behind me. I can't hear Varius moving at all, but every nerve starts firing. Every hair starts rising in anticipation of his touch.

With every second that passes, my body grows more and more taut until I can't take it anymore. Surely, he must've crossed the room already to me? I start to turn, but two strong hands grab my shoulders and hold me still.

I tense, my muscles locking as I fight the reflex to stomp

on his instep, then turn to elbow him in the kidney, followed by a punch to his solar plexus.

"You're scared of me," Varius says tightly, pain and guilt flowing through our bond.

"You tortured me," I say. "That doesn't normally make a girl trust you won't hurt her. Next time, try chocolate and flowers."

"So you *do* want chocolate –" he starts, confused.

"No!" My anger comes back now, the frustration that he still doesn't get me. "Oh my gods. Just undo the lace so I can get out of this thing."

As he starts to work on the back of my corset, I can feel his irritation with me, and that pisses me off more. I'm not being fucking unreasonable. Just because I was willing to fuck him a moment ago doesn't mean I was ready to forgive him. It's not my fault if he came up here expecting me to be all loving and serving and back to being what he was used to having just because I had a moment of weak horniness. People have hate sex all the fucking time. I'm allowed to have hate sex.

Dammit. He *tortured* me. He raped me. He's forcing me to live with *That Bitch*. To see her every day, knowing she came from what he did to her. Did he suck on her large tits? Did he stroke himself inside her mouth? Kiss her? How long was their foreplay? Did he imagine me at all? Or was he glad to fuck someone who wasn't so flat everywhere? Fuck. Khalid's girl is so beautiful, and I'm just plain fucking Jane.

"I hate you." The words flow out before I can stop them.

"I know." He tugs on the lace, unthreading a section of it from my corset.

"I'm going to dedicate our entire marriage to making you miserable."

A flash of amusement comes down the bond.

"Don't laugh at me." I start to turn, my eyes hard, but the corset is mostly undone, and the dress has sagged just enough to trip me. I stumble into him. The dress is yanked down by my feet, and now the top of it sits around my waist. The fabric of his jacket presses into my bare nipples, and I suck in a breath as arousal mixes with my anger.

I want to fuck him like I hate him.

I want him to fuck me like he did that night I killed him.

As excitement shoots through me, so does confusion. I didn't like that at the time. But now I want it?

That doesn't make any fucking sense.

Fucking *blood bond!*

"Stop messing with my head!" I shout as I shove him away from me. But my dress is still tangled around my feet, and all that does is make me fall backwards. My arms flail out, but he's already caught me. I'm bent over backwards as if he's dipped me after we've danced. His eyes are intense on mine. My heart is beating rapidly inside my chest. I can't breathe even though the corset is now free.

My pussy is slick with desire. *For him*, and I hate it.

I hate him.

I hate the whiplash of emotions I'm having.

"Get off me," I snap.

Or at least I try to, but the words never come out.

So I stay in his arms, staring up at him as he looks down at me. His gaze holds mine, then dips slowly down my neck to my naked breasts.

I suck in a breath.

His hand slides up my body, hovering half an inch off my skin, to settle over my breast. My nipples harden, so damn sensitive even though he isn't touching me. But I didn't come earlier, so it's not taking much to push me back to that edge of ecstasy.

"Can I touch these, baby?" he says, his voice raspy and harsh. "Will you let me pinch this nipple while I suck the other one into my mouth?"

A small noise escapes me, and the arousal on his face is

breaking through my resistance. He looks like he'll spend all night worshiping me. His jaw clenches as he struggles with his control to wait for my answer, and my eyes immediately go there. Fucking hel, that should not be that hot.

He inhales. His eyes darken, and I am acutely aware that he can smell the changes in my arousal. Clenching my legs together, I try not to squirm.

"Micha," he begs. "Let me touch you."

I swallow hard, torn between two desires. But when his head was beneath the scrunch of my dress, I couldn't see his eyes. I don't know if I can fuck him with it meaning nothing now, not while he looks at me like this.

But I want to. Gods, I want to reduce him to nothing like he has me. Where I can just use him and discard him. Take what I want and leave the rest behind – all his bullshit, all his promises. See him as nothing but his sex organs. Make *him* the breedmare. Make this marriage meaningless, take back the only control I can have.

"Okay?" I breathe, not quite confident I can pull this off though.

"Is that a question?" Varius groans, his words so tight in their control.

"No?"

"*Micha*." That word is the epitome of torture, but his hand still hovers above me, not moving the slightest way towards me.

I clench my teeth as every nerve in my body vibrates on a pinnacle of absolution and damnation. "*Fucking touch me,*" I hiss.

His palm grazes my left nipple just as his lips lower over my right. I arch into his mouth, but before I can fully feel the softness of his lips, he freezes. Some fucker has knocked on the door. I swear to the gods, if that's Aleric –

"Varius," Rudy knocks in Morse code.

Cursing, he straightens and turns. The lack of hesitation

stings, and I twist in the opposite direction, calling myself a fool. I make sure to pick up my skirt this time. As Varius strides towards the door, I grab the dress for the reception party, a white regal looking piece that hugs my body, which has been left out on the bed, and head for the bathroom.

I stop, though, as I pass the dresser. Yanking open the top drawer, I grab the stuff I want, then head into the ensuite.

I don't need him for a release.

All I need is a toy. That's all his dick is to me right now anyway.

Fucking asshole.

FORTY-FOUR

HIM

I've never wanted to hit a brother more than I do in this moment.

Including Talon.

Because as Rudy is signing away in utter frustration about having just learned from Maddox that he's to marry Micha's sister, I can smell my wife's increasing arousal. I can hear the vibrations of her nipple clamps, the soft moans she's trying to bite down even behind the closed door of the bathroom. If I knew this was what Rudy wanted to talk to me about, I never would've answered the door.

But Rudy is like a son to me, and I'm always worrying about him given how his innate magic works. He's assaulted by everyone's fears, their worries and paranoia. We are all wolves in sheep's clothing, ready to turn on our allies at the smallest opportunity; being around us will not be easy for him. He'll have night terrors tonight. Maybe even for a full week, a month.

And when he's that beaten down, that exhausted from lack of sleep, his magic is harder for him to control. He'll have to isolate himself, step into the Plane of Shadows so no one's fears will come alive. The last time he had to do that, he was gone for months. His fear of being forgotten in that dark hole full of monsters is still capable of affecting Khalid from all that way, so he can't come back until he's able to control it.

It breaks my fucking heart, knowing that my desire to marry Micha and his desire to be my best man will lead to all that suffering, which is the only reason I haven't shut the door in his face.

But fuck, I can hear her moans getting louder.

"You knew you would have to marry one day," I cut in.

"But she doesn't even know sign language!" he signs in exasperation.

"You have six years before you wed. She can learn in that time."

"What would we even talk about? I'm almost double her age."

"Twenty-six to her sixteen is hardly double –"

"Fucking close enough."

"– and by the time she's of age, you'll be thirty-two. Half plus seven. You're fine."

He glares at me. Half plus seven is the equation we all decided on when we were discussing age gap relationships at some random point in time. You take half the age of a person, then add seven, and that's the youngest they can date without it being creepy.

"Well, what if I'm gay?" he finally says, and at any other time, I'd be proud he's finally come out to me. But one, I've known for years. And two, his whining is cockblocking me.

"You don't have to have sex to have kids these days. Come in a cup, and we'll sort the rest out." I start to shut the door as the smell of Micha's arousal fills my lungs.

His jaw locks as he sticks his foot out. "It won't be fair to her to be stuck in a marriage with someone who could never love her."

"Would you rather marry Vlad?" I sign in exasperation, needing to get this conversation over with before she comes.

He freezes. His jaw goes slack. He knew I knew he was gay, but he didn't know I've known he's been fucking the vampire for the last two years.

"Think about it," I say as I shut the door in his face, then stride towards the ensuite. I try the handle, but it's locked.

"Baby, open the door," I demand.

She whimpers, and I can hear the wet slurp of a toy as it slides in and out of her.

"*Micha.*"

I rattle the handle, but I don't force my way in. I can sense her heartbeat is lower down than my cock, and I can hear the nails of her hand scraping into the wood of the door. She must be facing me as she rides a dildo suctioned to the tile floor.

"Let me in, baby. I can make you feel so much better than that damn toy."

She presses the control on the vibrating clamps and cries out.

"Just open the door then, love. Let me at least watch." My cock is so damn hard. The taste of her is still on my lips, and I'm craving the intimacy I want with my wife.

"Fuck...I'm going...to come..." she moans.

I rattle the door again.

"Let me lick your pussy while you ride the toy," I say. I undo the button of my pants and pull down the zipper. I wrap my fingers around my cock as her breaths pick up in pitch and pace. "I could take your ass at the same time."

My hand slides down the hard length of me. I hiss in a breath as my cock jumps; it's too damn sensitive. I'm not going to last long at all. "Let me fill you with my cum, baby."

"No." Her voice is sharp, final. "If you want to fuck me tonight, you can't come now."

My hand stills. "What?"

"I didn't fucking stutter."

My teeth clench. I pump my cock in my hand one last time, then release it with great effort. "Fine. But open the door."

"No."

She scratches her nails into the wood, using it to brace herself as she fucks the dildo faster. I can hear her wet pussy sliding up and down it, the harshness of her breathing as it picks up. I can even sense the quick beat of her heart, and I know in another few seconds she's going to orgasm all over something that isn't me.

Fucking.

Hel.

I'm going to tear that godsdamn dildo to pieces as soon as she opens this door.

She isn't trying to stay quiet now. Her cries are loud, and she's banging on the door. I squat down and press my palm against this side of it so I can connect us at least in one way. The vibrations move through my arm as she hits it one last time, and I just know her legs are shaking.

She screams, and the only fucking relief I get is she calls out my name. No doubt she did it to rile me. But it gives me comfort too; at least she can still bear to think of me.

Groaning, I lean against the door as my cock throbs in pain, my own orgasm so fucking close. "Fuck, baby, let me hold you," I rasp.

She doesn't say anything, but I can hear her breathing hard, her head leaning on the other side of the door.

Closing my eyes, I fight the urge to reach a hand down to my cock. I want to slide inside her tonight. I want to make love to her as my wife. I just want to fucking hold her and know that we will be okay.

When the door opens, I rock back on my heels, my knees on the floor in front of me. She stands above me in her white reception dress, the wet pink dildo in her hands. Fuck, she looks every inch a goddess. *My* goddess. The one I will spend the rest of my life worshiping even if all she wants to do is smite me down.

"Gods, you're beautiful," I rasp.

Her cheeks heat as she blinks in shy embarrassment. She shuffles from foot to foot for a second, and I know she's trying to build courage for whatever it is she wants to do.

She had that same nervousness when she stood on stage in the karaoke bar. When she tried to buckle the collar around my neck. Its weight is suddenly prominent on me, and pink or not, utterly feminine or not, I will wear her mark with pride.

I am the property of Micha fucking Shadow.

She takes a small step forward so she's standing right in front of me, her feet between my spread knees. Then she raises the dildo to my lips, and I open my mouth without hesitation, craving the taste of her in any way I can get it.

Her lips part as she watches me. She breathes heavily, her eyes hot with a building need. I want to reach out and grab her, to exchange the dildo in my mouth for the lips of her pussy. But I know she isn't ready yet. She needs to have full control of the situation. She doesn't trust me anymore.

So I will do nothing but sit here and hold her gaze while I suck the taste of her off a dildo I'm so godsdamn fucking jealous of.

"Varius..." she breathes. But then she blinks and shakes her head. Forcing a smile, she pulls the dildo from my lips and waves it around awkwardly. "You know, you bought a lot of toys, but I didn't see a strap-on in there."

My eyes narrow. "No."

"Even if I –"

Fuck. I'd let her. If that was the only way I could have

her.

But she cuts herself off as she rolls her lips in, a smile dancing in her eyes. Then she tosses the dildo at the bed.

I twist as she does so, pulling a throwing knife hidden under the cuff of my jacket. The blade spins through the air, skewers the damn toy, then pins it to the headboard with a satisfying *thud.*

I turn back to her and rise. Her mouth is open. "What did you do that for?"

"It touched you."

Her eyes narrow as she shakes her head, and her earlier amusement vanishes. "You're such a fucking –" she starts to seethe, but then she cuts herself off. Her jaw locking, she shoves past me.

"Micha –" I say, wondering what the fuck has set her off this time. Every time we seem to take a step forward, all she does is shove us back.

"Go fuck yourself," she snarls as she heads for the door. "Oh, wait, you can't," she sneers. "Because you stabbed the fucking *dildo*!" She grabs the door handle. "Oh, I know. You can use the stupidly thick stick that's already up your ass!"

She yanks open the door, but I dart over to her and slam it shut with a hand. As she tries to throw her right elbow into my ribs to get me to back off, I catch it with my other hand, then yank her around. Her left fist swings for me. I block it with my right forearm, wrap my fingers around her wrist, pull her arm out, and duck under it. I lift her over my shoulders as I straighten and toss her towards the bed. She bounces on it hard, then flies up to tumble over the side, but with a burst of speed, I'm on the mattress. Grabbing her arm, I yank her onto the bed and cage her with my body.

"Get off me," she seethes.

"I will after you tell me what's wrong. We need to learn to talk to each other, Micha." While I was reading all those articles about how to apologize, I also clicked on some links discussing the key to long-term relationships, and they all said the same thing: *communicate*.

She glares at me without a word, and the tightness in my chest starts to strangle me. "Fuck, monster. I want to spend the rest of my life with you and all the rest of my lives, but I can't do this alone. You have to help me –"

"Why?" she snaps, her eyes blazing hot.

"Because I love –"

"No, why does it fucking matter if you get me to like you in this life," she asks sarcastically, "when all my memories will be wiped in the next?"

"Because I don't want you to hurt at all." Knowing she'll have something to say to that, I hurry on, "I fucked up and hurt you. I know that. I can't change that, but I am trying to fix it, Micha. I am trying to become the person you need."

She glances away from me, and my stomach drops.

"You don't trust me when I say you're mine, so I will show you. I will spend every day for the rest of my lives showing you that you are mine. That I will protect you and fight for you and *learn* for you. If you need something, tell me, and I'll provide it." Her eyes dart back to me.

"I love you, little monster," I murmur. "And I know you don't believe that right now, but I will show you every day until you do."

I lean down to kiss her lips only to stop a breath away. I promised her I wouldn't touch her unless she wanted me to tonight, and she needs to be able to trust my word whenever I give it.

"You want to prove to me that you're sorry?" she says, her eyes serious and intense.

I nod.

"Then cut off your cock and fucking choke on it."

FORTY-FIVE

HER

"Is that what you really need?" Varius asks flatly. "You can't forgive me unless I mutilate myself?"

My blood is pounding in my ears. I'm not thinking right; I know it. Because there are alarm bells ringing in my skull, a little voice telling me I'm going too far, and yet, the words that come out of my mouth are, "Yes! Khalid cut off his hand for hurting his girl, and you've done nothing!"

"Khalid can speak magic. If I cut off both my hands," Varius says tightly, "I can't protect you."

"Protect me?" I screech. "You won't be able to hurt me! I begged you to stop."

He flinches. Grief crashes down our bond.

"I cried and screamed, but my pain didn't matter to you."

"It mattered –"

I shove at his chest. "You kept going! You hammered that screw into me over a hundred times. You shaved off my fingers. So don't tell me you cared –"

"Of course I cared, but I thought you were Antonio's whore," he explains.

"Fuck you."

"Yeah, fuck me," he snaps. "I fucked up. I know that, but dammit, monster, I am *trying*. I am trying so fucking hard to apologize. I spent days researching the best wand for you instead of looking for Talon despite the secrets he had on this Family."

"You didn't do that for me. You were procrastinating because you didn't want to kill him."

"Of course I didn't want to kill him! He was my brother. I loved him!" He clenches his jaw. "Fuck, Micha. I promised to protect him when Caden walked out on us. He supported me in the moments I doubted my ability to lead this Family. He took a bullet for me when he was only sixteen. So no, I didn't want him dead. He was my brother.

"But I ordered the hit on him anyway because of what he did to you. I didn't try to hunt him down because *you* were more important." He presses his forehead to mine. "Fuck, little monster. I got married the day after he died for you –"

"You married me for yourself. Because *you* wanted to feel safe that I could never leave you." My anger flares as I turn my head from him until he lifts his.

"That's not –"

"And you didn't even vow to do anything other than take me as your wife, so fuck off. *I'm* the one who had to vow to worship you and cherish you and become your slave."

"You're not a slave –"

"Then what am I?"

"You're my wife!" he roars.

I stare at him as he breathes heavily above me.

"Fucking hel, Micha. You're my wife," he rasps. "I told you I am yours as much as you are mine."

"So not at all."

His dark eyes grow cold. Then he's rolling out of bed and

yanking me with him. "Since you're clearly not in the mood to talk like an adult –"

My spine stiffens.

"– we're going to go downstairs, dance the first song, and then talk to our guests so they don't ditch us for Antonio. You are going to stay by my side, act every inch my fucking wife, and then I'm taking you upstairs to fuck you until you are ready to forgive me."

"The hel –"

"You *are*."

My nostrils flare with the force of my anger, but even I'm not stubborn enough to refuse him right now. He isn't my guilt-heavy husband who's trying to convince me he loves me. He's Varius fucking Shadow, the Boss of the Shadow Domain, a man who's to be *obeyed*.

"But first, little monster, you're going to sit on my face because we could both use a fucking stress reliever."

My jaw clenches. I might not be able to deny him given my station, but to hel if I'm going to willingly comply.

"Sit on the edge of the bed," he says, each word a fucking warning, "and hike up your dress." His eyes are piercing and too damn dangerous.

But it isn't fear that's coursing through me.

I resist for a second.

He takes a step towards me.

I sit my ass down.

He waits.

I pull up my dress.

"I hate you."

"I know." His tone softens. "But right now, you're going to be a good girl and spread your legs." He removes the black tie around his neck, but he leaves the pink collar on. Then he shrugs off his dark-red jacquard jacket.

I tense the muscles in my legs so I don't squirm while watching him. But when his stare turns even more intense and punishing, I part my thighs as my mouth waters. He nods in approval, then steps towards me.

"Now tell me to please lick your pussy."

I glare at him in stubborn refusal. Unfiltered desire curls a corner of his lips as he glances down my body.

"I could be down on my knees right now with my tongue buried in your pussy. I could be humming on your clit, there for you to use and command. Don't you want me on my knees, Micha? You just have to say the words."

My pulse quickens as I think about him being tied and at my mercy. He'd hate that. But I might need it...

"You could be sitting on my face with my finger rimming your ass as I slide my tongue between your lips. Or maybe I'll play with your nipples, rolling them between my fingers as I suck on your clit. I could be worshipping you, Micha. I could be everything you want me to be *if you just tell me.*"

My blood rushes through my skull. My heart aches for the bridge of intimacy he's offering; it's been so godsdamn lonely this past week. My eyes latching on to the collar he's wearing, wanting to see it for the sign of ownership it is, I rasp, "Get on your knees and lick me until I come."

He groans. "As you wish."

Dropping to his knees, he buries his face between my legs. His tongue flicks up and down the outside of my pussy. A leisurely action with no desire to go inside. No rush. No ditching of the foreplay to get to the good stuff. He takes his time building me up, and I dig my nails into the sheets to try not to make a noise. He likes it when I moan, so I won't. He doesn't get that part of me anymore.

Especially since it's only been a week since he fucked another woman in this very house.

The entirety of my body stiffens. I start to imagine him doing this to her.

Does he know what she tastes like?

Is he comparing me to her?

"Stop thinking, Micha," he growls.

The fact that he's tuned into me enough to realize I'm too tense calms me down a little. The fact he used my name helps even more. I try to trust he's here with me, that this act between husband and wife is actually that. But all I keep thinking about is: what does Khalid's girl sound like when she comes? I don't know the answer to that.

But he does.

Fucking hel. I can't do this. There's no intimacy here. No bridge left –

"Micha," he growls as he lifts his eyes to mine. I try to move away from him, but he grabs my hips and holds me still. I don't try to push him away. As much as I want to, part of me is desperate for this. To regain the connection we've lost. To pretend, even for a moment, that we're not broken past the point of fixing.

"Let me take care of you, baby."

I stiffen at his use of a nickname. *Is that what he called her?* He does like to talk as he fucks.

"I can feel how tense you are. Just look into my eyes and let me make you feel good."

I tremble at the idea of him wanting to look at me, to *see* me rather than imagine her. My eyes dart down to his, and I suck in a breath at how focused his gaze is. On me. There's not a flicker of distraction.

"Good girl. You keep your eyes on me just like that, Micha."

I relax a bit more at the sound of my name.

"That's it, baby."

I stiffen again.

"That's it, Micha," he corrects, catching on, picking up on the pain I don't say. And my heart squeezes tight with the knowledge that he really is here with me. He isn't thinking about anyone else.

"Gods, you're so fucking beautiful, Micha," he murmurs,

keeping his eyes on my face. "I love the way you smell." He inhales deeply, and the hunger on his face intensifies. "Now I'm going to lick you until you come. But you keep your eyes on me. Let me see that beautiful face."

My throat closes with a barrage of emotions as he starts to lick me again. His tongue slides between my lips, lapping me slowly before settling on my clit and swirling. I groan as I dig my fingers into his hair. My breathing turns heavy, and my eyes grow half-hooded as he starts to hum, but his gaze never wavers. His attention stays on me. Whenever I tense, my jealousy and doubt hounding me, he massages my ass, urging me to relax. As soon as I do, he hums his approval and his eyes light up like I'm the most beautiful thing in the whole world.

He builds me up to the edge of orgasm over and over and over again, but every time I get close, I start to think about *her* and how he made *her* feel like this.

I hate her.

I hate him.

How could he do that to me?

My body tightens as all I can see is their hips slapping together.

My arousal disappears as I watch them come at the same time in my mind. His hands on her breasts. Hers on his hips.

I want to claw out his fucking eyes as he looks up at me, but as soon as that thought hits, I cry out. The bond between us opens like a damn – and I realize seeing him come with someone else was the price he needed to pay.

His fingers dig into my ass as he growls with utter need. My thighs squeeze around his head as all of his love and devotion and arousal comes flooding into me.

My back arches.

My fingers scrape his skull.

I fist his hair and ride him hard as all his emotions ride

me.

I get a flash of an image in my head – of me as I am now, panting on the edge of the bed as he kneels between my legs. My eyes widen as I can feel his cock throbbing hard in his pants, almost painfully. He rocks his hips, and I can feel it. The intense pleasure. The need for release.

I scream as mine hits.

I jerk back.

He groans. His fingers digging into me, he doesn't stop licking my pussy.

His tongue strokes me a few more times before his lips lock over my clit, and he starts to hum. Grabbing a fistful of his hair, I try to shove him off me. It's too intense. The mix of our emotions is too much.

But he doesn't stop. Doesn't give any mercy until I'm a mess of emotions that leave me shaking and crying.

"Micha?" he murmurs as he crawls up my body. I throw my left forearm across my face as I fall back onto the bed and cry harder.

"Shhh." He lies on his side next to me and pulls me into his arms. He presses a kiss to my forehead. "I'm sorry, little monster. I'm so sorry."

But I don't feel bad at all. I feel too good, and I try to explain that, but all that comes out are raspy sobs that leave me shaking against him.

I cling to him, rubbing my face into his shirt, making it wet and messy. I try to pull my head back and apologize, but he places a hand on the back of my neck and holds me still.

"It's okay," he murmurs. "It's okay. I'm so sorry, Micha. I thought... I thought this would help us heal together. I'm sorry, monster. I'm so sorry."

I shake my head against him, trying to explain that the bond has strengthened considerably, that I can feel not just his emotions from time to time, but I can feel *him*. I can see a bit of what he's thinking, what his body is feeling. He's holding me in his arms, and I can feel me trembling against him. I can feel his fear that he's lost me. His crushing guilt. His determination to make it right.

Grabbing hold of his shirt, I rip it open. Buttons pop free in every direction, and as they're sailing through the air, I lean down and bite his naked chest. He hisses in a breath as I draw blood. Sucking it into my mouth, I lift my arm up to his lips. He hesitates for a second, but then he's biting down on my wrist.

I dig my teeth in harder as the bond between us snaps tight. A delicious warmth floods through me. I sag against him, breathing heavily.

"Micha...I need...to be in you," he groans as he rolls me onto my back. His hands go between us, fighting with his belt. I try to help him, desperate to have him inside me, to fill me completely. My lips find his, or maybe his find mine. All I know is that we're kissing like our lives depend on it. His hands cup my breasts as I finally manage to undo his belt. Ripping at his pants, I pull his cock free.

He groans as he wraps my fingers around him. Then he's pulling me off him and placing my hand above my head. "Fuck, Micha. I'm not going to last, and I want to be inside you."

I whimper as he rubs the tip of his cock against my wet pussy. He slides his head between my lips, back and forth a bit before he finally pushes in. Panting and rasping, I arch my back as he fills me.

"*Fuck*!" he groans as he collapses on top of me, and I can feel the pulse of his cock as it empties his seed inside of me already. "Gods. Shit. Fuck. Micha. You feel so fucking good."

He squeezes my breasts, pinching my nipples in between his fingers.

I whimper against him, needing him to move, to hit the back of my womb like he always does. To make us feel like we used to.

"Fuck," he hisses. But then he starts to move. I cry out as I wrap my legs around him. He buries himself deep, then withdraws, then pushes his cock all the way in. I lift my hips, meeting his pace. Fast hard thrusts. A primal need that neither of us can contain. Our bond intensifies, our arousal mixing into one.

"Fuck, Varius..."

"I love you, Micha."

I cry out as my orgasm breaks me. Tears burn my eyes as I can feel the intensity of his love for me. He actually meant it, every word he's said to me this last week. The pain and grief and fear that he's lost me. The determination to win me back. The terrifying love he can't control. He loves me. And he is trying.

He's trying so fucking hard to fix what he's broken.

Wrapping my arms around his neck, I close my eyes and cry.

He rubs my clit with a finger as he continues to fuck me hard and fast, chasing his own release. His hips are bruising the insides of my legs, but I don't care. I just need him close to me.

Groaning, he shoves in deep one last time, then arches back as he grabs my hips. I open my eyes to stare at him as he comes. I've never seen anything more beautiful.

My lips falling open, I lift a hand to his face. He presses his cheek into my palm, his eyes closed, and shudders. Then he collapses on top of me, his heart going as hard as mine.

"I love you, Micha," he murmurs as he kisses me on the forehead.

I hug him tight as I feel a large weight lift off my chest. The pain isn't gone. The forgiveness isn't there.

But we are finally starting to heal.

FORTY-SIX

HER

By the time we fix our clothes and make it outside, the party is in full swing and most of the nibbles are gone. Even though no one has started dancing yet, the music from the live band is loud, and the chatter is non-stop. Guests mull around in their four-figure dresses and suits. Red and white roses decorate the light-gray stone tiles around the pool. In the rays of the setting sun, white wisteria and red Chinese paper lamps hang from lines that have been stretched across the patio.

Eyes turn towards us as we step through the double glass doors of the living room. Maddox whistles from over by the pool, and the rest of his brothers soon join in, clapping and hollering and acting like a bunch of idiots bowing down to the king of the frat house the next morning. My cheeks heat as I glance at Varius, but he doesn't seem embarrassed at all.

Then again, he is still wearing the pink collar despite it

being heavily stained with the cum I squirted everywhere while I was riding his face. I tried to get him to take it off when he changed his shirt, but he refused. So there it sits around his neck, the bow crinkled and damp and smelling like me.

My blush spreads further as I duck my head. Reaching over to me, he lifts my chin. My lips part as I glance at him, but his attention is on my father, who has just come over to greet us.

"Congratulations," Stefaan says, bowing his head. "I am honored to have you as part of my family."

"We are honored to have you here. How was the trip through the mountains?"

His lips tighten. "We transported in." Bio transportation magic is rare. Not only is it a hard skill to learn as a witch has to memorize every particle inside the circle before they can cast the spell, but the risk of things going wrong is too great. One small miscalculation on the caster's part could have their client's eyes left behind or their body morphed together with the rocks that accidentally got transported with them. It doesn't matter that all transporters must now be trained and licensed by the SCU – one of the rare rules of theirs that we all follow; the fear of permanent pain and disfigurement trumps low statistics.

For Stefaan to have decided to use one, he must have calculated that there was little chance they'd survive if they drove through Death Hunt territory, which includes most of the mountain ranges on the east coast of America.

"Have they started attacking you?" Varius demands, and I can feel his paranoia that he wasn't informed. He must have spies in the werewolves' territory. Have they all been killed? Or worse, turned?

Stefaan hesitates for a second. Then he straightens his spine. "No. They've been killing our competition." A silent show of what an alliance with them could mean for the

Blacks. Varius might've given them territory and the means to start dealing Ricks and Vs, luxury sex drugs, which will increase their income greatly, but turning on us now won't make them lose either of those things.

I tense, my eyes darting across the crowd, wondering if the assassins he brought with him are actually here to kill us. I spot Andrea Turner in a long black dress, talking to Rudy. Her hands move freely as she signs, but the fact that she isn't holding a weapon at the moment means nothing. Rudy is a cleaner, not a fighter, and Varius will sacrifice his life to save his brother. I know how much Rudy means to him – the same as Lou means to me. Andrea can have a knife to his throat before Rudy's eyes can even signal to his brain that she's moved.

And then there's Jaclyn Hoscheid in a dark-blue gown with a slit down the side. She's talking to Sharee Smith, who is wearing a green dress that flares out at her hips and stops at her knees. Jaclyn is an amplifier, able to increase the strength and magic of her allies. Sharee is a telekinetic. She isn't as strong as Enoch or Ezriel, but she can bend light and sound waves to turn invisible and move without a sound.

I know Father brought six others with him, but I don't see them. Are they innocently obscured from view given the density of the crowd, or are they lying in wait, planning an attack?

They'd have to take out Khalid before they can touch Varius, but now that he's bonded to his girl, his attention might be divided. I don't know if I trust his ability to protect my husband when she's here.

My skin prickling, I wish I had my fucking magic. Or at least a knife, but I can't hide one in this dress, and wearing one openly is a sign of mistrust of our allies. Varius has a few on his body though. I step closer to him, ready to grab the one he has under his jacket if shit turns crazy.

"We'll send an escort back with you," Varius says, as if

he's worried about my father rather than suspecting him of betraying us.

Stefaan shakes his head. "Thank you, but I would rather you keep your men here to watch over my two daughters. Antonio has not neared our territory himself, and seeing the other guests here, I'm not the one he will go after." His eyes find Aleric, who's flirting with a woman I don't know. She's glaring at him though, which makes me instantly like her.

"Besides," Father says with a bit of a smile. "Without Lou with us, I do not fear making it back without casualties."

I smirk. She's so useless in a fight. My eyes search for her as they continue to talk. Varius gets information on William Florsley, the man who's supposedly after me for not having assassinated his kid like I said I would years ago.

My sister's talking to Dayne near the pool. She glances over at me and smiles with a big wave. Excitement lights up her eyes. I take a step towards her, not having seen her in forever, but Varius' hand on the back of my neck stops me from going further. He pulls me back to his side without looking at me at all.

My eyes narrow in annoyance. But I'm not dumb enough to fight with him here, where he'd be forced to punish me in front of all these people. They might be our allies but only because they believe we can win against Antonio. If they smell any hint of weakness from Varius, we will no longer be a worthy investment for them to support.

So I wait impatiently while he continues to talk with my father. Then, when Stefaan finally leaves, I wait some more as another guest takes his place. I spend the next hour with my husband's hand collared around the back of my neck. His thumb strokes my skin, sending delicious shivers down my spine every few minutes. My nipples start to harden against the fabric of my dress, and I shift on my feet to relieve some of the sudden restlessness coursing through my legs. None of the guests who have come up to us have addressed me, so I've not had anything to concentrate on other than his touch. The pink collar around his neck isn't helping things either. It should look ridiculous, but he's wearing it without shame, and that level of confidence is freaking hot.

Dropping his hand from my neck as he converses with three of his capos, Varius then cups my ass. He massages me without breaking conversation. My cheeks heat as I stay dead still, trying not to give anything away. Thankfully, we haven't made it that far out of the house, and there's no one behind us.

But his hand doesn't just stay on my ass check. It starts to roam, two fingers dipping between my thighs from the back. I subtly bite my lip to stop a moan from escaping, but by the number of vampire heads turning towards me, it's a useless gesture. If Varius can smell me when I'm aroused, then so can all of them.

Fuck.

His fingers rub between my pussy lips a few more times before he lifts his hand to my waist. I start to breathe a sigh of relief, but then I realize his hand hasn't gone to my waist at all. It's slipping through the side of my backless dress to come around and cup my naked breast. Not even trying to hide the fact that he's groping me, he starts to play with my nipple. The conversation doesn't break at all.

The three men leave, but more just take their place. I'm starting to grow too hot as Varius keeps rubbing my nipple in between his fingers. He tugs on it every so often, keeping it hard and making it far too sensitive. When he pulls his hand out to once again pay attention to my ass and pussy from the back, I lean into his side and bury my head into his chest.

I'm mortified that he's touching me somewhere so public, but at the same time, I've never been more turned on. There is an increased thrill to doing something you shouldn't be.

Biting my lip, I struggle with something I really want to do. But his fingers are merciless, my own desire is too, and I can't resist. I move my hand forward to cup his cock. He's rock hard in his pants, and I stroke my fingers down his length, only to immediately stop, my hand burning from doing something so naughty.

Feeling the eyes of everyone on me even though no one seems to have noticed, I blush hard.

Once the guests we were just talking to move away, the live band starts to play "All of Me" by John Legend. My eyes widen as I realize this is the song for the first dance. *Shit.* If Varius touches me that intimately right now, I'm going to be screwed. What if I come in front of everyone? My sister and father are here. I'd never be able to look at them again.

"Varius, wait," I start as he pulls me through the crowd to the frosted panel of glass that's been placed over the pool. "I can't –"

We step onto the dance floor; suddenly I can't breathe. Everyone's eyes are on me, including Lou's. *Fuck.* I search for Dayne, trying to silently plead with him to save me. But he doesn't. His eyes aren't even on me. They're on Quinton, who's getting cosy with Vlad. My best friend narrows his eyes on the man he claims to not like, and I narrow mine on him.

"Fucking useless best friend," I mutter with a scowl. For now it's too late for me to be saved.

We have stopped in the middle of the dance floor. Varius looks into my eyes and wraps a hand around the nape of my neck. My pulse beats against the rough surface of his palm. It picks up in intensity as he forces me into a dip. He holds me low as he runs his other hand down my body, between my breasts to the V of my thighs. My eyes widen. He isn't even going to try to hide it.

He cups my pussy through my dress, and I grab his wrist even as my body begs me to let him do whatever he wants to me. "Everyone's watching," I hiss.

"Good. Then they can all see that you are mine." Pulling me upright, he kisses me on the lips, then turns us around the room in beat to the song. He touches me inappropriately every chance he gets, and I can feel the hard bulge of his cock whenever he presses up against me. Fuck, I'm getting wet. All the vampires must be able to smell me.

In a piss poor attempt to distract him with conversation, I blurt, "When did you learn to dance?"

"When I was a teen –" He spins me away from him, then pulls me back in. His hand goes to my waist. "I thought it would get me laid." He grabs my ass.

"Ah, and when it didn't, you learned to shove knives up vaginas," I say with a nervous laugh. He did that the first night we met. The sex after was wild – something my body is remembering all too well.

He chuckles as he turns me around so my back is flush against him. "No," he murmurs in my ear as he rocks our hips together. "Then I learned to sing." His hand runs down my body. "Though these days, I mostly just hum." He cups my pussy, and my mouth runs dry as a bolt of arousal hits me hard.

I try to pull away, to force some distance between our bodies, but he spins me in place so now we're facing each other. His cock rubs against my stomach as we dance. I try to think of something else to talk about, but all I can think about is sex.

Fuck.

His nostrils flaring, he dips me. His eyes run down my body. Arousal pulses through our bond, and I can almost feel what he wants to do to me. How he'll peel off my dress slowly, follow the fabric with the touch of his lips. Down my belly to my pussy, where he'll bury his tongue between my legs as he lets the dress fall to the floor. In front of all these witnesses.

My legs shaking, I stumble into him when he pulls me back up. I place a hand over his chest, and he places one of his over mine. Wrapping his other arm around my waist, Varius holds me to him. His cock jerks against my stomach. My breath catches as I look into his eyes, and for a moment, the world stops.

Then the sound of applause breaks into our bubble, and I blink rapidly as I realize that the first song has ended. Other couples are now joining us on the dance floor.

"Congratulations, bruh!" Maddox shouts as he spins a woman towards us, his hands on her hips. She's wearing a black dress that ties around the back of her neck. The front of it dips in a narrow V all the way down to her belly. Half of the skirt rises above her knees in an asymmetrical cut. She's heavily bruised and scarred across her body, and fresh claw marks run across her shoulders and upper arms. Her long white hair is still damp from a recent wash, and she smells like soap. Chains bind her hands and feet, with more around her waist. Her vibrant purple eyes spit fury above her Hannibal-esque mask.

"She bites," Maddox shouts in explanation, with a grin that says he's into that.

"I told you to kill her," Varius replies when he and Zita get close.

"I'm killing her mentally." Maddox's smile turns wicked. "Then I'll kill her physically."

She lunges forward to headbutt him in the nose, but he grabs her throat and stops her mid-attack. "If you want my attention, love, try flashing your boobs."

Hauling her to him, he kisses her mask, then he unties the straps of her dress so the top half of it falls down, baring her breasts completely. The only reason she isn't completely naked right now is because of the belt around her waist.

Feeling Varius' eyes on me and the cold jealousy through our bond, I turn my head so he doesn't kill her. My jaw tics as I'm annoyed at his hypocrisy all over again. He did a hel of a lot more to Khalid's girl than just look at her. I might be letting him fuck my brains out again, but that doesn't mean I've forgiven him.

Fucking neanderthal.

"There, now you have all of my attention," Maddox says. He cups her right breast. "Now what did you want to tell me?" He pretends to listen for a moment, nodding every so often even though she says nothing. "What? You want me to fuck your face while you're hanging upside down from a tree?"

She growls behind her mask.

"Of course I will, love. I'll even eat your pretty little pussy at the same time. Now congratulate the lovely couple so we can take our leave."

She growls words I doubt are well wishes, but Maddox seems pleased enough with them. He turns to me as we all continue dancing. "Welcome to the family, sis."

I beam. "Thanks…bruh."

"Ha!" He whisks his captive away, dragging her towards the woods. My blood heats, knowing what they're about to do. Varius' eyes narrow on me, and I am intensely aware of the flush of my cheeks. He's always been paranoid of my relationship with Maddox, so if he thinks his little brother has just turned me on, will he kill him?

My pulse spikes. I fish for something to say that'll cool his jealousy. "Varius, I –"

"I *love* the way you smell," Aleric says from beside us. "What is that? Cocoa and cum?"

He's dancing with Sau, and his hands are all over her body. He's smiling at her, but if looks could kill, he would be gutted, speared through his anus, and set on fire. I've never seen Sau be anything more than the welcoming hostess in public, so to see her so openly hostile with an ally we need has taken me by surprise.

As if feeling my stare, Aleric turns his head to look at me. "Thank you for the invite," he says with a grin. "I'm having a lovely time."

"Thank you for coming," Varius responds emotionlessly.

"Oh, I haven't come yet." He turns back to Sau and winks extravagantly. "Though I'm certain I will soon."

"Come while you're dancing with me, and I'll cut it off," Sau hisses.

"Oh, but how can I possibly not, love, when you talk so dirty to me?"

She pretends to stumble, then stomps on his foot with her heel. His grin only widens as he groans, "Oh, fuck, yeah, baby. Do that again."

As they move away from us, I glance at Varius. "Um... should we intervene?"

"No," he says tightly, though our bond tells me he wants to. "He has my permission."

My eyes widen. I know he's mad at his mother just as much as I am, if not more, but she is the only midwife I trust with our child. If our daughter turns out to be a hybrid, anyone else will kill her and then me while I lay there in labor.

I turn my head to keep an eye on her, but Varius grabs my chin and forces my attention back to him. "She's the Reaper of the Sired, Micha. She'll be fine."

He goes back to touching me intimately every chance he gets. Then his lips find mine, and his hands squeeze my ass. His tongue strokes mine.

When he pulls back, my eyes dart to the people around us as I subtly try to keep my cool. If he keeps touching me like this though, I fear I'm going to throw myself at him without shame. My body is all too familiar with what he can do for it, and I'm craving any sort of connection with him after the week we've spent fighting.

His hands squeeze my ass as he lifts me up. He settles

my pussy over his erection and rocks into me. I grab hold of his shoulders as I stare at him with wide eyes, my blood rushing through my skull. "Put me down," I hiss.

"As you wish." He sets me down, but just as I breathe in relief, he spins me so my back is to him, then shoves me away from him. As I stumble forward a step, I realize we're at the edge of the party. He smoothly maneuvered us here while we were dancing.

"No. I want to see L–" I start as I turn back around, but he grabs my arm and hauls me in for another deep kiss.

He lifts his lips after a moment, panting hard, but his head stays tilted towards mine. "You can either run, little monster, or I can fuck you right here, but either way, I'm going to fuck you."

He releases me, and I stumble back, breathing hard. I take a few more steps in reverse, then pivot on my heels, kick them off, and run.

A few people in the crowd whistle and clap wildly, but I don't dare look over to see who is teasing us. It's probably his brothers and Dayne. But then I hear my baby sister yell, "Get it, girl!"

My cheeks on fire, I run faster to get away from the utter embarrassment. Not wanting to get fucked somewhere they can all hear, let alone see, I don't slow down in the slightest when I reach the woods. Tree branches whip across my body, tearing into my dress with delicious stings. The grass and twigs get crushed underfoot. My lungs pump hard, as do my legs, but at the sound of a predator coming up behind me, I suddenly find more energy.

I dart around a tree, then stumble over a root in the dark. But my assassin training kicks in, and my honed reflexes have me rolling back onto my feet before I really register that I've fallen. Taking off again at full speed, I breathe the hot summer air into my lungs.

I can hear Varius behind me, his steps heavier than mine,

the whips of the branches louder and more numerous. But I can also feel him, the arousal through our bond, the way he can sense me through his special abilities. I can feel my own heartbeat through him, and I wonder how the hel I could ever escape such a predator.

A primal fear rushes through me, giving me more to pull on. Frantic, I dart around trees and duck under branches. I think about heading for the lake, wondering if he can swim. I'm a good swimmer. He has a lot of muscle. It could work...

But when I turn towards its direction, he's right in front of me. I throw myself to the left, my feet scrambling on the ground. I fall to my hands, then fling myself back up. I take off in the opposite direction, expecting him to grab me with every step I take, but he never does.

I run until my legs ache. Until my lungs and heart feel at their limit. He appears in front of me every so often just to scare me, and that added uncertainty is making me panic, the primal part of my brain screaming that I'm not going to make it out alive.

I stumble from exhaustion but still try to keep going, my hands and knees dragging me along the forest floor. Fear floods every nerve, and it only amplifies when I'm picked up by a warrior. I start to yelp, but a hand is shoved over my mouth. My back hits a tree. My eyes widen as a towering presence fills my line of vision. And then his hand slides down to my throat, and he covers my mouth with his lips.

Arousal jerks beneath the fear. The two mesh together, amplified by the other's presence. I moan as I cling to him, and he pushes up my dress. He releases my neck to rip off my underwear and the plug he placed inside me before we came down from his room. His old cum rushes down my legs. He pushes it back inside me with two fingers. I arch between his body and the tree as he hits my G-spot over and over and over again.

I cry out against his mouth, but he silences all noise with

his lips and the tightening grip of his hand around my throat. The lack of oxygen makes me dizzy, adding to the rush of sensations I'm experiencing. Frantically rocking my hips, I chase a release that'll leave me wrecked.

He groans into my mouth. His tongue dances with mine. Reaching around my neck, he unties my dress. Shoving the fabric down past my breasts, he lifts me higher up the tree with the fingers he has in my pussy, and then lowers his head to lock his lips around my breast. He cups his free hand over my mouth, trapping in my cries.

I buck against him, needing more, begging him with my body. My legs move restlessly around him as I try to find that glorious release.

But he keeps me on the edge, moving his fingers too fast for me to come. I whimper against his palm. He groans with his teeth around my nipple. Then he pulls me back down the tree. Leaning in so his lips meet my ear, he sucks the bottom of my ear into his mouth and bites down hard. I cry out against his hand. He licks the side of my face before saying, "Don't make a sound."

Spinning us around before I can make sense of that, he steps away from the tree. He maneuvers me like I don't weigh a thing. He sits upright on the ground with his legs spread out in front of him. I'm still lifted in the air with his hands gripping my thighs, my knees bent up to my chest. Kissing the back of my neck, he lowers me onto his hard, throbbing cock.

I bite my lower lip so I don't cry out.

"Good girl," he murmurs in my ear. "Stay nice and quiet as you watch my cock enter you."

He pulls me down further, and my hands fly over my mouth, trying to keep the noises in. My gaze darts down to watch his cock slowly starting to fill my pussy. I take the full head of him in, then slide down even more. My nipples grow hard. My body grows flush. Panting against my palms,

I watch through half-hooded eyes as he pulls me down fully.

I'm stretched so much. He's in so deep. Moaning, I sag against his chest and drop my hands. He releases my thighs to grab my breasts, pinching my nipples in between his fingers. I bite back a cry. He murmurs in my ear. "Now look ahead, little monster."

I do without question, knowing I will find pleasure from obeying. My eyes widen as I see Maddox and Zita in front of us though, never having imagined that. They're a fair few yards away. My pussy spasms around Varius' cock as my jaw drops.

"You like the view?" he growls, a jolt of jealousy coming down our bond. Danger screams inside my skull as I realize he herded me here. He must have been able to smell them or sense them through their heartbeats.

"Do you want to join them?" he demands as he shoves a hand between my shoulder blades and pushes me down. I reach out automatically, my hands landing on his knees to hold myself up. He grabs my hips and lifts my ass off him. I know I should be paying attention to him first and foremost, but I can't seem to rip my eyes away from the scene in front of me.

Maddox has Zita hanging upside down from a tree just like he said he would. She's fully naked, and her body is covered in old scars – the bites and claws of werewolves. She must be an omega – a pack's punching bag, her body a canvas to their violence. There are also new wounds that are still bleeding – whipping lines from whatever Maddox's been doing to her.

Her legs are spread, her ankles tied to a branch above with some rope, and in the moonlight piercing through the branches, I can see her pussy gleaming with wetness. My own grows wet too.

Maddox steps up to her, also fully naked, and grips his cock. His member is almost half the size of Varius', I would suspect, but the confidence he moves with more than makes up for it.

"Nah...I think I like you better with the mask." Maddox's words whisper on the wind, so faint I almost miss them. As he turns, I suck in a breath, wondering if he can see us. But his eyes are on the ground.

"I asked you a question," Varius growls as he digs his fingers into my ass. He slams me down all the way on his cock, and I almost cry out before I bite my lip. My nails dig into his knees, drawing blood. I'm shaking so much, all my muscles feel weak.

"Do you want to join them?"

My pulse spikes. I shake my head, not wanting Varius anywhere near another woman.

"Are you fucking lying to me?" he growls as he lifts me off him.

I shake my head again.

He slams up into me as he pulls me down. This time I can't fully trap my whimper. My head jerks up as a small cry escapes me, but Maddox is facing Zita again with the leather Hannibal-esque mask dangling from his fingers. He puts it back on her despite her attempt to resist him, jerking her head back and forth. He grabs a fistful of her hair to hold her still, then straps the mask on. There's a hole in it now though, circular and right over her mouth.

My heartbeat picks up as Varius' cock moves fast and hard inside me. My nipples are hard, sensitive buds as they sway in the night air. My mouth waters as I watch Varius' brother step up to Zita with his hand on his cock again. He forces his dick through the hole in her mask. His ass and leg muscles tighten as he starts to thrust into her.

"Are you imagining yourself in her place?" my husband growls as he picks up his pace, slamming me down so hard, pain radiates through my womb. He's hitting the back of it, bruising it, and he's moving so fast now, I fear he's going to rub me raw.

I hang my head as I shudder on his cock. My entire body is shaking as it begs for a release, but I need him to play with the outside of my pussy to get it. My nails dig deeper into his knees. I try to shift my weight to one hand, but my balance instantly disappears. Biting my lip, I whimper.

"Answer me," he snaps, slamming me down all the way onto his lap so his hands are free to go around me. One wraps around my neck. The other slaps my pussy. I jump from the unexpected smack. Panting hard, I shake my head.

"But it's making you hot, isn't it? Watching my brother fuck that whore?"

I squirm on his cock, but I can't deny it. My eyes find the couple through the trees, and my pussy spasms as I watch Maddox lower his head down to her cunt. He licks her as he fucks her face, his hands wrapped around her head as he pounds into her. "Yes," I pant, my legs shaking.

Varius' jealousy flares so violently that I fall forward on a gasp. He shoves me down the rest of the way. My face hits the ground. He kneels behind me. Pulling out of my pussy, he pushes the cum plug in, and then slams his cock into my ass.

I cry out, unable to stop myself. His hand lands on my ass, and the smack resonates through the trees. There's no way Maddox doesn't know we're here now. My cheeks flush as Varius fucks me like an animal. He grunts and growls and leans down to bite my shoulder and neck. I scream as he rearranges my insides with every thrust of his cock.

"Watch them like the whore you are," Varius snaps as he grabs my chin and forces my gaze up.

Maddox is fucking her faster now. He still has his tongue buried between her legs. He thrusts in deep and stays there, and the excitement of seeing someone else come brings me to the edge. My whole body grows hot, the flush spreading across every nerve.

Zita jerks away as Maddox grunts. Then he steps back, and I can see her spitting out his cum. He takes another step back, then drops to his knees. Confusion keeps my orgasm away as Varius continues to pound into me from the back.

But then I realize what Maddox's doing when his body cracks and breaks, and shadows swirl around his feet. When he finishes shapeshifting, my jaw drops off completely. I thought he might just be increasing the size of his cock, but he's changed the entirety of his body into that of a werewolf in its wolf form. He's now twice her size, if not more.

"That's it, you beautiful whore," Varius groans as he rams his cock down my ass. "Come on me while you watch him fuck her." He grabs my throat and leans back to sit on his calves. He pulls one of my arms back as he jackhammers into me, penetrating me so deep. I cry out as he releases my throat and rubs my clit instead.

"That's it. Good girl," Varius grunts behind me. "Come like a beautiful little whore."

With an animalistic growl, Maddox grabs Zita's body in his big meaty paws and yanks her down from the tree. She cries out as the skin on her ankles are undoubtedly rubbed away. He spins her around so she's upright, turns to face us, and then spreads her legs wide. Giving us a show.

My breath catches as my eyes drop to her pussy. The large head of his cock, much bigger than her forearm now, pushes inside her. She screams as she's forced to take his thick girth, but there isn't any blood pouring down her legs from any tearing. He must have given her a V, a succubus potion that allows her to take monster cocks.

My breaths come out hard and fast. Varius releases my arm to cup my breast and pinch my nipple. Overwhelmed, I cry out, and my orgasm crashes through me just as Maddox shoves his cock all the way in. I can see the outline of it beneath her skin, reaching up to just beneath her breasts. The end of his cock blossoms out into a knot, and he fucks her hard and fast just the same as Varius is doing to me.

I scream and jerk on his cock. He pulls out of me, moves the cum plug to my ass, and then lines his cock up with my pussy again. I try to stop him, but he throws me down to the ground and shoves in. He fucks me so hard, my body sinks into the cold forest floor.

Digging my nails into the soft earth, I am helpless to do anything but let him rut me like an animal. My pussy is rubbed raw, my ass is well smacked, and I am on the verge of falling asleep, my body too well fucked to stay awake.

Grabbing me by the throat, Varius yanks my head back up. "You watch them like a good little whore," he demands. I open my eyes to see Maddox's wolf cock sliding in and out of her body. "That's it. Good girl. Let me give my fucking payment to the blood bond."

My pulse spikes as my eyes widen. Getting my second wind, my heart expanding in my chest, I turn my head to look at Varius. Dark eyes stare back at me, his face twisted with jealousy.

He gazes into my eyes. His breaths get harsher. Then with a hard smack of my ass, he finally comes inside me.

He falls forward on a groan, and I collapse beneath his weight as he fills my pussy. I shudder beneath him, my entire body feeling so damn delicious.

But he doesn't let me bask in it. Doesn't give me a break at all.

Hauling me to my feet, he growls sharp words into my ear, "Run, little monster. *Run.*"

FORTY-SEVEN

HIM

I wake up on my side with my cock still inside her. We moved from the woods to Maddox's room last night. After watching her come with her eyes on my brother, I needed to own her completely. So I fucked her all night in his bed, with Marrabelle, his weird little sex fiend pet thing that lives in an empty fish tank on his dresser, masturbating as she watched us.

My chest still tight with the jealousy I haven't been able to get rid of, I roll us over so Micha's on her stomach and I'm above her. She's still asleep when I start to fuck her, pounding her little, tiny body into his mattress. She wakes up part way through, wrapping her arms around his pillows to moan into them, and that just builds my jealousy more.

Khalid needed us all to fuck his girl for his blood bond to snap into place, but all I needed was for her to come while watching someone else. I want to kill Maddox, the little shit, and his girl Zita, but I know doing so will void the payment, so I settle for destroying his room instead. I took her on every available surface last night and then some, marking her entire body as fucking mine. Her pussy is sore, and her thighs are heavily bruised from the pounding of my hips. She doesn't even try to match me anymore, just lies there as I fuck her hard and fast and feral until the bed breaks. She's just a little sex doll for me to use.

Grabbing her throat, I turn her head to kiss her. My tongue steals inside her mouth. My other hand wiggles between her and the mattress to play with her clit. She gasps against me as I work to force another orgasm from her.

"I can't…" she pants against my lips. "No more…"

I fuck her harder. The broken planks of the bed beneath us crack in rhythm to my thrusts. She groans. Mewls. Her fists tighten in the sheets. When she starts to shake, I know she's getting close.

"That's it, Micha. Come for me," I growl as my balls slap against her ass. "Squeeze my cock like the whore you are. That's it. Good girl. Who's my good fucking whore?"

She screams as she comes all over me. I pump into her a few more times before pulling out, grabbing my cock, and lining it up with her ass. I push in deep with one hard thrust, and she thrashes beneath me on another scream.

I fuck her hard, slapping her ass until it's red and sore and I'm filling her with my cum. Digging my fingers into both her cheeks, I arch back with a groan. My balls are completely empty, but she's so fucking full from all the loads she took last night that it doesn't even matter. Our thighs are soaked, the bed is ruined, and the entire room smells like it's been scent-marked by an incubus. Maddox will probably move out of the house after this. A good thing because I don't know how long I can live with him before I snap and kill him.

Collapsing on top of her, I bite her neck with a low

growl. She whimpers as she clutches the sheets. I start rocking inside her again even though I'm no longer hard. I just can't get enough of her.

Pulling out, I roll her onto her back and settle between her legs. She moans as I lick her slowly, too tired to even thread her fingers in my hair.

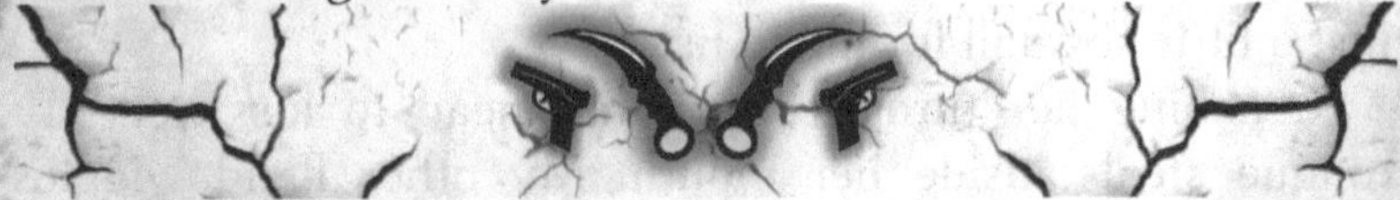

A couple hours later, I manage to get Micha down for breakfast. She finally has her appetite back after a week of barely eating, and I watch her with pride as she finishes her plate of bacon and eggs while she talks to her sister. She hasn't touched her glass of water though.

"Drink," I say.

"I'm not thir–"

"Finish it."

Lou snickers, and I'm certain Micha kicks her under the table given how her sister then winces and sticks out her tongue.

Sighing, Micha grabs the glass and raises it to her lips.

"Good girl."

Lou coughs, as does Dayne beside her, but my attention moves to the rest of the people at the table. When my eyes skirt past Maddox, my hand settles on my butter knife. The fucker shifted into a wolf last night, and although I know that must have already been planned given Zita was able to take his cock rather than get split in half, a dark voice inside my head is telling me he did that just so he could see better, hear better. Smell Micha's pussy so much fucking better.

Her hand lands on my lap, and I realize she can feel my jealousy. I suspect our blood bond strengthened last night with one of us having finally made payment, but I still can't fucking feel it. *Dammit.* What if I never get to?

My muscles tight, I grab her hand, then release the knife

in my other. I am the Boss of the Shadow Domain, and I am in control.

"Lou, Dayne, leave," I say as soon as I notice they've finished eating. Lou stands immediately, but Dayne glances at Micha first. I haven't told him I'm bringing him into my Family yet, so his loyalty isn't to me. Though I suspect, even after he says his vows, Micha will always be his priority.

She looks at him, and he rises. A spark of jealousy ignites at how well they can communicate without words, and she squeezes my leg to tell me to cool it.

I slide her hand up my thigh. My cock twitches beneath her palm. She slams her glass down and coughs as a blush heats her cheek. Lou looks back at her with a weird look, and Micha covers her mouth with a hand. "Wrong pipe," she says.

I grin.

Lou looks at me, then blushes herself as her head whips back around.

As soon as the two outsiders leave the room, I let her go. All eyes turn to me, my brothers understanding that I have just called a meeting.

"Aleric told me yesterday," I sign with my hands, getting straight to the point, "that Cara has had a breakthrough." When he wanted me to show him to the bathroom, it turns out he wasn't just being a total prick. "She thinks she'll have the disease perfected in another day or so."

"How do we deliver it?" Leno asks.

"She'll coat some weapons with it."

Enoch groans. "You mean swords, right? She's putting it on fucking swords and not bullets."

"Yes."

"Why?" he whines. "A gun is so much easier to use."

"The spell is unstable, and she doesn't want it mixing with black powder."

He grumbles beneath his breath, but he accepts that

answer.

"Can I have it on a knife?" Maddox signs.

I nod.

"What effect will it have on us?" Leno asks.

"If it doesn't get into your bloodstream, then nothing. If it does, you will experience dizziness, severe stomach pain, diarrhea, a boil-like rash, seizures, burning in your mouth and nose, vomiting, breathing difficulty, blindness, deafness, and complete paralysis from your neck down. Some of these symptoms might be permanent, so don't cut yourself."

"Shit," Enoch groans.

"It's a magical disease that bypasses a werewolf's natural resistance to magic, bruh. Of course it's going to be nasty," Maddox teases. He turns to me, and my fingers itch for the butter knife beside my plate. Or perhaps I'll use the fork...

"How long does it take to take effect?" he asks.

"Twenty-four hours," I say, reaching for the control I'm known for.

"What the fuck? That's useless," Enoch blurts, then signs it with his hands.

"It's the best she can do without making it so strong it kills us just by being breathed in."

He doesn't have anything to say to that.

"How are they testing it?" Leno asks.

"Aleric has been supplying her with wolves."

"Bitten or born?"

My jaw tics. I have the same worry; their level of magical resistance isn't the same. "Bitten."

"Shit, so it might not even work on Antonio?"

"If his dosage is higher, she says it should. So we'll need to attack him all together and stab him as much as we can."

"Fuck."

"Which is why I've ordered a shipment of silver through the portal."

"The SCU –" Mother starts.

"Are not the priority right now. If we can make a net, we can kill him. Next month is Siome's birthday –"

"Who?" Ezriel asks.

"Antonio's dead mate. He visits the place he proposed to her every year on her birthday, which is the first of July. So we have until then to make a plan to kill him and any super werewolves he's already infected."

"Where did he propose?" Ezriel asks warily.

"The crocodile farm."

"What the fuck?" Leno yells.

Maddox laughs, and just the sound of it makes me want to beat his fucking face in. For him to have any happiness at all right now is pissing me off.

Enoch shakes his head, forcing my attention back on him. "It's impossible. He owns the territory up and down Matanzas River. As soon as we try to cross the bridge, he'll have us. We could fly in, but invisibility won't work given they can smell us. If they figure out our destination, it won't matter where we land; they'll just be waiting for us at the farm."

"You forget we've allied with the vampires now, bruh," Maddox says, rocking his chair back. "We can just phase in."

Enoch opens his mouth, then closes it again. "Oh, yeah."

"Idiot."

"Cuntfucker," he spits back.

"Why, yes I am," Maddox says with a grin, and I damn near grab a knife as I think about Micha having watched him do just that.

"Shit," Enoch mutters as the rest of the table laughs at his poor combination of words.

Breathing out, I force myself to focus on the details of this meeting. "According to Cara," I say, "if she had to create a cure for the disease, that'd take her three or four weeks, but for anyone else, she suspects it'll take months. So we need to kill him in five weeks' time, or we might not get another chance to ambush him." Antonio is not a man of habit outside of visiting the alligator farm on her birthday and visiting the place she died on her death date every year. Having him followed isn't possible either – not if we want to see the men who take that job again. With Siome's death anniversary being nearly a year away, it will be too late to ambush him then.

"Shit, okay then," Enoch says, though he shakes his head in despair.

The mood around the table is grim.

I glance at Micha. Her glass is only half empty. I nod at it. She scowls at me but brings it up to her lips grudgingly.

With the fun shit out of the way, I turn to Khalid. After he killed Talon, he got back home in the middle of the night. The next day, we were all rushing around to get ready for the wedding, so we didn't get a chance to speak. He holds my gaze with dark eyes, and my paranoia shifts harshly in my stomach.

"Tell us what happened with Talon," I say softly.

All heads turn towards him.

"I killed him," the reaper says without emotion. "I stuck a knife in his throat and ripped it out."

"Shit."

"Was it quick?" Maddox asks.

"Yes."

He closes his eyes briefly in relief, but Micha's glass hits the table with a *clonk*. I glance at her, my eyes hard. This is not the time to express her anger. Clenching her jaw, she looks away from me.

"Did you take him into your shadows?" Rudy asks, his hands trembling.

Khalid nods, and the tension around the table eases a little. In the end, despite his crimes, Khalid still viewed him as a brother. In the confliction of emotions inside of me, my happiness over that is equal to my paranoia about what that means. If Khalid sided with him in the end... like Talon did after Vinny died...

"Did he say why he did it?" Enoch wonders.

"He believed Varius being Boss has led to too many dead. Vinny" –Talon's best friend– "was merely the last straw."

My lips tighten. The reaper's gaze turns to me, and for a moment, I see anger there. Accusation and regret. My heart rate spikes, but I do not release his gaze.

"Was he sorry at all?" Micha asks, her words pushed out tightly between her lips.

Releasing my gaze, he turns to her. "About you, no."

It's harshly said, but she accepts it without emotion. I doubted she expected anything else, but hope is a damning thing to have.

My phone buzzes with a timer, and I rise as I turn it off. Eyes flash around the table, judging me over how abruptly I'm discarding Talon's death. But although he might've been my brother, he set up my wife, and I'm not ready to forgive him enough to mourn.

"We're heading to the portal," I say, pocketing my phone. "Khalid, Maddox, Leno, and Micha, you're with me."

My wife looks at me in surprise, but she said she wanted everyone to know I have claimed her, so they will. She will accompany me to every meeting, every part of the business. The capos won't appreciate a woman's presence, but I don't give a shit about them.

All I care about is her.

Holding out my hand, I wait for her to rise.

FORTY-EIGHT

HER

The portal's on the west side of town, located under one of the Shadow warehouses. The first floor is a stereotypical room full of shelves that contain landscaping machinery, equipment, spare parts, and supplies. Witches and humans, not all of whom are involved with the Family business, stack shelves and pack orders. The floor manager rushes over and leads us into his office. He shuts the door behind him, then uses his magic to remove the floor behind his desk to reveal a set of metal stairs.

As I peer into the dark hole, Varius' paranoia flares down our bond. Khalid descends, and the urge to stab him in the back, to eliminate a stronger threat before he eliminates me is making my fingers ache with need. I clench them into fists as I glance at my husband. The hairs on my nape rise. His paranoia's been ricocheting off every nerve all morning, making me anxious that something's about to happen.

His jaw tight, he nods at me to enter after Leno. He'll go

next to protect my back. I nod at him ever so subtly, letting him know that I understand we might have to fight our way out of here. I just don't know if he's paranoid because we're going into a dark hole with no door he can open or because he doesn't trust his brothers. Does he have a real reason to be on edge? Or is this just because Talon betrayed him and now he doesn't know who to trust?

Knowing I won't get any answers out here, I descend into the dark.

The metal steps clang beneath my shoes. My pulse stays steady as all my nerves fire. I touch the gun I have strapped to my waist. Varius is right behind me, and I relax a little from the feel of his presence.

Nothing lunges out of the dark to get me. Khalid, Krypto, and Leno are already continuing on, their backs to me, so there's no immediate threat from them either.

Releasing my gun, I follow them down a hallway that's only wide enough for one person to walk through at a time. The floor's uneven, and I have to concentrate on my footing so I don't stumble. The dullest of bulbs hang above us. Their ambience overlaps and creates multiple shadows per person, making it hard for our eyes to adjust. The back of my neck prickles. Claustrophobia starts to set in. *Fuck.*

"Is the rock too hard to work with?" I ask, trying to keep my mind occupied so I don't shove past Leno and Khalid to run to the exit like a little bitch. Or worse, draw my gun and shoot them in the back. Varius' paranoia is stressing me the fuck out.

"Nah," Maddox says from behind Varius. "This is the last stand to stop whatever comes out of the portal."

"I thought the other side was controlled by the Ezwail'ik Family?"

"It is," Leno says. "But the werewolves on Blódyrió fall under the Craving on the full moon."

"*Fuck.* All of them?" The SCU keeps on top of Craved

sups on Earth, but I saw a mad werewolf in North Korea while Dayne and I were on a job there. We had been hired by a Russian politician to kill the diplomat who'd slept with his youngest daughter. While in Pyongyang, we heard whispers of a *gumiho* (what they believed her to be) being experimented on. They were torturing her to see how fast she could heal and which wounds hurt her the most. When we found her, they'd forced her to change into her wolf form and were in the process of skinning her alive for her pelt. She fell into the Craving right after we killed the guy behind the glass, and she ripped her way through the entire compound.

We missed our extraction to go save her, so I was really annoyed when she ended up saving herself, then tried to kill us. Unfortunately, with her under the power of the Craving, we couldn't let her live once she reached the exit. She would have slaughtered her way through the entire city, perhaps the country, killing without discrimination. If an undercover reporter caught wind of her before the SCU arrived to clean up, then our entire world would've been blasted open.

So I killed her. It wasn't an easy fight, and by that point she was heavily malnourished, dehydrated, and already half dead from all her wounds. If she'd been at full power, I would have struggled even with Dayne's help. Being under the Craving gives a sup extra strength. They do not heal any faster, but their wounds bleed less and their pain resistance skyrockets. In short, they become pure killing machines.

To survive an entire night when half the population goes bloodthirsty at once? Fucking hel.

"No, most of them chain themselves up with silver before nightfall," Leno says. "But some of them like to spend the night out hunting in the mountains or other uninhabited places."

"And let me guess," I say, stepping over a lump in the floor, as if a tree root has grown under the tile, "the portal on the other side is in the middle of nowhere?"

"Yep. And then you have blood moons."

"I've heard of those," I say, but then I pause. "What are they again?" My knowledge of Blódyrió or any of the other Seven Planes other than Halzaja is sorely lacking. And I only know a bit about the plane of the angels and demons because Lou is a summoning progeny and is obsessed with eknor demon culture.

"It's when the moon turns dark red, triggering all the werewolves and vampires to fall under the Craving," Varius says, and I turn my head to look at him. I like the fact that he's answering me too. He normally ignores me in public so no one knows I'm his weakness. A slow smile curls my lips, lighting me up on the inside.

His eyes heating, he grabs the back of my head. My feet root to the floor while he steps up to me. He ducks his head, and his lips cover mine, kissing me until I'm breathless.

I start to reach for him, but he pulls back, then nudges me to keep moving. I stumble forward even though all I want to do is ride his cock right here, right now. Our blood bond has strengthened substantially since last night, and his arousal is amplifying mine.

"The blood moon's cycle can't be tracked," he continues as we walk, and I focus on that rather than leaning against the wall and telling him to get down on his knees in front of me. He has teased me with the idea of having him at my mercy too many times, and mama *wants* it.

"It's random and comes without warning."

Wait, what are we talking about again?

"Some people say it happens when Artemis comes down for a hunt."

Oooh. Yeah. Now I remember. "Wait. Artemis as in the Goddess of the Hunt?" I ask, turning my head. "That can't be true, can it?" The gods haven't been seen on any of the Seven Planes in...forever, as far as I'm aware. Granted, my knowledge of these things is actually pretty bad. If it doesn't have anything to do with my family or job, I've been too busy to pay attention to it.

He shrugs. "There are hundreds of thousand dead when the blood moon ends, so perhaps."

My jaw drops. I stumble over a bit of rocky ground, and I turn to catch my balance. Keeping my eyes on my feet, I say, "*Fuck*."

"Most of those are probably due to the two billion wolves and vampires going crazy in an instant all at once," Leno adds. "The wolves don't have time to chain themselves up, the vampires can phase, and no one's activated the wards. It's an absolute massacre in every village, which is why all the large settlements on Blódyrió only allow vampires and werewolves to enter during the day, year round."

"Shit. That sucks. It's their home world."

Leno shrugs. "They never had huge cities before people migrated over anyway. I don't think many of them care."

"Mmm. So do Craved sups find their way to the portal often?" I ask as Khalid nears a bend in the narrow hall.

"Once a decade or so," Varius says. "But we don't want to be caught off guard."

The hallway turns, then widens into a corridor. Now five people can walk side by side. It stays like that for a long stretch before rounding another corner and expanding once more. It does this a few more times until twenty people can fit side by side. They're choke points, I realize, places where the defending party can hold off a much bigger army.

"So if there's only one wolf coming through every ten years, what's with the design?" I ask.

"It was made during the Great Extinction, and no one's ever decided to change it."

I whistle as I feel the weight of history all around me. The Great Extinction happened around two thousand years ago if memory serves, when a vampire called Sebastian the

Ancient Destroyer teamed up with a descendant (a child of the gods, who are not gods, just like gods are not the titans they hail from) known as Rakian the Rise of Ragnarok.

In their war across the Seven Planes, they completely destroyed one world, Persic, causing it to continuously fold in on itself like a paper fortune teller. Earth was cut off from the rest of the Seven Planes in an attempt to save it, and Christianity was born to make them forget the old gods and the world they were no longer to be a part of. Gaera, once a plane of picturesque paradise, created by the elementals, fell into decay. Its rivers started drying up. Its forests and plains started dying. I assumed the planet would've been close to uninhabitable by now, but considering my wand came from there, I guess it's still stable enough to hold life.

"That's really cool," I say.

The corridor soon opens up into a cavern, its manmade material giving way to natural stone. Rugged brown walls arch into a ceiling of stalactites that hang a few feet down. At the back is a wall made of swirling pink and orange mist. Dozens of men in store uniform laze around the place. They are all here for security if shit hits the fan, but for now, they are just bored out of their minds.

"I thought portals glowed?" I murmur as we approach.

"Only when they're about to be used," Leno says.

"Ah." I swallow the rest of my questions as a muscular man with a shaved head and face tattoos comes up to us. A dragon curls around his left eye, and the name Daymara is written in cursive on his cheek.

"Boss," he says as he looks at Varius. "What can I do –"

"Get everyone out."

He hesitates a second, then turns and yells for everyone to get upstairs. There's a moment of confusion given the gate is just starting to glow.

"Out, now! Boss' orders," the man repeats.

The atmosphere changes instantly as they realize that it's

Varius fucking Shadow who's just entered. Everyone jumps to obey, and the cavern starts to clear.

"We'll be up until you come up," the soldier says as he turns to leave with his men. "Or if any of the protection runes are activated."

I glance at the runes he's mentioned. Fifteen blue circles cover the floor in front of the portal. On closer inspection, I realize they're not fully complete, with a gap of a few inches left on each one. They're similar to a summoning circle for eknor demons, but the runes around these will be to stop outside forces from breaking in rather than the other way around.

The five of us split, so Khalid, Varius, and I step inside one of the circles, and Leno, Krypto, and Maddox wait in another. They won't activate until a witch casts a spell to delete that gap.

Lifting my eyes to the portal, I watch as it grows ever brighter until it matches the intensity of the setting sun. The surface of it ripples like water, and the first silhouette starts to push through.

It's humanoid and nowhere near as tall as a werewolf in wolf form, but it could still be a vampire under the Craving. Werewolves might have unmatched speed, but vampires can phase. They could reach us in the blink of an eye.

Fuck. I wish I still had my magic.

My teeth clench as my anger at Varius comes bubbling back.

"When did you claim her?" Khalid demands as another silhouette joins the first.

The question is so out of the blue that it puts me on edge. But then Varius' paranoia slams into me, and I have to curl my toes to fight the urge to run. My hand brushes against a knife as I shift subtly towards my husband.

"This isn't the time," he says.

"I killed our little brother and came back to a wedding,"

the reaper says softly. "You will give me the fucking time."

My pulse spikes as two predators face off.

The urge to stab Khalid before he can react makes my fingers twitch. His gaze shifts to me, and I freeze.

"A little more than a week ago," Varius says tightly. "But I loved her before then."

My eyes widen as sudden giddiness breaks through my fear. "Oh my gods. Did you fall first?"

I turn my head to look at him while keeping Khalid in my peripheral. I'm excited, not stupid.

His lips move so subtly, it can't even be called a twitch, but I can feel his love for me, the joy he gets from seeing my excitement even as he keeps his eyes on the cold gaze of the reaper. "Karaoke night," he says, and I preen.

"Bonding night."

"You're bonded?" Khalid demands, but neither of us get the chance to answer as the first creature steps out of the portal.

All of our gazes go to the white-haired man who's built like Henry Cavil in *The Witcher*. He's soon followed by a woman with a neck so skinny it makes her head look too big. An image of one of those bobble head toys pops into my mind, and I roll my lips in, chastising myself for being rude.

"Henry" disappears back into the portal immediately as... Fuck. "Bobble Head" –I'm so going to Hel, but gods, if I don't go there laughing– walks towards us. Her head bobs as she moves, and I am dying on the inside. I keep my face completely expressionless though. As an assassin, wearing masks is all part of the game.

"Varius," she purrs as she stops in front of him. Using her right hand, she taps first her left shoulder, then her right in an off-world greeting. She doesn't once acknowledge Khalid or I.

"Zara," Varius says, way too friendly for my liking. He repeats the gesture. I wait for him to introduce me, but he never does.

Forcing a smile, I say, "I'm Micha," just as she's about to say something. She ignores me. "His wife," I add.

"You got married, and I wasn't invited?" Zara says with a pout.

"It was last minute," Varius supplies.

"Ahhh." She nods knowingly, then looks at me like I'm some baby-trapping hoe. But it's the fact that Varius doesn't correct her that irritates me the most.

"I –"

"Let us talk, Micha." His tone is cold, flat, and final.

Clenching my teeth, I swallow my words. We might be married and bonded now, but I know he won't hesitate to punish me. My lack of control reflects badly on him and the Family, and he is all about the fucking Family.

She smiles triumphantly, and my jealousy simmers so hot I can't feel anything else. The portal glows softly behind her, and I focus on that as she and Varius *talk*.

Dozens of people come through the portal. A quarter of them are Zara's men. Of those that remain, two thirds are carrying backpacks, marking them as the people we are smuggling in. They'll be forced to work for us for the next five years before they're given IDs and set free. All the fees they've already paid go to Zara's Family as off-world money means nothing to us. We get their labor.

Maddox starts to lead them upstairs to get them out of the way. Varius doesn't want anyone here to witness the exchanging of silver so we can take Antonio by surprise.

My eyes fall on those that remain. These are the poor bastards that the Blood Fangs have demanded. One of the stipulations of our treaty is that they get to use our portal to buy and sell humans six times a year. So they gave us a list of six women to pass over to Zara's Family to round up and collect a few weeks ago. They will then supply six humans as payment. Aleric wanted to come exchange them himself, but Varius refuses to let any outsiders enter the warehouse.

"Who's missing?" Varius asks as he nods at the group of seven girls surrounded by Zara's men.

"The succubi killed herself last night," she says, looking annoyed. "We can add one to the next batch, though, if you still want one. Alternatively, we've brought two fae with us as a replacement. They're twins."

He heads over to them. My stomach twists as I follow, urging me to set them free, but vampires have to eat. If these people don't die to feed them, then someone else will. *Just think of them as cattle, Micha.* No one would bat an eye at farmers buying stock.

A young woman catches my eye. She looks terrified.

I look away.

Pigs have the intelligence of a three year old. Some of them play video games for fun. I wince. These facts aren't helping me as much as I hoped they would. I stop, unable to get all the way to Varius.

Bobble Head Bitch notices and smirks at me. Grabbing one of the twins by the arm, she hauls her in front of the Boss of the Shadow Domain.

"Fae blood might not be as sweet as succubi, but it packs more of a punch."

"What Court is she from?"

"They're both rejects, so probably half-bloods."

Disinterest comes down our bond.

"But we can leave them here," Zara hurries on. "You can take a bit of blood to your client and see what he thinks?"

He thinks about it for a moment, then nods. She smiles at him in a way that makes me want to stab her in the face. "I'm glad we can still please each other," she purrs.

Anger pushing me on, I manage to walk the rest of the way to Varius. Neither of them look at me. "They'll count as one," he says, his full attention on her.

Her smile tightens. "Of course."

Pulling out his phone, he sends a text to Maddox, telling him to bring down the six women we left topside. While we wait for his return, Zara leads us over to the crate of silver. When Varius confirms he's happy with it, she shuts the lid. By that time, his brother is back, leading the six women for the exchange. They're all chained together, linked by collars around their necks.

Zara smiles wide as her men swap which group they're guarding. "It was a pleasure doing business with you," she says as she bows her head at Varius, but I'm short enough to notice that she's taking the opportunity to run her eyes all over his body.

My jaw tightens as I fight the urge to hit her. Just a few more seconds, and I'll be out of her damn company.

But just then an image pops into my head of her down on her knees, sucking his huge cock. His hand is in her hair as he thrusts inside her mouth. *"That's it, baby,"* he grunts. *"You're taking me so well. You're going to swallow for me, aren't you?"*

My chest tightens as I realize she's a telepath. She smirks at me, her smile hidden from Varius by the bow of her head.

"That's just one of the many things we've done," she says telepathically. *"You might have his name, you fucking bitch, but I'll always have his cock."*

She sends another image to me, this time with his cock in her pussy. She's sitting on his lap, and he has his face buried in her boobs. His hands are gripping her hips, guiding her to go faster. *"Fuck, Zara. Your cunt feels so good. Ride me just like that. Fuck, baby. You're going to make me come. Yeah. I'm going to come in your tight little pussy."*

Straightening, she smirks at me.

"Until next time," she purrs as she reaches out to touch my husband.

But I move faster, fueled by pure *rage.*

Pulling out a knife, I stab her in the fucking face.

FORTY-NINE

HER

Or that's what I would've done if Varius didn't grab my arm, twist my wrist, and force me to drop my knife, which he catches in his other hand.

Zara stumbles back in fear and rage as I scream, "You bobble head bitch!"

I go to swing for her with my other arm, but Varius hauls me away from her, choosing her side over mine, and oh my gods, if I thought I could get away with it, I would kick him in the fucking balls. The utter asshole keeps telling me I'm his, only to keep pulling this shit when it comes time to actually proving it. Fucking hel, when am I going to learn all he is is a smooth talking liar?

"Apologize," Varius hisses.

As I stand heaving in stubborn refusal, Zara recollects her composure. She looks at me smugly, then takes a step forward, no doubt confident in the fact that she's won. I look crazy, and my own damn husband is holding me back from kicking her ass.

"Yeah, tell me –"

"I will handle my wife," Varius cuts in.

She shuts up immediately, and now it's my turn to smile smugly.

"*Micha*," he demands, his voice low and deadly. Regret and disappointment come down our bond, and I know he'll have to punish me if I don't say the words. My chin lifts. Fuck her. I'd rather take the punishment.

Varius' lips touch my ear. "You will cause a war with her Family. She is Ryker Ezwail'ik's only child."

Fuck.

I clench my teeth. I really want to stab this bitch in her face, but I won't start a war just because she's being petty. I'll prove myself to Varius that I can be level-headed enough to rule alongside him. Oh, look at me, growing up and not letting one brash moment ruin the rest of my future.

Father would be so proud.

Relaxing my jaw, I smile sweetly. "I'm sorry for trying to show you my knife, Zara. I just thought you'd like to see how pretty it was close up."

"Do you think I'm dumb?"

"Considering you decided to show me images of you fucking my husband while I was within stabbing range? Uh, yeah."

"Why you little –"

"Did you break into her mind, Zara?" Varius says softly, and the blood instantly drains from her face.

"Of course not. That's –"

"Kill her," he says flatly. "I'll deal with the rest."

He releases me, then disappears from my side. There is a second of disbelief from both me and her, especially since Varius left me my eight-inch knife. The horror and shock on her face pleases me greatly, but I know watching her life fade will please me more. Smiling evilly, I step forward. She throws another image at my mind, trying to trip me up, but she's a weak telepath with no capability of stopping me.

"Iris!" she screams as she backs up, but no one is coming to help her. It's thirteen to four, but these are the infamous Shadow brothers. One of them on their own could take on all her soldiers.

So I advance without worrying. It's time to have some fun. To get out all the stress that's been building up inside of me for the past few weeks. I can't kill Khalid's girl, but I've just been given the green light to kill her.

Her face paling, she spins around and tries to run for the portal, but I jump forward and grab her arm.

"You wanted my man," I say as I force her back around. "Then let's see how well you can take eight inches."

I shove my KA-BAR into her stomach. Her eyes widen as she gasps for air. I move the hand I have on her forearm up to the back of her neck. Leaning in close, I murmur, "You must know how much he loves to pull out all nice and slow." Pulling the blade out, I leave in just the tip. "Before going in hard and deep." I thrust the knife back into her.

She screams like the whore she is. Her hands push at my chest in a pathetic attempt to stop me. Pain wets her eyes as she silently begs me for mercy.

"And you must know he can go for hours." I pull out the blade until it's just the tip again. Then ram it back in.

She screams once more.

Then whimpers when I stab her again in the same place. My hand stays on the back of her neck, holding her still in my rage and jealousy. Holding her up when her legs give out.

"You thought you could hurt me by sharing that shit with me?" My teeth clench tight as the pain I'm pretending not to feel ricochets around my chest. "I will show you *pain*," I whisper.

I shove her away from me. She falls backwards and hits

the ground. She's full-on sobbing now, terrified and bleeding out like a stuck pig.

"Please..." she rasps. "Please.., I'm... sorry."

"You're *sorry*?" I sneer. "You practically fucked my man in front of me, and you're *sorry*?"

She cries harder.

I want to carve her to pieces for the shit I've "seen" her do with my husband. The images are replaying inside my skull, and the jealousy eating through me is making me see red.

"But you know what? Okay," I say as I squat down at her feet. "I'll let you crawl back home to daddy if you do one thing for me."

She looks at me with hope-brimmed eyes as her hands feebly press on her stomach. "Any...anything."

"Fuck this knife like it's Varius."

Her eyes widen.

"I'll even let you pick what hole he goes in." My fingers tighten on the knife as the image of her down on her knees sucking his cock comes back to me in intricate detail. "So what do you say, Zara? You want to swallow him like you showed me?"

She shakes her head as she starts to sob. She's so fucking weak and pathetic. She can't even experience a bit of pain to save her own life. Always hiding behind daddy's name and the belief that no one will punish her for being a bitch.

Well, this time she messed with the wrong woman.

I might not be Varius' all the way. But he is *mine*.

"Or would you rather ride him up your cunt?" I point the blade at the V between her legs. "Pick or I'll do them both."

"Please!" She shakes as she sobs. Turning over onto her stomach, she tries to drag herself to the portal.

"My choice it is."

Grabbing her by the ankle, I yank her towards me. She screams as her nails try to dig into the floor. I aim the knife at her cunt and pull her towards me some more. The blade now points past her knee.

"Stop! Please!" She sobs as her hands scramble for a grip. "I'm –" She breaks off on a scream of terror as I touch the tip of the knife to her inner thigh.

"What was it he supposedly said to you? 'Your cunt feels so good. Ride me just like that.'"

"No. I was just –" She screams as I slowly stab her. The knife cuts smoothly through her flesh, but it's quickly halted by her pelvic bone. Her legs spasm as she convulses; she's going into shock. I grab her hip and yank the knife out, then ram it in again in one fast, hard movement. The pelvic bone can't stop me this time. The knife slams in all the way to the hilt.

She cries out, but she barely has the strength anymore. Her sobs are broken and weak. The pain she's feeling must be overwhelming. But it's nothing compared to watching the man you love fuck trash like her.

I feel like I've actually walked in on them. Her telepathy might not be strong enough to cause my brain to bleed or my nerves to fry, but her talent is more than enough to have made me smell and see and hear every fucking thing that would've come with walking in on the scenes she showed me.

I felt the metal of the door handle in my hand, the carpet beneath my bare feet. The air smelled like hours of sex had just taken place. It was so strong I could almost taste it on my tongue. I heard the wet slurp of her pussy as she took him and the harsh panting of them both. And gods, I heard those fucking *words*. *"Your cunt feels so good. Ride me just like that. Fuck, baby. You're going to make me come. Yeah. I'm going to come in your tight little pussy."*

Pulling out my knife, I slam it into her again. Over and over until her pussy is a shredded mess of meat that will never feel my husband's cock again. "Fucking *whore*."

She's lying there in silence now, in too much pain to move. Blood pools around her lower half and is splattered all over me. The knife is slippery from how much coats my hand. I pull it out one last time, and more bits of her vagina fall out of the hole that was her pussy.

Breathing hard, I move up her body. I kneel over her waist, my legs straddling her. Grabbing a fistful of her hair, I yank her head and half her torso up, arching her back so she can look at me. She stares at me with glassy eyes that are almost lifeless. She's lost a lot of blood. Too much to survive without a healer now.

Recalling the image of her deep throating my husband, I line the knife up with her lips so the edges of it are pointing up and down. She doesn't fight me. Can't. She's on death's door, but she isn't there yet. Tears fall down her face. She'll feel this.

"Swallow, bitch." Holding her gaze, I shove the knife deep down her throat.

FIFTY

HER

Blood gurgles up past her lips.

I hold her gaze coldly, then yank the knife forward. The edge of the blade catches on her lower teeth and jaw, so it takes me multiple attempts of slamming it down like a lever as I fist her hair to hold her up. Blood splatters down onto the floor. The tip of the knife starts to poke out of her back. I finally make it through her jaw, splitting her chin down the middle. Opening up her throat so all her life can bleed out.

Shoving her onto the floor, I look at her in disgust.

"So...you get all your rage out, bruh?" Maddox asks, and I look up to see all of the brothers standing around me. Leno is looking a little pale, but Maddox looks kind of proud and in awe. Khalid looks indifferent, but Varius looks fucking *pissed.*

"No." I say, glaring at my husband. The image of him fucking Bobble Head Bitch morphs into that of him with Khalid's girl. My fingers tighten on my knife. "You and I need to have a chat," I growl.

Zara might've been a bitch, but she's given me one thing I needed – the courage to confront him about *That Bitch*. There's no detail he can tell me now that'll be worse than what I've seen.

"Yeah, we fucking do," he says tightly. Reaching down, Varius pulls me to my feet, then drags me towards the exit. "Deal with her," he snaps over his shoulder at his brothers.

"What the hel is your problem?" I snarl as I try to tug free. His hand tightens like a vice. "You're the one who told me to kill her. I tried to apologize."

"You goaded her," he snaps.

"She showed me the two of you fucking! You would have killed her if she'd showed you me, you hypocritical –" He spins me towards him, yanks the knife out of my hand, and tosses it. Then he grabs both of my biceps and hauls me up towards his mouth. My legs instinctively go around him just as his lips crush down on mine, stealing my breath and my words but not my fire. I shove against his chest and bite his lips, but he just grabs my throat and cuts off my air. My lips are forced apart as I struggle to breathe.

"I'm going to check if you're wet, little monster," Varius growls as he strangles me. "But you better fucking not be."

Striding over to a wall, he slams my back against it. I try to fight him off as he keeps me up with a thigh between my legs and his hand around my throat. He shoves my dress up, sticks his other hand down my panties, and pushes a finger inside me.

He hisses in a breath as I squeeze around him. Pleasure pulses through me as I arch off the wall.

"You fucking whore." He shoves more fingers into my pussy, stretching me enough to tear.

I cry out without a sound. My head grows far too dizzy. My vision starts to blur. He finger fucks me hard and fast, growling words that I don't catch. I pass out and then wake up to find his hand no longer on my neck and his fingers no longer in me. Now it's his cock, slamming into my pussy as he fucks me hard and fast and brutal.

I suck in air. My sore throat causes me to gasp. He turns his head to look at me, his eyes hard. White hot jealousy slams into me.

"Did you like imagining yourself pegging her?" he snaps as his hips bruise my thighs in hard delicious thrusts. "I saw how you fucked her with that knife. It turned you on, didn't it? Made you so fucking *wet*."

"You're...delusional," I choke out.

"Don't lie to me!" His fist slams into the wall. "I felt how wet you were. You were fucking *soaked*." He rams into me, breathing hard.

My eyelids flutter as I moan and arch back. My fingers dig into his broad shoulders. "I'm wet...because you touched me...you damn neanderthal."

"Bullshit."

"I killed her, Varius."

"You raped her with that knife. You were wishing it was a dildo, weren't you? Or your own fucking dick if you took a Rick." He buries himself deep inside me as he shakes with jealousy. The guy is fucking crazy.

"Of course not! I just wanted to fuck her up so you could never slide your dick into her again, you ass."

"I've never touched her," he growls as he slides out of me and forces me around to face the wall. I push my ass out to him as he grabs my hips.

"She showed me otherwise," I say.

"She lied." He presses the head of his cock against my ass. He doesn't push in, just rims it.

"And how the fuck would I know?" I shout as I turn my head to look at him. "You've already slept with one whore! What's one more?"

"You are the only person I've slept with!" he roars as he

shoves his cock into me, tearing up my ass, but I welcome the pain. Need it to control my rage. Pushing back on him, I fuck him as hard as he fucks me.

"You fucking *liar!* You slept with Khalid's –"

"No, I didn't."

"Bullshit!"

"I swear to the fucking gods, Micha. You are the only person I have ever slept with." He slams in all the way as he grabs my chin and forces me to arch back. I stare at him in anger, but it slowly fades under the intensity in his eyes.

Holy shit. He's telling the truth.

My jaw drops. "Then why didn't you tell me?"

"Because I didn't think you cared." His hand feathers down to my throat as he starts thrusting into me hard and deep. "I couldn't *stand* the thought of you telling me that," he hisses. "How you didn't care if I fucked another woman because I wasn't yours anymore." His eyes burn bright and wet, and my breath catches on fire from the heat of them, the flames eating up all the oxygen in my lungs.

"Fuck, monster." He sags against me, pinning me to the wall with his bulk as one arm bands around me to stroke my pussy. "I have 'Property of Micha Shadow' tattooed on me," he says, his voice a lot lower but no less ragged, no less raw and honest than it was before. "Those are not meaningless words. I'm *yours*. I'm fucking yours, little monster, and the thought of you rejecting that, I couldn't bear it. I couldn't lose the hope that one day I could make you fall in love with me again.

"So even though you clearly hated me and tried to kill me and even though you cut off my fucking claim on you, I held hope that as long as I didn't hear you say that I wasn't yours..." He swallows hard, and a tear slips free. "It was all I had to hold on to, monster."

My lips wobble as I stare up at him. There is so much raw emotion in his eyes, so much fucking pain and misery.

Caused by *me*. Because I was hurting. Because he hurt me.

I shake my head. "They're bonded," I say. "That couldn't have happened if –"

"Khalid's always been extreme," he cuts in half-bitterly, half-lovingly. "When he asked us to fuck his girl while he watched, I took it at face value that that was the payment. Because I couldn't imagine sharing you with anyone. The pain of just thinking that..." He clenches his teeth. "I'll kill anyone who touches you, Micha." He fucks me slowly until he calms back down. It takes a while, but I don't rush him. I need the extra time anyways to wrap my head around what he's saying.

He groans, then comes inside me. He breathes heavily, his chest beating hard against my back.

"But then I found out from Maddox that he also asked Talon to fuck her before all the shit went down, but he did not need him after. So I put the pieces together.

"Khalid's payment was never about us fucking his girl – a carnal act without meaning. It was about him being afraid she'd fall in love with one of us and leave him. He thinks she's too far out of his league. That she's beautiful and pure while he is the reaper."

"He isn't just a reaper. He's a person. My person." Her earlier words come back to me, and shame hits my cheeks.

"It's why he needed his brothers to do it. So he could see her laugh with us after. So he could wake up every morning and fear this would be the day she realizes she can do so much better than him." He shakes his head. "He didn't need Talon anymore because he knew she'd never fall in love with him."

I swallow as I tremble beneath his body. "But Khalid still needed you –"

"He did. Which is why he can never find out I didn't do it."

"But you said he watched –"

"I convinced him to wear a blindfold. Like I said, he's always been extreme. I told him that if he watched us, he'd know who made her scream the best. Then he wouldn't get as jealous if he saw her laughing with a different brother. But by not knowing if she was talking to the one who made her come the hardest..." He looks at me sadly but without regret. "I hurt him further so I didn't have to hurt you."

My breath catches. Tears fall down my cheeks.

"I stood in the hall with them, but Maddox went in for me. He slipped into his shadow so no one could hear him shapeshift. Then *he* fucked her, Micha, not me. And then he went in again at the end, being extra sure to let her know it was him so both his turns felt different."

"But you smelled like her."

"The whole fucking floor smelled like her. I swear to you, Micha. I never touched her."

His dick slips out of me as he steps back, and the wet heat pours down my legs. He turns me around and hugs me tight. "I'm so sorry that I left you believing I fucked her all this time. I just couldn't bear the thought of hearing you say, 'It doesn't matter,' or 'I don't care,' when I told you I didn't."

I roll my lips in, breathing hard through my nose as my body shakes. I squeeze my eyes shut and hold him to me. "I'm sorry," I say into his chest. "I only told you that because I didn't think it would matter if I said no. You already chose your brother over me; I couldn't handle you doing it again, and I..." I trail off, feeling too vulnerable.

"Yes?" he murmurs as he strokes my back.

I don't say anything for a long time, and I can feel his fear that I'm blocking him out again, but I'm just trying to figure out how to word what I want to say without sounding like I'm crazy.

"I wanted you to choose me."

"Like a test?"

"No. Like… I didn't want you to not do it just because I told you not to. I wanted you to not do it because *you* didn't want to." I blow out a breath in frustration. Explaining shit is hard. "I didn't want to have to beg you to not cheat on me. I just wanted to know I mattered."

"Of course you ma–"

"You'd just tortured me, Varius." I try to pull away, but his arms lock me to him. "You tortured me, you left me for hours, and then you said you had to fuck another woman!" My anger rises. "How the hel was I supposed to know you cared about me? That I mattered?"

"You're right. I said something stupid. I'm sorry."

I clench my teeth, annoyed that he's apologized. I'm so fucking angry, and I just want to scream a bit. But now I can't.

"What's wrong?" he asks.

"Nothing."

"I can tell –"

"I'm just angry, okay?"

"With?"

"Everything."

"Ah."

I scowl into his chest, but he just holds me.

"Well, how about we go home and have a shower, and I wash all this blood off you? Then I'll draw you a bath and give you a back massage?"

Fuck, that sounds nice.

"Maybe," I grumble.

He doesn't make a sound, but I can feel his laughter as he picks me up and carries me out of the building.

FIFTY-ONE

HER

I sit in the bath between his legs. He washed the blood off me, running the cloth along my body while I stood under the spray of the shower. Leno and Maddox are currently dealing with the portal situation, questioning Zara's soldiers (the boys knocked them out instead of killing them) to try to see how often she got in touch with her father and where she went on the full moons. Depending on what they say, we *might* be able to stage her death to have been caused by a werewolf under the Craving after we dump her body back on Blódyrió.

With a little sigh, I lean against Varius' chest. His fingers rub between my pussy lips, slow and gentle. It isn't sexual. It's just touching for the sake of touching. A need to be connected while our souls try to heal from all the pain we've suffered through.

"Why did you let me kill her?" I finally ask, realizing I have no idea why he did it. I turn to look at him, but he nudges me back around.

"She touched you without my permission," he says as he cups a breast and teases my nipple under the warm water.

"No, she –" My jaw drops as I twist to face him. "You're such a neanderthal! You got jealous she touched my *mind?*"

"I told you, Micha. Every part of you is mine. Now face forward so I can hold you." He manhandles me, twisting me around until my back is flush against his chest again. His hand goes back to rubbing my nipple.

I swat him away. "You have issues, you know that?"

"I know. I married them."

"Hey!" I start to turn around again, but he stops me by pushing two fingers into my pussy. I suck in a breath as I lift my hips.

He chuckles as he pulls them out again, then goes back to just petting me. I smile as I sag against his chest.

Lifting a hand to my stomach, I think about the little life beneath my palm.

"We're making a baby," I whisper.

His hand rises to cover mine. "Can you feel her kicking yet?"

I shake my head. "I'm only fourteen weeks. It'll take another two at the earliest; though as she's my first, I might not feel her for over a month or two." *If she survives that long.* I'm still at a high risk of having a miscarriage. Babies don't develop a magical immune system until the twentieth week.

He squeezes my hand.

I force a smile even though he can't see me. Sau is the best healer on this side of the Atlantic, perhaps even in the entire world. She's going to be fine. A warmth blossoms in my chest. I can feel the truth of that statement. I might not be a foreseer, one who catches glimpses of the future, but there are some things a mother just *knows*.

My smile turns genuine with giddiness. I'm going to be a

mother. "What do you think about Bambi?" I ask softly as I run my fingers across the back of his hand. My heart flutters with sudden nerves. Most parents don't think of names until after the twentieth week, but I know our baby is a fighter. She will make it to term.

"Like as a movie?" he asks.

"No, as a name."

"I guess it's fine for a deer..."

I smile. "No, for our baby."

The fact that I can't feel his utter refusal to call our child this even when he's so clearly against it makes me feel all warm and fuzzy. Awww. He's trying so hard to not hurt my feelings.

"Deer are only ever prey," he says slowly. "She needs a stronger name." His confidence comes back. "Like Rafiki."

"Rafiki," I say flatly.

"Yes," he says triumpantly.

"I'm not naming our baby after a baboon."

"But he knows the way."

My lips twitch. "No."

"Scar? That's a cool name."

"He was the villain."

"You just raped someone to death with a knife."

I open my mouth, then close it. He has a point. "Still no."

"Baloo?"

"*Varius...*"

"It's a good name."

"It's a terrible name. People will be asking her how to spell it forever because it just sounds like Blue."

"We can tattoo it on her forehead," he deadpans.

I roll my lips in, but I can't stop the giggle. "No."

"Hmm. Jiminy Cricket? He survived getting eaten by a whale."

"No."

"Thumper?"

"That's a bunny! You're going back to prey animals."

"He's a rabbit, and rabbits are not prey animals," he says seriously. "I have seen *Monty Python.*"

"*No.*"

"You're right. People might mistake what rabbit she was named after. We should just go for the full title of The Killer Rabbit of Caerbannog."

I laugh, loud and free. A flood of happiness comes down our bond as he chuckles with me.

"I love you," he murmurs as he bands his arms around my chest.

I shake my head to clear it of giggles. Turning to look at him, I smile. He leans towards me for a soft kiss.

"You damn neanderthal. I love you too."

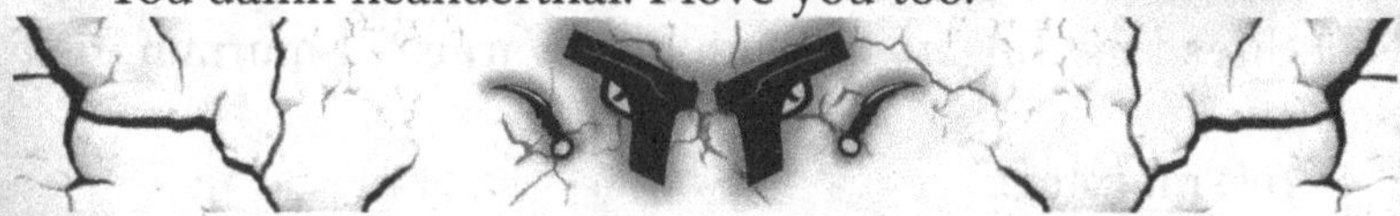

After our bath, he drys me with a towel, then leads me to the bed. He rubs lotion all over my skin as he gives me a full body massage. I lie on my front as he kneads the tightness out of my back, sighing contently into my pillow.

His hands work from my shoulders down to the top of my ass, then they go up again. Then down again, and with each cycle, they get a bit lower. My eyes peek open when he gropes my ass. His hard dick rubs between my cheeks.

"I thought I was just getting a massage," I say.

"You are," he replies as he rocks his dick back and forth. He pushes my ass cheeks together. "Your ass is a part of your body and a very *fine* part too." He slaps it, and I curl my toes.

Shuffling down my legs, he lines his dick up with my pussy. Then he grabs my hips and pulls me onto him. I moan as he fucks me slowly, but I don't meet his rhythm. I'm too relaxed to want to move.

He doesn't seem to mind.

He pulls out of me slowly, then pushes in just the same. He's taking his time, feeling every inch of me on his dick, rubbing me sensually rather than fucking me hard.

I close my eyes again as I moan into his pillow.

He builds me up slowly, never changing his pace. Just a soft, gentle climb up to the top that has me falling off it with a small, shuddering cry.

Collapsing on top of me, he slides one hand under my body to cup my pussy.

I sigh, loving the feel of his weight squishing me. Like a comfort blanket that's oh so warm and protective.

Eventually though, he gets too heavy, and I wiggle so he knows to get off. Rolling me onto my side, he keeps his dick in me as he cuddles me from the back.

I thread my fingers through his. "Varius?" I murmur, half asleep.

"Yes, monster?"

I hesitate a few seconds even though I'm the one who started this conversation. As much as I want this, I don't know if I *should* want this yet. It hasn't been that long in the scheme of things since he hurt me. Am I an idiot for taking him back this quickly?

But it's not like either of us thinks we're fixed, perfect, back to normal or how we used to be. We're nowhere near that, and we know it. But we're on the path towards it. And this is just one step in that direction.

"Will you tattoo me?" I murmur, now suddenly awake and no longer relaxed.

He stills. "Are you sure?"

I nod.

"Of course I will." He pulls his dick out of me as he rolls away, and his cum floods all down my thighs. He pulls me to the edge of the bed so my legs are hanging over it. Then he walks over to our dresser to get the tattoo gun he bought a couple months ago.

Gods, that feels like forever ago...

When he turns around, his eyes find mine, and there is a vulnerability there I never expected. "If I do this, Micha," he says slowly. "You can't ever cut it off. It'll break me."

My eyes mist as my breath catches in my chest. I didn't realize how much that had hurt him. "I'm sorry," I say. "I'm so sorry."

"It's okay."

"It's not," I say. "I hurt you too, Varius. And I'm sorry. My intention wasn't to punish you. I just needed..."

"I know," he says. Then he swallows. "But if you're sure..."

I nod. "I am."

An abundance of joy comes down our bond as he walks back to me. "I love you," he says as he kneels between my thighs. He sets everything up with the tattoo gun, then starts to draw a character over my pussy. Then a word. Then a name.

Tears burn my eyes as I wiggle my fingers down by my side when he's finished. He threads his fingers in mine and squeezes.

"I love you, monster."

"I love you too."

Although we might not be anywhere close to being okay, I can finally see a future where we *could* be.

We'll just need to work on us one day at a time.

I squeeze his hand.

But we *will* get there. I know it.

Because he is irrevocably *mine*.

And I can finally believe that I am *his*.

Property of Varius Shadow

FIFTY-TWO

HIM

My claim is back on her body.

I want to trace my fingers over it as I crawl onto the bed and pull her into my arms, but I don't want to irritate her skin. My blood chills at the memory of finding her in a pool of blood, her pussy cut up, and a knife held to her wrist. I remember all the pain that hit me when I found out what she had done and *why*.

I swallow hard.

Her little hands come up to grip my forearm. She doesn't say anything, and I wish I could feel what she's feeling, but the blood bond still hasn't snapped into place for me. Now that she knows I didn't fuck Khalid's girl, she still owes her payment for us to complete it.

Where we are in our relationship though, I don't think we'd survive it. So I won't push for it yet. I'll just need to trust her at her word that she won't hurt me like that again. It is a terrifying feeling to give that much of myself to anyone, that risky hope; she could use it to destroy me with a single action.

But losing her would be worse.

I kiss the back of her head. When she doesn't react, I lift my head up a bit to look at her, only to realize she's fallen asleep. Sighing, I lay back down.

But I don't dare sleep too. I know the reaper will come tonight. There's not a doubt in my mind that he knows I'm a hybrid.

He was watching me while we fought Zara's soldiers, clocking how fast I moved and what I could sense when I wasn't looking. His shadows swirled around my feet too many times, like he was debating about whether or not he should suck me under. Being in that plane won't be a death sentence for me though. I might be a hybrid, but I'm also a Shadow. My blood will still protect me from the monsters that roam there.

The reaper doesn't knock when he enters. He slips under the door in his shadow form. I sit up, grab the gun hidden behind the headboard, and wake Micha as I do.

"What's –" She stops, no doubt sensing the predator at the foot of our bed. She turns to him quickly. "Khalid."

He's rematerialized in his normal form.

"You're not wearing your mask," I say. The reaper always kills with a four-horned skull covering his face.

"Do I need it?"

"You're in my room in the middle of the night."

"Because you didn't come downstairs for dinner, and we need to talk." He pulls a chair out of his shadows and sits down. "I know you're a hybrid," he says, leaning forward and cutting straight to the point. "I would've talked to you sooner, but Mother made me believe you didn't know. It wasn't until I noticed you wouldn't show me your back or get near my shadows when we fought Zara's men that I knew."

My hand tightens on the gun I'm holding beneath the covers. He isn't like me; one shot to the heart will kill him.

"Relax," he says, his eyes dropping to my lap to tell me he knows about the weapon pointed straight at him. "I'm not here to kill you."

"Why not?"

Confusion flashes across his eyes as he looks back at me. "You're my brother."

Surprise flashes in mine. "So was Talon."

"Talon was a coward who hurt our girls. You've never put this Family in danger. You've fought to protect us since you were a kid. You are not a hybrid to me, Varius. You're my brother, and that's all you'll ever be."

Fuck. He might as well have hit me in the solar plexus with those words. "Who knew you were so sappy?" I say, my voice rough.

"*Kira,*" he says without hesitation or shame, and I shake my head. Of course his girl knows.

"So why are you here?" Micha asks, and I stiffen. I don't want his attention on her at all.

He keeps his eyes on me, knowing me too well. "Because you've bonded, and Varius' curse will break if he falls in love."

My whole world freezes. I haven't told Micha that, and my heart is pounding as I wait for her response.

"But he is in love," she says confidently. "So that can't be right."

Neither of us say anything.

She looks at me. "Varius...?"

I don't want to take my eyes off someone who can kill her, but I can't avoid the pain in her voice either. My throat tightens as I turn my head towards her.

"It's a specific type of love," I say.

The lurking pain in her eyes is killing me. "What does that mean?" she asks softly, but I can hear the crack in her voice, the wavering confidence in what we have.

I push all my love down our bond. "I know you can feel that, Micha," I murmur as I cup her cheek. My other hand keeps the gun pointed at the reaper. "I love you. More than I ever thought it was possible to love someone."

"So then he's lying," she says.

"Maybe, but the love Mother described is not one I'll ever feel."

"Why not?"

"Because it means I'll have to be willing to let you go," I growl. "And that is never going to fucking happen."

"What?"

"I'm never letting you go."

"No." Her eyes flash with irritation. "What does that have to do with love?"

"Mother says it's proof that you love someone more than yourself. I have to be willing to give you up so you can find happiness without me." My hand moves to the back of her neck. "But I will kill everyone on this damn planet just so I'm the last one left for you."

She smiles. "That sounds like love to me. Your mom's just dumb."

"I love you, Micha. Never doubt that." Leaning forward, I kiss her lips, but I keep my eyes open and my brother in my peripheral.

He stands abruptly as he sucks his chair back into his shadow. "If you think it might break, V, tell me. I don't care if you turn, but you could lose control when you change, and I don't want you attacking the people in this house if you do."

With that, he leaves.

Micha flops back onto the bed with a strong exhale. "I think I'm finally starting to like your brother. He still scares me, but he's alright, huh?"

I stretch out beside her, laying the gun on the bedside

table. "Yeah," I say, still surprised over his words to me. "He's alright."

"*You are not a hybrid to me, Varius. You're my brother, and that's all you'll ever be.*"

Fuck, I think as I close my eyes. That's hitting me right in the feels.

FIFTY-THREE

HER

I dig my toes into the carpet of the living room and buzz with pure joy and excitement. At breakfast this morning, Varius told everyone he was going to swear Dayne into the Family. I didn't know he was doing this. I thought my best friend was only visiting for a couple of days. To find out that he's going to be here forever is making me giddy.

Standing in front of my best friend, Varius says, "Show me your power."

Dayne holds up his hands. Electricity sparks between the fingers on his right hand. Red energy swirls between the fingers on his other as the runic tattoo on his left shoulder glows softly.

"Will you use your magic to protect the interests of the Shadow Domain?" Varius demands.

"I swear it."

"Show me your weapons."

Dropping his hands, Dayne removes a gun and a knife

from their holster and sheath. He holds them up in front of him.

"Will you use your weapons to protect the interests of the Shadow Domain?"

"I swear it." He puts them away as Varius asks, "Will you keep the secrets of the Shadow Domain?"

"I swear it."

"Will you respect your brothers?"

"I swear it."

"Then hold out your arm, and repeat after me."

Dayne offers his right hand out, palm up.

"If I betray my vows to this Family."

"If I betray my vows to this Family."

He carves a stylized S into my friend's palm beneath his middle finger.

"If I betray the Boss before me."

"If I betray the Boss before me."

A second S connects to the first at an angle, sixty degrees off its base, pointed towards his thumb.

"If I betray my brothers and uncles."

"If I betray my brothers and uncles."

A third S connects the first two to make a triangle.

"Then I will die under the reaper's blade."

"Then I will die under the reaper's blade."

Varius draws a drop of blood from the side of his finger. Then he squeezes it over the carving on Dayne's palm.

"You now live for the Family," Varius says. "Until death."

"I now live for the Family," Dayne says. "Until death."

"Oh my gods, yes!" I squeal as I throw myself at Dayne. He laughs as he catches me. Varius' jealousy comes down our bond, and I narrow my eyes at him. If he even thinks bad thoughts about my friend, I will bite him.

His jaw tics, so I squeeze my bestie extra hard before pulling away. I smile. "It's good to be Family again." I punch him in the shoulder. "Why didn't you tell me?"

"I only found out last night," he says, "when you were too busy getting your insides rearranged."

I blush.

He grins. "And I like seeing you all excited. You're cute."

I narrow my eyes at him, then at Varius as I feel his jealousy hitting hard. His hand wraps around the back of my neck, and he pulls me to him.

"Thank you," I say as I wrap my arm around his waist. His grip loosens a bit, but he doesn't look at me, his focus on Dayne. "You will be her bodyguard from now on. If she steps out of this house, you better be with her."

I groan. Dayne smiles. He's going to be insuffereable.

"Yes, Boss."

"You'll be working with Quinton anytime she's off the property."

His smile fades, and mine shoots up. Oh, I am looking forward to teasing the two of them and putting them in awkward situations. I just know Quinton was all up on Vlad at the wedding reception just to get a reaction out of Dayne. It didn't work, but give it time. I have never seen him so irritated by someone that he's already fucked. Usually, that has always gotten them out of his system. The fact that Quinton is still in there is making me excited.

He gives me a look to tell me I better behave myself. My grin widens. This is going to be so fun.

"Now leave us," Varius says. "I need to discuss something with my wife."

As soon as Dayne's gone, Varius turns to me. "Khalid has banned you from going to any more meetings."

"What?"

"He says you're too volatile, and we can't keep killing our allies."

"But I apologized to the bitch! You're the one who –"

"I know. And I'm sorry I messed that up for you, but you will still help me rule this Family, Micha. You'll just have to do it from the shadows."

My jaw tightens. All of this just feels like he's trying to hide me all over again. Nothing but sweet words and no actions to back them up. "Whatever," I say as I cross my arms. "You just don't want to change tradition. Women are nothing b–"

"I risked starting a war and losing hundreds of million a year for you," he says sharply. "I sure as hel will change a damn tradition for you."

I don't say anything, still not quite trusting him. But I nod so he knows I'm not blocking him out.

He sighs, then kisses my forehead. "I need to go meet Aleric. We need to figure out a plan to kill Antonio, but I love you, Micha."

I nod again. He tenses as he waits for me to say the words. They sit heavy in my chest, not wanting to come out, not because I don't love him but because I no longer want to speak at all. We still have our issues. I still have my fears, and sometimes they get overwhelming.

"I love you," I finally murmur, but he's already gone. So I get out my phone and text him.

With us at war with the Death Hunt, I don't want him to ever leave the house thinking I'm mad at him. That could be the last thing he ever thinks of me.

My throat tightens as I grip my phone hard. A sudden feeling of deja vu hits me.

Every time my life starts looking up...

No!

Jumping to my feet, I head over to the gym to work out my nerves. But it doesn't matter how many times I hit the bag or spar with Sau, I still can't shake the feeling that our time together has already started to run out.

FIFTY-FOUR

It's time.

After a month of RECON, planning, and training with Aleric's men in the dark of the night, my brothers and I are gearing up to go after Antonio. We are in a warehouse on the west side of town, waiting for the vampires to phase in to join us. Micha and Krypto are safe at home with Mother, but all my brothers are here.

"Do you think," Aleric asks as he suddenly appears and tosses a sheathed knife to Maddox, "that if I took a Rick, I could fuck one of those super werewolves without dying?"

Six other vampires phase in, all carrying the weapons Cara poisoned for us.

"What?" Leno asks, and everyone groans over the fact that he took the bait and asked a stupid question.

"Their cum's poisonous to us," Aleric says. "But if I take a Rick, then it's not my dick, is it? Which means it's not vampire dick."

"I think it's still your dick," Leno says, actually giving thought to it.

Aleric waves him off, then pulls out a red vial from his jacket pocket. "Maddox, let me drink this and then you tell me –"

"I'm not studying your dick, bruh."

He tosses the potion to my brother. "Then study yours and let me know." He pats his pocket. "I've brought extras with me."

"Does everyone have their weapons?" I cut in before my brother can decide he's curious about that now too. With a grin, he slips the Rick into his pocket for later. I've been handed a machete in a leather sheath and a strap, and I slide it onto my back.

Everyone nods.

"Do you have the silver?" Vlad asks, and I head over to the box we've brought with us. The amount of silver we got through the portal was only enough to make a net and a couple of chains. We would have struggled to bind Antonio with just that. But it turns out Zara wasn't Ryker's daughter at all. She took advantage of the fact that we didn't know her home tongue and none of her men knew English. She was nothing more than a pathological liar. Luckily, Lou is fluent in Geish (as well as seven other languages) and was able to communicate with them. No one, it seems, liked Zara. They just fought back because they thought we were going to kill them all.

So now we have two nets, half a dozen chains, and some powder to throw in their faces. There are also twelve small balls for the twins to use with their telekinesis. If they can bury one inside a werewolf, it's game up for the wolf until they can dig it out.

Enoch and Ezriel take a net and six balls each. Then each of my brothers suck two chains into their shadows. Leno sprays us with a potion that smells like alligator musk so the wolves won't be able to smell us as we wait.

"Let's goooo!" Aleric sings. Grabbing my arm, he phases us across town.

We appear inside one of the alligator pens, only a few feet away from a massive reptile. The creature scurries into the water where it feels more comfortable. I stumble away from Aleric as my body shakes, and my stomach churns. Phasing isn't easy on the body if it isn't built to do it.

Rudy and Vlad soon appear beside us. Their bodies are tense, and they part quickly. Rudy drops to his knees as he heaves. I help him up. He nods his thanks before he casts an invisibility spell around the four of us, and then we wait.

I smell him before I see him. My eyes track to the start of the boardwalk. It takes a few seconds before he appears, but then there he is – the fucker who hurt my wife and caused me to hurt her even more. He will not be leaving here alive.

He steps onto the boardwalk on his own, leaving behind his guard of six women and two men. Aleric stills beside me, and for the first time, I truly see him for the beast he is. My blood chills as I glance at the hunger in his face.

A crocodile moves near the middle of the boardwalk, and I wonder if that's where Maddox and Khalid are. My little brother needs to be within a few feet of his target to be able to shapeshift into them. We might have been robbed of our main stash of alexandrite, but we still have enough to craft three more soul dolls, and we only need one of them to kill Antonio.

With luck, it'll be that quick and easy, and I can go home and tell Micha the threat to our child is over. But only a fool relies on one plan when they only have one shot to pull it off. So the rest of us are here as Plan B. Cara is infecting his car's AC unit as Plan C. It won't be as effective, and it will take a lot out of her to keep it alive without a host, but if he drives for more than thirty minutes with it on, then it will weaken him considerably. We might get another chance to kill him then, if we can figure out which safe house he's recovering at.

I tense, my muscles ready to explode into action as I watch him cross the boardwalk. There is a collective weight in the air, an electric current of anticipation. My eyes dart back to where I hope my two brothers are. I can't see them under the cloak of magic, but that means he can't either.

Antonio walks without hesitation, but he isn't fast. He moves leisurely, his head down, lost in his memories. He suddenly looks up to peer around the watering hole full of crocs and gators.

There's something wrong.

Aleric phases away just as Antonio stops. The werewolf drops to his hands and knees, shifting in an instant. He's a second too slow. Aleric appears on his back, his hands going around the werewolf's face, gouging into his eyes as his teeth aim for his neck.

The eight soldiers Antonio brought as guards all start to shift, their bones cracking, their skin splitting. Vlad and the other vampires phase to their locations, working in pairs to kill three of our foes by ripping their heads from their bodies. Plants shoot forth out of the nearby shrubbery and grabs hold of a fourth werewolf mid-change. They haul her towards the water. Until her change is complete, she can't control her limbs. The crocodiles will tear her apart.

As Enoch and Ezriel cast a ward around the entire area to keep our fight secret from humans, Maddox rushes under the boardwalk towards Antonio. He's in the form of a six-foot croc. All he needs is a few minutes – minutes Rudy is keen to buy as he focuses his magic on the alpha, bringing his fears to the surface.

A woman screams, and I snap my head to the left, for an instant thinking it's Micha. It sounds exactly like she did when she was strapped to that chair. My pulse skips a beat as I look for her, but then it settles as I watch half a woman, her body missing from the waist down, drag herself across the boardwalk towards Antonio. Her intestines trail a line behind her, and there are wails coming from it. High-pitched. Child-like. And I realize I'm staring at Siome – at the twisted memory Antonio has of her death.

Knowing he will never leave Micha alone for the sins of my mother, I rush towards him to help Aleric. The Boss of the Blood Fangs phases away just as Antonio tries to grab him off his back. He appears behind the half-dead woman and stomps on one of the fetuses with a smile on his face. Antonio roars as he charges him.

I quickly scale the boardwalk behind him and unsheathe my machete. Shadows seep out of the cracks in the floor. The sound of clicking and hissing coming from it tells me it's the reaper. He's the only one of us who can call the monsters to the surface. He wraps around Antonio's back left foot, but before he can start climbing up his leg, the wolf bends down and bites it off.

I lunge for the right, knowing he's going to jump into the water. Shadows can't form there, but even with my secret speed, he moves faster. Throwing himself off the boardwalk, he leaves part of his foot behind.

The crocodiles go for him as soon as he hits, dragging him under in a feeding frenzy. The murky water gains a tinge of red, and I place my hands on the railing as I peer over it. My eyes search the sea of scales. Aleric grabs my arm, and we're suddenly on the other side of the swamp. I fall to my knees, the second round of phasing affecting me even more than the first. It's a cumulative pain, but I push back to my feet just in time to see Antonio emerging from the water. Aleric clearly knows him well.

The two Bosses clash, too fast to really watch. Antonio is moving with all the power he's recently gained from eating hybrid babies, and Aleric is phasing with the precise skill of an experienced killer. He grabs Antonio's arm and phases a step to the left. He can't hop far with the beast who doesn't want to go with him, but he doesn't need to. Phasing a step away or a mile makes no difference to the effect it has on one's body.

I charge forward with the poison-lined machete. If I hit Aleric, it could severely wound our side, but the month we have practiced training alongside each other has helped me to learn his movements.

I dart around their blur of bodies, and every time the wolf goes to bite Aleric Zadar, I slash at him, demanding his attention. He snarls at me as he swipes. His claws rake into me but only surface level. I might not be anywhere near as fast as him, but he doesn't want to fully lunge at me. Doing so will leave him open to be attacked by the bigger threat.

A person on our side screams in sheer agony, and I know they're dying. I don't turn to look to see who it is though. Rudy will defend our brothers. He'll sacrifice his life to do so, and he can't scream.

So I keep my focus on killing Antonio. I dart forward as he and Aleric return from another quick phase. My machete swings up, then down right over the vampires' back. I'm using him to hide my attack, just like we trained, and he phases away right as I'm about to hit.

The blade slices into the werewolf, cutting deep. He kicks out at me, and I go flying, pain searing across my chest. But thankfully, he kicked me with his severed foot rather than the clawed monstrosity he was balancing on. A direct hit from his other leg would've ripped open my chest, possibly killed me.

I hit the ground hard. The air in my lungs whoosh out. Another wolf charges me, moving at a speed that nearly matches Antonio's.

I lift the machete to swing at him. My ribs protest, and that blast of pain makes me a fraction too slow. The wolf's mouth covers my face as he slides into me, but just as his teeth are about to close, his head flops to the side, and the rest of his body follows. I scramble to my feet to see a large silver bullet get pulled out of the werewolf's splattered brain with telekinesis. When the bullet 'waves' at me, I know it's Ezriel who saved me. Enoch might complain about doing any work ever, but he at least has the ability to stay focused.

Tightening my fingers around my machete, I turn back to continue my fight with Antonio, but I don't see him or Aleric. Someone screams behind me. Then two more do the same in quick succession. I spin around, seeing if it's him doing the killing.

My eyes widen at the sight in front of me. The last two of his soldiers aren't werewolves. They're fully grown hybrids, monstrous beasts standing over nine feet tall. Fangs drop down like they do on sabertooths. Their claws are like that of a giant sloth, and their build is as heavy as a tank.

Three bodies litter the ground between them. Khalid is dragging a fourth one out of the combat zone. My pulse kicks up as I realize it's Enoch. My brother's chest is ripped open. His head lolls to the side, unconscious.

Ezriel and Leno are fighting one, alongside two vampires. Leno is wrapping tree branches around its limbs, molding them like vines, Ezriel is wrapping silver chains, but they're not burning it like silver should. The vampires phase like gnats around it, stabbing it here and there with blades.

The other hybrid is only fighting Rudy. It slashes him apart with its claws, tearing great big chunks out of his skin. Its teeth latch onto his shoulder, but he stabs it in the eye with the broken sword he has in his other hand. The beast howls as it releases him. Half his shoulder is missing, but Rudy moves like it isn't. He powers forward, hacking the thing apart with both his swords, one broken in half, the other not.

He dances around the creature like a god of the dead, using his magic to keep going. He fears being trapped in a decaying body, forever alive, forever forced to suffer. He will be the sole survivor.

A sudden gasp of air has my head snapping towards the water. Aleric punches out of the surface, then he's gone in the next second, having phased to land beside me. He's bleeding profusely from multiple bite wounds. "The fucker dragged me in," he rasps.

Then he's on me in the next second, his teeth sinking into my wrist holding the machete. My first instinct is to hit him, but I rein it in. He is one of our strongest players, and I need him in the game if we're going to finish this.

"Where is he?" I demand as my eyes search the water. All the reptiles are moving away from us, having finally clocked that we're too dangerous of a prey, so it's hard to pick out someone swimming beneath the surface.

"I don't know," he says as he lifts his head. His eyes flash blood-red as he licks his lips, and I suddenly realize what he can discern from having drank from me.

"*Son*," he says with a harsh stress on the word.

My pulse spikes as my stomach drops. I rip my arm away from him. "This is not the time."

He smiles, accepting that. Then he laughs and grabs my arm. I spotted Antonio at the same time he did, on the other side of the swamp. We appear not too far in front of him. Knowing I'm going to drop to my knees and heave, I roll into the motion to take out the werewolf's legs. He tumbles over me, and Aleric is on him in a flash, landing on his back and ripping chunks off it with his claws.

Antonio starts to push up as I roll around to look at them. Aleric isn't a big man, and Antonio is a werewolf. It will not be a hard endeavor. Then he'll get away, his speed not one I can match, and I will be forced to rely on Aleric to give chase. But I want to kill him.

I want to be the one who makes him suffer.

He hurt my girl. I need to kill him for that.

Launching myself forward, I shove my machete through his calf with all my strength. He howls as the blade pierces through the concrete below him. I draw another knife I have on me. This one isn't lined with Cara's poison, but I don't need her magic if I can cut off his head.

I scramble forward. Aleric clocks my intention, and he focuses his attack on one of Antonio's shoulders. He severs the muscles and tendons. The werewolf falls to the ground as his arm can no longer take his weight. He snarls as he tries to grab Aleric off him with his other hand.

Aleric grabs it and twists, keeping the werewolf's arm locked so he can't defend his head. All he has now are his teeth, but they can't protect his nape. Raising my arm, I swing the blade into his neck. He falls forward as the knife bites deep into his flesh. It lodges into his spine, and I twist as I rip it out. Blood sprays all over me. My ribs protest in pain, but I ignore them. I slash at him again. Aleric rolls off him as the wolf no longer needs to be held down. With one more swing, I sever his head completely.

For Micha.

For me.

For our baby girl yet to be born.

Lifting my head, I look at Aleric, expecting him to have questions or to make a dumb dad joke, but he isn't staring at me. His eyes are narrowed on the body in front of us.

"What is it?" I ask, a sliver of unease moving through me.

Without a word, he grabs hold of the body and phases. I turn back to the others, looking for Vlad to ask him what the hel his Boss might be up to. But then I see Aleric. He's reappeared near Maddox. He shoves the body in front of him, and I race over, that sliver turning into a cord that knots thick in my stomach.

My blood rushes through my skull as I catch the words, "Is it him?"

Fuck! Of course it is!

But when I get there, Maddox is squatting down beside Antonio's headless body with a frown on his face. Khalid walks over to him, as does Vlad and Ezriel. Leno is tending to the wounded.

"Maddox!" I snap, terrified of the answer.

"Give me a sec, bruh," he says quietly.

My heart racing, I start tracking the wounds on the alpha werewolf – the partially missing foot, the slices across his chest and back. I try to decide if they're the same or just close fucking matches.

No.

They have to be.

It has to be him.

But the doubt is curling in my stomach.

Did he switch with a patsy when he was under water? Or was it the wrong person from the start, just spelled to look like him?

Maddox's face pales as he looks up at me. "Some of his DNA markers are different."

My heart seems to claw its way out of my chest. I spin towards Aleric. "Take me home," I snap.

Because if Antonio left mid-fight, then he only came here to make sure none of us were *there.*

"He said he would come for our baby, Varius."

"I won't let him."

Fuck! I promised her that. I fucking promised!

As Aleric grabs my arm, I pray that I'm not too late.

FIFTY-FIVE

HER

"I need to tell you something," my sister says, her voice squeaky as she sits down in the armchair beside me. I'm instantly suspicious of what she's about to admit to.

"What did you do?" I ask, my eyes narrowing.

"Nothing." She shakes her head. Her hands twist in her lap. "Well, no. I –"

My eyes widen. I jump to my feet as Varius' panic comes down our bond. I've never felt him terrified before. "Sau!" I scream as I run out of the living room.

"Micha!" Lou gasps as she follows me. "What –" Her confusion disappears as she full on yells, "Dayne! Get off the toilet!"

I skid into the kitchen and spin towards Sau.

"What's wrong?" she asks. She's in the middle of pouring blood onto the counter. A dark energy shifts under the grain and eats the meal it's given.

"Can you feel Varius?" I demand. When Khalid almost

died a few months ago, she felt it. She's connected to her children in some way I don't understand.

"No. Why? What's wrong?"

"Have you felt him in danger before?" The words are rushing out, almost quicker than my thoughts.

"Yes. Every time he was attacked." She looks grim, and I see the realization in her eyes. "Get everyone down to the basement. I'm bringing out my monsters."

I spin on my heels and grab Lou's arm just as Dayne skids into the room. "What's going –"

"Mole rat." It's our codeword for 'you cannot help; you will get in the way; you helping will get us killed.'

He curses as I shove Lou towards him. "Take her to the basement and stay there. Do not open the door for anyone. I need to get my wand."

"Micha!" Lou shouts.

But I'm already running through the living room to head upstairs, and Dayne is pulling her towards the basement. I need my wand. I'm useless without it. Charging into our room, I aim straight for the weapons cabinet. A movement outside catches my attention though. I turn my head as I continue to run, but then my feet root to the floor in horror.

"They have a witch!" I shout towards the open door as my stomach drops to my feet. Leno's plants in the meadow in front of the house, our first line of defense, are curling up and dying, starting from the far end. Like a black wave of death, the spell rushes towards us. I spin on my heels, practically throwing myself at the cabinet. I yank open the doors to grab my wand.

Pulling up my shirt, I point the kezja horn at my stomach and give it a few rapid flicks while saying, "*Elfesi navis.*"

Warmth floods over my belly, protecting my skin. I can't put a spell on my baby herself. She's too young. The magic will kill her faster than Antonio can. I point the wand at my back and repeat the spell. My skin will be like stone. Not impenetrable, but it's all I know. I haven't bonded with the wand fully yet. I haven't relearned all my spells.

"Shit!"

Grabbing a knife with my free hand –I don't have time to load a gun– I run from the room.

Dayne meets me in the hall.

"You need to be in the basement," I yell.

"Varius will kill me if I hide without you. If I'm dying either way, it's going to be by your side."

I grit my teeth. "Lou?"

"She's in there with the dog."

"Fuck. Come on."

As we hurry down the stairs, I catch sight of Stormie's back (Enoch's fiance, who arrived just a few days ago), but she's rushing towards the basement with Khalid's girl. I turn for the kitchen with Dayne. My mother-in-law is still standing at the counter, but this time, both her hands are hovering over it.

"They're killing all the pla–"

"Arise."

My eyes widen as a massive praying-mantis, scythe-like claw rises out of the counter in a swirl of pitch-black ink. More of that ink pours off the counter on all sides, crashing to the ground and curling up like the mist at the bottom of a waterfall. Sau steps back as another claw shoots out of the counter. I want to keep staring, but my assassin training kicks in. Focus. React. *Move.*

"They have a witch. She's breaking through the wards."

She ignores me as she looks at Dayne. "Go down to the basement."

"Not with Micha."

"Then take her."

"Sau! You can't take them on your own. Antonio nearly killed you."

"He won't this time."

I glance at the monster climbing out of the counter, but I don't hesitate for long.

"Come on," I tell Dayne as I peel out of the kitchen. We rush through the house, and the hairs on my neck rise. The memory of the last time I did this assaults me. My blood chills. Panic flairs through me. He promised to come back for my daughter.

I won't let him.

But whatever was killing the plants was moving fast. The werewolves will be here as soon as they break through the property ward. How they can send a spell through it, I don't know. My mind flashes back to the ward I set up around the basement the last time. Antonio walked straight through it.

Shit.

The basement safe room isn't going to save anyone. The ward's weaker than it was when I broke it; whatever witch they have on their side is strong. Still, what other chance do we have?

This is going to be a war between super werewolves and Sau's monsters. We'll be nothing but canon fodder to both sides.

"Shit," Dayne says from behind me, and I turn my head to find him looking out the window. I twist back around to peer through it.

"Fuck."

My heart rate increases. The plants are all dead, the ward is down, and there is a hundred-odd werewolves charging straight towards us. They'll be on us in seconds. Pure terror comes down our bond. Fear for my safety. *He knows.*

Followed by determination and a need for violence. *He's coming –*

A sudden shockwave shakes the house. I start to fall over, but Dayne catches me before I can knock into the wall.

"What the hel was that?" I ask, but the answer is out the window. A black dome has shot up around the property. Not around the house itself but behind the wolves. Their witch is trapping us all in here. Varius' rage tells me he didn't make it in. *No!*

"It's Sau's," Dayne says grimly.

"What?"

He nods at the wolves. They've slowed down a little, and they look more restless. "They're afraid," he says.

"Why would she..." I close my eyes briefly. Of course. If her boys come back and try to fight them, they'll die. If her monsters escape and run through St. Augustine, the seven archangels will come down to smite us all. There's no back-up for us. Either Sau kills them all with her monsters or we die.

She's just saved Varius...and I can't hate her for that.

I love you. I push that through our bond, hoping that he can feel it.

"Shit, I can see why she's named," Dayne breathes, and I open my eyes.

My jaw drops as I watch a massive shadow form in front of the house. The first row of werewolves run into it and immediately get attacked by the monsters inside. They're dragged down on howls of pain. The second row jumps back and snaps their teeth, but the third row barrels into them and shoves them forward.

Monstrous tentacles, claws, and teeth reach up out of the dark. It's like Sau's rung a dinner bell, and all her kids have come to feast. They grab hold of the werewolves and use them to drag themselves up. Monsters of all shapes and sizes now rip free and turn on the other wolves in a frenzy.

"Come on," I say. We need to get down to the basement. If one of them sees Dayne, they'll attack him just as fast as they will our enemies. He doesn't have Shadow blood in his veins.

But just as I turn from the window, I whip my head back. I thought I saw a person out there, someone with wild red hair. Is it their witch? Did they see us?

Shit!

"Come on!" I race for the basement; Dayne's right beside me. The glass behind us shatters. I risk a look behind me, needing to know if it's their witch or a wolf or a monster to know what evasive action I need to take. My eyes widen at the speed the thing's moving. It must be one of the super soldiers Antonio's made.

"Don't stop!" Dayne shouts as he throws up a pale-blue shield behind us. It reaches across the span of the hall. The werewolf slams into it and bounces back. He growls at it, then rakes his claws back and forth across it. Sparks fly off as he keeps shaving his claws, the magic burning everything that touches it, but the ward *is* starting to break.

We're not going to be able to outrun it. I stop and turn, then lift my wand. Power curses through me. It's hot and mad and fueled by a mother's fear.

"Micha –" Dayne says as he swings towards me.

"Drop the shield," I order.

He curses, but he lifts his hands to do so.

The shield comes down just as I release my spell. It rips down the wand, lighting up a trail of purple lines within it, then explodes out the tip in a sharp line.

The wolf snarls as it races forward, but then it howls as the spell hits it square in the face. It stops in its tracks as purple flames consume it within seconds. It's only a few feet from us, having crossed all that distance in a split second.

"Damn," Dayne says as it crumbles to our feet. "When did they get that fast?"

"Antonio's been giving them –" I break off on a scream as Dayne sags forward, blood pouring out of his mouth. A human hand I know all too well is poking out of his belly.

"Sau!" I scream as I turn to fight Antonio. I know she'll be too late for me, but I'm hoping she'll heal him.

I flick my wrist to call on another fire ball. Although he

is still touching Dayne, I can control each individual flame. They will not hurt my friend.

But Antonio grabs the wand just as it starts to fire. He shoves its tip towards Dayne. My eyes widening, I focus on dousing the flames before they can touch him.

While I'm distracted, Antonio yanks the wand out of my hand and tosses it away. Then his fist slams towards my jaw, but all my training with Sau has given me quicker reactions than I had before. I lean away, and the blow he was going for ends up more as a graze. Unfortunately, with his power, that still hits fucking *hard*.

My head whips to the side as I stagger in front of Dayne. I try to focus through the pain and double vision.

Antonio still has his arm through my friend, so for now he's keeping all his blood in.

My eyes widen, though, as I notice Dayne's lifting both his arms. Clocking what he's going for, I pretend to stumble around. If I attack Antonio, he's going to rip his arm free, but if he thinks I'm helpless, he'll take the time to gloat.

"I told you I'd be back for you –" His words turn into a sudden clenching of teeth. The smell of burning meat hits the air as Dayne electrocutes him with both hands. I lunge past them, dropping my knife as I scramble for my wand.

I snatch it up and turn, already preparing a spell before I aim. A blast of fire starts to shoot out of the tip, but Antonio is already gone, having fought off Dayne's magic and ripped himself away. I swing the wand to my left, where I just manage to catch a blur of motion before he slams into me. I don't get the chance to release the spell.

It seems it doesn't matter how much I trained with Sau to be able to track her movements; Antonio is simply too damn fast.

The back of my head hits the wall with a *crack!*

My vision narrows, then blurs.

His blood-stained hand goes around my throat and lifts

me off my feet. "Where's your magic gone, Shadow whore?"

Cupping my hands I smack both his ears. As he releases my throat, I wrap my legs around his waist and shove my thumbs into his eyes. I press down hard, but before I can blind him, he grabs both my wrists and wrenches them back.

Crack!

I cry out as bones poke out of my skin, and my knuckles hit the top of my forearms.

He tears me off him, then throws me at the wall. I hit it and slide down. Ribs break. A lung's punctured. More agony shoots through me as I land on my wrists. Vomit is forced out of me. I start to go into shock.

This is the end.

I know it.

Closing my eyes, I cry over not having finished my bond with Varius. At least then I could find him in the next life.

Tears roll down my cheeks.

I'm sorry, Varius.

I'm sorry I'm not strong enough to survive...

Ignoring the pain, I press an arm to my stomach, trying so hard to feel my baby one last time. The spell I cast on myself is still there, protecting her. Tears burn my eyes. Will it protect her long enough for Sau to get here? Can she save Rafiki when she's not even nineteen weeks old?

Rafiki... What a stupid name.

But gods, if she lives... I'll gladly name her whatever he wants.

Just let her live.

Please.

A little foot kicks inside my belly. My eyes snap open as I hear her urging me on.

Get up, ma. The fight ain't over yet.

Gritting my teeth, I focus on the magic inside of me. I need my hands or my wand to use it though.

But I don't need either with black magic.

I just need to be willing to sacrifice a human.

Luckily, there is an army of werewolves I hate outside.

Opening my mouth, reacting on instinct, I start to invoke the darkness that always surrounds us witches. I touch it, and it feels ancient, all-powerful. It feels my veins and urges me to let it free.

But it isn't an incantation that comes out of me. It's a blood-stained gasp as Antonio's foot slams into the arm protecting my belly. My vision narrows as agony threatens to send me into the dark.

I dig my nails into the world of consciousness.

My arms are burning nerves of molten fire, dragging me back down. But I can't leave my baby.

I'm the only one here to protect her.

Kneeling down in front of me, Antonio grabs my arm. I'm struggling to breathe, wheezing from my punctured lung. My chest is half-collapsed, deformed from its injuries. I'm pretty certain I have a concussion. I'm bleeding from multiple places, both inside and out.

Yet, still I try, reaching for the dark magic inside of me.

He yanks my arm away. My eyes roll back into my head as he slams it on the floor. The sound of ripping flesh hurts my ears, and I open my eyes to see he's shifted his hand into that of a werewolf's.

My heart pounds rapidly as I realize what he's about to do. I want to scream, but my throat is too crushed and bruised.

"Heal her a bit, Eduardo," Antonio purrs. "I want her awake for this."

A hand touches my forehead, and warmth flows into me. My worse wounds start to heal. I open my mouth to try to take advantage of the opportunity, but Antonio shoves his hand into my stomach, easily breaking through my magic, and all I can do is scream.

He gropes around inside me, searching for the life I'd sell my soul to protect. I pray to every god I know, offering them anything and everything, but I've already given them my magic. There's nothing else they want.

White light flows through me as Eduardo keeps me from passing out.

Please....

Please...

"Varius!" I scream, trusting him to save me. "Varius!"

But he doesn't come.

Antonio jerks his hand out, revealing a bloody fist.

He opens it to show me my little baby girl in the palm of his hand, still inside her amniotic sac.

"No!"

He poises a claw over her.

I struggle to reach her, to help her in some way, but my body is broken. My arms are useless. I reach for the dark magic once more, but my words falter on another scream as I watch him tear open the only thing still keeping her alive, still allowing her to breathe.

Her partially-formed lungs try desperately to work. She's trying so hard to survive despite everything that's stacked against her. She's too young for this world. She's too fucking young!

"Don't..." I cry as I watch her struggle. "Don't...please."

Leave her alone.

"Please..."

He laughs at me, cold and cruel. "I begged Sau to save my mate and pups, and do you know what she did?"

I reach a broken arm out to my baby, wanting to hold her, to take her from him. But my hands are still destroyed. My wrists are still snapped back. He grabs my broken hand with his free one and clamps my knuckles into my arm. I cry out in utter agony.

"*Nothing*," he hisses. "She let them die."

"I'm not...her," I whimper.

"No. But you are a Shadow whore."

Releasing me, he grabs Rafiki by her head and lifts her up. She's still breathing, and my heart trips in my chest.

"Please..." I cry. "Please don't –"

"Do you know how my pups died?" he asks without emotion. "They were eaten by the monsters in her shadows."

I scream as he lifts her above his head and then opens his mouth.

I keep screaming as he lowers the bottom half of her between his lips.

I keep screaming long after he bites her in half, after he sucks out her organs and intestines and the last flicker of her life.

I scream.

And I scream.

And I scream.

His eyes widen as he swallows. "That's not a witch," he says as he jumps to his feet.

He drops Rafiki to the ground, letting her splatter like a blob of ice cream.

My scream becomes all that I am. Broken and raspy. My vocal chords snap as I keep my eyes on my little girl.

I never got to hold her.

I need to hold her.

She needs to be held by her mother at least once.

Sobbing, I will my body to move. To reach my little girl.

I need to hold her.

I need to hold her.

"Heal her enough to transport. She's coming with us."

White light flows around me. My wrists snap back into place. The bones shift back to where they belong. The rest of my wounds are fixed, but all I'm concentrating on is the fact that I can move my hands again. That I can hold my little girl before I'm taken away.

But just as my fingers are about to stroke her little head, Eduardo steps on my hand. I cry out, not from the pain of all my bones being crushed beneath his heel but because I know I will never get to hold my daughter.

I sob as he drags me away from her. I dig my nails into the floor, trying to claw myself back to her. She's so small and alone.

She needs her mother.

She needs her mother!

But instead, I'm picked up by Antonio and hauled over his shoulder. I beat his back. I scream at him to let me go. I should be doing more. Fighting properly. But my strength, my ability to think clearly is all gone. All I know is grief.

Heart stopping, unsurvivable grief.

And then the world is gone as I'm transported out of the Shadow home.

FIFTY-SIX

HIM

As soon as the dome falls, Aleric phases me inside the house. I barely got a second to look at the war zone outside, but that was long enough to sear it into my brain. Over a hundred bodies littered our property. Werewolves torn to pieces by grotesque monsters before they themselves were eventually ripped apart. Dead plants lay all around them – so much death where it used to be picturesque. So much violation where there used to be peace. How could Micha have possibly survived?

Intense agony rips through me when Aleric lands inside Mother's bedroom. I've phased half a dozen times in the last hour. My body's screaming in pain, and I drop to the ground like a fucking stone. All my muscles are on fire. My bones feel like they're constantly fracturing until they mimic the cracks in a window.

Aleric's presence is that of a predator above me. You can't be weak in this life. You can't do anything that even *seems* weak.

You can't cry. Can't go to therapy. Can't crawl on your hands and knees. But I don't have the strength to get to my feet. So I crawl towards the heartbeat I can barely detect.

I do it without caring another Boss sees me.

I don't care about his judgment. The embarrassment. I don't even care that this moment of weakness might mean he turns on our Family later, thinking it is there for the taking. I don't care about the future casualties.

All I care about is getting to my wife as fast as I can.

I don't have time to wait for the pain to subside.

So I dig my fingertips into the carpet and drag my spasming body across the room. I pull the door open and crawl through the hall. I push out my senses, trying to detect her heartbeat or just smell her blood.

I detect the latter. A lot of it. She's near the basement stairs. There's a heartbeat there too, but it isn't hers.

Screaming in utter agony, I drag myself towards her presence. I can imagine her lifeless eyes as she lies in a stagnant pool of blood. I can imagine her eyes aren't even there anymore, ripped out by the harsh rake of a claw across her face. I see her so broken and beaten, she isn't recognizable to anyone but me. She's been torn apart. Her chest plate ripped open. Her face gnawed off.

Those images curb stomp me in the back of the head. I drop my face to the ground and scream.

The pain in my muscles and limbs has been replaced with a terrible ache, an exhaustion that's begging me to give up, to not force myself to see her body. Because deep down, I already know that's what I'll find.

Just a body.

Not my stubborn, sarcastic wife.

"Noooo!"

I push myself up. My muscles and bones protest, but I bite through the pain. A hand grabs my shoulder and pulls me the rest of the way to my feet. Ducking under my arm, Rudy helps me stagger down the hall.

More heartbeats flood around the house. One kneels down by the faint pulse that isn't hers. Two more race down the stairs to the basement – Khalid and Leno no doubt, checking on their girl and dog who should hopefully be there. I can't sense them through the magic of the ward.

Tears burning my eyes, I suck in a breath before we turn the corner. Rudy squeezes me with the arm he has around my waist. My heart in my throat, I take that final step. And then I can *see*.

Mother is kneeling over Dayne, her hands glowing over a fist-sized wound in his stomach. The hole is just like the one Micha had when I found her in the basement. Antonio was here. And he came for her.

Shoving away from Rudy, I lunge for our mother. "You were supposed to protect her!" I yell. I grab her by her hair and pull her to her feet. I don't care that she's in the middle of saving Dayne. He might be family, but he isn't my *wife*.

"Where is she?" I roar as I shake her. "Where is my wife?"

"She's alive!" she says, and my grip loosens as my chest is hit with too heavy of a blow. "Antonio took her. I tried to stop them –"

I backhand her across the face hard enough her hair rips out of her skull and stays in my fingers. She stumbles away from me. "If you tried, you wouldn't be here!" I shout.

I go to lunge for her again, but my body can't move. I'm trapped by the power of Ezriel's telekinesis. I struggle against him, gnashing my teeth and spitting in fury. I feel like an animal. A basic beast who only wants one thing.

"Where is she?" I scream.

"I don't know," Mother says as she turns back to me. She doesn't heal her swollen cheek from where I hit her. "I only got here after they already cast the transportation spell."

I scream as I strain against my invisible binds. Ezriel is holding every atom in my fucking body. My eyes turn to him. He still has strength to stand, but I can detect the harsh beat of his pulse. He's worn out from his fight with the hybrid and werewolves. If I keep pushing, he'll break. Then I can kill the bitch in front of me for not having been by my wife the entire time.

"You should've made sure they got to the basement!"

"I know!" she says. "I'm sorry. I thought I stopped them all before they got to the house. If I'd known they had a transporter –"

"Look at the plants!" Even the ones inside the house are all dead. "They obviously had a fucking witch!"

Not many witches know how to work a transportation spell, but I don't care. She should've known Antonio would have something up his sleeve.

"He took my wife! You let him take my fucking wife!"

I pull against the binds of my prison again. All my muscles strain for release.

"Enough," Khalid says softly but firmly as he moves between us. He faces me, his mien dangerously calm. "Mother, finish healing Dayne," he orders. "We don't need another casualty. Then get out of the house."

She doesn't say anything as she obeys.

Khalid clasps my shoulder as he looks me in the eyes. "We're going to find her, Varius. We're going to tear apart every single one of his compounds if we have to, but we will get her back."

"He's going to torture her." My voice breaks, a cracked and raw insight into the state of my soul.

"I know. But your anger isn't going to save her."

I crumble beneath that truth. I'm doing nothing to help my little monster.

Closing my eyes, I force myself to breathe.

Khalid squeezes my shoulder again, and I shudder.

"We're going to find her, brother, and we're going to bring her home."

Latching onto his promise with trembling hands, I nod. I just hope she's still alive by the time we do.

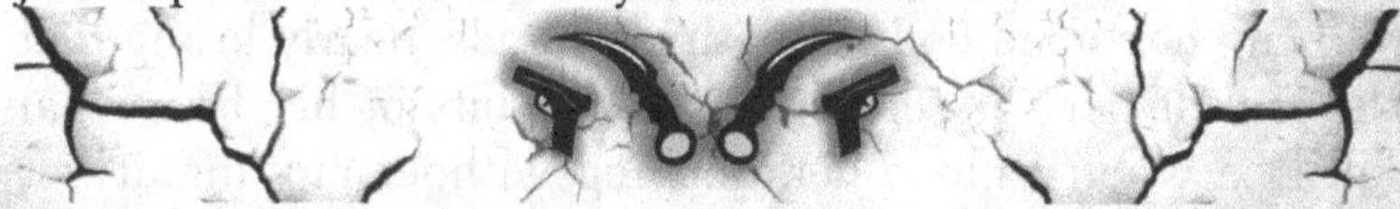

I'm numb by the time Mother is well gone and Ezriel releases me. Everyone has left me alone in the hall. Dayne has been moved to somewhere more comfortable for him to recover. He hasn't regained consciousness, but Mother said he was stable and that he had been out by the time she had gotten here, so there's no point questioning him.

I should've let him tattoo a tracking rune back on her. Fuck. I never should have had her burn the first one off out of paranoia that someone could use it to find me through her.

I should've –

Cutting that thought off, I force myself to focus rather than despair. I move from the spot where Dayne was to the biggest pool of blood that smells like her. I breathe it in, trying to feel her presence where it no longer is. Then I shift my focus to the other scents in the area, documenting the bastards I need to kill. There's Antonio, there's a male I do not know, and then there's –

My heart stops as I smell a mixture of her and me.

Dropping my head, I frantically scan the floor.

For a moment I convince myself I'm imagining it, that Bambi isn't here.

But then I realize I'm looking for something too big, and I drop to my knees to search again. My eyes latch onto a tiny, tiny body on the floor. Her head isn't much bigger than a golf ball, and it's been caved in, deformed. Like she was dropped from a great height. Bits of her brain has leaked out, and the lower half of her body has been ripped off. No organs remain to tumble free. I want to search for the rest of her, but I can't tear my eyes away from her little face.

My stomach churns as I reach for her. My body shakes. She needs her mother, but all she has is me.

I cup her small body in both my hands, nearly losing it at the feel of her shattered skull, at the bits of her brain that fall free when I move her. Sobbing without any dignity or care, I cradle her to my chest.

She's so small. So fragile.

My heart squeezes as I stare at her face. Her head is so big compared to the rest of her. She hasn't grown into it yet, and now she never will. She will never experience all the life she had ahead of her. Never fall in love. Never see her mother's radiant smile. She'll never even feel me holding her. Never know that I love her.

I love her so damn much even though I'll never get the chance to know her.

Cradling her against me, I rock back and forth and sob.

My chest burns with pure agony. My eyes feel heavily swollen. "I'm sorry…" I sob as I stare down at my little girl. "I'm so sorry I failed you… I love you, Bambi. I love you even though you have a dumbass name. But you can blame your mother…" I break off on uncontrollable tears. My hands shake, making her whole body tremble. "I love you…" I rasp. "Daddy loves you." I bring her little head up for a kiss. The cold brush of her skin breaks me, but I don't pull away. She needs to know I love her. "Daddy –"

I cry out as a sudden pulse rips through my chest, like a defibrillator paddle being touched to a dead body. I gasp as I shift Bambi into one hand so I can place the other on the wall. The pulse comes again, and my heart jerks painfully. Like it's dying from being targeted by some dark spell.

Fuck. Did Antonio leave a trap on my daughter to kill me?

Despite the fact that he clearly must have, I still refuse to let her go though. She is my baby. I can't.

"Help!" I yell, but the word is more of a croak as another pulse slams into me. I lean against the wall and close my eyes, gasping through the pain. My chest is trapped in a closing vice. I slam my free hand on the wall, trying to breathe. I can't die before I save Micha. I can't die!

The pulse hits one more time, multiple times worse than all the others. Pain explodes through every nerve, lighting them up, scraping a hot poker against them.

Micha!

I scream in agony. Others shout around me. I can sense their presence, their heartbeats like grating nails on a chalkboard.

Micha!

My mind reduces into a single pinpoint, a single purpose as the curse on me breaks. It consumes me until I know nothing else.

Micha!

Roaring, I open my eyes and jump to my feet. A deep hunger fills me. A need to kill, to drink the blood of my enemies.

And everyone around me is an enemy because they've taken *her.*

Attacking the nearest one, I scream, "Where is my fucking wife!"

EPILOGUE

HER

I collapse onto carpeted ground, spasming in pain as the transportation spell deposits me inside a building. Antonio has fallen to his knees and dropped me, but I don't have the strength to try to get away. I don't have the energy or the care. They killed Dayne. They killed my baby. All I want to do is curl up in my grief.

"You are a Black, Micha." My father's voice is firm.

"And a Shadow." Varius' is warm, believing in me.

But they're both wrong.

All I am is a broken mother.

"It's time for you to be more than just a Shadow whore," Antonio says as he hauls me up by the back of my neck. He tries to put me on my feet, but I refuse to walk. Can't. So he throws me over his shoulder.

"I was going to kill you," he explains as he carries me down a bare hall with white tiled floors. I should be taking note of where we're going so I can create a floor plan, but my mind is too numb to think.

"But now you're too valuable. It's rare to be able to birth a hybrid. Out of the hundreds of women I've tried to breed, only three of them have been able to do it."

For a moment, I don't care what he's saying. They are words without meaning. Just empty air.

But then awareness hits me, punching past my grief. He just took my child from me. To hel if I'm going to let him breed me so he can rip more of them from my arms.

My rage ignites inside me, growing hot, spreading all the way through my body and mind. It kills my grief, chokes it on the fumes my rage creates. Screaming, I kick my feet, aiming for his balls. He grunts as I hit them. Then he rolls me off his shoulder with an arm around my waist. He holds me in the air horizontally. I snap my knees into his stomach. I swing my fists into his side. Pain radiates up my wrists, the fractures not fully healed, but I don't stop. Opening my mouth, I go to bite him.

Grunting, he pivots and slams my head through the wall. The plaster gives easily, but the wooden beam behind it does not. Intense pain shoots down my neck and spine. My eyes roll back. My vision fades. He pulls me out of the wall and then drops me to the ground. I don't have the awareness to catch myself, and my cheek hits the floor hard.

Grabbing me by the ankle, he drags me down the hall.

My body has been through hel and back and hel again, but I refuse to let it drag me under. I'll claw my way to the surface on broken, bleeding nubs if I have to.

Forcing my eyes open, I will myself to move.

But just as I start to, I'm thrown through a door, which is then slammed shut behind me. I hit the ground and roll. Dragging myself up to my feet, I spin around. The hairs on my neck prickle. There are other people in here, but all my focus is on Antonio. His face appears on the other side of the barred window inside the door. There is no glass, so I hear him easily.

"I'm going to enjoy watching you try to fight them," he says with a sneer. "Know that I'll be jacking off while you do."

"You fucking —"

I stop at the sound of multiple things moving behind me. The hairs on my neck rise.

He smiles, a pleasurable sneer that leaves me cold.

Spinning on my feet, I raise my arms, adrenaline pushing through my exhaustion. But it is an impossible sight before me. There are over a dozen men in this old cafeteria, and all of them are looking at me like I'm their ticket out of here.

"You know the rules," Antonio says cheerily. "Shift before you fuck her. You'll have a better chance of impregnating her that way."

My heart slams in my throat as I quickly scan the room, looking for a weapon. But the tables are too big to wield, and there aren't any chairs, just benches attached to the tables. There might be knives or utensils in the back of the room, but there are multiple opponents standing in my way.

Shit.

"Welcome to your new life, Shadow whore," Antonio purrs as I hear the pull of a zip. "Now be a good girl and put on a good show for me."

Ignoring him, I focus on the blood bond. I draw strength from Varius' presence inside of me, even if it is just more pain.

Because I can use pain.

I can wield it like a weapon.

After all. I am a Black.

My hands fist.

And I am a fucking Shadow.

NEED A 0% SERIOUSNESS PALETTE CLEANSER?

Suggestion: *My Queen, My King*

I wasn't really having sex with my executioner; I was seducing my executioner to kill him, and that sounded infinitely better. Classier. Way less slutty.

OR A SLIGHTLY MORE SERIOUS ROMCOM WITH HATE SEX?

Read: *To Love and to Perish.*

"I have learned necromancy just to kill you over and over again."

"Awww. That's so sweet. No one's ever obsessed over me that much."

"I'm not – No, die!"

WANT TO KNOW HOW MICHA SURVIVES?

Follow me on Facebook for updates of the last book in Varius' and Micha's trilogy.

WANT TO READ THE GOOD TIMES BETWEEN VARIUS AND MICHA?

Read *Tethered Souls.*

All he wanted me for was a womb…

WANT TO KNOW HOW KHALID MET KIRA?

Read *Cursed to be Mine.*

I've stalked her for two years.
I've made myself a key to her house.
And now it's time to make her mine.

AUTHOR'S NOTE

Hello everyone!

If you've made it to the end of *Broken Souls...* I'm sorry.

I know a lot of us read to escape, but a lot of us also read dark romance to heal the parts of ourselves the world has ripped apart, and sometimes we just need to know that no matter the horrors we go through, no matter how absolutely terrible our lives become, there is hope of a HEA (and they will get one in the next book).

That our failure to save or simply protect those we love, including ourselves, does not define us.

That our pain does not have to leave us crippled, though rarely will it ever disappear. Our shoulders just become broader to carry that weight.

You are perfect in your imperfections.

Don't ever forget that.

RESEARCH NOTES

I know a lot of you reading this are mothers. I know miscarriages and loss of pregnancy is a major trigger and a controversial thing to include in books. But I did not write the ending to be a shock factor. I wrote it because that is what Antonio decided to do, and writing is not just an escape for me. It isn't really a choice. I either get the shit out of my head, or my dreams stay nightmarish helholes where I can feel, sense, smell, taste, etc everything.

And so here we are, at a miserable ending where Antonio can just rot in hel.

But if there is one thing that should come from this, it should be a wider understanding of a parent's grief when they lose their child either through miscarriage or after they're born.

10-20% of known pregnancies result in miscarriages[1]. By the age of eighty, 18% of American parents have lost a child, with that number higher for minorities[2]. There are so many people around us suffering, and that grief does not go away as the years pass. It might fade. It might become a bit more bearable, but it sits there heavily, and understanding that, understanding our friends and neighbours and the strangers we pass by in the street with not even a smile... That compassion can be

[1] https://www.washingtonpost.com/health/2022/08/02/miscarriage-risk-pregnancy/

[2] https://evermore.org/key-bereavement-facts

SPOT ANY ERRORS?

Please let me know by emailing me at:
authormirandagrant@gmail.com

WANT TO IMPACT THE REST OF THE SERIES?

Drop me a review! Tell me what you loved and want more of or what you hated and want less of.

WANT TO LEARN ALL ABOUT WIPS AND NEW RELEASES?